TALES FROM THE
OLD BLACK AMBULANCE

TALES FROM THE OLD BLACK AMBULANCE

AN ANTHOLOGY

J. D. BLACKROSE

GUSTAVO BONDONI

RICK DUFFY

A. G. HILTON

LARRY HODGES

TALLY JOHNSON

MACKENZIE KINCAID

EMILY LAVIN LEVERETT

ROB MacGREGOR

GAIL Z. MARTIN

JASON J. McCUISTON

JENNIFER R. POVEY

CLARK ROBERTS

ANGELA ROQUET

TIM WAGGONER

AND

ROBERT W. WALKER

EDITOR

JASON T. GRAVES

PROSPECTIVE PRESS
Winston-Salem

PROSPECTIVE PRESS LLC

1959 Peace Haven Rd #246, Winston-Salem, NC 27106

www.prospectivepress.com

Published in the United States of America by Prospective Press LLC

TRADEMARK

TALES FROM THE OLD BLACK AMBULANCE

ISBN 978-1-943419-87-6

Printed in the United States of America
First Prospective Press printing, May, 2019

The text of this book is typeset in Athelas
Accent text is typeset in Fueled by Schlitz

TABLE OF CONTENTS

DED
SOCIETY

LARRY HODGES

"AND NEVER GO NEAR THE WALL!" REVEREND BRYAN THUNDERED, POUNDING his fist on his tombstone. One of his eyes popped out, revealing a substantial maggot colony in the opening. Several in the congregation gasped; most were too modest to show off their own. It jolted Charles awake from his daydream about football. By the bright moonlight he saw the Reverend's maggots. He'd never seen such a collection!

The Reverend smiled and popped the eye back into its socket on his gray face. Goo dribbled down his cheek. "Sorry—didn't mean to flash everyone," he said to the residents of Dedland who were gathered about his tombstone for Sunday services. Off in the distance an owl hooted from the surrounding trees.

The sermons bored Charles, which was why he usually slept through them. He'd rather play with Toby, his pet rat, which lived in a hole in Charles's stomach. It tickled when he nibbled on Charles's insides. He could hear Toby's rapid heartbeat, like raindrops on a tombstone.

Charles had his own maggot infestations, and was somewhat proud of the one in his right armpit. But only in the privacy of his own coffin would Charles take off his tattered shirt and examine the growing colony, which was working its way into his chest. The shirt had once been bright red, but time, mildew and various infestations had taken their toll, making it an attractive spotty brown. His leather breeches and boots had long ago been taken over by brown and white mold. Green goo dripped from his ears and a cut on his cheek. Unlike most of the Ded, Charles had a full head of wavy brown hair that fluttered in the breeze, the envy of others.

Reverend Bryan continued his sermon. "Why must you never go near the wall?"

"*Because it's dangerous!*" said the congregation in unison.

"If you go past the wall, what will happen?" the Reverend asked.

"*You'll fall off the edge of the world!*"

The Reverend gave a toothy grin, which came easily to him as he had no lips. He still had most of his teeth, which were stained a pretty brown. Much of his face had eroded away, revealing the skull beneath. He wore a long, loose cloak, which at one time must have been black, but was now stained gray and brown. He had a deep, rich voice with a touch of a drawl. A fat worm stuck out of his neck, swaying side to side slowly. Charles wished he had one.

"The Great Caretaker created us in his image, gave us Dedland, and we can wish for no more. It's the *truth!*"

"*Truth! Truth! Truth!*" the congregation chanted.

"Amen!" the Reverend said, finishing his sermon. He absentmindedly flicked on the ever-present cigarette lighter in his hand as the congregation said "*Amen!*"

Sitting next to Charles were Susannah, whose stomach always seemed to be bothering her, and fat old Robert, who listened more attentively. None sported a better grub collection than the one Robert had in his forehead, or displayed the variety of molds covering Susannah. Charles's coffin and tombstone were next to theirs, and he often attended Sunday services with them.

The Reverend flicked off the cigarette lighter and continued. "Tonight we have a special welcome to the latest Ded, who the Caretaker has given us this past day. I welcome you all to join us for the wake in one hour."

Charles got up to go, along with Robert, Susannah, and of course Toby, now perched on his shoulder. Charles and some of the others had agreed to get up a game of football after church. Charles had been around a long time before football had been introduced, but he'd quickly come to love the game.

"Hi, Charles!" It was Barbara, one of the few other Ded who were small. Barbara was only shoulder height to Charles, just as Charles was shoulder height to most of the Ded. She was a recent arrival, appearing in Dedland only a few months before. The Caretaker seemed to favor her, as sometimes when they got up they'd find he'd left fresh flowers on her tombstone. The dandelion flower that had recently begun growing out of her head matched the faded yellow dress she was wearing, which was covered with bloodstains.

The front of Barbara's neck looked like it had been sliced across by a sharp object, though of course no one had actually sliced her; she had been created that way. Charles even remembered her wake, when she'd first opened her eyes. He'd never seen a Ded with such an opening in their throat. Since that time two other girls Barbara's size had shown up with the same sliced throat, Suzy and Collette. It was very strange, he thought.

"Would you like to play?" Barbara asked.

Charles and Barbara often played together, but while he preferred action games like football, rock tag and heart attack, she preferred playing with her headless doll collection. She was better company than most of the Ded, many of whom spent their time talking about the weather, the latest bug census, or new breeds of fungus.

"Not today," he told her. "We're playing football over by the Smith tomb. Want to join us?"

"*No way!*" she exclaimed. "I don't want to hurt Dandy." She threw up her arms protectively over her dandelion—too quickly. Her momentum knocked her head backwards. Since the front of her neck was sliced across, her head connected to her body only by the skin on the back. Her head fell over backwards, with the back of her head smacking into her back with an awkward thump. "*Oops!*" she said, and reached behind and pulled her head back into place. Fortunately, Dandy hadn't been hurt.

Soon Charles and the others had a lively game going. Charles's team was losing badly. "I'm getting the Willies," Charles said, and left to find the two. Soon afterward, with Willy Arnold and Willy Brown on their team, they caught up.

Suzy and Collette came by to watch. Charles glanced at their throats, each matching Barbara's. He wondered about their origins. Since all three had identical cut throats, was this related in some way? Was there any reason why some people resembled others? Just as the three girls had matching throats, some said that he looked similar to Susannah and fat old Robert, with the same nose as Susannah, the eyes of Robert, and the rest of his face a mix of the two. Why had he been created that way?

"C'mon, Charles!" Willy Arnold said, and his attention returned to football.

With the score tied 56-all, Charles went long for a pass, dodging back and forth among the tombstones. Stumbling among gravestones and mud, he broke free of the Ded covering him and ran into the end zone. Arnold, the quarterback for his team, saw him and threw his head as hard as he could. It was a perfect pass and Arnold's head landed in Charles's outstretched hands. He slipped in the mud, landing on his stomach in the end zone. *Touchdown!* Toby squeaked. As Charles got up, the rat crawled out of his stomach and fell to the ground.

"Great catch!" Arnold's head said.

"Awesome pass!" Charles said. Charles returned Arnold's head to its waiting body and the two exchanged high-fives. Charles wanted to keep playing, but someone began yelling for them. It was time for the wake.

Charles didn't want to leave Toby behind and so he took a few minutes to search for his pet, which he soon found. But Toby had been badly injured. His head hung from his body at an unnatural angle, and blood was coming out of his mouth. Not sure what to do, Charles put Toby back in his stomach. He headed for the wake, knowing he'd be late.

"I see that Charles has decided to drop by," the Reverend said. The worm in his shoulder seemed to tilt toward Charles, as if staring at him. Charles looked at it enviously. Crickets chirped in the background.

"Sorry, Reverend." Charles had been to many wakes. They were always a little exciting as you never knew who the Caretaker had buried during the previous day. Several Ded were digging into the new grave and soon the coffin was visible. Reverend Bryan opened it.

It was a woman. She was horribly wrinkled, with snow-white hair and wearing an ugly white dress. *It won't stay white for long,* Charles thought.

Reverend Bryan stood over the woman as the Ded gathered about. The Ded began slapping their legs with their hands, slowly building it up, faster and faster, louder and louder. The ones with flesh on their legs and hands made a smacking sound, while those with mostly bone made a higher pitched cracking noise. Then Reverend Bryan raised his hands and all were silent.

"Only the Ded can wake the Ded," Reverend Bryan said, holding up the lit cigarette lighter. Then he flicked it off and leaned over the woman. "*Wake up!*" he cried, slapping her in the face with a loud *crack*. The chirping crickets went silent.

The woman's body jerked and her eyes popped open. She looked alarmed as she sat up. As she surveyed the onlooking Ded, her alarm grew, and she let out one shriek after another, as most new Ded did. This went on for some time, but she calmed down as the Reverend spoke with her in soft, reassuring tones.

She was still looking about rapidly, her mouth an "O." She tried mouthing some words, but nothing came out.

"Relax," Reverend Bryan said. His eye chose this inopportune time to fall out again. He popped it back in, and only a little goo rolled down his face this time. "We're friends. We're the Ded!"

"I see," she said. "Dead people, you say. Am I one of you?

"*Exactly!*" Reverend Bryan said. "We are all Ded." It had been a successful wake, and soon the Reverend and others would give her the usual orientation and she would enter Ded society.

Later that night Toby died from his injuries. Recent rain had replenished Charles's tear ducts, and so tears streaked down his face as he buried the rat next to his own tombstone. He'd perform the wake for Toby himself the following night.

He returned to his tombstone. He stared at it for a bit. It said: "Charles Darwin, Feb. 12, 1809 - Apr. 19, 1821." He glanced at the two adjacent tombstones. The first said, "Robert Darwin, May 30, 1766 -Nov. 13, 1848." The second said, "Susannah Darwin, 1765-1817." Although he'd learned some simple reading skills from the thousands of tombstones in Dedland, he had little idea what any of it meant. He'd heard that the small Ded, like himself and Barbara, had numbers that were close together. His were only twelve apart, while Robert's and Susannah's were 82 and 52 apart. Barbara's was only eight apart. There were also a few tiny ones, not much larger than an owl, with the numbers sometimes zero or one apart. They cried constantly.

He also knew that the second number had something to do with when the Caretaker created the Ded person. The most recent Ded had 2012 as the second number. He wondered why the Caretaker had given the same second name to Robert, Susannah, and himself. He'd been a Ded longer than Robert and almost as long as Susannah, and a lot longer than Reverend Bryan. The previous Reverend was still here. After many hundreds of years there wasn't much left of him.

Where did the Ded come from? The question had been bothering him recently. Did the Caretaker just deliver Ded bodies during the day while they slept, to be woken up by the Ded at night? That's what the Reverend said, but it seemed suspect to Charles. He remembered when Barbara first showed up. Why was she smaller than the others, with her head nearly cut off? Of course, many of the Ded had heads that came off sometimes, including Charles, but Barbara's looked like someone had actually cut into it with a knife. Why would the Caretaker do that? But what did he know of the ways of the Caretaker? Perhaps the Reverend would know. He yawned, and was soon comfortably back in his coffin, as were the rest of the Ded. The dark would be gone soon.

❧ ❧ ❧

Charles was up within minutes after the dark returned. He easily pushed open the lid of his coffin, pushing soil aside, and climbed up to the surface.

He dug Toby up. Not bothering with the formalities, he shouted, *"Wake up!"* and poked the rat. With a jerk, Toby came awake. He no longer had a heartbeat.

Susannah stuck her head out of the dirt over her coffin. "Not so loud, you'll wake the Ded," she said. Yawning, she pulled her head back below ground and went back to sleep.

Toby looked confused, so Charles picked him up and put him in his stomach. Soon Toby was nibbling on his insides, and the ticklish Charles couldn't stop laughing. He wondered if Toby was now one of the Ded. The Ded are created that way, in the Caretaker's image, according to the Reverend. They just need someone to wake them up so they could begin their existence. But if the Ded were in the Caretaker's image, did the Caretaker look like the fat and old Robert, or the smaller Barbara?

The whole Toby episode got him to thinking about Ded origins again. Dedland had many living creatures, such as rats, mice, raccoons, birds, bats, snakes, and of course all types of insects. When they died, they would wake up again if someone performed a wake. But they were no longer alive, of course. Their hearts no longer beat, they no longer had a high body temperature—in the case of the rats, mice, raccoons, birds and bats—and they no longer needed to eat, drink or breathe. They were just like the Ded, except they were just animals. The Ded were different. Weren't they?

If these animals were first alive, and then died and became "animal Ded," then shouldn't the Ded also have started out as living creatures? What were their origins?

He asked Reverend Bryan.

"I'm glad you came to me," the Reverend said, fiddling with the unlit cigarette lighter. The worm in his neck seemed to nod in agreement. "We must always look for truth, whatever it might be. No, Charles, the Ded were never alive. The Caretaker created us in his image." Some slime was dribbling out of his nose. He wiped it away with his hand. He still had three of his fingernails, but the other seven fingers ended in rotted flesh. "We are not like animals."

"How are we different?" Charles wanted to know. He was stroking Toby, who no longer was soft and warm. His body was harder and ice cold. Charles liked the new version.

"We just are," Reverend Bryan said, a maggot crawling out from behind one of his eyes. "Besides, where would these so-called 'Living Ded' come from?"

"From outside Dedland, outside the walls."

Reverend Bryan stared at him, and both eyes popped out at the same time. The Reverend squatted down, feeling about blindly for his eyes. Charles picked them up and handed them to the Reverend, who popped them back in.

"*Outside the walls!*" the Reverend thundered. "There is no such place! Anything there would fall off the edge! Only birds, bats and flying insects can fly past the walls and not fall!"

"How do you know about the edge?" Charles asked, backing away slightly at the Reverend's sudden anger.

"Because the Caretaker is perfect and created the perfect Dedland. Why would he ruin his perfect creation by creating something which could only be less perfect?"

Charles found that logic hard to argue with. Still, he persisted. "Remember the eclipse we had last month? The moon was low in the sky, yet the shadow of Dedland against the moon was a perfect circle."

"So?"

"Don't you see?" Charles said excitedly. "If Dedland were a flat circle, as you say, then since the moon was low in the sky, the shadow should have been an oval. So Dedland must be a sphere."

"Then why doesn't the ground curve?" Reverend Bryan asked. "And if there were lands beyond the walls, wouldn't everything fall off it as the world curved downward? *You must face the truth!*"

Charles didn't have answers to these questions. The Reverend shook his head. "I don't know where you get this gibberish, but understand this. I've studied this for years. Dedland is a flat circle, 1500 feet across, surrounded by walls. Outside the walls there is nothing, *nothing!* If you go outside the walls, you will fall off the edge and fall for eternity. The Caretaker put the wall there for a purpose, to keep us safe. If he wanted us to look out, he wouldn't have made them so high."

"I just don't believe it," Charles said. "There has to be something out there. I'm going to look."

Reverend Bryan stared at Charles. "You are *not* going near the wall."

Charles was stubborn. "I'm going to."

That was too much for the Reverend. He flicked the cigarette lighter on and held the flame close to Charles's face, close enough that he could feel its heat. "Go to your coffin and stay there the rest of the night. If you go to the wall, you will burn for your disobedience and blasphemy." The Reverend turned and stormed off. Charles had never seen him so angry. He still wanted to go over the wall, but perhaps he'd better do as the Reverend said for now. He didn't want to burn. He went to his coffin and spent the rest of the night playing with Toby.

❧ ❧ ❧

The following night Charles woke up and yawned, and dug his way out of his grave. As he pulled himself from the dirt, something grabbed his head roughly. Before he could react, a thick rope had been put about his chest, under his arms. Then he was shoved back into the dirt.

"You ain't going nowhere," a rough voice said.

Charles popped his head back up and looked about. Four Ded surrounded his grave. He recognized them. The four hung out together by their graves on the outskirts of Dedland, and pretty much stuck to themselves. They attended church, always sitting in the back. They all wore dark sunglasses. Their long, black trench coats were riddled with holes.

Charles tried climbing out again, but they shoved him down again. "What are you doing?" he asked.

"Reverend's orders, you ain't goin' nowhere," said the shover.

"You mean I'm a prisoner?" Charles asked.

"No, you just ain't goin' nowhere. Now go back under and stay." Two of them shoved him down hard. The shover held the other end of the rope.

Could the Reverend do this? Apparently so. *It was so unfair!* He'd been here a lot longer than the Reverend, and yet he'd treat him like this.

He could dig a tunnel and escape. Except for the rope around his chest. It would take him a long time to chew through that. What he needed was a better chewer.

Toby squeaked.

It took Toby ten minutes to chew through the rope. Then Charles began to dig. He dug a few feet down, then turned in the direction he thought would take him to one of the larger tombstone monuments, about a hundred yards away. There were few other graves around it.

When he guessed he was under it, he tunneled upward. Soon he broke the surface. It had taken him several hours. Silently he popped his head above ground to look.

His dead reckoning had been accurate. He pulled himself up cautiously and hid behind the monument. Peeking around a corner, he could see the four guards by his grave.

The wall was a few hundred feet the other way. As quietly as possible, he crawled in that direction, ducking behind other tombstones as he made his way for the farthest wall, where there were no tombstones. Toby nibbled at his insides, and he barely managed to squelch his laughter. Nobody saw him.

Along the way he found a hoe by one of the more recent graves. Hoes, shovels and other digging equipment were the tools of the Caretaker, to be left on the ground, unmoved and untouched, wherever the Caretaker chose to leave them. If Reverend Bryan found out he'd taken the hoe, he'd be in serious trouble.

He looked up at the wall. It was made of bricks and was about twice his height—about ten feet. He stood silently for a few minutes, looking up at it. There were several thousand Ded, the oldest of them about 500-years old. As far as he knew, none had ever done what he was about to do.

Standing on tiptoe, he thrust the hoe upwards and caught the top of the wall with it. Grasping the handle, he pulled himself up, hand over hand. Much of his flesh had rotted away, and what was left was pretty dried out, so he weighed much less than when he'd first awoke as a Ded so many years ago.

He reached the top and pulled himself up so he could straddle the fence. He didn't want to fall off the edge of Dedland. Once he was secure, he took his first look outside the walls.

Reverend Bryan was wrong. There was no edge in sight. Just a flat, gray area outside the wall, about fifty feet wide, and endless trees beyond that. Tossing the hoe down first so he'd be able to get back, he scrambled down on the other side.

He decided to follow the gray path outside the wall, and began a circuit of Dedland. The gray material was hard like rock, with two yellow stripes down the middle. Every few hundred yards an out-branching path would lead away from the walls, disappearing into the trees. Charles stayed with the path by the wall.

He decided that if Dedland was the area inside the walls, the area outside needed a name. He decided to call it Outside.

He was startled by sudden light and a strange sound. Turning, he saw a pair of yellow lights approaching rapidly. He'd never seen light from anything except the moon, the stars, and fireflies, and never anything this bright. According to Reverend Bryan, the Ded fall apart in the absence of darkness, which is why the Ded are so careful to be underground and in their coffins before the dark goes away.

Charles threw his hands over his head, shielding his eyes from the brightness as the creature bore down on him. Panicking, he dove for a tree on the side of the path away from the wall. Hiding behind the trunk and shielding his eyes as best he could, he peered around the side of the tree at the coming monstrosity.

It was like nothing he'd ever seen. He'd seen the full moon reflect light off a raccoon's eyes before, but these two eyes were far larger and brighter. The creature was blue, and much larger than any living thing he'd ever seen. The legs moved so fast they were just a whir.

The creature whooshed past. It had two red eyes on its back, not quite as bright as the front eyes. It disappeared into the distance.

Charles didn't move for five minutes. He almost turned back, then decided he had to see more.

He went back to where the path forked and followed the path away from Dedland for about ten minutes. The path curved sharply to the right, and he rounded the curve—and saw the double yellow lights from another of the huge creatures approaching. Once again he hid behind a tree and watched.

As the creature approached the curve in the path, it slowed down. Charles leaned out from behind the tree got a good look at it.

This one was red. What he'd thought were legs were actually dark, round objects spinning in circles. *What a wonderful way to move about!*

The creature came to a near standstill as it went around the curve. Its upper half was transparent, and Charles could see inside the creature. His jaw dropped at what he saw.

There appeared to be a Ded *inside* the creature. He stared at the Ded-like creature as he felt about the ground and found his jaw and put it back in.

The Ded-like creature glanced over and saw Charles in the shadows. It was a woman. She nodded in his direction and continued on past.

Charles glanced down at Toby, who was peering out from the hole in his stomach. If a rat could live inside him, could these Ded-like creatures live inside a larger creature?

He continued down the path. Soon he saw more lights, but these were attached to tall poles on the side of the smooth, rocky path.

He'd now been exposed to quite a bit of light and it hadn't bothered him at all, other than hurting his eyes somewhat. Reverend Bryan was wrong again.

As he continued to walk, more and more of the large creatures with Ded-like creatures inside went by. Some had more than one inside.

The trees on each side of the road came to an end and were replaced by strange structures. There were many more lights now. His eyes slowly adjusted to the increasing brightness.

He got his first close look at the Ded-like creatures living in Outside. They looked like fresh Ded, newly unearthed in a wake. He saw some getting out of the large creatures and entering the large structures. The large creatures were not really creatures, he realized. They were transportation devices for the Ded-like creatures. He'd call them transporters.

The Ded-like creatures had faces that were smooth and without character, their clothes were new and embarrassingly clean, and they walked about in a smooth fashion instead of the more jerky but rapid gait of a Ded. These had to be the "living" Ded he'd predicted.

He decided he'd call them the "Unded."

"'Scuse me, you okay?" The voice startled Charles and he spun about.

A large Unded dressed in blue stood there, smiling down at him. He had a shiny silver object pinned to his chest and wore a blue hat. Charles could hear a heartbeat coming out of his chest, like an animal, though a bit slower than most.

The smile quickly vanished and was replaced by a look of horror. Now his heart beat almost as rapidly as Toby's had.

"*Have you been in an accident?*" the Unded asked. The look of horror changed to terror. "*My God, the smell! And—your face! What happened to you?*"

Several other Unded approached. A woman shrieked and was pulled back by a man. Charles turned to them and approached them.

The man punched him.

Although it knocked his head off, it didn't hurt. Charles put his head back on, making sure it was on more tightly this time.

The Unded man drew his hand back to punch him again. Charles grabbed the arm and wrenched it away. There was a ripping sound and the arm came off. Blood squirted out of the man's shoulder, like an animal. Charles politely tried to hand the arm back, but rather than take it so he could put the arm back on, the man began screaming and ran away, like an animal.

"Hold it right there! Don't move!" It was the Unded in blue. Charles turned to him. He was holding something in his hand, which was shaking like Toby used to do on cold nights before he'd died. Charles took a step toward the Unded.

There was a sound of thunder. Charles put his hands tightly over his ears. Something shot into his chest and went through, leaving a hole and knocking Charles slightly back. There was more thunder and more holes as Charles was knocked backwards. After six of these, the blue Unded fumbled with the object in his hand. He seemed to be jamming something into it. Charles looked down and saw that the six holes looked like the holes in the four who had guarded his grave.

Charles thought he understood. Back in Dedland, he often played rock tag, where the object of the game was to hit your opponents with rocks. Here they had a more advanced version, where they shot rocks out of the strange device in the blue Unded's hand. Smiling, Charles approached the blue Unded. It was his turn.

The Unded didn't think so and fired two more of the rocks at him. That made eight holes in his chest. *Toby will have fun playing in those*, he thought.

He grabbed the object out of the blue Unded's hand—a rock thrower? He'd watched how the Unded had worked it, and now pointed it back at the Unded. He fired a shot into the Unded's chest and smiled at the backlash that knocked him backward. The loud noise was rather irritating.

A hole appeared in the blue Unded. Blood began pouring out. The Unded looked down at the hole, and then fell to the ground.

All about, the Unded were screaming and running away. Charles didn't understand. Had he violated a rule?

Two more Unded dressed in blue came charging out of a black and white transporter, their blue hats falling off behind them. They both held rock throwers, which were apparently okay for shooting at him, but not at them.

The two kneeled down by the blue Unded he'd knocked down with the rock thrower. One of them said, "Jim, get me the med kit." The other went back to the transporter and returned with a box. The other was holding the still Unded's arm and shaking his head. "Too late. He's dead." The one named Jim glared at Charles. The heartbeat of the still Unded on the ground had stopped.

The two Unded rose to their feet, holding up their rock throwers. Charles smiled back at them, trying to be friendly, and held up his own rock thrower.

The two began firing rapidly. The loud sound of these rock throwers bothered him. He approached the two, who backed away until they came to the wall of the structure behind them. Charles grabbed the rock throwers from them and tossed them aside.

The two blue Unded ran back to their transporter, which took off down the path.

Charles was now alone, other than the Unded lying silently on the ground, next to one of the strange structures.

The front walls were transparent. Inside a few Unded were hiding in the back. He'd seen how they operated the opening to the structure. Grasping the handhold in front, he pulled it open and entered the structure.

There was so much screaming that he quickly left the structure. *What was wrong with these Unded?* Several maggots crawled across his face as he contemplated.

He glanced over at the Unded lying on the ground. Perhaps he'd perform a wake on the Unded later on. But the man had been rude, so perhaps not. He picked up the Unded's blue hat and put it on. Charles liked hats. Many of the older Ded wore hats, while the more recent ones did not.

After picking up some of the pieces of himself that the rock throwers had knocked out and putting them back, he decided to explore some more.

He walked down the lighted path, sometimes stopping to examine the structures along the side. Everywhere he went the Unded ran screaming from him. Most were full-sized, but he saw a few his size and smaller. In the distance he heard loud sounds, sort of like the screeching of a bird, but much louder. Several times black and white transporters went by, and Charles realized the sounds were coming from them. These transporters not only had lights in the front and back, but had a light on top that flashed red, blue and white. The Unded in the transporters didn't see him and continued on past.

He came to a row of structures that were different than the earlier ones. These were mostly made of rectangular red rocks and had fewer lights. Transporters were sitting in front of all of them. He chose a structure at random.

It had a light in front, next to an opening. There were also a number of transparent openings. A light shown out of one of them, but from a higher level.

He'd learned how to operate the openings to these structures and so grabbed the handhold in front and pulled. Instead of swinging open like the other one, it resisted. He pulled harder and the entire opening tore out with a crash, along with the walls on either side. Charles tossed it all aside and entered the structure.

It was very dark inside. All those bright lights had made his eyes sore, and this was more restful to them.

He walked about, examining the many strange and inexplicable objects he found. Soon he came to a stairway. He followed it upward.

There were a number of doors there. He tried the first one, which opened to an unlit room. Inside he saw two Unded lying on a raised platform, sleeping. He looked them over. It was a man and a woman. The man was snoring very loudly. Looking closely, he saw that the woman had something stuffed in her ears. Charles smiled. Some of the Ded also snored, and the Ded in nearby coffins would stuff bits of clothing in their ears to drown it out. So this was one thing the Ded and Unded had in common. He silently left the room and closed the opening.

The next opening went into a smaller room. He examined himself in a large mirror on the wall. Several of the Ded had smaller ones, but none nearly this large. Below that he saw a pair of knobs, and turned one. Water shot out. He turned it back and left the room.

He could see light coming out from under the next opening. He quietly opened it and entered.

As his eyes adjusted to the light, he saw several items in the room. One was a raised platform. On it lay an Unded, who was smaller than the earlier two, about the same size as Charles.

There was light coming out of a book from the side of the platform. The Unded was holding something in front of him near to the light and hadn't noticed Charles yet. He knew that for some reason the Unded were horrified at the sight of him. He remembered the first Unded in blue had said something about his face. *OK*, he thought, *let's try something*. He pulled his shirt up so it covered most of his face. He still wore the blue hat he'd picked up from the blue Unded on the ground. He pulled it down low on his face.

"Hello?" he said. The Unded looked up. He was wearing a light blue floppy shirt covered with pictures of transporters. He had a blanket pulled over him to his stomach. "Please don't scream or anything. I'd just like to talk to you."

The Unded sat up, putting aside the book. Charles could hear his animal-like heartbeat. "Who are you? What are you doing in my room?"

"I'm not sure," Charles said.

"Was that you making all that noise a little while ago?"

"That was me, sorry."

The Unded tilted the light next to him so it shown on Charles, and looked him over closely. "Why are you wearing a policeman's hat, with your shirt pulled over your face? And why are your clothes all ragged and dirty? Are you a robber?"

Charles had no idea what a policeman or a robber were. "There's something wrong with my face and it scares people." *That was ironic,* he thought. *These Unded had horribly smooth faces, and his face was supposed to be scary?*

"If you don't show me your face, I'm going to scream for my mom and dad."

Charles had no idea what a mom or dad were, but figured they were the two in the other room. "Please don't. I'll show you my face. But you have to promise me something."

"What?"

"No matter what you see, no matter how horrible you think it looks, it's just on the outside. Please don't let it scare you."

The boy tilted his head. "I once saw a dead dog by the side of the road, covered with maggots, and that didn't scare me." The boy sniffed the air. "What's that smell?"

That was the second time someone had mentioned that. Charles had no idea what smell was. "I don't know. But I'm going to show you my face now. Remember, don't be afraid." He took off the blue hat and pulled down the shirt.

"*Wow!*" the boy said. He worked his jaw, and then frowned. "Are you the Living Dead? Are you going to eat my brain?"

Charles didn't really understand this. He wasn't alive, but he was one of the Ded. How could one be a Ded and also be alive? And what was that about brains? He had no interest in brains. His own had pretty much rotted away, but it didn't seem to serve any useful purpose, like arms or legs did.

"*No!* I'm not going to eat your brain. I'm Charles. This is Toby. What's your name?"

It took a moment, but the boy finally rasped an answer. "I'm Lee. What happened to you?"

"Nothing happened to me, but I can tell you where I'm from. Wanna hear?"

They talked long into the night.

At some point, Lee nodded off, and Charles made himself comfortable on the floor. He dozed off.

❧ ❧ ❧

Charles awoke with a bright light on his face. It was coming through what Lee had called a window.

Nothing happened.

This was far brighter than the lights he'd met up with during the night. It took a long time to adjust to the brightness. Lee explained that it was sunshine.

"My parents already left for work. They'll be back at lunchtime. They were pretty angry about the damage you did to the front door, but I didn't tell them anything. It's a good thing it's summer, or I'd have to go to school."

"What are parents? What's work, lunchtime and school?" There was a lot Charles had to learn about the Unded, just as Lee had a lot to learn about the Ded.

Lee now took Charles for granted and enjoyed playing with Toby. He solved the smell problem with a huge dose of what he called air freshener. Charles watched while Lee made and ate breakfast. He'd seen Toby and other small animals eat, but it seemed strange for something that looked so much like a Ded to eat like a common animal.

"I can't believe you live in *Parkland Cemetery!*" Lee said.

"I can't believe you *eat food!*" Charles said.

Charles soon learned about computer games and the two spent much of the morning at that. It was magic the way things danced about the screen at the touch of a button.

"What type of games do you play?" Lee asked.

"Football, rock tag and heart attack are my favorites."

"I know about football, but I like baseball better." He explained the game for Charles, then asked, "What's rock tag?"

Charles explained, and Lee grimaced. "That would hurt!" Charles was a bit confused. How could getting hit by a rock hurt?

"What's heart attack?" Lee asked.

"I'll show you," Charles said. He looked about for a suitable stake and found one. It was a little small, but it'd do.

"What are you doing with my pencil?" Lee asked.

"*Heart attack!*" Charles said with glee as he plunged the pencil deep into Lee's heart. "*You're it!*" Charles jumped back to avoid any counterattack by Lee.

However, Lee wasn't counterattacking. Strangely, he'd fallen back onto his bed, gasping. Blood gushed from the hole in his chest. Lee's heartbeat began to slow and then stopped. Charles didn't understand.

"What's wrong?" he asked. Lee lay still. Charles shook him. There was no response.

Charles stared at Lee's body for a long time. How fragile were these Unded. Then it dawned on him. The man he'd shot with the rock thrower before—a policeman, according to Lee—had also lain still, like Lee. Had they both died? Like animals? It was the only answer. He had killed them—was that a bad thing? It felt like a bad thing. Or was it?

If they had been killed, like animals, couldn't they be brought back as Ded if he did a wake? But Lee would need to be buried first for at least a few hours.

Charles heard the front door opening. *The parents must be back!*

"Lee? Come on down for lunch." He heard footsteps approaching.

Charles wasn't sure what to do. Lee wasn't about to come down, and Charles didn't think he'd get much of a welcome either. There was no time to hide, so he stumbled into a corner and stood silently.

"Lee?" The woman was at the door, looking in. She saw Lee covered with blood. "*Lee!*" she screamed and ran to the bed.

Charles heard the loud footsteps of the other one approaching. The man entered the room. "What's wrong?" Neither had noticed Charles, who was standing still by the closet.

When he saw Lee, the man's face turned white, like a newly arrived Ded. By now the woman had stopped screaming. *"Give me your cell phone!"* she exclaimed, and grabbed an object from his belt. She jabbed at it three times with her finger, then pressed something. A moment later she began speaking at it. "We need an ambulance at..." Charles couldn't quite follow the rest. The woman finally put the object down. Both of them were crowding around Lee.

"Excuse me," Charles said. Both looked up.

"What the hell?" the man exclaimed. He charged and grabbed at him. Charles easily ducked out of the way and pushed the man hard. The man went flying against a wall. A moment later the man stood up and again approached Charles, more warily this time.

His attention diverted, Charles didn't see the woman sneak up behind him and hit him with what Lee had earlier called a baseball bat. Charles's head went flying off. *That's twice today,"* he thought grumpily as he retrieved his head. *Enough of this.* He went to the window and punched it. The transparent material that Lee had called glass shattered. As he was hit with a storm of fists and baseball bats, Charles jumped out the window.

It was several hours and numerous other incidents before he found his way back to Dedland. He never wanted to leave again. The Reverend had been wrong, but he had been right in a way. Outside was no place for the Ded.

❧ ❧ ❧

The Reverend came to see him shortly after, and lectured him on Ded philosophy, religion, and truth. Charles hung his head while the worm in the Reverend's neck seemed to shake its head at him in contempt. The Reverend didn't know about his excursion and Charles wasn't going to tell him. His shirt had more holes than before, care of the rock throwers, but it was so torn up that the Reverend didn't note. Charles apologized and promised he wouldn't go to the wall. He was sincere and the Reverend believed him. The guards were removed. The rope, which Charles had retied around his waist with the portion left, was taken off.

Two nights later there was a new wake for two Ded. He was shocked when he saw that the newly Ded were the policeman in blue...and Lee! He got a look at Lee's tombstone. It said, "Lee R. Johnson, Jan. 5, 2000–Dec. 15, 2012.

I should have known this was coming, he thought. *This proves that the Ded come from the Unded. The Ded just don't remember their origins.*

Reverend Bryan performed the wakes. Charles stood in the back, not wanting to face the two, even if they wouldn't remember him. The Reverend held the policeman's wake first. Charles had learned from Lee about policemen, but he hadn't told Lee that he'd unknowingly killed one.

All went well until the policeman sat up and saw Charles. The policeman's eyes went wide as a look of absolute terror came over his face. He jumped up and ran away, screaming.

"That's one of the worst reactions I've ever seen," the Reverend said. He looked at Charles quizzically. Charles just shrugged his shoulders. Several Ded caught up with and restrained the policeman. When no one was looking, Charles quietly left, and hid in his coffin while the Reverend held Lee's wake. How had the policeman remembered him? The newly dead never remembered their past as an Unded. Was there something missing from his theory of the Unded as the origin of the Ded?

It was inevitable the two would meet, and they did so the next day. Charles was playing rock tag with Barbara. He pelted her with rocks and she gleefully pelted him back. He turned to look for more rocks and came face to face with Lee.

"*You!*" Lee exclaimed. Instead of horror, he was angry. "*You killed me!*"

"*You remember that?*" Charles gasped. Impossible! But it was true. Like the policeman, Lee somehow remembered. Charles had learned something new.

A Ded recognizes his murderer and then remembers the murder itself.

The killing took a lot of explaining by Charles, since Lee was still new to the ways of the Ded. He didn't remember anything else from his previous life, just the part where Charles had killed him. He finally calmed down and accepted Charles's apology. Charles mistakenly killing him was understandable, given his lack of knowledge about the Unded.

Lee found Charles's narrative about his previous life as an Unded less believable. "You're kidding, right?" Lee exclaimed. "I don't remember any of that."

However, Lee remembered much of his time with Charles, and when Charles prompted him, he began to remember what he'd told Charles. He remembered explaining about parents, work, lunch, school, and many other things. He no longer remembered these things directly, only telling Charles about them.

"I want to meet my parents," Lee said. Charles saw no reason why not. So the next night, off they went, sneaking to the wall where Charles had left the hoe.

Charles had learned from experience, and had borrowed a hooded jacket and sunglasses to mostly hide his face. Lee still looked enough Unded to pass as one. They made it to Lee's house without incident.

The reunion went off as well as could be expected. It was quite a shock for both sides. Lee had hoped he would recognize his parents, but they were complete strangers to him. For his parents, it was worse. First they had to accept that Lee, who so recently had been dead, now seemed alive, but was now Ded. Then they had to accept Lee's word that Charles was all right, even though he had maggots crawling on his face, goo coming out of his ears, and that he was quite obviously Ded...or from their point of view, dead.

Lee's parents started to hug Lee, but pulled back. "You're so cold!" his father exclaimed.

"Dad...Mom...I already explained to you," Lee said, exasperated. "I'm Ded!" This was very hard for them to accept.

Charles bit his lip hard. He'd almost pointed out that he'd been the one who'd killed Lee. A piece of his lip fell off.

Lee's parents were loving parents and soon had Lee in a deadly and tearful hug.

Dad was staring at Charles. "I recognize you—weren't you the one in the room when Lee was killed?"

Charles hung his head. "Yes, it was me. I'm sorry, I didn't mean to kill him."

"You bastard!" the Dad said. Charles saw the blow coming, but didn't react to the punch to the face. It knocked his head off again. He crouched to pick it up and put it back, but the Dad hit him again and again. Charles had learned that to the living, this was somehow painful, though of course to the Ded it just meant he was knocked around and damaged a bit.

"Stop it, Dad!" Lee said, getting between the two. He grabbed his Dad, and despite his much smaller size, had little trouble restraining him. The Unded had their good points, but strength wasn't one of them.

"He didn't know what he was doing," Lee continued. He explained the game of heart attack.

"So he just jabbed a pencil into your heart, and didn't think it would do anything?" Mom asked.

Lee grabbed a pencil off a table and jammed it into his heart, making a matching hole to the one Charles had created. "Doesn't hurt a bit," he said.

Both parents took deep breaths, but they seemed to accept this and the fire left their eyes when they stared at Charles.

Lee moved back home again. There was no way of explaining him to their friends and neighbors—who he didn't recognize anyway—so he stayed hidden. It was rather boring and he began to complain.

A few weeks later, he began to look more like the Ded than the Unded. Dermested beetles had taken a liking to his face. His parents came to accept that he would be better off living with his own kind rather than hidden in their house. Lee promised to visit often and returned to Dedland.

Since he'd only been in Dedland a couple of days before leaving, he hadn't really gotten to know anyone there and few noticed his disappearance. Those that did shrugged their shoulders and accepted it. The Reverend admonished him for missing church. Lee promised it wouldn't happen again.

Charles made his amends with the policeman, whose name was Bob, and returned the blue police hat to him.

Charles enjoyed having another person his own size and to play with, along with the two Willy's and the three girls with cut throats. They played a lot of football and rock tag. But Lee was dead set against playing heart attack. Two holes in his heart were enough, he said.

Lee, who was rapidly learning the ways of both worlds, explained to Charles that Robert and Susannah must be his parents. To Charles, they were just neighbors and friends, and he decided not to mention it to them. However, he vowed to spend more time with them. He wondered if the three girls with cut throats were also related? Lee explained the concept of sisters and brothers that he'd learned from his parents. Perhaps the three were sisters?

They let Barbara in on their secret. She was horrified that Charles had left Dedland, but had no problem believing them. She was awestruck by Lee and his past as an Unded. It hadn't quite registered with her that they were all former Unded.

🦇 🦇 🦇

On the night of October 31, the Ded awoke to the sounds of laughter, partying, and festive music. As they came out of their coffins they were surrounded by costumed Unded, who thought they were costumed performers and part of the festivities that Lee's parents had arranged near the front gate of Dedland, or as the Unded called it,

Parkland Cemetery. It was the first "Lee B. Johnson Memorial Halloween Party."

As far as Charles knew, this was the first time the Unded had ever entered the world of the Ded, at least during the night. He'd learned from Lee's parents that it was the Unded who buried the Ded, not the Caretaker—the Reverend was wrong. The Reverend hadn't been invited to the party, but there was enough noise to wake the Ded. He could barely hear the heartbeats of the Unded.

Many of Lee's former friends attended, including schoolmates and several teachers. None of the Unded recognized Lee, who no longer resembled his Unded self. He had taken on a gray complexion and Dermested beetles were still eating away at his face. A fat worm stuck out of a hole in his cheek; once again Charles wished he had one. Barbara said she thought Lee looked very handsome. Lee's parents decided not to introduce Lee to his past friends. How would they explain him? It was better to let them think what they thought, that he was just another kid with a great costume.

Mr. Vickers, a teacher from Lee's school attended, asked to say a few words. He was a tall, thin man with an even thinner face, and a long, thin nose. Charles thought his colorful Hawaiian shirt was something out of a nightmare, and that the man smiled too much.

"It's been many weeks since Lee was taken from us," Vickers began. As he spoke, both the Ded and the Unded gathered around. Charles stood next to Barbara, who was chatting with her fellow neck-slashed friends, Suzy and Collette.

"Why, Charles has a worm sticking out the back of his head!" Barbara exclaimed.

"I do not have—" Charles stopped, and felt around the back of his head. Something cold and sticky hung out of it. He had his own worm! "I'll call him Sticky," he said. "Now be quiet so we can hear Mr. Vickers."

"Sorry," Barbara said. She and the other two girls turned to Vickers. Charles heard Barbara gasp.

"We'll never forget him," Mr. Vickers was saying, shaking his head. He continued, but Charles didn't really hear as he turned to watch Barbara backing away.

"What's wrong?" Lee's mom asked.

Barbara's eyes were wide as she stared at Vickers, and the dandelion on her head seemed to stick straight up. Finally she whispered, "I remember. He's the one that killed me." She turned and ran.

Suzy and Collette were also staring at Vickers. They turned and followed Barbara.

Charles still only had a vague idea about the concept of killing, but knew it was a bad thing. He stared at Vickers, wondering if he should do something. After all, he'd learned that the Unded were pretty weak, and any of the Ded could pretty much overpower them, or even kill them—though he wasn't sure he wanted Vickers to become a Ded.

"*What's going on?*" thundered the Reverend. Charles hadn't noticed his arrival. Someone turned the music off, the dead silence now only broken by the chirping of crickets and the beating of the Unded hearts.

"It's the Unded," Charles explained. "From outside."

"There is no outside," the Reverend said. "Face the truth!" Then he stopped. "Who are these..." He didn't finish as he looked about, as if not sure what to call the arrivals. "These must be new Ded. But how..."

"They are not Ded," Charles said. "They are Unded, from outside."

"They are Ded! And there is no outside!"

"Then what's that?" Charles asked, pointing at the still-open gate.

"It's—" the Reverend began, but he stopped and stared at the gate.

"They—"

"*Leave now!*" the Reverend thundered, holding up the lighter.

The chirping crickets stopped. With a flick of his thumb, the bright yellow flame leaped out. Then he walked toward Charles. His eyes shone in the light, approaching like one of the Unded's cars in the night.

"Leave!" the Reverend thundered again. "Or *burn*."

"Where would I go?" Charles asked.

"Away from here!"

Charles took a step back. "No."

The Reverend took a long step and was all over him, the flickering lighter in his face. "Then burn." He thrust the lighter into Charles's hair. It exploded into flame.

Heat and pain shot through him. *Was this what Lee felt like when he'd stabbed him?* It was like nothing he'd ever felt. He dropped to the ground, clutching at his hair.

Something went over his head, and the heat died away, though not all of the pain. Lee's dad stepped away, pulling away the burnt shirt he'd used to smother the flames.

"You will also burn!" the Reverend cried, pointing the lighter at Lee's father.

"Stop it!" Charles said. "You always talk about the truth! Everyone, quiet!"

"What—" the Reverend began.

"Shut up!" Charles said. "Listen."

Everyone quieted. With the music off and the crickets quiet, there was only one sound left.

"Listen to it," Charles said. "The beating of hearts. Unded hearts." He knew the Unded couldn't hear it; they not only were weak physically, but they were practically hard of hearing as well. But to the Ded, it was like...raindrops on a tombstone. Like Toby before he died. The rat peered at him from the hole in his stomach.

"You can't deny the truth," Charles said. "The Ded don't have heartbeats. They are Unded. It's truth!"

"Truth!" someone said.

"Truth!" said another. Others joined in the chant, drowning out the heartbeats.

The Reverend flicked off the lighter, staring at the ground, and seemed to shrivel as the heartbeats and chanting continued. Finally he looked up.

"Truth," he said.

🐻 🐻 🐻

"Your honor," the prosecutor said, "unexpected eyewitnesses to all three murders have come to our attention."

"Objection!" cried the lawyer for Mr. Vickers as he leaped to his feet. The constant smile on Vickers' face dimmed a bit.

Charles sat among the Unded, unnoticed in the courtroom. Lee's mom had spent hours covering him with makeup and a new set of clothes, but the Unded still looked at him funny. Nobody paid him any attention now as the prosecutor and lawyer had an animated sidebar with the judge. When they finished, the prosecutor was smiling. The lawyer sat next to Mr. Vickers and whispered something, and for once, Vickers frowned. Then the prosecutor turned to the jury.

It's been several months since the Halloween party. The Unded at the party had left believing it was all part of the most realistic Halloween show they'd ever seen—only a few knew the truth.

Lee's mom had been teaching him how to read. Charles especially liked reading about animals. He had figured out on his own the origin of the Ded, that they came from the Unded. Now he learned that the Unded and all animals evolved from other animals, according the evolutionary theory of Alfred Russel Wallace. It was a fascinating concept. Were he and the other Ded at the top of the evolutionary tree? He wasn't sure.

He also liked reading history, especially ones that seemed to mirror his own introduction to a new culture, such as when Europeans had their first contact with American Indians. It was quite a cultural clash, that first contact. But it was nothing like what was about to happen, and this time there would be no Halloween party to explain it away.

"I call Barbara Stanton to the stand," said the prosecutor. For all intents and purposes, it was first contact. Unlike Charles, Barbara was not disguised in any way.

Pandemonium.

THE
PIPER'S
SONG

GAIL Z. MARTIN

THE FIRST INKLING SOMETHING WAS WRONG CAME WHEN THE WHITE GHOST Bikes began to clang and buck against the chains that bound them to lamp posts and street signs, wheels spinning without a breeze to turn them. Those whitewashed bicycles, symbols of riders killed in traffic, dotted the streets in and around Charleston, somber and usually silent memorials.

The second warning came from the roadside markers, the homemade crosses, and wreaths near the highways commemorating fatal accidents, the passing of loved ones. Calls surged to 911, reporting detailed accounts of car wrecks along the state routes and interstates, and all of them had two things in common. First, that the wreck details were completely correct, and second, that the fatalities had happened months, sometimes years, ago.

The last time those particular two sets of ghosts acted out, Charleston teetered on the edge of an apocalypse, beset by Nephilim raised by a long-dead hanging judge bent on fulfilling a vendetta. He and the Nephilim were gone—I knew because I'd been part of the fight to destroy them—and they weren't coming back.

What frightened the ghosts now, I didn't know but would make it my business to find out. Anything that terrifies the dead is more than enough reason to cause concern for the living.

"Can you read anything?" Teag Logan asked, standing next to me as I laid my hands on one of the Ghost Bikes that had started to rattle and clank on its own several hours earlier.

"I see a beautiful day, bright sun, music playing somewhere... the rider glanced to one side...then the crash, flying through the air, hitting the ground, darkness," I murmured, reading the strong emotions imprinted onto the bike by its dead rider. Not all of the Ghost Bike memorials are the actual cycles from an accident; some are purchased and painted as a tribute. The stand-in bikes weren't the ones causing problems, just the twisted and damaged ones that had been part of their riders' last moments.

"The memories of the crash are faded," I continued. "But the fear is new and strong." I strained to glean more from my connection with the bike's resonance and let myself open up to the memories that had sunk deep into the mangled steel.

The first vision had been of flowers and sky, sun and warmth, memories of life. Now, I saw through the eyes of the biker's ghost, the spirit that had remained attached to the place and vehicle that caused his death. The color and heat had faded from this view, leaving it cold and gray.

I had read the placard about the rider, George McMillan, a bicycle delivery messenger who had lost his life in a hit-and-run crash. Now, I saw through the eyes of George's ghost, surveying the landscape around me and feeling his fear. The ghost stood next to the ruined bike on a city side street, but all alone, separated from the living souls around him by the veil of death, present but unacknowledged. I got the feeling that George had made his peace with that, and wasn't ready yet to find out what happened if he sought out the light, and transitioned to the next stage of existence. He wasn't hurting anyone, but now, I knew that something had come looking to hurt George.

I heard the tune, a strange, mournful song that carried from a distance as if seeking an audience. George panicked, and I had to remind myself that I was seeing what had already happened, seeing the ghost of a ghost, so to speak, and that I could do nothing to calm the spirit or ease his fears.

The song grew louder, and George tried to run, but like most ghosts, he could only go so far beyond the object that anchored his spirit to this world, and the bike was chained to the light post. The bike shuddered and shook, wheels banging and chain rattling, but George could not flee. I tried to identify the tune, and couldn't quite retain the melody, although it played over and over, a hypnotic, compelling score. Perhaps it wasn't meant to be heard by the living, but it certainly affected the dead.

George clapped his hands over his ears and shook his head. "No, no!" he shouted, as the song grew louder. I had just decided that the strange tune was being played on some kind of reed pipe when George began to scream.

The images flashed past me, jumbled and chaotic, infused with George's utter terror. I glimpsed a presence, some kind of being, but only as an indistinct outline of a hunched creature upright on two legs. The music reached a crescendo, and George's ghost began to disintegrate in front of me, as if the song had the power to pull the ghost apart, bit by bit, until nothing remained.

The music stopped. George's ghost was gone.

"Cassidy!"

I followed my way back to Teag's urgent voice, and woke from my trance, leaning against the light pole, and removed my hand from the bike's worn seat. "Something hunted him," I said, drawing in a deep, shaking breath and trying to collect my wits. My connection to George's memories had been visceral, and I had felt the last lurch of his terror and the instant his consciousness was extinguished. Witnessing his unmaking, the violence against his spirit, affected me to my core. I wanted to scream, to collapse, to throw up.

Instead, I managed a wan smile as Teag placed a warm, anchoring hand on my shoulder and pressed a bottle of orange juice into my hand.

"Don't try to tell me about it now," he soothed.

"Is she okay?" A woman asked, stopping her morning jog to check.

"Low blood sugar," I murmured, hating to lie but knowing she really didn't want to hear the truth. "I'll be fine, thanks."

The woman jogged off, and Teag glanced around to assure that we were alone again, at least for the moment.

"I heard music in the dark, and saw a...thing...and then something tore George's ghost apart," I said, still breathing hard.

"You got a lot. More than with any of the other bikes."

I drank the juice gratefully and shook my head. "Not enough to make sense of what's going on, unfortunately. The last time the ghosts got upset, things went bad in a hurry."

I'm Cassidy Kincaide, owner of Trifles and Folly, an antiques and curio shop in historic, haunted Charleston, South Carolina that is a lot more than meets the eye. We get cursed and haunted objects out of the wrong hands, and we've saved the world on more than one occasion.

We also keep some important secrets, especially about magic. My magic is psychometry, the ability to read the memories and magic from objects by touching them. Teag has Weaver magic, and he can weave spells into cloth and data into information, making him one hell of a hacker. My business partner, Sorren, is a nearly 600-year-old vampire who was once the best jewel thief in Antwerp.

We're part of the Alliance, a coalition of mortals and immortals who protect the world from supernatural threats. When we win, no one notices. When we lose, the carnage gets blamed on natural disasters.

"Ready to head back to the store?" Teag asked. We had spent the morning checking out the Ghost Bikes and roadside memorials where disturbances had been reported. I'm not a medium, so I don't channel the ghosts, and I can't summon them, which means I have to rely on the spirits to make themselves seen and heard. Failing that, I can use my psychometry to pick up the resonance of their emotions before—and after—death, and then piece the clues together. It's a tedious process.

"Sure," I said. "We can pick up lunch and bring something back for Maggie." Maggie is our fantastic part-time assistant. She doesn't have any magic of her own, although she knows all about ours, but she's got sass and an awesome sense of humor. Maggie retired from teaching, then retired from retirement to help out with the store. I'm pretty sure she can honestly say that it's never been boring.

We picked up pizza and took turns eating and watching the front of the store. That's when I noticed the large wrapped rectangle leaning against the wall in my office. "What's that?" I asked Maggie.

"You or Teag had it shipped from that estate sale you went to last week," she replied with a shrug. "We have the two other cartons of stuff from there you brought back yourselves."

I remembered as soon as she mentioned the sale. Teag and I keep an eye on auctions and estate sales because they're a way objects with harmful resonance can make their way from person to person. We not only buy items suitable for the store to re-sell, but we also cull out problem pieces before they have a chance to cause havoc.

The mirror hadn't struck me as dangerous, merely unsettling. We knew very little about the old woman who had died, only that her home was full of beautiful, expensive, and odd items, a curiosity-seeker's paradise. The old house had been a solid brownstone in a nice part of town, and from the very sparse bio the auctioneer shared, Eliza Roberts had died at age 95, never married, and was the last of her family line. What had intrigued me was that while I saw very few religious items in the house, a fair number of pieces had possible connections to spiritualism. I didn't know whether or not Eliza had been a medium, but I'd lay money on the possibility that she dabbled in speaking with the dead.

"You're thinking something." Teag jarred me out of my reverie. "Spill it." He's my assistant manager for the store, but he's also my best friend and on occasion, bodyguard.

"After we close up, I want to get a closer look at that mirror and some of the other things we brought from the Roberts house," I said. "If the spirits are restless, maybe they'll contact us."

"Or you could just call Alicia," he suggested. Alicia Peters, a powerful medium, was a friend and an ally who had helped us on a number of occasions.

"Alicia's canvassing her side of the city for Ghost Bikes and roadside shrines, remember? So we'll hear back from her when she's done," I replied.

"You don't know how the objects will react to your magic."

"Do we ever?"

Teag sighed. "No. All right. Go help Maggie up front, and I'll get everything ready."

Fortunately, the rest of the afternoon passed quietly, but as I wished Maggie a good evening and locked the door behind her, I felt my nervousness ratchet up, wondering what would come from Eliza's mirror.

The rectangular looking glass had a dark mahogany frame. The silver backing had none of the signs of age that too-often marred a big piece, so the reflection showed clear and true. Teag had moved a more comfortable chair out of my office so I could have better support as I touched the mirror and opened up my magic. He's used to my psychometry by now, and more than once he's had to help me off the floor when a vision landed me right on my ass. I noticed he also made a pitcher of fresh sweet tea, which helps me recover from the huge energy drain that a difficult psychic connection can cause.

"I wove some new strips," Teag said, nodding toward several hand-woven fabric runners, each several inches long and a few inches wide, like overgrown bookmarks, which lay on the table. "They'll help ground and protect you, and this way, I can see what you see."

Teag could weave his magic into the warp and woof of fabric, creating powerful protection spells, but he could also create a psychic bridge between us so that he didn't have to rely on me to recount what I saw. That had saved my butt more than once when a vision turned suddenly dangerous.

"All right," I said, settling into the chair facing the mirror. "Let's see what's through the looking glass." In my left hand, I held one end of the woven ribbon and Teag held the other. I put my right hand on the cold pane, and like Alice, felt myself fall into another world.

Everything around me was made of silver and shadows, like a moonlit night. I knew I wasn't alone but feared to call out, unsure of whose attention I might draw. This place beyond the mirror was far colder than our break room, and when I glanced behind me, I saw my own face staring back at me, and the warm light of the real world setting it apart.

"Who are you?"

I startled and turned to face a woman whose somber black dress reminded me of the mourning clothes of a past era. I recognized the face. Eliza Roberts, the woman who had owned the mirror.

"My name's Cassidy. Are you Eliza?"

The woman nodded.

"We're not alone here, are we?" I could sense other presences all around us, just out of sight in the shadows. We stood in a pool of moonlight, distinct from the darkness all around. I did not want to leave the light or venture out of sight of the mirror and the way home.

"No. Mirrors harbor spirits. It's a safer place than many, especially now," Eliza replied.

"Do you know what's frightened the ghosts?" I turned slowly, scanning the darkness. I glimpsed eyes and pale skin, but no clear faces or forms.

"Not exactly," Eliza replied. "There's an old, strong power at work, one I don't recognize. I studied such things when I was alive. I've been able to see spirits in mirrors since I was a child, and since no one would teach me, I taught myself. But this new presence, it's dangerous and hungry."

"Hungry?"

"The entity is eating souls," Eliza said.

"So the ghosts it eats, what happens to them?" I felt the cold that surrounded me seep into my bones at the idea that even greater dangers existed after death.

"They cease to exist," Eliza answered. "At least, their consciousness is gone. They say energy never is destroyed. But they are no longer who they were, and they have not passed on to the next level, gone to the light. However you would phrase it."

Vanished, with a finality even greater than death. Many ghosts retained sentience after death and chose to stay behind to watch over loved ones, protect something important, or see justice done. I'd seen those spirits eventually find peace once their task was completed, moving on to whatever came next. To think of them being hunted, trapped, *consumed,* shook me on a visceral level.

"I offered sanctuary to those who sought it, here with me," Eliza said, gesturing to the shadows that surrounded us. "I couldn't save them all, but those who came, I protect."

No wonder the mirror gave off such a powerful resonance, disquieting but not evil. "I'll help you protect the mirror," I promised. "But please, tell me anything that might help us stop whatever is out there hurting the ghosts."

"The creature selects its victims," Eliza said, choosing her words carefully. "It preys on more recent spirits. The old haunts are rooted too deeply for it to disturb. It favors violent deaths. Few of those who took refuge here came from their sickbed. I believe creatures like this may have stalked battlefields, and now without that kind of carnage, it takes its pickings where it can."

Violent deaths—like the car crashes and bike accidents. I felt my anger rise. Those ghosts often stayed behind because it took time for them to process what happened to them in a single, traumatic instant. Even crime victims often had a few minutes before death to understand what was happening, but those from wrecks were alive one minute, dead the next, and wandered lost and confused until they finally figured out what had happened to them. The idea that a predator stalked them at their most vulnerable made me furious— and determined to do something about it.

"We'll find a way to stop this," I promised. "When we do, can the spirits leave here?"

Eliza nodded. "We are all free to move on from this place, when- ever we choose. I consider it a halfway house for wayward spirits," she said with a faint smile. "Go back to your world," she told me. "It's cold here, and you have work to do."

With that, Eliza Roberts turned and walked into the shadows until she vanished, leaving me alone in the moonlight.

"Cassidy!" Teag's voice called. "Cassidy, can you hear me?"

I closed my eyes, and let Teag lead me back to the warmth and light of the mirror, and through it, back to myself. I shuddered and drew a harsh breath.

"You're cold as ice," he said, letting go of the fabric ribbon to fetch me a sweater from my office, and a glass of sweet tea. "Here you go," he said, tucking the sweater around me and handing me the glass. I drank it down, and snuggled into the soft wrap, waiting to warm up and feel the sugar rush. Teag sat quietly, patiently biding his time until I had recovered.

"What did you make of all that?" I asked, hoping that our con- nection through the spelled cloth had given him a front-row seat.

"It's not the weirdest thing we've ever run into," he said, sitting back once he was sure I wasn't about to pass out. "We've seen dark witches drain energy from ghosts before, like cosmic batteries."

"They weren't particularly easy to stop, as I recall," I replied, and shivered. "But I don't think that's what we're up against this time. At least, not from what Eliza knew. She made it sound more like a creature, almost a psychic parasite, something that gravitates to natural disasters and wars where there's a lot of violent death."

Teag fetched me a hot cup of coffee with plenty of sugar, and I gripped the mug, warming myself from its contents. "Alicia should be back soon," I said, glancing at the time. "In the meantime, I've got a call to make."

My cousin Simon picked up on the first ring. In certain circles, he's better known as Dr. Sebastian Kincaide, folklorist, author, former university professor, and now the owner of Grand Strand Ghost Tours. "Hi Cassidy! Good to hear from you. Is this business, or pleasure?"

"Business, unfortunately, although it's always great to hear from you," I replied, putting him on speaker so Teag could listen. "We've got a situation."

"Tell me."

I explained about the Ghost Bikes and the roadside shrines, the spirit refugees in the mirror and the creature that tore apart George's ghost. Simon listened to it all with rapt attention. He knows about my gift and what we really do here at the shop, and his background with mythology and the occult—not to mention his own abilities as a clairvoyant and medium—have come in handy.

"I think it's a *maita*," Simon said when I finished. "I've read about them, but I've never run into one before."

"That's a creature I haven't heard about before," I admitted. "And I thought we'd seen everything."

Simon chuckled. "Probably not—although you do seem to see more than your share of cryptids and creepies. *Maita* come from African folklore, and there are varying tales depending on the tribal origin. Most agree that the *maita* begins as a cannibalistic witch and becomes a ravenous spirit after death—a soul eater."

Teag and I exchanged a look. "How the hell do we kill it?" Teag asked.

"That's the problem. There are ways to kill the living cannibal-witch to stop it from becoming a *maita*," Simon replied, and I was in awe of his encyclopedic knowledge. "Once it's become one, I'm not sure there's a way to destroy it—at least, for someone on this side of the divide."

"The divide?" I questioned

"The Veil," Simon replied. "Between the living and the dead."

That added a new wrinkle. "If someone were going to try to kill a *maita*, is there a type of weapon that might be better than others?"

"Cassidy, you can't be serious. Please tell me you're not thinking of going after one of these."

"It's kinda what we do, Simon," I replied. "And we have a pretty amazing group of friends. So, weapon?"

Simon hesitated and then sighed. "Iron works on most spirit energies. Probably not salt, because it's more of a creature than a ghost. I don't think silver has any special protection either. The only thing the legends say about killing a *maita* is that its power is held in special stones in its stomach. Cut open the stomach, spill out the stones, and the *maita* is destroyed."

"Do we have to do anything to the stones?" Teag asked.

"It wouldn't hurt to scatter them, although I don't think the *maita* can re-gather its energy," Simon replied. "Just please, be careful. The lore is very spotty; don't risk your life on it."

We thanked him and hung up, just as we heard a knock at the back door. Alicia Peters, a good friend, and a powerful spirit medium, stepped inside.

"What a day!" She and I both said in near unison and had to chuckle despite the dire circumstances. "You first," I said, as Teag pulled out a chair for Alicia and I went to get her some sweet tea. I filled my coffee cup as well since I figured it was going to be a long night.

Where my magic reads the memories and energy resonance of objects, Alicia is a true psychic medium, able to talk to ghosts. I wondered how much our experiences checking out the same types of memorials differed.

"The ghosts are terrified, and some of them have gone missing—been destroyed," Alicia said, sipping her tea. "They're aware that something is preying on ghosts, and no one knows when it might come for them. It doesn't feel like the power of a dark witch or a rogue necromancer. From what the ghosts could tell me—and it wasn't a lot of detail—it sounds like we have a creature out there feeding on spirits."

"Simon thinks it might be a *maita*," I told her and was ready to explain when Alicia frowned.

"That's really interesting. I'm surprised we haven't run into something like that before," she said.

"How's that?" Teag asked.

Alicia took another long drink of the heavily sugared sweet tea, letting it replenish her. "Charleston was one of the top ports for receiving enslaved individuals back before the Civil War. Some of those people came from the areas where belief in the *maita* originated. Just like with Voudon and Hoodoo, people brought their beliefs with them, and sometimes, they mingled with other influences to become something new and different."

"How do we fight it?" I asked. "Is this something Donnelly or Sorren could handle?" Archibald Donnelly is a mostly-immortal necromancer, and Sorren, my boss, is a vampire. Their special abilities—and the fact that both are extremely difficult to destroy—have come in handy when we have to battle bad nasties.

Alicia shook her head. "I don't think so. Simon told you that the *maita* has to be fought in the realm of the dead. It's not a ghost, so Donnelly wouldn't have any special power over it, and we don't even know if he could cross over to that realm and get back, given what he is. Same with Sorren—he's undead, not dead. I wouldn't want to risk having him enter and not be able to come home. There are plenty of stories about living people being able to go across and get back, if you're careful."

"We'll need iron knives," Teag said, "and I'll bring my silver whip, just in case. Protection charms, definitely. And something to guide us back, in case the path isn't clear."

"Us?" I questioned. I had figured I would go—if we could work out how to get to the frickin' *realm of the dead*—and that the others would stay behind to make sure I got home.

Teag and Alicia both glared at me. "Us," Teag repeated forcefully, and Alicia nodded. "We all go, or none of us goes."

"Okay," I relented. "But if this creature exists in the realm of the dead, we can't do anything until we know how to cross over—without doing it the usual way—so we can get back."

"I think I know just the place," Alicia said, giving me a grin I knew meant trouble.

❦ ❦ ❦

"I know this road. There's no bar here," I said as Alicia drove us down Huguenin Road, the avenue of cemeteries where more than a dozen graveyards held centuries' worth of Charleston dead.

"It depends on who's looking," Alicia replied as she parked along the side of the road. "I *am* a medium, after all."

"Whoa," Teag murmured as we got out of the car and stared at what my mind knew should have been an empty lot with the remains of an old foundation. Instead, a long one-story brick building stretched the length of the lot, running alongside the stone wall that marked the edge of Magnolia Cemetery, windows alight, and smoke rising from the chimney. A wooden sign proclaimed it to be "Hearseman's."

"I don't understand," I said, stretching out with my gift. I felt a strange resonance I'd never encountered before, something solid and yet *not*, real and other.

"For two hundred years, Hearseman's bar stood where you see it, and while it served everyone, it was particularly known for taking care of the men who dug the graves at all the cemeteries on this road," Alicia said. "The gravediggers, the groundskeepers, the landscapers, and the hearse drivers, as well as the priests and ministers who held the services—they all came to the pub when their work was over."

"But it's not there anymore," Teag protested. "At least, it wasn't—"

"It burned down seventy years ago," Alicia replied. "The fire went up quick and took a lot of the regulars with it, as well as the bartender. Times had changed, and some of the community fathers didn't think it was fitting to have a tavern adjacent to a cemetery. So the bar wasn't rebuilt. But it never really went away."

"It's a gateway?" I asked.

Alicia nodded. "Among other things. When conditions are right, and the ghosts are willing, Hearseman's is as real as you need it to be. It's a gathering place for spirits, and for those of us who can see them. And if you walk out the back door, you walk into the nether realm."

"How long will it last?" Teag asked, eyeing the old building skeptically. "We don't know where this *maita* is, or how to find it. What if we go through, and the tavern vanishes?"

"That would be bad," Alicia admitted. "We'd have to find another gateway, and while they're not uncommon, they're not on every corner. As for locating the *maita*, I suspect it's more likely that we'll find him sniffing around Hearseman's like a kid outside a candy store."

"If the creature is stealing souls, it's not going to be able to resist a big prize like Hearseman's," I said.

"I don't think the ghosts who anchor the tavern are at risk if the *maita* prefers to poach the newly dead, like trauma victims," Alicia replied. "But Hearseman's attracts ghosts, new and old, when it appears. And Reginald, the barkeeper, says some of the recent customers have wandered away and not been seen again."

"They're ghosts. Is that so strange?" I asked.

"Reginald sounded like he kept track of his regulars, and that the core group doesn't change a lot. I got the impression he kept an eye out for the newcomers. But when he said that customers told him about hearing strange music that called to them, that's when I thought it might be our *maita* at work," Alicia replied.

Teag pulled out a small cloth bag from inside his jacket. "Before we go in," he said and emptied three amulets into his palm. "I worked on these last night. They're kinda like beacons, to help us find our way home. Each of these has tendrils of energy that wind between the wearer and someone who serves as an anchor. The charm is woven using hair from both of you," he added.

Alicia and I had both given Teag a bit of our hair, something we would only do for a person we trusted implicitly because hair is such a powerful, personal connection in magic. Apparently, he'd made some house calls as well.

"Cassidy, yours is linked to Kell," he said, naming my serious boyfriend. "Mine, of course, is connected to Anthony," he added. No surprise there, since he and Anthony were a long-time couple. "And Alicia's links to Megan," he said, mentioning the medium's wife. "They have all agreed to allow us to draw on their energy, woven together with ours, to give us a lifeline in case we get separated, or we can't find our way back to the gateway."

I slipped the amulet's leather strap over my head and wrapped my hand around the charm. I could feel the thrum of Kell's energy and my own, and closed my eyes, appreciating that I had someone who cared so much about me.

"Hearseman's is a place for the dead, not the living, so all the standard warnings apply," Alicia said. "Don't eat or drink anything, either in the pub or beyond. Injuries that happen across the Veil are real back here, so be careful. Don't try to bring anything back with you that you didn't carry over."

Pretty simple, but myth and legend are full of people who couldn't follow the rules.

Alicia led the way. I concentrated on my touch magic as we headed for the phantom bar, since I can often sense a strong resonance through the soles of my shoes. One minute, the ground beneath my feet felt neutral, and the next, as I stepped over the transom, my gift went flooey for a moment, like a compass spinning without finding true north. The floor held my weight, the bar's patrons and furnishings looked solid, and the scent of pipe smoke, roasting meat, and beer seemed real enough. Yet my psychometry insisted that everything around me was not right, something other than it appeared. I just hoped I could tamp down the conflicting input from my gift before it gave me a splitting headache, or worse, distracted me in a moment of danger.

Hearseman's looked like a country tavern, the kind that welcomed working men and women with dirt under their fingernails and a sheen of sweat from a hard day's labor. Given the bar's true age, there was no TV and no recorded music. The buzz of conversation, punctuated by occasional guffaws, filled the space. Photographs around the room showed proud drivers with their fancy hearses, from the Civil War on up through the bar's lamentable demise in the 1940s. Those opulent hearses were quite probably the most dignified transportation the deceased would have ever known, and many a mutual aid society or beneficence organization took great pride in being able to send one of their own off in style.

Some long-time patrons were immortalized by the tools of their trade, shovels scrubbed clean enough to shine, fastened to the wall with a plaque commemorating those who wielded them. A few aged photographs showed dozens of men with dour expressions and somber black suits standing in rows for the camera, the proud gravediggers of the cemeteries of Huguenin Road. I glanced at the ghostly patrons. Some were black men with arms of corded muscle, sitting next to beefy white fellows and Jews with yarmulkes and forelocks, sharing a bottle or a pack of cigarettes. A few hard-worn women gathered at their own table, their tanned faces and broad hands a testimony to a life of hard work. Despite what might have been common elsewhere when the tavern physically existed, Hearseman's was open to all those who helped the dead cross over, regardless of color or creed.

"Hello, Alicia," Reginald greeted the psychic from behind the bar. None of the regulars bothered to turn around. "You've brought friends."

"Just passing through," Alicia replied. She looked around at the patrons. "You've got a full house tonight."

"People gather when they're frightened," Reginald replied, raising one eyebrow with a knowing look. "I'll hold us here as long as I can, but best you be on your way and get back fast as you can, you hear?" He gestured toward a hallway that led into darkness.

Alicia thanked him, and we followed her down the shadowed corridor. The sounds of the tavern faded quickly behind us, making me wonder just how long the hallway extended. I thought we might pass the kitchen or some other rooms, but the passage was long, narrow, and unbroken until we came to a door at the end.

"Ready?" Alicia asked as we paused by the exit. When we nodded, she opened the door, and we entered the realm of the dead.

From the books and movies I'd consumed since I was a child, I expected something that looked like black and white photographs, or perhaps a true underworld of caves and tunnels. Instead, I stepped into a blighted landscape of dead trees and withered plants.

"Is this the afterlife?" I asked, thinking that religion down through the ages had gotten the details terribly wrong if this was the endgame.

"No," Alicia replied. "It's an antechamber for souls that are too conflicted to move on. Spirits that want to leave our realm, but don't feel ready to go to the next level, so to speak."

That made me feel marginally better since I didn't want to vacation in this bleak place, let alone spend eternity here. My psychometry found an uneasy truce with the strange land underfoot, registering it much the way it did a cemetery—unquiet ground.

"How do we know where to look?" Teag asked. We had all pulled out our iron knives and other weapons when we left the back door of Hearseman's, and now we stood back to back, surveying this strange, forbidding terrain. No birds sang, no leaves rustled, only the skeletal clicking of bare branches in the cold wind.

"There!" I whispered, afraid that if I spoke aloud, it would stop the music. "Can you hear it?" The notes of a flute carried through the air, beautiful and poignant, calling for me to follow. My spirit lurched at the sound as if it might be tempted to leave my body, and I clamped my hand around the amulet to ground myself.

"I hear it too," Teag echoed, and Alicia agreed a second later. They looked as uncomfortable as I felt, torn between wanting to follow the music and find the *maita*, and the sense of self-preservation that insisted on running the other way.

"Look!" Alicia pointed, and I saw that we weren't the only ones to fall under the sway of the music. Two ghosts appeared ahead of us, too far to catch up with but still in sight. "Go back!" Alicia called out to them. "You're in danger!" But the ghosts kept on walking, managing to stay far ahead even when we picked up our pace.

Then we saw the piper. The creature had a distorted body, with arms and legs too long and gangly to be right, and a hairless head with bat-like ears. The face might have been human once, but now the features were contorted, the nose pushed in and wrinkled, eyes slitted, mouth protruding like a lamprey with rows of sharp teeth that were visible when the *maita* paused its playing. A distended belly hung down with the weight of the spelled rocks inside. The monster raised its flute, which looked like it was made from a hollowed human bone and began once more to play its tune.

"The ghosts look like they're in a trance," Teag said quietly. "They're heading right to him."

"I wonder why it pulls some and not others," Alicia mused.

"Now's the time," I urged, "while he's focused on dinner."

We spread out and rushed forward, counting on the *maita* to be distracted by the ghosts, because the lifeless landscape offered us no cover. I veered right, Teag went left, and Alicia headed straight for him. Teag had his coiled metal whip, and while the silver might not do extra damage, the sharp edge of the thin blade was dangerous enough. Teag and I both had our iron blades ready, and I also had my athame, a wooden spoon with strong positive resonance from which I could pull power.

Alicia was our secret weapon, and while she also carried a knife, it was her ability to call spirits that might give us the advantage we needed. We closed in on the *maita* just as it reached for the first of the two mesmerized ghosts, sinking its claws through the insubstantial form and yet somehow snagging the wraith to draw it forward toward its maw.

Teag launched himself at the creature, striking with his iron dagger and landing a deep blow to the *maita's* side. I dove forward at nearly the same instant, driving my knife through the *maita's* tough hide and into its back. Neither of us could get a clear shot at the belly of the beast, where we needed to land the killing blow.

Realizing its danger, the *maita* let go of the ghost it had snared and turned its attention to Teag and me. Its sharp teeth chattered, and its dark eyes watched us, and then it sprang at Teag, moving faster than its heavy belly suggested might be possible. It snapped at him with its teeth and grabbed for him with its clawed hands. Teag lashed out with the metal whip, cutting a deep gash across the *maita's* chest but not low enough to make a difference. Behind me, I could hear Alicia calling out to the ghosts, asking for their help to bring down a threat bigger than any spirit could evade on its own.

I lunged at the creature, slashing with my knife, managing to land a blow close to its stomach, but not close enough. Teag and I wove and dodged, trying to steer clear of those sharp claws and pointed teeth, and still inflict the damage necessary to destroy the *maita* and save the ghosts.

That's when I realized it had grown much colder, and when I looked up, I saw that a host of spirits had answered Alicia's summons. They surrounded us, watching as Teag and I battled the monster, managing to wound but not yet kill the *maita*. The creature lunged for Teag, ignoring the slash of his knife and the slice of his whip and took them both to the ground, its sharp talons raking across Teag's chest.

I leveled my athame, drew on its resonance, and sent a blast of cold energy at the *maita*, tearing him off Teag and sending him sprawling. Teag staggered to his feet, bloody but alive, and we both went after the *maita* before it could regroup.

The ghosts surged forward, massing around the downed monster. Individually, the spirits were at the *maita's* mercy, but collectively, emboldened by Alicia, they were far too many for the creature to threaten all at once. The spirits swarmed over the *maita*, keeping it on the ground, and Teag and I approached warily, looking for our opportunity. I slipped my athame back beneath my sleeve, and gripped my knife tighter, ready for the right moment.

The creature struck out against the ghosts, flailing with its sharp claws and kicking with its taloned feet, snapping its teeth and shrieking as the wraiths dodged its blows and fought back against the monster that stalked them. Teag circled around, coming in above the downed *maita* and then rushing forward to drop a loop of his sharp metal whip around its head, as I mustered my nerve and dove for its bulging belly.

I plowed through the cloud of ghosts that were keeping the *maita* down, feeling as if I were sinking through icy mist. The gray revenants were corpse cold, frigid as the tomb, and my whole body shuddered and shivered as I brought the iron knife down two-handed and sank it hilt-deep into the creature's distorted abdomen.

The *maita* let out a piercing shriek that felt like someone raked a scalpel along my bones, but I couldn't stop now. I had to trust that the ghost would keep the creature's hands and feet away from me and that if Teag's whip didn't decapitate the *maita*, it would at least give it something else to fight against. Using all my strength, I ripped downward with the blade, opening the monster from chest to groin. Black ichor spilled out and with it hundreds of smooth stones of all sizes, each with a faint, sickly glow.

The *maita* bellowed in pain and fury, and one of its feet caught me on the thigh, ripping into my leg and sending me sprawling. Alicia's voice rose, shouting for the ghosts to keep fighting, and their numbers grew, a surge tide that nearly hid the monster from my view.

Teag gave a final jerk on his whip and stumbled backward as the *maita's* head came free, rolling clear of the ghosts. I crawled back into the fray and steeled myself for the freezing cold as I came back to finish the job.

A heap of glowing stones lay slick with foul black goo, spilled out between the *maita's* legs. I swept them away with one arm, sending them out of the creature's reach, and then fell on its body, digging into the cavity with my hands to make sure all of the stones had been removed, no matter how tiny.

Alicia found the bone flute that had fallen in the struggle and crushed it underfoot.

Bleeding and freezing, I startled as Teag laid a hand on my shoulder. "Come on, Cassidy. It's done. We need to go home."

He helped me to my feet, and when I tried to put weight on my injured leg, I cried out. Teag leveraged his uninjured shoulder under mine. "Quite a pair we make, huh?" he asked, and I could see he was as dead tired as I felt.

"Alicia?"

"Right here," she said, and then held both hands up in blessing, murmuring something that I didn't catch but which made the ghosts pull back from the *maita's* corpse. They regarded us in a somber, gray line like spectral soldiers.

"Thank you," Alicia said to the spirits, and Teag and I added our gratitude. "The creature is gone. It can't hurt you anymore. Take what rest you can." She lowered her hands, and the spirits dispersed, some vanishing in a blink and others drifting away.

When they were gone, I could see the monster's body. The head lay several feet away, severed by Teag's sharp whip. The magic stones had been pushed far away from the corpse, and we scattered them even further.

"I wish we could burn the body and those stones," I said.

"Not sure how you start a fire in the realm of the dead," Teag said with a pinched smile.

"Can something else find the stones and use them? What if there's another one of those things out there?" I asked, as the reality of the fight finally caught up with me. I was covered in blood from my hands to my shoulders, spattered with gore everywhere, and bone weary.

"Then we'll deal with it, when—if—it happens," Alicia replied.

We turned around, in the direction I was certain we had come from and saw nothing but a gray, blighted horizon.

"Where's Hearseman's?" My voice sounded hollow.

"It's still there," Alicia said, "the ghosts are watching it for me. But we need to get back. Reginald can only hold the gateway open for so long."

"How—" I started to ask, and then I remembered the talismans, our very own ruby slippers to take us home.

I closed my hand around the amulet, and I felt the warmth of Kell's concern and the life energy of the tether Teag's magic had woven.

"Ready?" Teag asked.

"Very," Alicia replied, and I nodded fervently.

We made slow progress, me with a bum leg and the others on

the brink of exhaustion from the fight. Without the amulet, I would have despaired, because the way back seemed to stretch much farther than when we had come. Whether that was true or just a trick of the strange realm, I didn't know, but when the lights of Hearseman's finally came into view, I nearly cried in relief.

"Is it done?" Reginald asked as we made our way out of the long corridor and back into the pub. Despite the fact that we looked like we had come from a war, none of the patrons paid us any heed.

"It's over," Alicia said. "The *maita* was destroyed."

"Thank you," Reginald said, taking in all of us with his gaze. "We owe you a debt." He inclined his head toward the door. "Now, you'd better get going. It's time for us to move along."

We hobbled out the door and into the night. I had no idea how long we had been in the realm of the dead, but I was hungry, tired, and thirsty, and all I wanted was to go home.

To my surprise. We found three cars waiting on the darkened street. Anthony, Kell, and Megan stood huddled together and sent up a quiet cheer as he headed toward them. I looked over my shoulder and saw that the plot behind us was once again empty land. Hearseman's had gone to wherever good ghosts went to drink, and I hoped I didn't have reason to visit it again.

"We brought food, water, and first aid supplies, plus some whiskey—for medicinal purposes, of course," Kell said as he came to relieve Teag of helping me hobble. Anthony was a step behind him, heading for Teag like a guided missile. Megan rushed for Alicia and pulled her into a tight hug, murmuring into her hair. I felt like we were returning from deployment back to our waiting loved ones, and perhaps that wasn't too far off the mark.

The shadowed length of Huguenin Road held Charleston's dead in its many cemeteries. I hungered for light and warmth. "Let's get out of here," I said. "For the rest of the night, the world is going to have to look after itself. We're officially off duty."

FEED THE STOVE

J. D. BLACKROSE

MARY SHOVELED COAL INTO THE POTBELLY STOVE KEEPING HER EYES AVERTED from the furnace door, hoping to avoid conversation. The giant stove was in constant need of feeding, be it coal or wood, to provide heat for the downstairs and to Mary, who had tended this stove all of her twenty years, the furnace was a fierce taskmaster.

Pa said it was "a gen-u-ine Hatfield from the Gem line," which Mary knew was true because Hatfield Gem was stamped right on the front. All she understood is that she'd never slept through a whole night since it was her job, her only job, for her entire life, to keep the stove fed at all times.

Mary's hands, face and clothes wore a thin layer of coal dust. Her lungs were black with it although she didn't know it, and the same blackness seeped into her soul. She did know that but she didn't care.

"Mary!" her mother called.

"Yes, ma'am," Mary replied running into the kitchen where her mother was boiling eggs, grateful the stove had kept quiet. Mary couldn't believe the chickens still were laying, but it was her brother Jacob's job, his only job, for his entire life, to make sure they did.

"Watcha doin' girl?"

"About to go down the hill to get more coal. We'll need it to see us through the next week or so. Abe says its gonna get cold and windy."

"That man's knee has never failed us yet. Okay, you go get the coal. Wheelbarrows where ya left it. And Mary..."

"Yes'm?"

"Don't be dilly-dallying talking to that Deihl boy. You know how your Pa gets."

"Mom, Otto's not a boy. He's a full grown man."

"Humph. Doesn't matter."

"Matters to me. I'm an old maid now. Otto Diehl is the only man left alive who's interested in me."

"We've talked about this, Mary. Pa has made this plain. Your job is here, helping your dad, me and your brother. No one else can feed the stove like you do. If you left, who would do that job? We'd all freeze come winter. Do you want that to happen?"

"No, ma'am."

"I'm sorry, girl, but with your two older brothers dyin' off of..." Mary stopped to wipe at her eyes. "And your eldest sister gettin' married without our permission, you and Jacob all we got left. We best stay together."

Mary didn't meet her mother's eyes and she plodded outside to grab the wheelbarrow, the damn thing rolling in the correct direction almost by itself. Mary thought of her Pa, deep in the mine chipping away at the mountain from the inside. Mary wondered what would happen when the mining company finally dug out the center.

Would the mountain fall in on itself or slide apart in pieces, sending slabs of rock over the town, erasing the town as the miners had erased its innards. Seemed fittin' to be the latter, thought Mary.

She passed the "Welcome to the Coal Mines of Black Hills, PA" sign, hanging from one corner, squeaking back and forth with the wind. It was only a few more yards to the coal shed where Otto worked.

"Heya, Mary," said Otto, when he saw her. He doffed his wide-brimmed hat. "How much you needin' today?

"Abe says we headed for a cold spell, 'though full winter won't be here yet for a month or so. Guessin' I need a whole wagon full, maybe two." Mary gazed at the sky and noted the thick clouds rolling in despite the modest temperatures.

Otto bent down to retrieve a shovel, his biceps bursting from his gray shirt and his tight backside framed by his worn tan workpants. Mary admired the view but pulled her face back together when he stood.

"Ya'll only have the one wagon and that means you be makin' two trips," said Otto. "Don't 'spect many more people comin' in today so I'll bring a second wagon fur ya, if that be okay?"

"You sure? That's not necessary," replied Mary, twisting her neck to look up at him. She hadn't realized how tall he was.

Otto blushed. "Well, Mary, it'd be my privilege, if you let me."

Mary peered down at her shoes like they had turned into a snake. Her head was busy thinking. What would Momma say if she let Otto help her with the coal? Is that the same thing as bringin' a boy home?

She shuffled her feet back and forth and decided even it was, she'd do it. Let Momma say something when she was only doin' what' right by the family. She bobbed her head in agreement.

The way back seemed shorter than the way there and before Mary knew it, they were in front of her house. "I'll help you load it up in the coal bin, Mary," said Otto, staring at her with warm eyes.

Mary ducked her head, wondering if she'd been too forward with the conversation, as her Momma would say.

Momma stepped out on the porch, hands on her hips, back erect, steel bun in place and a fake smile plastered on her face. Her eyes bored into Mary like termites into wood. Mary could feel her mother's disapproval squirming into her body, worming its way through every cell. The restriction that had loosened during the talk with Otto drew so tight she couldn't breathe.

Her Pa rounded the house from the back, home early. The afternoon breeze died out like a snuffed match. Mary's legs twitched with the need to run.

Otto doffed his hat again and stammered, "Hello, Ma'am, Sir. I'm helpin' Mary with the coal, seein' as she needed two wheelbarrows full. I'll just help you get it loaded in the bin, Mary, and be on my way."

Pa's raspy voice carried across the stillness. "That's very nice of you, Mr. Diehl, but no need to help Mary get the coal in the bin. That's her job and I'll thank you to let her to it. Don't *you* have a job to do?"

"Yes sir." Otto turned to Mary. "It was nice talkin' with you, Mary."

Mary didn't dare respond. Pa cleared his throat and Otto back peddled out of the yard like his pants were on fire.

Mary managed to whisper, "Otto was helpin' me so I didn't have to make two runs."

"No, he was hopin' to make a run with you, nasty girl. Now get that coal where it needs to be and come into the kitchen. Your Momma's got potatoes to peel." Pa turned on his heel and walked into the house. Jacob, about to exit, stood sideways as his father elbowed his way through, then scuttled out with his head bowed, shoulders hunched.

Mary turned her back on the house, so angry her hands were shaking, unable to cry, her fury depriving her of tears. She was touched when Jacob ran his hand over hers and whispered, "I'm sorry, Mary."

She squeezed her nails into her palms. "Me, too, Jacob. Where you goin'?"

Jacob made a face. "Chicken coop o'course. That's my *job*." Mary nodded in understanding and gave his hand a squeeze. Then they both looked back at the screen door and fled to their different corners of the yard.

After filling the coal bin, Mary carried several buckets worth of coal into the main room and shoved the first one into the stove. The Gem model sighed in happiness.

The second bucket of coal slid down the Gem's throat and was swallowed whole.

Mary considered a third bucket but decided to wait until later in the evening when the chill would be on full-force.

But I'm hungry.

Mary squeezed her eyes and fists, taking a sharp breath, muscles rigid.

Mary-girl, I'm hungry.

"I'm not listening!"

Mary scurried out of the room into the kitchen and focused on peeling potatoes for all she was worth.

Dinner was at twilight, the four of them eating boiled eggs and potatoes, and Mary and Jacob both gazed at their plates hoping not to catch their father's eye. Pa folded his hands and led them in prayer, "Bless us, O Lord and these Thy gifts, which we are about to receive from Thy bounty, through Christ our Lord. Amen."

Momma served Pa two whole potatoes and two eggs, which she had peeled for him beforehand. She served Jacobs two potatoes and one egg and Mary one egg and one potato. She served herself too, limiting her serving to potatoes only.

Mary chewed in deliberate small bites trying not to make a sound. She noticed in the silence that her brother did the same. Pa reached out his black-stained hand, black no matter how much he washed it, and snagged the last egg. Mary had hoped he wouldn't want it as she was still hungry and had reached for it, but jerked her hand back since her father claimed it.

"Whatcha thinkin' little girl," asked Pa. "You wantin' this egg?" He waved it in front of her face like he was baiting a dog.

"No, sir. I was goin' to offer it to you."

Momma interrupted. "Of course Pa should have it. He's the one who does all the hard work in that coal mine to support the family. We must make sacrifices."

"Damn straight," said Pa, stabbing a finger at Mary. "I spend my days in that gloom, riskin' life and limb, knowin' any moment could be my last and I want my damn egg."

Mary nodded but thought about how hard her Momma worked and how she herself could never get a full night's sleep because she had to feed the stove, and the most un-Christian notion occurred to her, which was that they all worked hard and things should be more evenly shared. She shut the thought down quick as it came, promising God she would not disrespect her father again.

Mary exhaled as she and her Momma cleaned up the plates in silence, not realizing until that moment that she'd been breathing so shallowly that she was dizzy from lack of oxygen.

Momma headed upstairs with an extra quilt and Pa followed. Jacob made his way upstairs too, but Mary stayed on the couch as always, knowing that she'd have to mind the stove the night through. The crickets were quiet this evening, the air heavy with something she couldn't quite place, and the dark smothered her, laying thick on her chest.

She knew it was coming.

Mary-girl, I need more.

"What is it you need?"

"Food, nourishment, sustenance, life."

Mary shoveled another bucket of coal into the stove.

Mary-girl, do I have a name?

"Your name is Gem. Says so right on your front." Mary's eyelids drooped.

That's nice. If I have a name and you have a name, then we can be friends.

"Yes." Mary's consciousness submerged as the stove plundered her mind, looking for weak spots. Her thoughts grew sluggish.

The coal is good, Mary, but not filling.

"What do you need, Gem?" Sluggishness liquefied to nothingness.

Let me show you.

A vision rose in Mary's head. She jolted back. "I can't do that!"

Of course you can, Mary-girl. Or I stop working and your Pa comes down with the belt.

"Can't it be anything else?" Mary begged.

The room cooled several degrees and Mary heard her parents' bed squeak.

"Okay, okay! I understand."

Keep it cold, Mary-dear. That will help.

Mary walked into the kitchen in a daze, opened a small trap-door, climbed down the ladder and grabbed a bucket of ice water from the root cellar. She scrambled up the ladder and gathered the other items she needed. Sitting in front of the stove she dunked her right foot into the ice water.

We must make sacrifices, Mary-girl.

Quick, Mary-girl. Now.

Mary removed her foot from the ice, held it to the floor with her left hand and placed a cleaver on her right pinkie toe.

She moaned. "I don't wanna."

Mary-girl, you have no choice. This is your job, your only job, for your whole life.

Mary cut her toe off.

Gimme, gimmme, gimmmeeee!

Mary threw the toe into the stove.

Quiet as a mouse, Mary wrapped her bleeding foot with a clean dishcloth, dunked it back into the ice and went to sleep for the rest of the night.

She woke early enough to hide the evidence, dumping the bloody water behind the chicken coop. She cleaned the knife and wrapped her foot in a white bandage which she covered with a thick sock. The stove was humming along, still warm.

Momma descended the stairs, eyes bloodshot, skin sagging with fatigue.

"Momma, are you sick?"

"Didn't sleep well, Mary, thanks for askin'."

"Why didn't you sleep well?"

Momma ran her hands over her face. "Let's get breakfast started. Room's nice and warm. You did good with the stove last night."

"Thanks, Momma."

Mary followed her Momma into the kitchen and couldn't help but notice that her Momma walked gingerly, like she was aching all over. Mary's foot ached in sympathy.

"Momma, you sit down. I'll make you coffee."

Her mother was in such a bad way that she didn't argue but settled herself in a chair and gave a short nod of thanks. Knowing her Momma was a private woman, Mary didn't ask questions but made coffee, sliced her mother's homemade bread into thick portions and toasted them in the oven. She retrieved a jar of the blackberry jam they'd canned during their short summer and placed the food on the table.

Pa strode in and plopped himself down at the table and ate breakfast without a look at anybody. Then he put on his coal miner's hat and took his leave. Jacob trailed in next, taking careful, quiet steps, head swiveling back and forth confirming that his father was gone.

Mary pulled out some toast she'd hidden and the three of them ate in silence.

The temperature dipped enough that there was ice on the porch and Jacob ran to the chicken coop terrified he'd not put enough straw into the corners to keep the hens warm. Mary limped into town with fifty cents and the hope of buying fresh milk.

She was surprised when her sister Charlotte slipped out from behind a stall.

"Hi, Mary," Charlotte said, holding out her hands for a hug. Mary collapsed into those arms glad to have a body to hold on to.

"Is it just as bad?" Charlotte asked, pulling Mary's chin up like she was a five-year-old.

"No, we're doing okay," Mary replied, crossing her fingers behind her back and sending up a plea to God not to mind her lie.

"You sure?"

"Yes.

Charlotte leaned in close and whispered, "I have news. We're having a baby."

Mary gave her sister another hug, unable to remain bitter in light of such happy news.

"Mary!" called a male voice, and the sisters turned to see Otto walking to them, flowers in hand, but when he got within arms' reach of Charlotte and Mary, he froze.

"Otto, those are beautiful flowers," said Charlotte, blinking back her tears so Otto wouldn't see. "How ever did you grow them in this weather?"

Otto stammered, "Well...we...we have a greenhouse and my mother likes these. They tolerate the cold..." He shoved them at Mary. "They're for you." His face was red enough for anyone to think he was having a heart attack.

Mary stood still, not sure what to do, so she looked at her feet.

"Mary...?" Otto said.

"Mary, take the flowers," Charlotte said, giving Mary a bump with her hip.

"Yes, of course."

"You like them?" he asked. "They're poppies. My mother loves their color."

"No one has ever brought me flowers."

Otto grinned.

"I'm glad I can be the first. You know I'd do anything for you, Mary."

Mary's heart beat fast and her feet itched with the need to flee, but she smiled and said thank you again.

That night Gem made another demand, swearing that she'd stop working and rouse Mary's father. Desperate, Mary complied. Her left toe went into the fire.

Mary could barely walk the next day and was finding it hard to balance without both pinkie toes. Her mind sank further into despair, shadows building at the edges, pushing out any light that was left. She hobbled to the coal mine and met Otto again, refusing his help but taking one barrel of coal. She couldn't possibly make a second trip.

"You don't look good, Mary. Let me know if there is anything I can do. I'd do anything for you, you know that, right?"

Mary could only nod.

Gem demanded more that night.

I'm starving.

"I've already given you my two pinkie toes."

A finger then.

"Please don't make me."

Do you remember the first time your father beat you?

She'd been eight. Her Momma hadn't got out of bed that day and wouldn't let Mary in to see her. Charlotte knew it was the mine's quitting time and was hiding with baby Jacob.

Pa stomped through the door, throwing the screen door so hard it ricocheted off the wall and lost a spring in its hinges. He bellowed for his wife demanding dinner. When Momma didn't come down he grabbed Mary by the neck and shoved her toward the ice box.

"I do everything for you and your Momma! Is it so hard to make sure I have a decent meal when I get home?

Mary did the best she could but she was young and supplies were limited. She gave him a cold boiled turnip and the rest of the stringy chicken they'd had the night before, holding the plate up for him. He took one look, threw the plate across the room, picked her up and lay her over his knee.

The first strike was with an open palm. The second another slap. The third a punch in the lower back. She didn't make a sound, remembering that Charlotte said crying made him happy.

Pa removed his belt to up the ante.

He whipped her across her back.

He whipped her across her legs.

Again. Again. Again.

When she still didn't make a sound he threw her on the ground and whipped the bottom of her feet.

Mary was separate from the pain, floating among the stars. The flick of the belt on her feet brought her back.

"I'm sorry, Pa!" she cried. "I'm sorry!"

The whipping stopped. Mary was distantly aware that her mother had hobbled down the stairs and pulled her husband to her and toward their bedroom. Mary passed out.

Mary's mind fractured, a piece flying off to a far corner of her brain, waiting to come out when the time was right.

Mary recalled beatings at ages nine, twelve, and fifteen. Each thrashing shattered her brain a bit more and those shards lurked in the background, ready for their time.

They decided the time was now.

Memories flooded Mary's mind, not only the beatings but the bruises on her mother's face, Charlotte's safe spot so well-hidden that no one else could locate her, a cat with its whiskers burned off. Jacob crawling under the table to get away from Pa's dinner-plate sized hands. The memories brought clarity.

Mary collected the ice, the cleaver and the rags and chopped off her left pinkie finger. It went into the fire and Mary slept the rest of the night.

The next night required her other pinkie finger. The following an ear lobe. The next a thumb.

Mary's mind was now a jumble of faceted slivers, iced with pain and the knowledge that she couldn't survive the stove. The blackness sunk through her whole body, covering her heart, settling in her belly.

She sacrificed a slice of her calf only to wake in agony horrified to find that the stove was cold. She shoveled coal into Gem, begging the stove to come back to life.

"Traitor! I gave you what you wanted."

I need more.

"I'll find a way to get you more, just get warm!" Mary hissed.

Promise?

"Promise."

Mary retreated to the kitchen and made bread, kneading and thinking, thinking and kneading. Rolling, braiding, starting more yeast. The house smelled good, a clever disguise for what lay beneath.

As the last loaf went into the oven, it came to her. So simple, she thought. It was right in front of her the whole time. She walked to the coal mine.

"Otto, would you be willing to come to dinner? I think it is time for you to get to know my parents."

Otto's face lit up and he held her hand, nodding yes.

Mary whistled all the way home.

She retrieved what was left of his flowers out from where she had hidden them so they could sit in a vase on the table. She trimmed some of the stems, petals and leaves, boiled water and got to work preparing for Otto's arrival.

Momma was out in the back yard, laying compost on the garden for the winter. She cradled one arm to her chest and was doing the task one-handed. Pa wasn't home yet.

Otto greeted her with a kiss on the cheek. Mary patted his cheek in return. Her mind was blank, dedicated to her plan.

"Mary, do you think..." Otto asked.

Mary turned to him, face serene.

"That I could ask your father for your hand tonight?"

The words burbled through Mary's brain, a thick stream of sound that oozed its way in. What he said made no sense. Why didn't he see her missing pieces?

She smiled and inclined her head.

"Wonderful, Mary, I promise I'll make you happy."

She patted his cheek again and handed him a drink, grateful she'd kept the poppies.

When Otto collapsed to the ground, Mary yanked him by his feet until she reached the trap door. She squeezed him through the opening and pushed, his body landing with a thunk on the root cellar floor.

She hummed her way through dinner, drawing concerned looks from Jacob.

That night, she eased herself down to the root cellar, finding blood on the ladder and pooled on the floor. Otto was still breathing but he was going to die soon. She didn't have much time.

She cut his hand off and fed it to the stove, who purred like a kitten after receiving the sacrifice. The stove told her to cauterize Otto's wound with fire, so she did.

Otto roused in the morning, screaming in pain, but that was taken care of with more poppy syrup.

That night, she cut off his foot.

The third night he was awake and hyperventilating. The pain from his destroyed limbs making him crazy.

Mary brought him some water and despite his anguish he used his good hand and swallowed in one gulp. She handed him some bread and he ate that too.

"Mary, what is happening? Tell me what is happening. Who is doing this to me? Get a doctor. Get my family. HELP me!"

"You said you'd do anything for me, Otto."

"Yes, yes..."

She caressed his cheek. "You are helping me now. Here, drink this."

More poppy syrup. She'd slipped into the Deihl hot house and stolen some more flowers. She fed him poppy syrup over the next day, keeping his pain at bay, addicting him to the drug one dose at a time.

When she went down the next night, his eyes were dilated and his stumps were bloody, the bandages shredded by an attempt to escape. He rocked back and forth, mewling until she held the glass to his lips and he drank.

He lost his earlobes that night and drank his medicine by day.

"Otto..."

"Yes, yes...I need. I need..."

"I know and I'll give. What should I feed the stove tonight, Otto?"

"My nose, Mary. Take my nose." So she did.

Otto disappeared piece by piece. He was legless and armless. He'd lost his nose, his earlobes and his lips. He was delirious from addiction, blood loss and dehydration. He gave the only thing he had left.

"Take my heart, Mary. Take my heart."

With Otto gone, the stove was antsy, wanting its flesh, used to it now. Mary satiated it with a whole chicken thrown in alive, but that only banked the stove's need.

Mary-girl. It's time to get your father. If anyone deserves it, it's him. That Otto was a nice guy.

"I don't know how, Gem."

Think of something.

Mary couldn't find a solution. The stove did as it threatened and went cold. The snow fell and icicles built up on the windows.

Her father pushed her against the stove in the morning. "What's wrong, girl? You have one job, it's your only job and you can't do it? Why's it so cold in here?" He took her head in both hands and banged it against the stovepipe. Mary slumped to the floor.

The mind shards shrieked. They rioted, their facets flashing rainbows that floated across her awareness. She looked at her father and in her mind the rainbows formed a jewel, a hard diamond reflecting her face, and she saw her own evil in the refraction.

The soot in her belly rose up to choke her. The blackness in her heart snapped it in two. The shards of memory in her mind let her see her crimes.

What had she done? What had she done? Oh, God, poor Otto. She clambered to her feet, ignoring the blood streaming from her skull.

"What did you make me do?" she yelled, pushing Pa with both hands.

Pa's eyes narrowed, feral, needing to kill. He had a reservoir of ink-black hate that was straining to be released. He lunged, teeth bared, his mind a ticky-tacky scorecard of slights, hurts, insults, and impotence.

Mary had lived through many such assaults and to her practiced eye, his attack was predictable. Timing it, she side-stepped, using his momentum to hurl him forward where the stove was waiting, door open wide. She shoved her father into stove's cold maw and as he descended the fire flared to life.

Mary rotated to see her mother at the top of the stairs, one hand to her heart, the other to her mouth. Jacob skidded to a halt behind her, his face a mask of fear and hope.

Gem whispered. *There is only one way.*

Mary squared her shoulders, blood flowing down her neck and arms. "I'm sorry, Momma, but we must make sacrifices. Feeding the stove is my job, my only job, for the rest of my life."

She threw herself in after her father, the stove snapping shut after her. She never heard her mother scream.

Charlotte returned home for the first time to hold her mother as she wept. Jacob, not knowing what else to do, went out to the chicken coop to do his job, his only job.

He entered the coop, shoulders stooped, his mind a mass of slithering snakes and snapping teeth. He looked at the chickens and stopped dead.

All of the chickens stared at him, unblinking, moving in the same manner at the same time, synchronized as one.

Jacob, we're hungry.

THE DEVIL'S CHAIR

ROB MacGREGOR

I EASED INTO THE PARKING LOT BEHIND THE OLD BRICK BUILDING THAT HOUSED the *Deland Star-Journal*, my first job out of college, my third day on the job. So far I'd spent two days writing obituaries for town folks who hadn't died yet. They'd been well known community leaders and were in failing health. Thanks to my diligent work, we were now ready to put them on page one before their bodies cooled down.

Today, hopefully, I would get a real assignment. I wouldn't feel like I was really a reporter here until I saw my byline, Thomas J. Reed, on an article.

I'd hoped to get hired as a reporter by the *Orlando Sentinel*, and had an interview the week after I graduated. The personnel director was impressed that I'd been editor of my college paper, but after he looked over my resume and clips, he said, "Tom, my advice for you is to go out and work for a year on a small town paper. Then give me a call. But I can't promise anything. You know how it is these days with tight budgets."

I was disappointed, but a couple of days later I saw that the *Star-Journal* was looking for a reporter. The editor hired me twenty minutes after I walked into the newsroom. Three others had already applied, -but I was a local boy and already knew the town. It was entry level job in journalism and the pay wasn't great. I'd already vowed I would start looking for a new job in six months. Meanwhile, I would do my best to make an impression here and get some good clips.

My roommates at Redman, the private college in this central Florida town, had a good laugh when they heard that I wasn't leaving "Deadland" yet for a big city newspaper job. Chas and Dane could be real assholes, but I could tell they were glad I was sticking around and paying rent on our three-bedroom apartment a few blocks from campus. They both had another year at Redman and were several weeks into the fall term.

I walked into the office by the rear door and ambled over to my desk. The *Star-Journal* was published twice a week and had an editorial staff of four, including James (Flash) Gordon, the editor, the only one in the newsroom at the moment. Gordon was in his fifties, with bushy salt and pepper hair and a droopy mustache. He had a middle-age paunch gained from twenty-some years on the copy desk of the *Philadelphia Enquirer*. For the past decade, he'd moved from paper to paper, city to city, and had landed in Deland a year ago. It didn't take long for me to realize that he had a somewhat jaded sense of humor, which I appreciated.

I waved to him. "Morning Flash."

"Tom, love your obits, but you gotta tone down the dark humor. These folks in Deland won't appreciate your Mark Twain-esque writing style."

"I was just trying to be creative with a...deadly dull topic."

"I get it. So I got an assignment for you that will allow you to go full bore into your darkest graveyard sensibilities."

"Oh, yeah? Tell me."

"First, you need to do one more obit this morning about someone who actually died last night and was-well known in town. After that, I want you to take a drive over to Cassadaga. You know about it?"

"Sure. They worship spooks there, right?"

Gordon dropped his head back and laughed. "You are definitely the right one for this story. We need a page one yarn for our Halloween issue coming up. Don't take the easy route, like going on their phony ghost tour. If there are such phantasms, as some folks attest, I doubt that they're standing around waiting for the ghost tour to come by. Find something edgier that will captivate our readers and leave them wondering who the hell is the guy who wrote this wild story."

"I got it, Flash. It'll be fun."

"You want to include some background on the weird town, of course, but keep it simple. You're not writing a paper on local history."

Actually, I already had an idea. I knew more about Cassadaga than I was letting on. In years past, a handful of costumed Redman students had literally terrorized residents of the spiritualist community on Halloween by racing through the narrow streets, screaming like banshees and dancing and drinking on the graves in the local cemetery. That annual extracurricular activity came to an abrupt end when one of the old Victorian houses burned to the ground one hallowed eve. The arson was never pinned on any Redman students, but enough suspicion was raised to permanently end the tradition.

Last Halloween, I'd decided the Halloween issue of the *Redman Diary*, as the paper was called, was a good time to look back at the college's strange connection with the spiritualist community. But the administration nixed that one fast. I grudgingly abided and instead wrote a page one opinion piece about the history of college newspapers and the threats against their First Amendment rights by self-righteous school administrators. That didn't go over well either, but they let it pass.

Now a year later, my new editor was sending me to Spooksville. After compiling the obit on old Dan Cummings, a two-term mayor of Deland in the 1970s, I told Gordon about Redman's link with Cassadaga, thinking he would love the local hook. I was wrong.

"Forget that, Tom. That's ancient history. Besides, Delanders don't give a shit about what you privileged private school kids did on Halloween way back when. Like I said, get something current. Or something old and make it current."

Now that I was working on the paper, I had to stop thinking about Deland as Deadland. But ironically, the only people I'd been writing about so far were truly Deadlanders...or soon to be. At least I'd be getting out of town to write about more dead people. "How about a first-person story about a midnight visit to the Cassadaga cemetery? There's a spooky urban legend about that place. It's called the Devil's Chair, and..."

"Stop. Don't tell me anymore. Go get the story. I like it already. I want to read it. First person is fine. But don't do anything illegal. You got that? If the cemetery closes after dark, get permission from somebody. Tell them you're on official business from the *Deland Star-Journal*. Show them your new press credentials," he added with a laugh.

"Okay, I'm heading out. I'll text you updates."

"Don't bother. Just get the fucking story. You can text your girlfriend. Or take her with you. And keep track of your expenses."

Not a bad idea, I thought as I walked out to my Prius. Samantha had actually told me once that she wanted to get a reading in Cassadaga. We could get a room in the old hotel and spend the night.

Like my roommates, Sam was a senior at Redman and lived in the dorm. She was in psychology right now, her last class of the day. I texted her.

Me: *What are you doing this afternoon?*

Sam: *Writing a paper for art history.*
Me: *I got a better idea. A trip to Cassadaga.*
Sam: *Really? I'm in. Call you after class.*

🦇 🦇 🦇

"This is so exciting, Tommy. I've never had a reading. We can get dinner in the hotel restaurant. My friend, Darlene, said they've got good Italian."

I'd picked her up from the dorm, and now we were just a few minutes from Cassadaga. "Yeah, sounds good." I was glad that Gordon was covering expenses and I just hoped that included dinner for two...and the hotel room. After all, I would be working late tonight.

"She also said I should get a reading at the house across the street from the hotel."

"Maybe if I can work it into my story, I can get the paper to pay for it."

"Oh, fuck that, Tommy. I don't want you blabbing about my reading in that gossipy newspaper. I'll pay for it myself."

"Sorry. It was just a thought."

She lifted her blonde hair off the back of her t-shirt, a habit of hers, especially when she was annoyed. "Yeah, I know, a bad one."

Twenty minutes after departing we arrived in Cassadaga, and I drove slowly through the narrow hilly streets lined by old wood-framed houses with picket fences and placards at the gates offering mediumship services. A forest of tall pines framed the town. I pulled into the parking lot in front of the Cassadaga Hotel, a two-story Mediterranean-style structure built in the 1920s. We walked up the steps to the front door and entered a lobby that was right out of another era, complete with antique furniture .

"This is so cool," Sam declared. "What a great assignment for your first article." We peered in at the restaurant, which included a bar, then looked around a New Age gift shop featuring books, crystals, candles, incense, and Cassadaga t-shirts.

"Are you interested in a reading?" the woman behind the counter asked. She wore a billowy purple dress that reached her ankles.

"Not right now," I replied. "Where do we check in to get our room?"

"Right here with me."

Our first-floor room was small and basic with three doors. One opened to a hallway leading back to the lobby, another opened to an expansive porch that stretched the entire side of the hotel, and the third went to our bathroom.

Sam set down her bag, sat on the edge of the bed. She looked around, unimpressed. "I've seen closets bigger than this room." She quickly added: "I want to go get my reading. What're you going to do?"

"Get directions to the cemetery, I guess, and look around some more. Are you going to come with me after your reading?"

"Can't we just relax?" She smiled and patted the bed.

"Sure, later. I want to run over there and get some pictures before dark."

"Okay, fine. But I'm not going there at midnight with you. That's too creepy. I've heard those stories about that Devil's chair."

"Yeah? What have you heard?" I knew the basics of the legend, but I wanted to hear what Sam recalled.

"The story I heard is that the chair was built for an old man whose wife and daughter died in a fire. He came and sat in the chair facing their graves for hours every day. They say you can still see his ghost there sometimes."

"So why's it called the Devil's Chair?"

"Because if you're foolish enough to sit in the chair at midnight, the devil will talk to you. And if you come back in the morning, you will see the devil."

"Do you know the part about the beer can?"

"I heard something about it."

I pulled a can of Budweiser out of my pack and held it up. "Supposedly, if you sit there at midnight and leave a can of beer for the devil, in the morning it will be unopened...but empty."

"Well, I'd rather see that beer can than the devil in the morning...or at any time."

We walked out to the porch and I wished Sam luck with her reading. I hoped she would find someone who was an actual psychic or medium, and not someone playing at being one. As she disappeared across the street, I noticed the woman who had checked us in standing near the door to the lobby. She was smoking, holding an ashtray in her hand. I decided to see if I could interview her for my article. After all, I had no idea if I would find anyone in the cemetery to interview—at least anyone who was alive.

"What do you want to know?" she asked as I approached.

"Is it that obvious I was going to ask you something?"

"You look like someone who has questions. Maybe that's what you do, question people. Then you try to make sense out of the answers."

"That's good. You a psychic?"

"I do readings here in the hotel, along with tending the store and checking people in to their rooms. I cover most of the bases here, but I don't wait on tables in the restaurant or make coffee at our coffee bar."

"I'm a reporter for the *Deland Star-Journal.* Can I ask you a few questions?"

"About?"

"Cassadaga, of course."

"Wait."

She closed her eyes, while continuing to hold her cigarette above her copper ashtray. I pulled my phone out of my pocket and started my recorder. I also snapped a surreptitious photo of her. The ash on her cigarette was lengthening when her head jerked up and the ash fell into her copper ashtray. "No, you want to ask about the cemetery."

Okay. Had she overheard Sam and I talking? Or was she, well, an actual psychic? "That's part of it. I'm writing an article for our Halloween issue. Can I record our conversation?"

"Only if you promise to send me a copy of your article."

"May I use your photo?"

"Yes, but make sure you call me the hotel manager and a practicing psychic-medium."

Whatever, I thought, then snapped a couple more photos of her with my phone. I pulled out one of my cards. "E-mail me at this address on Halloween and I'll send you an attached file."

She held the cigarette between her lips for a moment, took the card, and slipped it into her dress. She exhaled a cloud of smoke. "What do you want to know?

"First, your name."

"Cassandra Carmichael. But you can call me Cassie."

"How did you know I wanted to ask about the cemetery?"

"Stuff pops into my head. Sometimes it's a voice, other times it's an image. I saw you standing by a gravestone. Or actually sitting by one." She shook her head. "What is it about you and dead people? I see them around you."

I shrugged. "I've been writing obituaries."

Cassie frowned. "They're telling me to warn you to be careful, or you might get what you're looking for. Does that make sense?"

"I think so. I'm planning to go to the cemetery tonight at midnight. Will I be able to get in?"

"Sure. If that's what you want. No one will stop you. I'll say this: If you go, you'll have an experience you'll never forget."

It sounded like a warning.

🦇 🦇 🦇

Dinner. The food was good, but I could hardly eat anything. All I could think about was my upcoming midnight journey and planting myself in the Devil's Chair. I was both excited and nervous, remembering what Cassie had told me. Sam was talking about her reading, but I was having a hard time focusing on what she was saying.

When she'd returned to the room from her reading, she'd been unusually quiet. She said she wanted to think about what she'd been told and would tell me about it later. All she revealed was that she'd cried.

We drove to the cemetery, located on a hill outside of town, so I could take a few photos with my digital camera and orient myself. I needed to be able to find the Devil's Chair in the dark. As I'd expected, Sam refused to sit in the chair, but I snapped a few pics of her standing behind it. "That's all," she said. "Let me see them." She slowly swiped through the images examining each one closely probably to see if there were any spooks lurking in the background. She didn't look happy in any of the photos.

We wandered around for a few minutes, looking at the old graves, some dating back to the late nineteenth century, but Sam was getting more and more uneasy. "Let's get out of here," she said, noting that the sun was low in the sky and she didn't want to be here even at dusk. We wandered through a grove of trees en route to the car and both of us abruptly stopped when we heard a sharp screech like an animal under attack. The sound shifted to a howl, then laughter. A man and a woman burst out the trees. "Gotcha, didn't we!" the woman crowed as they stepped out of the shadows. "Sorry about that. We couldn't help it."

They were a few years older than Sam and me, both slender and dressed in black. Their lips were painted black as well and they wore heavy eye make up. Their multiple piercings sparkled and their tattoos seemed to come alive in the warm light of the descending sun.

Sam took a couple of steps back, but I responded in a friendly manner. "Yeah, you got us. I bet you're headed to the Devil's Chair."

They both answered. "How did you know?"

"Hey, mind if I take a couple of photos of you two by the chair?" I told them about my assignment.

"Of course, that's why we're here." Again, they both spoke simultaneously.

That was strange, and it was enough for Sam. "Thomas, give me the keys, please. I'll wait for you in the car."

"Sure. Just don't drive away," I said and squeezed her arm. "I'll be there in a few minutes."

With that, my new companions and I headed for the infamous chair. "Can I get your names?"

"I'm Bela and this is Lugosi."

Great. Bela Lugosi. No doubt Flash would give me a hard time about those fake names, but I'd tell him it fit perfectly for a Halloween story. Lugosi sat in the chair and Bela sat on his lap. I took a dozen shots as they mugged for the camera. "Where are you two from?" I asked.

"Transylvania, Louisiana. It's a real place."

🦇 🦇 🦇

"Hello, Tommy, are you even listening to me? You said you wanted to hear about my reading and I'm trying to tell you."

"Sorry. I'm just preoccupied with my article. So the reader told you that you were going to dump me for someone else? Is that what she said?"

"No, she said I would find my true love next year. I'm hoping it will be you."

"That doesn't sound very promising to me. Is that what made you cry?"

"No, it was about my relationship with my sister. She nailed it."

I'd heard about the issues between the two sisters and didn't want to get Sam started. "Maybe the reader didn't know that you'd already found love."

"She called it lust."

I choked back a laugh. "Oh, sounds like she tuned in on something."

I could see that Sam didn't find any humor in that comment. Change the topic, I thought. "Hey, do you want to see those photos I took of that freaky couple sitting on the Devil's Chair? I can pull them up on my phone."

"No, I don't. I've seen enough of them. Did you notice they weren't wearing any shoes?"

"No, I didn't see that."

"Really? How did they get there, anyhow? I didn't see any other car."

"Maybe they parked off the main road and walked up."

"Yeah in bare feet. Why would they do that?"

"Who knows? They're weirdos. Hey, you sure you don't want to go back with me at midnight?"

"No way. I don't think you should go, either."

"Seriously, Sam? I'm not afraid of ghosts, because there's no such thing. They only exist in stories."

◖ ◖ ◖

I arrived at the cemetery at ten to midnight. In spite of what I'd said to Sam, I couldn't help feeling somewhat uneasy walking among graves. The crunch of leaves and twigs underfoot seemed magnified and made me conscious of the silence and the sleeping bones lost in eternity six feet below. The silver moonlight cast shadows from the gravestones, enhancing the eeriness. I would write about these sensations in my article, while noting that I was a non-believer. That would make my sense of uneasiness more interesting, I thought.

I approached the red brick chair at 11:58. I scanned the graveyard, looking for any shadowy movements or shimmering visions. I couldn't help wondering if those neo-goths were hiding somewhere again, ready to jump out and frighten me the moment I sat down. But the graveyard felt empty. It was just me and all the dead.

I settled into the Devil's Chair, made of red bricks. It had a broad back, a broad concrete seat wide enough for two people. Sort of like a throne, but not really. It was just a local urban legend, I told myself. Nothing was going to happen. I wished it was Halloween tonight. There probably would be some activity here, maybe a few costumed visitors prancing through the graveyard, something to report. But stories about Halloween appeared before the designated day. No one was interested in reading about Halloween events after it was over, unless the reports concerned poisoned candy and razor blades turning up in the kiddies' bags, abandoned houses burning to the ground, or gravestones knocked over or marred with graffiti.

I reached into my pack and pulled out the can of beer I'd brought along. I was tempted to pop it open and guzzle it down. Maybe I would even toast the non-existent devil. But I'd already decided to play along with the legend. So I set it on the arm of the chair.

I should've brought a cushion to sit on. The chair was uncomfortable and I wondered how the old man had sat here for hours. I adjusted my position and leaned into the backrest. In spite of the hard surfaces, my head nodded after a few minutes, and I was overcome with drowsiness. I'd stayed up reading late last night and now my shortage of sleep combined with two glasses of wine at dinner was taking its toll.

Voices. I caught my breath, jerked awake. Was it a dream or had I really heard people talking? I looked over my shoulder and saw the same couple entering the graveyard. They each had draped an arm over the other's shoulders and they were weaving like drunks. I slid off the chair, crouched low, and when I saw they weren't looking my way, I darted over to an old oak tree and ducked behind it.

I would turn the tables and see if I could scare them. As soon as they approached, I would jump out and scream and wave my arms. I imagined they would turn and run or probably stumble and fall. The murmur of their voices grew louder. It was strange that they would come back, but then, that was what I'd done.

"Look, someone left us a beer," Lugosi said.

My back was pressed against the trunk of the tree. They were only twenty feet away. Perfect timing. My heart was pounding. *Do it now,* I told myself. I leaped out, waving my arms, and started to let out what I hoped would be a blood-curdling howl. But I caught my breath and my scream died in a gurgle. The Devil's Chair was empty. I looked around and couldn't believe that they'd somehow managed to move away without my noticing it. I hadn't frightened them away. They were gone before I'd stepped out.

"We're here for you, Tommy." The simultaneous chorus from the two had issued from directly behind me. I spun around, but no one was there.

My phone vibrated. A text from Sam.

Get out of there, Tommy. Those two we saw are dead. They were murdered outside that cemetery back in the mid '80s.

Again the chorus spoke from behind me: "Stay with us, Tommy. Stay with us."

This time I didn't look back. I raced for my car, and their voices echoed in my head. "Tommy, Tommy. Stay with us. Stay with us."

ₐ ₐ ₐ

Sam and I sat at a table on the porch the next morning with coffee and pastries. We were packed and ready to leave Cassadaga. "Look, I found it, Sam. They were murdered here in 1986 and they were from Louisiana. Here's their picture."

"My god, they look almost the same, except her hair is blue there and he's got a goatee."

"Remember, I told you their names and they said they were from Transylvania. There really is a Transylvania, Louisiana. And her name was Bela and his was Luigi."

"Now you've got a story to write, Tommy. Except you don't believe in ghosts."

"I know. That makes it more interesting. I'm a non-believer—or at least I was—but then I saw something. Too bad there's no proof of it."

"What about the pictures you took of them on the Devil's Chair?"

"Shit, I completely forgot." I pulled out my camera and flicked through the pictures of Sam standing behind the chair and a few others I'd taken. I came to the final ones, and stared at the empty chair. "They're gone. It's just pictures of the chair. So, like I said, no proof."

Sam shook her head. "Let's get out of here."

"Wait. We've still got to go back to the cemetery. I want to see if the can of beer is there, empty and unopened. I still don't believe in the devil, but that would be proof of something."

"Yeah, the devil," Sam responded.

From nearby someone laughed. I look up to see Cassie, who wore a long white dress and held a cigarette and ashtray in her hand again. "I guess you had an experience, Tom."

"Yeah, I did."

She took a deep breath, dropped her head back, exhaled. Her eyes glazed as she stared at me. "The beer can will be your proof, but not the way you think it will."

I thanked her, and we headed on our way. En route, Sam explained that Cassie was the one who had told her about the murdered couple. "She lives in the room next to us. She was smoking on the porch after midnight when I talked to her. She said both of them were shot point blank in the forehead. A handyman who worked in the camp was a suspect, but he committed suicide, and no one was ever arrested.

❧ ❧ ❧

We walked up to the Devil's Chair for the final time, and the beer was still there and unopened. I rubbed my hands together. "Now to see if it's really empty." I picked it up and was disappointed. "It's still full. It's just an unopened beer."

"Are you sure?" Sam asked.

"Of course, watch." I shook it up several times, held it at arm's length and popped it open, expecting the foamy brew to shoot out.

Instead, a warm red liquid bubbled over my hand and dribbled in front of the Devil's Chair. I dropped the can and looked at my hand. "Shit, it's blood, Sam!"

"You got some on me," she gasped, wiping her arms. "Oh my god, look!"

She pointed at the foot of the chair. Two small pumpkins, the size of softballs, rested in front of each leg, and they were splattered in blood. I picked up one, then the other. Splotches of blood formed two eyes, a nose, and a grinning toothy mouth.

"Wow! I've got to get pictures."

I set the pumpkins on the chair and fumbled in my bag for my camera. But by the time I was ready to shoot the pumpkins, the blood—or whatever it was—had started to fade. I snapped several photos, but when I looked closely at the images, there was no sign of any facial features on the pumpkins, no sign of the blood.

"No! Not again."

Sam reached for the camera. "Let me see."

She swiped through the photos, and caught her breath. "The legend said that you would see him in the morning. Look!"

I peered over her shoulder. To the left of the first photo of the pumpkins was the last one I'd taken of Bela and Lugosi. And now I could see them faintly, ghostly images, and I could see the back of the chair visible through them. Both had a single black hole in their foreheads.

"Proof," I whispered.

CADDY MAN

GUSTAVO BONDONI

"WHO ARE YOU SUPPOSED TO BE? JOHNNY CASH?" A FAT GUY LOOKED DOWN at me from the top step. The lights glistened off the top of his bald, sweating head.

I gave him my best tight-lipped smile. Attire which matched black with black tended to generate the same jokes over and over. "No sir. I'm the driver. Mr. Gianbattista sent me because the regular guy is indisposed."

"What happened to him?"

I shrugged. "For all I know he was used as a human sacrifice in an ancient ritual. I'm just here to take the stiff."

That got a laugh. "Knowing Jimmy, he probably got drunk and took some woman home with him last night, and now he's hiding from her husband."

"Whatever."

"You know where the church is?"

"Yeah." It was kinda weird, thinking that the body was being crated to the funeral from the city morgue... but I guess that came with the territory when you were a mob underboss. When your time came, it was unlikely to be peaceful.

I followed the fat guy and another, thinner gangster into the building. The body had already been released and the undertakers had done their work. Bobby the Ferret was nowhere to be seen... instead, I took delivery of a beautiful mahogany casket on a trolley.

We wheeled the coffin to the delivery ramp.

"I'll get the car," I told them.

I'd double parked around the corner; nobody would ever ticket a hearse outside the morgue; that was terminally bad karma. The engine emitted its deep-throated growl and I eased it to where the corpse was and got out.

"Wow," fatso said, all mockery gone from his face. "Nice wheels. The Ferret would have loved that. Going out in style. Will you come for me when I get mine?"

"You hire me, you got me," I said. "Here's my card."

"Thanks, man. What kinda car is that, anyways?"

"That's a 1964 Cadillac hearse," I told him.

"Sinister, dude. They don't make them like that anymore. The guys are gonna love this one."

"Thanks."

We loaded the body into the back, struggling with the heavy casket. At some point between the sixties and today, someone had decided to change the loading height of hearses and ambulances, and the gurney didn't quite match loading bay of the car.

Fat guy held up a hand. "Wait up. The cortege is on the way. They'll pick you up outside the building."

I would have preferred to deliver the body in private, but this was a mob funeral... even in this enlightened twenty-first century there were

"Oh, man. He killed me. Jimmy."

"Heather, do you know who I am?"

Her eyes took a long time to focus on me. "You? What are you doing here?" At least she dropped her arms to her sides. Whether that meant she was comfortable with me or contemptuous, I preferred not to speculate on. "Are you here to help me?"

"I've already brought you back from the dead. Doesn't that tell you something?"

"Oh, thank goodness for that," she said. "I need a fix so bad."

I exulted. This was the part I'd read about, the part that had drawn me to this particular piece of black magic. I smiled. "I'm sorry. I can't help you with that."

"You can't? Of course you can't. You were always the square one. You wouldn't even drink a little too much at parties. Well, don't worry, I can get it somewhere else."

"That's not the reason. I can't help you because the heroin won't work for you. When you died, your heart stopped. Your blood isn't flowing. The heroin can't move through your body."

"Who gives a shit? Just get it in, that's all. I just want to feel it inside. You don't know what it's like, having to get your fix and not getting it. It's hell."

"Once it gets inside, it won't work. That's what I'm trying to tell you. No matter how many times you shoot up, you won't get any relief. You'll always feel exactly the same way you do now."

"But I need a fix."

"Get one. It won't help you."

Realization that I wasn't lying to her hit her and her fawning, do-me-a-favor-and-I'll-make-it-up-to-you face disappeared to be replaced by the anger I'd grown to know so well of late. "You bastard. Why did you bring me back, then? I can't live like this."

"I can hurt you, so don't."

"Is that why you brought me back, to hurt me?"

"Do you deserve it? Don't lie, now, I know everything."

Her voice turned pleading again. "You don't know what it was like. I needed my fix. Any addict would do anything to get her fix. Much worse things than I did. All I did was fuck a few guys."

"More than a few."

"So what? It's easy for you to judge me. You just don't know what you're talking about."

I sighed. "I didn't bring you back to hurt you. I'm going to let you hurt yourself, hopefully as much as you hurt me. And I don't care about all the men you slept with when you were on drugs. I get it. You were just a junkie, and you couldn't help yourself. I forgive you every single time you betrayed our love." I gave her a hard stare. "Except one. The first one. The first time you took Jimmy up to our house. That's why you're here."

"I was lonely. You were gone every night."

"Because you asked me to get a better-paying job so we could afford rent on a better place. If I'd known what you wanted to do in our new place I would have told you to fuck off." I spat on the ground. "Enjoy your new life."

I turned to go.

"No. Don't leave me."

I walked faster. I was pretty sure her dead and dried leg muscles wouldn't be able to keep up with me.

"Please! Don't leave me here."

I didn't turn back.

"I love you!"

My fists clenched of their own accord and tears rolled down my cheeks. If she said my name, I would have stopped and canceled the

BONE WHISPERS

TIM WAGGONER

KEVIN BLANCMORE SLOWED AS HE APPROACHED THE OLD GRAVEYARD. IT had been almost forty years since he'd been here last, and the place looked as if it hadn't changed in the slightest during that time. It was not a thought that provided comfort.

Kevin braked and pulled his Nissan Altima—on which he was two payments behind, not that it mattered anymore—onto the side of the road in front of the graveyard's black wrought-iron gate. There was no parking lot—the graveyard predated the road by nearly a century, he guessed—and Kevin scarcely had enough room to get his car off the road. There wasn't a lot of traffic out here in the coun-

TALES FROM THE OLD BLACK AMBULANCE

Kevin turned off the engine and pulled the keys out of the ignition, but instead of getting out of his vehicle right away, he sat for a moment, staring out the windshield and listening to the car's engine tick as it began to cool. He wasn't sitting there because he was afraid, though he supposed he had good reason to be. And he wasn't nervous, not even a little. He felt nothing, and that was the reason he sat behind the wheel of his car, hesitating. Considering what he had come here to do, or more to the point, to *find*, he should feel something. A moment like this...well, it was why the word *momentous* had been created, wasn't it? It was potentially life-altering in the profoundest of ways and should be marked as such, if only inside his own heart. But just because he was aware that he should feel something didn't mean he would. It seemed he was as dead inside as any of the graveyard's residents, and all that remained was for the rest of him to catch up.

He unlocked the driver's side door and climbed out of the car.

The weather in southwest Ohio in early June could range from cool and mild to hot and sweltering. But that was Ohio, where the weather changed as often as people's minds. Unfortunately for Kevin, it felt more like mid-August, the air steamy, thick and damp. Even worse, he still had on the suit he'd worn for Nancy's graduation, and the instant he emerged from the Altima's air-conditioned environment, sweat began beading on his forehead and pooling beneath his armpits. He considered leaving his jacket and tie in the car and rolling up his shirt sleeves, but even though he would be more physically comfortable, he decided against it. A momentous moment like this called for a certain level of formality, so the suit would stay on and he'd just have to endure the discomfort. He could do that; after all, he'd had a lot of practice. An entire lifetime's worth it seemed sometimes.

Let's have a nity party for Kevyy-wevyy, he thought. *One, two,*

front of the graveyard—*Looks like the county's behind in their mowing*—and stepped up to the gate. The graveyard was enclosed by a salmon-colored brick wall that measured five feet high, nine feet on either side of the gate and at the wall's four corners where conical black-brick turrets pointed skyward. Kevin thought the graveyard's designer must've been going for a somber yet dignified effect, and he couldn't say the man had missed. The gate was in fact a pair, held shut by an ancient rusted padlock. Not locked, though. The padlock hung open on the gate, just as it had done during Kevin's childhood. He wouldn't have been surprised to learn that the padlock rested in the same exact position that it had then, untouched by hands all these long decades. Human hands, anyway.

A metal plaque was bolted on the turret to the right of the entrance, its surface dingy, the letters worn some but still legible.

QUAKER BRANCH MEMORIAL BURIAL GROUND. EST. 1957.

Kevin knew the date referred to the construction of the wall. The graveyard itself was much older.

He took hold of one of the gate's bars, careful to grip a section where the black paint hadn't flaked off too much—*Didn't come all the way here to get tetanus,* he thought, almost smiling—and pushed. The gate resisted at first, the bottom edge digging into the ground, and he gave it a bit more muscle. Finally, the gate budged a few feet, giving him enough space to slide through, even with his less-than-modest gut. The gate hadn't made a sound when it moved, no slow creaking or harsh grinding, and Kevin recalled that it had been similarly silent the last time he was here. Now, just like then, he was vaguely disappointed. A proper cemetery gate should open with some manner of sinister sound to establish the appropriate atmosphere.

Once inside, he paused to look around. Large oak and elm trees bordered the outside of the graveyard, making it impossible to see to the ground that bare patches of dry earth peeked through. There were a good number of gravestones, over a hundred, he estimated, and they were roughly divided into two even sections. On his left were the newer stones, dating from around the time the outer wall had been constructed. They were larger, more varied in type, and the legends engraved upon them were still readable. To Kevin's right was what he thought of as the old section. Here the headstones were much smaller, set closer together, and more uniform in shape. They were colored either stony gray or chalk-white, their edges softened by the passage of one season after another and the elements' less-than-tender ministrations. Kevin knew from previous experience that the inscriptions—those that remained legible, that is—were both simpler and somehow more elegant than those in the newer section. WILHEMINA MOTE, B. 1834, D. 1867. JACOB HOBBLIT, B. 1856, D. 1859. The birth and death dates were almost always closer together in that section, as well. Sometimes too close.

Past the newer section, nestled against the graveyard's east wall, sat a simple wooden building, its sides gray, boards fraying in places as if the structure had been fashioned from cloth instead of wood. Two windows were visible from this angle, a door set between them, a small plaque affixed to the right of the door. Kevin couldn't make out the words from where he stood, but he didn't need to. He knew what the plaque said, could recite it from memory. THIS BUILDING IS A REPLICA OF A QUAKER MEETING HOUSE THAT STOOD ACROSS THE STREET FROM 1803 TO 1849. ERECTED BY THE BOY SCOUTS OF AMERICA, ASH CREEK TROOP, 1962.

The plaque didn't mention the fate of the original meeting house, and Kevin had always wondered what had happened to it. Had it burned down? Or simply grown old and fallen apart? *Happens to the best of us*, he thought. *The worst of us, too.* He also wondered

"So he was up there two, three times a week, and he'd let us know his progress. You know how it is when you're shooting the breeze late at night. Did she let you do this and that. I can't remember the details, so don't ask. There was a bunch of us telling stories, some true, some bullshit, so I don't remember. All I can tell you if you really want to know is that Jimmy always got what he wanted in the end."

I grunted.

"So one day he asks for some smack. I asked him why he wanted it, and he told me it was for a girl. Prostitution is big business for us, so we told him who to get it from. I never deal the stuff myself. Godfather doesn't like it. We didn't know it was for Heather until he brought her around one night."

"You met her?"

"Yeah. We all did. And before you ask, yes, we all fucked her, too. She'd do anything for a hit."

I ground my teeth. "Tell me."

"Just imagine it, kid."

"I don't want to."

"Then screw you. We were all sitting around one night when Jimmy walks in with this blonde girl. He counts us and says. 'You'll earn seven hits tonight, Heather. All you gotta do is suck seven cocks and swallow' and she says 'can I start with one and you give me one hit?' and he laughs and says 'nope. All seven or nothing.' She was on us so fast we barely had time to unzip our flies."

I swallowed. He was right. That was all I could take. I knew he wasn't lying. I didn't know how I know, I just did. I drove in silence for a bit.

"How did she die?" All I knew was that one day she didn't come back. I thought she'd run off with someone, so I bought a gun. I wanted to pay them a visit, not to hurt anyone, but to get her back. I still loved her then. But my questions around the neighborhood hadn't led me to a love nest but to Jimmy. That was when I realized she wasn't coming back, ever.

And the more I learned about her, the more I understood how badly she'd betrayed me.

He shrugged. "The same way they all do. Couldn't scrape up enough for her next hit and no one would give her one. The Johns hate hookers that cry. They want the girls to pretend to like it. She wouldn't pay, and she was in over her head. Jimmy told her to get the money from wherever. He probably gave her a couple of days, but the next time I heard about her, she was in the trunk of Jimmy's car and he needed help burying the body."

"And you helped."

"It's what we do. After all, the fact that she was gone was a clear message to anyone else who wanted to mess with the mob. And no body means no crime. The cops wouldn't worry too much about one missing whore. They never do."

Silence reigned again.

"Do you remember exactly where she is?" I said at last.

"Of course."

"So it's true what they say? You haven't killed too many people?"

"I try to avoid it when I can, but that's not the reason I remember. I've been at plenty of buryings. Dozens, maybe. And I remember where each and every person got planted. Think of it as a survival strategy."

"What?"

"If I know where the bodies are, and someone wants to whack me, and I get wind of it, I can go to the feds and make them wish they'd never been born. So they gotta be careful."

"Wouldn't it make you more of a target?"

"Nah. Doesn't work that way. You can't just go out and hit someone like me. You gotta get all kinds of permission. And the mark always finds out."

"They got you in the end."

The dead guy sighed. "Yeah, they did. I got careless, or they got lucky. Or maybe it was an unsanctioned hit. Anyway, I know who did it now, so they're all toast. Not much the commission can do about i either." He peered at the road. "Here we are, it's just past those trees.

We rolled to a halt. He'd pointed at a couple of small sapling along the grassy verge of the road. Beyond that there was a solid dark green wall of underbrush. "How far in do we have to go?" I asked.

"Maybe thirty yards."

"All right. Hang on."

I gunned the motor—a puny thing compared to the mighty racer in the Caddy—and pointed the nose between the little trees. Then I accelerated in a cloud of tire smoke and a screech so loud it almost covered Jimmy's screaming. We roared into the thicket and I winced as the tree on the right ground along the side of the car. Eventually, the undergrowth stopped us dead and we pushed the doors open.

"Subtle," Bobby said.

"Shut up, I told him. You're dead, so you don't get an opinion. I didn't want to leave the hearse out there. Someone might have gotten curious."

"No one ever comes this way. That's why we use this place."

"Besides," I said, not knowing why I was even bothering to defend myself from a man who should, by rights, have had a ton of soil on top of him by now. "I want Jimmy nearby. I didn't really understand the way it worked, but I think his suffering somehow drives the magic that brings people back to life."

"Can you bring as many people back as you want?"

"No. The spell only allows for two."

"Damn. Would have been a useful party trick. She's over here." He led me across the overgrown, uneven ground to a small grassy clearing. "You got shovels?"

"In the back. Guess who's nominated to dig?"

"Yeah," he said. "No need to harp on it. I know how these things work. Shit flows downhill." He went to the back of the hearse and opened it. Jimmy's screams filled the placid countryside and I breathed. I'd forgotten to check on whether the rough ride through he foliage had killed him. His condition was delicate after all.

But luckily, the dark sorcery had done its job and he was still alive and screaming.

"Man, you really cut him up good. Why isn't he dead?"

"Same reason you aren't."

Bobby nodded and started digging. Pretty soon he had a nice hole in the ground.

"This is almost fun. It doesn't feel like work at all, I'm not even tired yet."

"I don't think you need to worry about being tired anymore. But I imagine the whole decomposing and falling to bits part of it will kinda suck."

"Will that happen quickly?"

"I hope not. Remember who we're digging up there."

"Yeah."

The shovel hit something. "Here we go."

I helped him clear the dirt off of a black suitcase. It was one of those big cloth things for budget travelers that you can buy at Walmart. I'd seen thousands of them go through the warehouse.

"You put her in a suitcase?"

"Much easier to explain a suitcase than a body if you happen to get stopped by the cops. Can you believe that idiot Jimmy had her covered in garbage bags?"

"I can believe just about anything when it comes to Jimmy," I told him.

I let him pull the bag out of the hole.

"There goes my best suit," he griped.

"Dude, you're dead. I would think that would give you some kind of a sense of proportion."

"This was a really, really good suit. Made by a tailor in England."

He finished hauling the bag out of the hole and I saw that the bottom half was stained and wet. I also gagged at the smell.

"Open it."

They'd padlocked it, so I went back to the car and brought a bol cutter I found in the glove compartment. I gave it to the mobster and he sawed through the thick cloth. Inside, dark gray garbage bags covered the body. "You guys don't recycle, do you?"

That got me a surprised look and a smirk. "That's for pansies, man. You try that in front of the boys, they'll start lookin' at you funny. It's a good way to end up dead."

He tugged at the bags. Soon, I saw hair, hair I'd run my hands through and smelled after making love. I didn't want to smell anything that came out of that suitcase now, that was for certain.

I took a step back. "Lay her down on the grass."

She was wearing a pair of denim shorts. I loved those shorts because of the way they showed off her legs, but I thought she only wore them in summer. It was early spring now, still a bit chilly.... And it had been chillier still when she died, probably a couple of weeks ago.

She wasn't wearing a top or a bra, and I clenched my teeth. There was a small wound below her left breast. It had bled in a line which fell across her stomach and stained the waistband of the shorts. Whoever had stabbed her knew what he was doing because there wasn't another visible mark on her.

Her skin was pallid and grayish on one side and a sort of dark maroon on the other, where the blood had pooled. The cool earth had kept decay in check, I suppose, because she didn't look like a zombie—I had expected her to have lost large patches of skin, maybe to be able to see her teeth through her cheek. That hadn't happened yet, but the skin did look a little flaked, like if I touched it, it would come off in my hand. Her face looked disappointed, as always.

I took another step back.

"Well, there she is. I did my bit. Can I go now."

"Yeah. Are you going after the guys who offed you?"

"Of course."

"Good. Hope you give 'em hell. You still won't tell me who did it?"

I raised the glass again. The noise subsided. We could still hear his agony, but it wasn't as distracting as before.

"How long is this going to take?"

I looked down at my phone. "The app says we have an hour."

"All right. Wanna tell me what this is about?"

"My wife."

"Yeah, I knew that. But I'd think we did you a favor offing her. She was a slut and a junkie. I wouldn't be surprised if she'd been taking all your cash to pay for her fix."

Rage colored my vision for a second, and I almost crushed the dead man's heart. My hands clenched and unclenched on their own, itching to share the pain. But then I got a hold of myself. I sighed. "You didn't know her when we met. She was the sweetest kid in school."

"They all are at that age. But you sure picked a bad one. What happened?"

I most certainly wasn't planning on telling a mobster my sob story, but somehow, this guy seemed that he actually cared. Or maybe he seemed that he no longer counted. He was dead, it was like talking to a ghost. It didn't count.

"That piece of shit in back happened."

"Jimmy, huh. Yeah, he was always getting into trouble with other guys' wives. If he didn't have the mob behind him he'd have ended up dead in a ditch a long time ago. But those things don't happen by themselves, your wife had something to do with it."

"You sayin' it was my fault?"

"Not really. Maybe it was hers. A lot of girls get bored holding the fort at home. You gotta have someone watching them. And then have someone watching the watchers."

I suppose that's the kind of paranoid thinking that gets you promoted in the mob and keeps you breathing. And maybe he was right. I hadn't done any of those things, and look where it had gotten me.

"I suppose. Most of my coworkers had the same kind of trouble.

I used to work the night shift at the Walmart warehouse and then I got the night shift at the morgue."

"Yeah. I know how that is. Cold beds don't stay lonely for long."

"I....I suppose I could have lived with it if it hadn't been for the drugs. That was when I realized what was going on. When I saw the tracks."

"You should have kicked her out on her ass."

"I loved her."

We drove in silence, broken only by Jimmy's bouts of screaming, until I finally couldn't bear it any longer. I needed to close the gaping wound, even if it killed me.

"Tell me about it. How she died."

"You really want to know? Some shit is better to bury."

"I want to know. From the beginning."

"You're an idiot."

"Just tell me."

"All right. Jimmy liked to get the girls he screwed hooked on heroin. That way he could share them out or rent them to his clients. He loved it when he could say 'how's it feel, fucking some poor sucker's wife? Worth every penny, huh?'"

I gripped the steering wheel harder. My knuckles turned white, and he must have noticed. "Do you really want to hear it?"

"All of it."

The dead guy shrugged. "It's your funeral." Then he laughed. The sound was awful. "The first time we heard about her was maybe two years ago. Jimmy came in boasting about this tight piece he'd met at the convenience store. Claimed to have screwed her brains out and had her yelling all night. Said he never met such a wildcat. You still want to hear this?"

I didn't know why he wanted to spare me. Or maybe he didn't. Maybe he just wanted to make me earn my suffering. I didn't understand how the wiseguys thought when they were alive, I certainly wasn't going to be able to figure out a dead one. "Just tell me."

zens-to-be. Or maybe it had just been one more damn thing to do to earn another meaningless badge.

Looking at the meeting house—the *replica*, he reminded himself—Kevin experienced a flash of memory, so intense and visceral, for an instant it was as if he'd traveled back in time forty years. He was inside the meeting house, sitting with his back against the door, tears streaming down his cheeks. On the other side of the door was an excited snuffling accompanied by the sound of claws scratching against wood. From time to time there came a *thump*, both felt and heard, as something heavy shoved its body against the door in an attempt to force it open. And of course there were the sounds of his sobs and his plaintive whispered pleas. *Go away, please go away...*

Kevin gave his head a single sharp shake to dispel the memory, but while it retreated, it didn't go far. He felt moisture on his face, and he reached up and wiped it away, telling himself that it was only sweat and almost believing it.

The memory reminded him, as if he needed to be reminded, that there was one part of the graveyard he had up to this point assiduously avoided looking at: straight down the middle, back against the south wall. It wouldn't here now, not after all this time. So there was no reason not to look, right?

But the hole was still there, looking just as large as he remembered it. A three-foot circumference around which were scattered a number of old broken headstones, looking as if at some point they'd been flung forth from the hole and allowed to lay where they landed. And next to hole, sitting back on its hind legs and gnawing a length of bone held clutched in its front paws, was a groundhog the size of a sheep. The creature looked at Kevin with its glossy black eyes, completely unfazed by the human's presence, regarding him impassively as it chewed on the bone, its teeth making soft *shhh-shhh-shhh* sounds.

Up to this moment the air had been still, but now a breeze moved through the graveyard, causing the branches in the trees that surrounded the outer walls to sway. The soft rustling of their leaves sounded to Kevin's ears like a chorus of whispering voices all saying the same thing.

Welcome back.

❦ ❦ ❦

Kevin pedaled his bike faster, not caring that he couldn't see the road clearly through the tears in his eyes. Maybe if he went fast enough, the wind he kicked up would dry them. Or maybe he'd end up getting creamed by a car because his vision was blurred. Either way would be fine with him right now.

Houses flashed past: trees in the yards, cars in the driveways. Ranches, two stories...the same sort of homes that you'd find in town, except there was more space between them out here—sometimes as much as an acre or two. Though Kevin technically lived in the country, it was still close enough to town that there weren't many farms around, certainly none within a mile or so. It was late August and he'd be starting fourth grade next week, not that he cared. He'd used to look forward to the beginning of the school year, but not anymore. Now he didn't look forward to anything.

The wind blowing against his face was hot and dry, and while it blew the tears from his eyes, its heat stung his face. He wondered if he was sunburnt. Probably, he figured. He'd been out long enough. He couldn't decide whether he liked the pain, couldn't decide whether to keep feeling it or ignore it. He decided to worry about it later.

He'd been out riding since breakfast, and his Yellow Submarine t-shirt was soaked with sweat and clung to his scrawny body like it was glued to him. His shorts were damp too, and he could imagine another kid seeing him, calling out, "Hey, did you pee your pants?" and then bursting out with mocking laughter. Kevin would have to toss his clothes into the washer whenever he finally got home. He had to wash all his clothes, his sheets and pillow cases, too. And he had to do the dishes, both his and his mother's. If he didn't, the sink would become so full that cups and plates would slide off the mound and crash to the kitchen floor.

He wondered if his mother had any idea he'd been out this long, and if she did, was she worried? Not that she'd get out of her chair, let alone leave the house, if she was. Sometimes Kevin wondered what would happen if the house caught on fire. Would his mom just keep sitting in that old chair of hers, staring at the TV even after the air had become so filled with smoke that the screen was no longer visible? Would she sit there while the flames drew ever closer and began licking at her flesh? Maybe.

She hadn't liked leaving the house when Dad was alive, but he usually had been able to coax her outside. But now...

Kevin didn't want to think about *now*, so he pedaled faster and concentrated on the stinging wind biting into his face.

Eventually he realized he was hungry, and he figured he might as well go home and make himself some lunch. He didn't care about food anymore; it was all so much tasteless mush to chew and swallow. But if he didn't eat, he'd become so hungry that he wouldn't be able to ignore his growling stomach, shaking hands, and throbbing head. It was easier to just eat and get it done with so he could avoid the annoyance. He'd ridden that day without any particular destination, just traveling up and down country roads, riding just to ride, pedaling so he wouldn't have to think or feel. But he was on Jay Road now, only about a mile from his house. He could be home in only a few minutes—if he took the shortest route. Unfortunately, that would be riding past the old Quaker graveyard, and Kevin wasn't sure he wanted to do that.

He'd been to the graveyard a few times before, but always with his father, never alone. It had seemed scary back then, but because he was with his dad, it was fun-scary, not scary-scary. But since his father died—almost a year ago, now, though it sometimes seemed to Kevin to be much longer—he hadn't wanted anything to do with graveyards and cemeteries, or anything else that related to death in

"Do I look like a snitch?"

"How should I know. You're the first dead guy I've ever met. How the hell would I know what a dead snitch looks like?"

He chuckled at that. "I'm not going to tell you. But if you read the papers, you should be able to figure it out after all is said and done. I don't need to worry about the cops anymore, so I'm going to kill them in a way that will definitely make the front page."

"Good luck, then."

"Can I take the car?"

"Sure. If you can get it out of here. But you need to give me a second."

I pulled the paper from my pocket and read the next incantation a couple of times to myself. Then I said it out loud. "Fanto amb tro-lo."

Jimmy's screaming, which had filled the clearing, stopped dead.

And heather moved her arm.

"All right. You're good. Get the hell out of here."

Bobby turned and walked towards the hearse. He made a hell of a lot of noise getting it out, and took a long, thrashing while, but I wasn't paying any attention to him. My eyes were locked on the corpse coming to life on the ground, the woman I'd loved since high school.

She moved one leg, then the other. She sat, slowly, groaning as if in terrible pain. She tried to straighten her head, which had been bent to one side so she would fit into the suitcase, but as soon as she succeeded, it fell back.

With a gut-wrenching cry she tried to get to her feet. She stumbled, took a couple of halting steps to one side, caught herself on a bush and then stood up.

"Hello," I said.

She jumped. So nothing wrong with her ears, then. Funnily, her first instinct on hearing an unexpected voice in the wilderness was to cover her bare tits. "A little late for that, don't you think."

going to be a hundred cars paying their respects. No worries, I'd prepared for the eventuality. This wasn't exactly a standard-issue hearse.

It was a beautiful, sunlit day as we drove out of town. They'd chosen a country church in a distant suburb, an old colonial town fifteen miles outside of Atlantic City with a Catholic church. A perfect place to pretend that Bobby the Ferret was something other than a vicious hoodlum.

I drove around sedately, listening to the rumble of the racing V-8 under the hood and enjoying the fall colors; orange and red adorned the trees and glowed brightly in the sun. A long line of cars snaked behind me.

We passed the place where I would have turned had I been alone—a wooded country road that led off into some hills—but I drove on. I most certainly didn't want half the mafia on my ass when I turned.

But that was why the car had its engine. I gunned it a couple of times, turning the gentle rumble into a roar, and then, burning rubber just to give the grieving wife and kids in the car behind me a good show, I took off. Unless they had a Ferrari in the cortege, nothing was going to catch me.

They tried, though. A couple of cars shot out of the group and attempted to hold position, but they disappeared from my mirrors after just a few miles. It figured. The hearse was moving at more than a hundred and fifty miles an hour.

I turned off the main road and dialed it way back. This wasn't the time to draw the attention of the fuzz. They'd ask me some harsh questions to which the only honest answer would be that yes, I did have the stolen body of a murdered mobster in the back of the hearse, and no, I didn't care to explain why.

The GPS on my phone led me to the side road down the scenic route. I was in no hurry, and besides, I didn't want to use the big two-lane for fear of running into the funeral invitees. I didn't think they'd be pleased to see me.

In due time, a long black car came into view. It was a hearse, but a modern thing, perfectly boring and aerodynamic. The kind of thing no self-respecting human being would be caught dead in. I got out of my own big black car and walked over to the modern atrocity.

As soon as I opened the back gate, the access to where one would normally lay a coffin, the sound of agonized screaming filled the air. Good. That was exactly what I needed.

"Hi, Jimmy," I said. "How are you feeling? Lovely day, isn't it?"

Jimmy really wasn't in a state to make small talk. He'd been bound hand and feet, and then tied spread-eagle to the little silver handles inside. He couldn't move. The skin of his gut was sliced open in a cross pattern, and the flaps had been moved out of the way by using fishhooks and taut line which was tied to different parts of the car interior. It was a crude but remarkably effective way of keeping it out of the way.

A bunch of burning coals had been placed on different parts of his intestines and organs, per the ancient instructions. At first, I thought they would go out as soon as the copious amounts of blood washed over them, but it seemed the magic words had done their job. They still hissed where they were, as hot as when I'd started. It looked really painful.

He noticed I was back. His eyes widened and he got control of his screaming long enough to whisper: "Kill me. Please kill me."

"Oh, no, not yet," I replied. "I still need you for a while. You'll die when your usefulness is done, not a second sooner." Then I spat in his face. That wasn't in the instructions I'd found on the internet, but I supposed it wouldn't do any harm.

A piece of paper from my pocket held the next set of words. I read them to myself a couple of times. Having seen how powerful the incantations were, I really didn't want to screw this next bit up. "Hu Falopa Nac Amini," I intoned.

Jimmy convulsed and began screaming again. That was probably a good sign.

I returned to my own hearse and opened the back gate. Man, I could never get over how much better stuff was in the sixties. There was thumping on the coffin. That would normally have made me nervous as hell, but this time, it was exactly what I wanted.

I popped the latch on the outside and the dark brown lid flew open. The ugly mug of Bobby the Ferret glared at me from a sitting position. Being shot in the head hadn't improved his looks.

"What the fuck is going on?" he roared.

"You're dead, Bobby," I told him. I wasn't really in the mood for chitchat, and I know you weren't supposed to talk crap about the dead, but Bobby had always been an asshole, even when he was just a kid.

He thought about that for a while. "Yeah, makes sense. I remember the feeling of the gun on the back of my head and then nothing until I woke up in the dark." He tilted his head. "Don't I know you?"

"Yeah. But you wouldn't really know my name. I was just a working stiff in your stomping grounds."

He grunted. There were thousands like me in the neighborhood. Unless we got into debt or ratted them out to the police, they left us alone. We left them alone for health reasons. "So why am I breathing?"

"You're not."

He blew onto his hand, or at least tried to. His lungs didn't cooperate. "All right. So why am I talking to you if I can't move my lungs?"

"Magic."

"Really? Well, I don't care. I'm outta here." He climbed out of the coffin and crawled out of the hearse. Even in his best suit he looked like death warmed over in the sunlight.

"You can't go. I need you."

"Who's gonna stop me? You? I'm dead, remember? You can't hurt me, and I want to go even a score. Someone killed me, and I can't just take that lying down."

He made as if to leave, so I closed my fist, imagining that I was crushing his heart. He grunted and stopped. "I can hurt you. I can give you pain like you never felt before. And I will, partly because I never liked you and partly...well, we can talk about the other bit later. But we can make a deal. If you help me out with something, I'll leave you alone to go get your revenge. How's that sound?"

"Depends. Are you a cop? I ain't ratting anyone out."

"Nah. I just want to know where the bodies are buried. Well, one particular body, anyway."

He gave me a suspicious look. "Who?"

"Heather Farina."

He relaxed immediately. "That bitch? Why?"

"She was my wife."

He thought it over for a while. "I suppose there's no real harm in that. I show you where she is, and you let me go?"

"Yeah." I'd keep my word, too. I didn't like him, but I had no real beef with Bobby. No skin off my nose.

"All right. You know how to get to the Black Horse Pike?"

"No, but my phone does."

He shuddered. "Always hated those things."

I walked to the modern hearse and opened the door.

"Why are we taking that piece of crap? Let's take the Caddy."

"We can't. Half the police in the state are gonna be looking for that one. Besides, there's something in here that I need."

Bobby grunted and we mounted up. As soon as he sat down, he looked at the dark window that separated the space for the casket from the space for the driver. "What's in the back?"

I lowered the black window and screaming filled the cabin, along with the stench of burning flesh. Bobby craned his neck to get a better look.

"Is that Jimmy?"

"Yeah."

"Good. He was always a prick."

"I know."

"Can't you make him shut up?"

any way. But if he wanted to get home fast, he'd have to go past Quaker Branch.

He almost took the long way. But it *had* been almost a year since his dad had succumbed to lung cancer, and Kevin *was* going to be in fourth grade, was practically a fourth-grader already. He figured it was time he started acting his age. He bet when Dad was a kid, he wouldn't have been afraid to ride past the graveyard.

That settled the matter. Kevin turned off Jay Road onto Hoke. His road—Culver—branched off from Hoke...right after the graveyard. He thought about pedaling his ass off and flying by the graveyard at super-speed, but if he did that he'd zoom right past Culver. There was no way he'd make the turn going fast; he'd end up in a ditch or sprawled on the street, scraped up and bleeding. He didn't care if he got hurt, but if he were injured, he'd have to clean and dress his own wounds, and he didn't feel like doing all that work. So he slowed as he drew near Quaker Branch, telling himself to keep his gaze fixed straight ahead and not look as he went past. But the graveyard was on his right, and it was set so close to the road that it was hard not to look. And there were memories within those walls...memories of him and his dad. In the end, he couldn't *not* look.

When he did, he braked to a stop in front of the black gate without being aware he was doing so. Through the gate's bars, on the far side of the graveyard, a large animal sat back on its haunches, its round head turned toward Kevin, wet black eyes staring at him. Its fur was brownish-gray shot through with coarse silver-white hairs, and it held something in its forelegs...something curved, white and smooth. At first Kevin thought it was a giant rat—the creature looked to be three feet tall, if not larger—and it was plump, almost round as a beach ball.

Kevin's imagination whispered through his mind. *You know how it got so fat, don't you? It's got tunnels all through the graveyard. It's broken into the graves, gnawed through the coffins, and—*

Kevin clamped down on those thoughts, clamped down hard. It wasn't a rat, it couldn't be. Rats didn't get that big...did they?

The creature, whatever it was, continued sitting there and staring at him, completely motionless. Kevin might have thought the animal was some kind of statue, or maybe stuffed and mounted by a taxidermist, so still was it. But despite the absence of movement, he knew it was alive. He could feel intelligence looking out at him from those wet-black eyes, gauging, judging...

Then Kevin realized what it was that he was looking at. Not a rat, but a groundhog. Still a damned big one, though.

So it's a groundhog, his imagination said. *It still could've dug tunnels in the graveyard, still could be feeding here. Look at what it's holding...does that look like a rib to you?*

The idea was ridiculous. Groundhogs didn't eat meat...did they? Kevin wished his dad were here. He'd know. More, he'd tell Kevin that the groundhog had probably just burrowed its way underneath the wall around the graveyard, and or maybe squeezed its furry bulk between the bars of the gate. It was just curious, just exploring. It didn't live here, didn't have tunnels here, and it certainly wasn't eating the remains of people, some of whom had been dead for more than a century. But Dad wasn't here to tell Kevin these things, and for some reason, they didn't sound as convincing when Kevin told them to himself.

The groundhog continued sitting and staring, but now it began to move. It brought the smooth white curved thing it held toward its mouth and—eyes still fixed on Kevin—began to chew on one splintered end. Even though the groundhog was at least two hundred feet away, Kevin could hear the sounds it made as it chewed as clearly as if it were sitting right next to him. Soft *shh-shh-shh* sounds, almost like someone brushing their teeth.

It wasn't a bone, couldn't be!

Before he realized he was doing so, Kevin started yelling at the groundhog.

"Get out of here! Go!"

He expected the animal to startle, drop the bone, and go running off in the galumphing-undulating way groundhogs had when they really wanted to move. But this groundhog just continued to sit, stare, and chew.

Shh-shh-shh, shh-shh-shh, shh-shh-shh . . .

Kevin opened his mouth to yell again, but before he could, the groundhog stopped chewing. It looked at Kevin for a long moment, and Kevin looked back, unable to tear his gaze away from the strange animal. And then the groundhog dropped the bone—if that's what it was—then fell forward onto all fours and began slowly coming toward Kevin.

Kevin's trance broke then, and he lifted his feet off the ground, jammed them onto the pedals, and got the hell out of there as fast as he could. He pedaled madly and by the time he reached his house, sweat dripped off of him like rainwater, and while he had no memory of doing so, he realized he must've taken the corner turn onto his road at full speed and not wrecked somehow. He remembered something his father had once told him.

It's amazing what people can do when they're motivated, Kevin.

"No shit," Kevin whispered.

◖ ◖ ◖

Kevin went out riding again after the first day of fourth grade. He didn't even bother going into the house after he got off the school bus. He just dropped his book bag onto the front porch, hopped on his bike, and took off down the driveway. He doubted his mother would know that he'd gotten home, let alone that he'd immediately left, and even if she did, he didn't care.

Kevin didn't have many friends, and none of them were in his class this year. He'd seen Mike Todd and Steve Tomlinson out on the playground at recess, and while he'd been tempted to tell them about the groundhog in the graveyard, for some reason he hadn't. It wasn't that he feared they wouldn't believe him—although Steve could be skeptical at times. It just felt like he should keep the experience to himself, as if what had happened was private, just between him and the groundhog.

He hadn't been able to stop thinking about the giant ground-hog, kept hearing the sound of the creature gnawing on its bone, kept seeing it coming toward him across the graveyard grounds... The whole thing had been scary, sure, and he was scared now as he pedaled down Culver Road toward Hoke and the Quaker Branch Memorial Burial Ground. But he felt something else, too, something he hadn't felt in a long time: hope.

He remembered staying up one Saturday with his dad about six months ago to watch the late-night horror show, Shock Theatre hosted by Dr. Creep. They watched on the TV down in the basement because Mom was watching another movie upstairs, and she didn't want to change the channel. But that was okay. Kevin liked being down in the basement, alone with his dad, just the two of them. The film that evening had been *Thirteen Ghosts* with Vincent Price, and while Kevin didn't remember much of the story, he'd never forgot one scene where a skeleton came out of a pool to stalk a pretty blond woman in a nightgown.

During a commercial, Kevin had turned to his dad. "I don't like ghosts. They're creepy."

His dad put his arm around Kevin's shoulders and gave his son a gentle squeeze. "Yeah, that skeleton was scary, huh? But you know, I think there's something nice about ghosts, too. At least, about the idea of them. If you ever saw one, then you'd know that spirits were real, and that there's something more to life than just physical existence."

Kevin hadn't had any idea what his father was talking about, so he didn't say anything. But he understood now that his dad had al-ready been sick and knew that he was going to die. He also under-stood what his father had been talking about. He didn't know if there was anything like a heaven for him to go to once he was gone. He'd been scared.

That was why Kevin hadn't been able to stop thinking about the groundhog. The damned thing was weird, no doubt about that, but if it was supernatural somehow, that meant that there was more to life than most people thought, that magical things could happen. The groundhog wasn't a good thing, Kevin was sure of that, but if bad magical things were real, good ones had to be too, right? He remembered something else his father had once said.

Where's there's shadow, there has to be light.

Kevin was headed back to the graveyard to see if he could find that light, even just a hint of it. Because if he could...it meant that his father was maybe still alive somewhere, and not just a body sealed inside a coffin covered with dirt.

This time when Kevin reached the graveyard gate, he put down his bike's kickstand and climbed off. He walked up to the gate, shivering despite the temperature. He expected to see the groundhog come running toward him across the uneven grass, launch itself at the gate, claws scrabbling in the air as it tried to grab hold of him, curved flat teeth gnashing, eager to take a chunk out of his skin, tear away flesh to reveal the gleaming white bone beneath. Hard, fresh, young bone, so good for gnawing...

But there was nothing. The graveyard was empty.

For a moment Kevin considered getting back on his bike and leaving. Instead, he pushed open the gate, which made no sound as it moved, and walked inside. He expected to experience some sort of eerie feeling—a chill rippling down his spine, maybe a sense that he was being watched. But he felt nothing beyond the heat of the day and a slight breeze that moved the air around without cooling things off. Well, he was here. Might as well take a look.

He started walking toward the spot where he'd seen the groundhog sitting.

He saw the hole long before he reached it. It was so big, he was surprised he hadn't seen it from the road. It was located only a few feet from the graveyard's southern wall, and the ground here was mostly bare, with only patches of dry, dead grass. The edges of the hole were rounded and worn smooth from years of use. How old could the groundhog be? Kevin had looked up groundhogs in an encyclopedia at the school library, and according to what he'd read, the animals usually lived two to three years in the wild, but they could live as much as six years. But somehow the hole looked older, much older, as if it had predated the burial ground, a natural formation that had been here since long before any humans had ever set foot upon the continent. It was a crazy thought, of course, but he couldn't shake it.

Kevin walked up to the edge of the hole and peered down. It measured nearly three feet across, he estimated, and there was no telling how far down it went. He couldn't see further than a few inches down. After that, the dry earth of its walls gave way to inky shadow that seemed so thick Kevin wondered if a beam of direct light would penetrate it. He wished he'd thought to bring a flashlight. Then he could've checked for himself. He was thinking about riding home to get one when he felt cool air emanate from the hole. It wasn't a breeze, exactly; more like air leisurely wafting forth from somewhere far away. It was cool and musty-smelling, kind of like a basement but more so. A basement built deep within the earth. Miles deep. Miles *upon* miles. A soft sound accompanied the air, kind of like the hush of ocean waves breaking on a distant shore. No, more like the whispering of voices. Hundreds, maybe thousands. So soft that Kevin could almost but not quite make out the words.

He lost track of time as he stood there, looking down into the darkness, listening to the voices as they continued whispering, more urgent now, as if they were desperate to impart a message to him, but whatever it was, he wasn't getting it. Maybe if he stepped closer to the hole, leaned down, cocked his head to the side so that his ear was nearer the source of the whispering...

He got as far as sliding one foot forward when he heard a rustling in the grass off to this right. He snapped out of his trance and turned in time to see the giant groundhog running toward him. He had no idea where the creature had been hiding, but that wasn't important now. All that mattered was the damned thing was attacking.

The voices grew louder then, and Kevin thought he might have been able to make out what they were saying, but he was too terrified by the creature coming toward him. He screamed, his voice drowning out the whispers, and he whirled around and ran toward the Quaker meeting house. He didn't look back to see if the groundhog pursued. He didn't have to.

He reached the house, grabbed the metal handle bolted to the front door, and prayed it was unlocked. It was. He ran inside, slammed the door shut behind him, and dropped to the floor. He pressed his back against the door just as the groundhog slammed into the other side with a heavy thump. Kevin sat there, listening as the groundhog began scratching at the wood, tears streaming down his face, and he begged the creature to go away and leave him alone. But the scratching didn't stop. It continued and on and...

❦ ❦ ❦

Adult Kevin walked up to the groundhog. The damned thing was even larger than he remembered. He didn't question whether it was the same creature. Of course it was. The beast sat only a couple feet from its lair. The hole looked the same as it had the last time he'd seen it, with the exception of the headstones scattered about. After he'd escaped the groundhog by breaking one of the meeting house's windows, climbing through, and running like hell for his bike, Kevin had returned to the graveyard one last time. He'd knocked down some of the older, smaller headstones—ones he felt confident he could carry—and brought them over to the hole. He tossed them inside, wedging them into the hole, stomping on them to pack them down tight. He'd known it wouldn't stop the creature, which he'd decided might *look* like a groundhog but was undoubtedly something else, but he had to do it, if for no other reason than he could pretend that he'd stopped the thing. He'd expected the beast to come after him at any moment, but the groundhog didn't show, and he'd left the graveyard safely, telling himself that he'd sealed the creature off from the world and no one need ever fear it again. He'd known even then that it was bullshit, but it was bullshit he needed to believe.

Now, four decades later, he walked up to the groundhog and crouched in a squatting position in front of it. The creature made no move against him, nor did it seemed fearful. It continued gnawing on its bone as it regarded him with its wet black stare. Kevin stared back, gazing deep into the darkness within those eyes, and for a few moments he did nothing more. But eventually he began speaking in a soft, tired voice.

"My daughter Nancy graduated high school today. I didn't stay for her party, though. I...Her mother and I divorced when she was little, and Nancy's been uncomfortable around me ever since. Can't say as I blame her. I inherited my mother's less-than-sunny disposition, and I've battled depression all my life. And I don't think I ever recovered from the trauma of losing my father so young. At least, that's what all the therapists I've seen over the years tell me. It's been so hard for me. I can barely bring myself to talk with other people and, I can barely get out of bed in the morning. Medicine doesn't help. Just makes me groggier. But that's not the worst of it. A few months ago, I found out that I inherited something from my father, too. His cancer."

The groundhog remained motionless, but it stopped chewing the bone, and Kevin had the impression that it was paying attention to him. More, he had the feeling that it understood his words.

"No one knows. I didn't tell anyone at work. Didn't tell my ex-wife or Nancy. I wasn't planning on doing anything about it. Doctor says there's nothing *to* do. But as I was driving home from the graduation ceremony, I passed the highway exit for my hometown and remembered this place. Remembered you. So I turned around, got off the highway, and came here."

The groundhog cocked its head slightly to one side.

"To tell you the truth, I'm not really sure why I came here. Maybe I'm hoping that this time I'll finally find out whether there's anything beyond this life or not. Or maybe I'm just hoping that you'll make a fast end of me and spare me weeks of painfully withering away to nothing in hospice." He paused. "I guess the real reason I'm here comes down to one thing: I've got nowhere else to go."

The groundhog stared at him for a long time and Kevin stared back, sweat rolling down the sides of his face and the back of his neck. He wondered if he'd try to run this time if the groundhog attacked, or if he'd just stand here and let the creature do what it would to him.

Finally, the groundhog dropped the bone to the grass and fell forward onto all fours. Kevin's stomach clenched in anticipation of the beast running toward him, but he held his ground. Whatever was to come within the next few seconds, Kevin had at least answered one question for himself: he wasn't going to run.

The groundhog looked at him a moment longer, as if it were trying to come to decision of its own. Then it slowly turned away and began walking toward its hole. When it reached the edge, it stopped and turned back to look at Kevin, and then it crawled in, its large, furry body sliding into the opening with ease. And then it was gone.

Kevin stood there for a moment, trying to understand what had just happened. When he'd been a child, the groundhog had attacked, clearly trying to kill him. But this time it hadn't displayed even a hint of aggression. He was sure it was the same creature, no matter how impossible that might be, so why hadn't it come after him this time? Was he too large to be considered prey now? Too old? And then it came to him. It was neither of those things. The creature hadn't attacked him because there was no reason to. He was for all intents and purposes already dead, both inside and out. He was no longer an intruder to be run off. He belonged here.

Kevin walked over to the edge of the hole—which was larger now, to accommodate the groundhog's increased bulk—and peered into the darkness within. He felt the same cool air on his face as he had when he was ten, smelled the same basementy odor, heard the same soft whispers. Only this time, he understood their message clearly. It was an invitation.

Kevin thought it over for a moment, then he removed his suit jacket, folded it neatly, and lay it on the ground next to the hole. Then he got down on his hands and knees and followed the ground-hog into darkness. As he made his descent—fingers clawing moist soil, hard-shelled insects scuttling through his sweaty hair and beginning to crawl beneath his damp clothing—Kevin realized that his father had been wrong about one thing. Where there was shadow, there wasn't always light.

Sometimes there was just deeper shadow.

PEARLS BEFORE SWINE

ANGELA ROQUET

THREE YEARS HAD PASSED SINCE EMMA'S LAST VISIT TO LOCKWOOD Cemetery. She'd been thirteen when her grandmother died, and the funeral had been held on a sunny afternoon.

Even in daylight, the place had been creepy, filling Emma with a sense of dread as she wove through the old headstones that belonged to her family. But after nightfall, the cemetery transformed, like a furry moth shucking its chrysalis.

Shadows stretched and pooled behind every grave marker, and the older, moss-speckled tombstones glistened in the glow of lampposts scattered throughout the cemetery. The wind rattled the naked tree branches overhead. It howled and ripped at Emma's hair as if questioning why she'd come at such an hour.

It hadn't been *her* idea, she wanted to protest.

Kate, Emma's cousin, huddled beside her, their backs pressed firmly against their grandmother's massive headstone. The concrete angel that topped the monument leered down at them. *Judging* them, Emma was sure.

The light of the nearest lamppost didn't quite reach the Nader family plot, but she supposed that was why the men digging up her great-great-aunt Gretta had angled the hearse alongside the grave and left the passenger door open. The car's dome light spilled a sickly halo over the hole in the ground, but both men were deep enough now that Emma couldn't see them beyond the soggy hill of soil piled beside the grave.

They had to be getting close.

The thought tightened Emma's gut, squeezing until she tasted the meatloaf her mother had served for dinner at the back of her throat. She swallowed and prayed that she wouldn't vomit over her grandmother's grave. That had to rank somewhere above peeing *and* dancing, neither of which she'd ever dream of doing.

Kate snatched the sleeve of Emma's hoodie and jerked her back behind the headstone. Then she stabbed a red-tipped fingernail at the patch of damp earth between them, a silent order to stay put until it was time.

"We should call the police," Emma whispered. Her voice was low enough to go unnoticed by the men, drowned out by their grunts and the grating, scraping noises their shovels made. Still, Kate's nostrils flared.

"*Calm. Your. Tits,*" she hissed through clenched teeth. Then she tucked her platinum fringe deeper into the hood of her leather jacket before stealing a peek of her own at the men's progress.

Emma pressed her fingers over her eyes, hoping that when she opened them, she'd be back in her bedroom, warm and toasty beneath the heap of stuffed animals Kate liked to tease her for hanging on to. The girls were only a grade apart, but their friendship had taken a turn after Kate's sixteenth birthday, when she'd ditched their weekend slumber parties for dates with older boys.

The sting of rejection had felt like a mortal wound to Emma. She was shy and awkward, with red, unruly hair and a lazy eye. Her cousin had been her only friend. So, when Kate asked Emma to stay the night after months of dodging her calls and avoiding her at school, Emma jumped at the opportunity.

A decision she now regretted.

"I think I'm going to be sick. Oh, God." She laid her face against the headstone, letting the cold concrete soothe the panic burning her alive from the inside. "What if they have a gun?"

Kate exhaled a long sigh. "I should've called Amber for this."

The insult swelled a lump in Emma's throat, though she couldn't help but agree. She sucked in her bottom lip and swallowed again. The bitter tang that heralded tears mingled with the meatloaf, and a sweep of nausea stole her reply. Not that it had been an overly clever one.

The mention of Amber prodded the darkest, most insecure corners of Emma's psyche. She knew that had been Kate's intention—a means to manipulate her pathetic, pariah of a cousin—but Emma also couldn't deny that it was effective. She desperately wanted to regain Kate's affection, as malicious and superficial as the girl had grown over the past year.

The sound of a shovel hitting something solid made Emma's breath hitch, and the first hint of real fear dilated her cousin's eyes.

"You better have a key to this thing," a deep voice grumbled.

"Why the hell do you think we broke into that morgue first? *She-it*. I ain't no amateur."

"That's Wyatt, Chad's brother," Kate whispered. She licked one corner of her mouth, and then her voice dropped lower. "He's out on parole."

"What?" Emma squeaked. Kate clamped a hand over her mouth. Her nails bit into Emma's cheek, but she didn't let go until the sound of the men moving around in the hole broke the silence.

"We should *really* go back to your house and call the police," Emma tried again.

"We can't, okay?" Kate's jaw flexed, and she staked Emma with an annoyed scowl. "I told my dad I was staying over with you."

"Then let's go to my house—"

"No. We'll crash at Chad's after he fences the pearls."

"Chad's?" Emma's heart wilted as her slumber-party bonding plans went up in smoke. Then the rest of Kate's words caught up to her. "You're selling Gretta's pearls? But...what about protecting the family jewels? Wasn't that the whole point of this?"

Kate shrugged as her gaze slid away. "What good are family jewels if they're in the ground?"

"You lied to me." Emma couldn't even pretend that she was surprised. Her cousin's bogus story was too convenient. It had been gnawing at Emma ever since Kate told her how her loser boyfriend du jour's brother had *overheard* them exchanging family stories—namely Gretta's—and how they'd then overheard the brother call a friend to help him rob Gretta's grave.

It was all very...*fishy*, Emma thought. Especially now that she knew Chad would be doing exactly what Kate had insisted they were there to prevent.

Chad was a self-absorbed creep. Emma wondered if he'd even bothered to learn Kate's middle name or her favorite band—anything about her than her bra size—before sending her out to pickpocket his graverobbing, felon of a brother that he was clearly too chicken to tangle with himself.

"We're *so* going to hell."

"Yeah." Kate snorted. "But not for, like, a really, *really* long time."

"What if Chad's brother recognizes you? What if they come back to Chad's house and recognize me?" Emma asked, poking an index finger into her mouth to chew at the jagged skin under her nail. She'd reached the quick some time ago.

"They won't." Kate grabbed the hood of Emma's sweater and yanked it up over her tangle of bright, red-orange curls. "Just follow the plan. It's too late to puss out on me now. If you screw this up, I'll never forgive you."

If Emma screwed this up, forgiveness was the *last* thing she'd have to worry about. She blinked fiercely, clearing the blur of tears from her eyes. There was nothing to be done for the lump in her throat though, so she answered with a stiff nod.

Despite the danger and the lies, Emma knew she would do whatever her cousin asked of her. She wasn't a stupid girl—at least, not when it came to calculus and geography—but as cruel as Kate could be, Emma was a starving dog for any scrap of her attention. She was sure Kate had chosen her as an accomplice tonight for that very reason. Amber would have probably had the good sense to say *hell to the no* with one of her nasal chortles that reminded Emma of a parrot.

The sound of creaking hinges drew the girls' attention back to Gretta's grave.

"*Daaamn.*" Wyatt whistled, and his partner-in-crime loosed a muffled cough.

"Smells like old girl might've been buried with the clams along with their pearls." He snickered at his own joke, but it was muffled, too, as if he'd covered his mouth and nose with the front of his shirt.

"Shut up and help me get these off her neck," Wyatt said.

"I ain't *touchin'* her," his accomplice balked. "Pretty sure that's how zombie outbreaks get started, bruh."

"Then use the shovel to hack her head off—but don't fuck up the pearls or it's coming out of your cut."

Kate squeezed Emma's arm. "Now's our chance. Let's move."

Bile grazed the back of Emma's throat, but she swallowed it down and followed her cousin across the family plot to the side of the hearse opposite Gretta's grave. She held her breath the entire way, pinching her lips together to stave off the scream on the tip of her tongue.

This was madness, but Emma still clung to a fleeting wish. It wasn't a slumber party, and there would be no braiding of hair or baking brownies tonight, but if they managed to pull this off together, she hoped it would bridge the chasm that had formed between their respective sweet sixteens.

The whites of Kate's eyes glowed in the dark as she turned to Emma and held up one of her manicured fingers. They were too close to the crime scene for talk now—even if Emma's brain hadn't been on an endless loop of o*h my God, oh my God, oh my God,* she doubted her ability to form coherent words. It was all autopilot from here, following the instructions Kate had laid out for her half a dozen times on the long walk to the cemetery.

An awful crunching noise echoed up from the hole, and Emma had a horrifying vision of Gretta's mummified head being smashed in with a shovel. She snapped out of it as Kate cracked open the driver's door of the hearse.

Keys dangled from the ignition. The next step of the plan was green-lit.

More bone-crushing noises soon followed, disguising the sound of the back driver's side door as Emma eased it open, following Kate's lead.

There was no second row of seats behind the first, Emma realized too late. It was just a long, open space. Hardly big enough for the single casket that filled it. She hesitated at the sight, wondering if Chad's brother had stolen a body along with the hearse, but then Kate's lethal nails reached for her over the back of the front seat. She shoved Emma down behind the head of the casket not two seconds before the hatch door swung open.

"I sure hope that idiot brother of yours is right about how much these are worth," Wyatt's partner said. The unmistakable rattle of pearls slapped the wooden floor of the coach.

"Careful, asswipe," Wyatt barked from the open grave. "There's at least two mil there."

"There better be. If these turn out to be fakes or some shit, I'mma tell your PO where you buy your clean piss."

"Whatever, man." Strain pinched Wyatt's voice. "Come on. Help me get the bottom half of Granny Tut's lid open."

"What for?"

"You wanna wrestle Jimmy in through the top when we could just drop him in here?"

"Can't we lay him over her coffin?"

"We're gonna have a hard time packing the earth down and making it look undisturbed as it is." Wyatt growled under his breath.

"Oh, right," the other man said. "I didn't think of that."

"And this is why I'm the brains of the operation."

"Lay off, bruh. I'm coming."

He left the hatch door open and circled the car, heading back for the hole. Emma watched his shadow slice across the tinted windows and hunkered lower behind the casket—that she now suspected held a man named Jimmy who was either dead or soon-to-be.

Her brain resumed with its useless mantra. *Oh my God, oh my God, oh my God.*

"Get the hatch," Kate demanded—and not for the first time, Emma guessed from her scathing tone.

"Did you hear something?" Wyatt's voice echoed from Gretta's grave.

Emma stood suddenly, cracking her head on the ceiling of the hearse. Her teeth dug into her bottom lip, and she tasted blood, but she didn't cry out. The thump had been loud enough.

"Move, move, move," Kate chanted as she slid across the front seat and slammed the passenger door shut. She smashed her fist down on the lock before hopping back to the driver's side. "Get the pearls. Get them now!"

The hearse's engine sputtered and then roared to life as Emma stumbled toward the open hatch. She clutched her throbbing head in one hand and groped for the handle to the back door with her other.

"Hey!"

One of the men pounded on the side of the car and tried the handle. It sparked a jolt of panic in Emma's chest. She scrambled to beat the other man to the hatch. The door resisted for a split second, as though fingertips were just shy of making purchase on the outer handle, but then it slammed shut with enough force to send Emma sprawling over the foot of the casket.

"Do you have the pearls?" Kate rasped.

Before Emma could answer, a shovel connected with the back window, spiderwebbing the tinted glass. She shrieked and covered her head with both arms as another blow shattered the window. Bits of glass scraped her skin and peppered her hair.

"Hang on!" Kate shouted. The car lurched forward, the backend fishtailing in the mud.

The man with the shovel took another swing, but it fell short. He chucked it after them, and it grazed the frame of the car, eliciting another scream from Emma.

Then they were gone.

The car bounced over a shallow ditch and onto a side road. Kate howled victoriously. She shoved the hood of her jacket back and shot a manic, wide-eyed glance over her shoulder. "Please tell me you have the necklace."

The night air whooshed inside the car. It puckered Emma's skin and made her lungs ache. Her hands were shaking, but that had little to do with the cold. She patted around in the dark until her fingers grasped the smooth strands of Gretta's pearls.

"Got it!" Emma threw an arm out to steady herself as Kate rounded a corner too quickly. Glass crunched under her sneakers and unbalanced her footing—even more so than her cousin's erratic driving.

When Emma turned to head up toward the front seat, she froze. The casket lid was open. A man in jeans and a flannel shirt lay inside, eyes closed and hands folded over his stomach. A line of blood licked across his forehead before trailing down one cheek.

"K-kate?" Emma whispered, clutched the pearls to her chest. Her cousin glanced over the front seat again.

"Shit. I guess they really did it." Kate shook her head.

"Did what?"

"That's the guy who snitched and landed Wyatt in prison. Chad said they were going to kill him and dump his body. That's why they wouldn't let Chad come with them tonight. Even though it was *his* idea—" Kate sucked in a sharp breath and then coughed loudly, as if that would erase the accidental confession.

"I can't believe I let you talk me in to this." Emma edged around the casket, her eyes never leaving the man. Despite his ashen complexion and the blood, there was a handsome quality to his face. "He looks pretty good for a dead guy."

That earned a snort from Kate. "Says the cross-eyed virgin."

"I'm not cross-eyed." Emma glared at the back of the driver's seat, her skin searing despite the wind hissing through the window. "And there's nothing wrong with being a virgin," she added as she closed the casket lid, hiding the dead man from sight.

"You're right." Kate sighed, but the sound was more annoyed than remorseful. "I'm sorry. I'm just...kinda freaked out right now. Okay?"

"I wanna go home."

"Yeah, okay." Kate didn't even sound a little disappointed. It was as though she'd expected Emma to bail before the night was over. To *puss out*, as she'd so elegantly put it, and leave her to spend the night with Chad, minus a third wheel.

Emma changed her mind about climbing over the seat to sit beside Kate and instead dropped behind the passenger side, pressing her back against the cold leather. She changed her mind about a lot of things in that moment, including wanting anything to do with Kate.

They no longer had anything in common. Emma could see that now. Stealing from graverobbers was bad enough, but playing in the crosshairs of cold-blooded killers and then hijacking their murder victims was too much. It hadn't even seemed to faze Kate.

The hood of Emma's sweatshirt was still pulled up over her head, but her bright curls danced around her face. It was all too likely that Wyatt or his friend had gotten a good look at her. The fear of them coming after her would haunt her nightmares for years to come—the whole miserable night would, she was sure.

She let her mind wander into the future, as she often did when her loneliness became too unbearable, and envisioned how her therapist might analyze the experience. Surely such an event would qualify her for the good drugs. Or at least something to help her sleep.

Emma was roused from the mundane fantasy when Kate pulled off onto an unfamiliar street. "Where are we?" she asked.

"Chad's," Kate answered. "Duh. Where else?"

"You said you'd take me home."

"And I will, but I'm sure as shit not going to be stuck in this car with a dead body *by myself.*"

"Fine." Emma folded her arms, but she quickly unfolded them and scooted around to the other side of the car as the passenger door opened.

The dome light illuminated Chad's smirking face and his greasy mop of shoulder-length hair as he ducked inside. He leaned over, tongue dropping out of his mouth, and planted a sloppy kiss on Kate. She reciprocated with a low noise in the back of her throat. Before the kiss was done, Chad's eyes locked on Emma, and his gaze widened with startled outrage.

"Tha fuck is this?" he said, pulling away from Kate suddenly. Saliva webbed between their lips. "You were supposed to ditch her *before* picking me up."

"Yeah, well, we ran into a little problem." Kate's face flushed apologetically as she cocked her head toward the casket. "Guess who's in there."

"*Awww, man.*" Chad scowled at Emma as if it were somehow her fault there was a dead guy in the car with them. "We'll have to torch the hearse. If the cops find Wyatt's fingerprints in here with the nark who put him away, he'll go back to prison for sure. Then it'll be *me* he comes after next time he gets out."

"Yeah, good idea," Kate agreed.

"Where's the necklace?" Chad demanded.

"Emma has it," Kate said. "I told you she wasn't useless."

Emma thought she'd feel more pride at the compliment, but she didn't. Though her stomach clenched as Chad shot her another accusing glare.

"We'll have to wait and sell it tomorrow," he said. "Getting rid of all this evidence comes first." He held his hand open toward Emma. "Hand it over, Professor Moody."

The pearls lay across her lap. The three long strands were anchored to a single clasp, the opening plenty wide enough for the necklace to be slipped over one's head. Emma considered trying it on. Chad's name-calling hadn't inspired her to play nice, and the pearls were more hers than his anyway.

"These are a family heirloom," she said, sliding further out of his reach.

"Come on, Emma." Kate gave her a tight smile. "You're going to get a cut, too. How's five hundred bucks sound?"

Emma was sure that Kate had heard Wyatt tell his friend the pearls were worth at least two million. Offering her five hundred dollars was a slap in the face, but Emma didn't care how much they offered. What they were doing was wrong.

Chad scoffed and turned his sneer on Kate. "Not useless, huh?"

"*Emmaaa*," Kate groaned. "Fine, we'll give you a thousand dollars."

"No." Emma looped the necklace over her head. "You're not selling Gretta's pearls." Her conviction faltered as Chad produced a bulky handgun from his jacket pocket.

"Don't get greedy, Little Red." He looped his arm over the back of the front seat, lazily pointing the barrel at the floor. "You'll burn just as easily as anything else in this car."

"Chad!" Kate scowled at him but worry tightened the corners of her eyes. She was afraid he'd do—afraid that maybe he was just as wicked as his older brother.

Emma fingered the pearls and chewed her bottom lip, trying to decide if she was brave enough to call his bluff. Would Kate even care if her loser boyfriend shot her cousin dead right in front of her?

A thump and a muffled moan resonated from the casket, breaking the tense standoff.

"Holy shit!" Chad recoiled, and his back slammed against the dash of the hearse. "He's still *alive*?"

"We didn't know, I swear!" The horn of the car blared as Kate's elbow jabbed it in her haste to put more distance between herself and the casket.

Only Emma stayed put. Even a brain-eating zombie was preferable to Chad. Not that she was gullible enough to believe in such things. As proof, she popped open the lid of the casket.

"Don't—" Chad said too late.

The man in the casket, Jimmy, sat up and touched the side of his face where the line of blood had dried to his cheek. He squinted at Chad and Kate in the thin streetlight seeping through the windshield. His eyes settled on Emma last, and recognition lit his expression. "Em?"

"How... how do you know me?" Emma asked, one hand instinctively going to the pearls at her neck as his gaze fell on them.

"Who fucking cares?" Chad yelled. He leveled the gun at Jimmy. "He's a nark. We'll torch him with the car. Close the lid," he ordered.

"No way." She shook her head, causing the strands of pearls to rattle against one another. Then the gun aimed at her.

"Chad!" Kate grasped his shoulder. "I agreed to steal the necklace, not kill anyone."

"Bitch, did I ask you to pull the trigger?" he snapped and tried to shrug her off, but Kate refused to let go. Her free hand reached for the gun, pushing the muzzle away from Emma.

"If my cousin is found in the same car with your brother's nark, there's no way the police won't put two and two together," she hissed at him. "There's no way my parents won't blame this whole disaster on *me*."

Emma's heart shrank in her chest. Of course Kate wasn't fending off her would-be murderer for the sake of familial love. She just didn't want to get in trouble over it.

Rage overpowered Emma's sorrow, and she eyed the hatch door, wondering if she had it in her to make a run for it and leave Kate behind to deal with the bad decision she'd spread her legs and shed her dignity for.

Jimmy's gaze followed her line of sight and then darted back to her. His head dipped in a subtle nod as though he understood her plan and was ready to jump on board. He didn't want to hang around to get shot and barbecued either. *Go figure.*

A shot exploded in the car, sending Emma's shoulders up to her ringing ears. Her head snapped around, and she watched as Kate crumpled in Chad's lap.

"*No, no no, no...*" he wailed helplessly. But it was the sound of panic rather than grief.

Emma was too shocked to feel anything. Her brain refused to wrap around what had just happened. She blinked stiffly at the limp form of her cousin, waiting for her to sit up. To cry out in pain. To slap Chad. Anything.

That's when Jimmy's hand clamped around her wrist. He dragged her to the back of the hearse and threw open the hatch door, pulling her down after he'd jumped out. Emma let him. She didn't know what she was doing anymore. Without Kate to lead the way, she was lost. Worse than lost, she realized as headlights swept up the driveway, blinding her.

She heard Wyatt's voice as the car door opened. "Fucking Chad! I knew it."

Jimmy jerked Emma's arm toward the woods that bordered the dark lawn. "This way. Hurry!"

Another shot sounded inside the hearse. The bullet zipped past Emma's face. It hit the windshield of the other car. Wyatt and his partner flinched and squatted in the gravel drive.

It was hard telling who the shot was intended for, but it served to pull Emma out of her daze. Her legs began to work on their own again, and she followed Jimmy. They shuffled through a patch of thorny bushes and then leapt over a creek before racing past the tree line.

The moon flickered through the branches above them, but it provided little assistance. Dead leaves hid roots and rocks, and the larger trees were surrounded by saplings that snagged and tripped Emma in the dark. But anytime she fell, Jimmy was there to help her up.

Maybe he was a nark, but he wasn't a coward. Emma was sure of that much. She could have been dead right now. He could have left her in the hearse to fend for herself, but he hadn't.

A total stranger had done a better job looking out for her tonight than her own flesh and blood. The thought would have angered her if not for the instant karma Kate had suffered.

Emma tried to tuck away the memory of her cousin's lifeless body before it rendered her useless again. She didn't want to die. Not tonight. Not in the woods with a stranger—however nice he seemed.

After what felt like hours but was probably no more than ten minutes, the skinny trees gave way to larger ones that grew further apart, and evergreens filled in around them, offering more substantial cover.

Enough cover that Emma's stomach decided it was safe to purge its entire contents behind a downed tree. She wiped her mouth with the sleeve of her hoodie and followed Jimmy for a few more yards before stopping again.

"I can't go any further," she rasped. "I need a break."

"Here." He pointed at a wide tree, and they collapsed at its base, tucking themselves inside a nook formed by a pair of thick, raised roots.

Emma shoved her hood back, letting the cold air reach the sweaty nape of her neck. Her blood still boiled beneath her skin, but she refrained from peeling off the sweater. That was a good way to catch a cold. *Cool down too fast, you'll wake up hot in the morning,* Emma's grandmother used to say.

"Do you always wear fine jewels when committing crime?" Jimmy asked, panting.

Emma winced and wrapped a hand around the pearls. "I wasn't—this isn't what it—Wyatt stole these from my great-great-aunt's grave."

"Wyatt?" Jimmy looked confused.

"Yeah. You know, the guy you put away—clearly not for long enough. He was going to dump your body in Gretta's grave after he stole her necklace, too. My cousin and I hijacked the hearse before he got the chance, though. *You're welcome,*" she said between heaving breaths.

"Huh." Jimmy tilted his head back to rest it on the tree trunk. "And this auntie of yours, why would she take such a valuable to her grave? Did she not consider the risks?"

"It was a family secret—until my cousin spilled her guts," Emma explained. "The pearls have been safe and sound underground for over eighty years."

"Until now." Jimmy leaned around the side of the tree to glance back the way they'd come. Emma was sure Wyatt would be looking for them soon, but at the moment, all was quiet.

The woods were eerily still, all the creatures and bugs tucked away for the winter. Spring was still a month off, but the temperature was just warm enough to leave the ground soggy rather than frozen. Emma could feel the dampness seep through her jeans and hoodie. She tried to convince herself it was the reason for the shiver that had taken hold of her whole body.

"Hey," Jimmy said, cupping his hand over one of her trembling knees. "We're safe. Relax."

"I can't." Her breath wheezed, reminding her of the asthma attacks she'd had as a little girl. If she didn't get it together, she would save Wyatt the trouble and drop dead before he found her.

"Deep breath in... Slow breath out," Jimmy coached. Emma tried to look behind the tree, but he pulled her leg in closer to his. "You need to calm down before you hyperventilate."

"I can't," she repeated, feeling more pathetic by the second.

"Tell me about your auntie."

Emma swallowed and tried to push past the mounting panic eating away at her sanity, but her brain kept feeding her images of Kate and Chad in the front seat of the hearse. The shot still rang in her ears.

"Gretta, did you say her name was?" Jimmy prompted her again, giving her knee a gentle squeeze.

Emma nodded and licked her lips. Her breath was still heavy, but she hooked her trembling fingers under the strings of pearls dangling over her chest and held them up in the moonlight. They were all different colors. Silver and blue, pink and gold. A rainbow of fat, lustrous orbs.

"Gretta was engaged to a pearl dealer," Emma rasped. "He traveled the world to find the best and rarest varieties. And from those, he hand-selected every one that went into this necklace. Over two hundred in all—so the story goes."

"They're beautiful," Jimmy said, though when Emma turned to him, she found he was staring at her rather than the necklace. "Did your aunt not have any children to leave the necklace to?"

"No. Her fiancé was on his way back to the States when his ship was hit by a hurricane. Gretta died a month later. Everyone says it was of a broken heart. His body was never recovered, so she couldn't be laid to rest beside him. She asked to be buried with the pearls instead."

"How romantic." Jimmy placed a hand over his chest.

"I think you mean tragic." Emma frowned. Her breath had finally steadied, though a sharp pain still throbbed in her lungs. She rolled the pearls between her fingers. "My grandpa said she had crazy hair like mine. They named me after her—well, her middle name was Emily, anyway."

"A fine tribute. Wearing the pearls, I'm sure you're the spitting image of her."

Emma smiled. "Maybe so."

"What will you do with the necklace now?"

"I don't know. I just couldn't let them sell it. It felt...*wrong*."

"You should keep it. It looks good on you." Jimmy lifted a finger to tug playfully at one of her curls, and heat filled Emma's cheeks.

"I could never wear these in the public. They're *stolen* property." Her lips pinched as she swallowed the laundry list of excuses that sprang to mind. She never went anywhere fancy enough to warrant wearing expensive jewelry. And she didn't like drawing attention to herself—the hair and wandering eye did that plenty, and she hated every second of it.

"Do you suppose your auntie's fiancé bought them for the public's enjoyment?" Jimmy asked.

"Well...no... I guess not."

"Keep them for yourself then. Wear them when no one is looking." A grin tugged up the corners of his mouth. "Think of me when you do."

It was a silly request that Emma thought too intimate for a man she'd just met to ask of her, but she nodded anyway. It also reminded her of something she had forgotten as they'd fled for their lives.

"You never told me how you know my name."

Jimmy's smile grew sharper, and a mysterious light filled his eyes. "You wouldn't believe me if I did."

"Try me."

Instead of answering, he held his index finger up to his lips. Leaves rustled in the wind—*no*. The wind had died down. Something else disturbed the woods now.

Wyatt's gruff voice snaked through the trees. "I'm gonna fucking kill that redheaded bitch."

A branch snapped entirely too close. Emma stood, but Jimmy snatched her arm.

"We need to split up," he whispered.

"*What?* No." Emma squeezed his hand. Perfect stranger or not, she didn't want to be left alone in the woods.

"We have to," Jimmy said. "It's our only chance. I'll create a diversion, draw their attention. You know your way home from here, right?"

"Y-yeah, but..." Emma gave him a pleading look. "Come with me. They already tried to kill you once."

"Ditto, Em." He used the tree they'd been reclining against to stand and then kissed the back of her hand.

"Please, don't leave me," she whispered.

"I won't let anything happen to you. I promise." Jimmy touched her cheek. "Till we meet again."

Then he was gone. His parting was so sudden, Emma thought she'd imagined him disappearing into thin air. But then she heard more rustling in the underbrush.

"There!" Wyatt's partner called out. "Is that...?"

"Don't just stand there," Wyatt barked. "Move!"

Emma couldn't decide if they'd spotted her or Jimmy, but she didn't wait around to find out.

She tucked the pearls inside the collar of her hoodie and tore off through the trees. Branches ripped at her clothes and hair, and she stumbled over a downed limb, but she eventually made it to the road on the opposite side of the thicket. Once there, she ran as fast as she could down the blacktop, her pace never slowing.

Soon, the trees thinned, and her neighborhood came into view.

Emma cut through the alley that ran behind her house and quietly slipped inside through the back door off the screened-in porch. Her mother rarely locked it, but tonight, Emma flipped the deadbolt.

Then she crept up to her bedroom and stripped out of her muddy clothes. She stuffed everything thing down into one of her old bookbags from middle school before burying it in the back of her closet.

It wasn't until after she'd changed into her pajamas that she realized the pearls were still dangling from her neck. She turned to admire them in the mirror above her dresser one last time, and then slipped them off and hid them between her mattress and box spring.

She'd find a better hiding place later, after her brain had a chance to process everything that had happened. The events of the night were slowly catching up with her again.

Kate was dead. Chad and his psychotic brother knew who she was. Maybe even where she lived. The thought of them coming after her made her stomach roil, but there was nothing left to throw up. She'd left it all out in the woods.

Along with Jimmy.

He'd told her to go home, but Emma still felt like a coward for leaving him behind. She prayed that he was all right. Over and over, she whispered the wish to herself, though in her heart, she knew that she'd never see him again. The thought saddened her even more than the loss of Kate's friendship had, which in turn opened a fresh wound born of guilt and disloyalty.

Unrelenting tears flooded her eyes as she nestled into the mound of stuffed animals on her bed. She buried her face in them and cried herself to sleep.

A few hours later, Emma's door wrenched open, and her bedroom light flickered on. She squinted up at her mother's tear-streaked face.

"Oh, Emmy! Thank God you're okay," her mother cried. She clutched Emma to her chest and heaved a shuddering breath. "I thought you were staying the night with Kate."

"She ditched me for her boyfriend." Emma hoped the half-truth was excuse enough for her swollen eyes and stuffy nose.

"I didn't hear you come in, and your uncle Marty just called..." Her mother's voice dissolved into a choked sob.

"Mom?"

"Oh, sweetie. I have the worst news." She pulled away from Emma and sniffled. "That boy Kate was seeing, last night, he shot her."

"Is she...okay?" Emma's brain felt hazy as if her memories weren't her own. How could they be? They were too horrific.

Her mother's stricken expression was answer enough, even before she shook her head. "I'm so sorry, baby. He shot himself, too. They were found in his room this morning by his mom when she got home from work."

Emma drew in a ragged breath. She'd witnessed Kate's death, but Chad? She was sure his demise had been Wyatt's doing. Chad hadn't cared enough about Kate to feel *that* bad for what he'd done, and he'd been terrified when his brother had arrived. That wasn't the behavior of someone who'd lost the will to live.

"That boy was disturbed, and it must have run in the family," Emma's mother said. "His brother and another man stole a hearse last night, too. The officer who spoke to Uncle Marty said that they found it burned up outside of town with both men inside—and a third in a casket in the back."

Emma's heart sank, and the first real tears welled in her eyes. She wasn't sure how, but she knew it was Jimmy. Nothing made sense anymore. Her mother pulled her into her arms for another crushing hug, and she didn't let go for a long time.

Later in the day, when Emma's mother left to deliver a casserole to Kate's parents, Emma ventured from her bedroom and snuck into her dad's office. He was away in Chicago for work, but she suspected his trip would be cut short for the funeral. She wondered how close Kate's grave would be to Gretta's.

Thinking of Gretta, she returned to her task, combing through the family albums on her father's bookshelf. There was an old photo of her great-great-aunt that she remembered seeing a long time ago. Her grandfather had shown it to her when she was little—after she'd come home crying because a boy at school had said she was adopted.

No one else in her family had frizzy red hair, so she'd believed him. Until her grandfather produced the old photo of Gretta. Her great-great-aunt had been gorgeous, sitting proudly with the ropes of pearls cascading over her ruffled dress. Red hair styled in elegant pin curls. A bold, mischievous smile directed at the camera.

It had reassured Emma and given her the strength to face the boy at school again. She needed some of that reassurance and strength now. Her eyes snagged on old album, and she hooked her finger over the spine, pulling it free from the shelf.

A postcard slipped from the book. Emma picked it up and turned it over, noting the faded Australian stamp in the corner. The date, June 4th, 1937, was scrawled down one edge in curly handwriting. The message itself sent a tremor through her blood.

> *My dearest Em,*
>
> *We sail for home next Tuesday. By the time this reaches you, I shall be well on my way to your sweet embrace. I hope you are enjoying the pearls and think fondly of me whenever you wear them. Till we meet again...*
>
> *All my love,*
>
> *James*

GOOD
BOY

A. G. HILTON

The sun burned orange in its descent over the town of Brighton. The restraints of school had been unfurled a month ago, and the dog-days of summer had settled in for the children, bringing with them a languid humidity that dominated the days and afternoons filled with thunderstorms. Often, these days led to unbearable boredom, driving the boys and girls inside to escape the heat and the rain. But sometimes the winds would change and chance gusts from the north would bring milder climes, banishing the rain clouds— perfect for play.

One such evening found Brandon Cliff, eleven and small framed, ambling down the lonely road leading away from the neighborhoods of Brighton. He walked slowly, kicking pebbles aside as he went and stirring up puffs of dust which had begun laying a fine, pale coating on his sneakers and the bottoms of his jeans.

Momma's not gonna like that.

Oh well, *he* hadn't wanted to go out to this stupid place anyways. In fact, *he* hadn't wanted to move to this stupid town at all. And he bet that *she* hadn't really wanted to either.

Dennis had made her.

Even thinking the man's name put a bad taste in Brandon's mouth, like taking a bite of a rotten apple. Brandon hated him, hated the icky smell of tobacco that clung to his clothes and the scent of whiskey he carried on the weekends. Most of all, Brandon hated that Dennis thought he could waltz in and take Daddy's place.

But Daddy was gone.

For a moment he thought of turning around and heading back to town. How would Momma know any different?

But no sooner had the thought occurred to him, he felt ashamed. It was a *bad boy* thing, lying was. And he was a good boy. He'd promised Daddy he would be. Begrudgingly, he picked up his feet and continued toward his destination, a place the local kids simply called "The Field."

The Field, less grand than its name implied, was a weeded lot at the edge of the woods. All the kids in the surrounding neighborhoods would be there. Everyone came on the nice summer evenings to play soccer, baseball, or simply horse around.

It would have been a completely unremarkable spot save one detail; it shared a border with some private property and an old house. A house belonging to a peculiar resident of the town, a recluse and undertaker, Mr. Arthur Night.

The "Graveyard-Man."

Having only moved to Brighton in the most recent school semester and being purposefully slow on the uptake, Brandon had yet to pick up on many (any) of the town nuances. But from the beginning he had heard the whispers about the old creep that lived in the house at the edge of The Field.

Stories abounded about Night, as they often do about people who are withdrawn or strike others as different. Night's eerie profession did him no good in these regards. Nor did the strange stories which circulated about the Night family in general, particularly those concerning Arthur's aged mother who, after dealing with a chronic illness (or perhaps a good old case of the crazies if you believed some of the other rumors), had disappeared without explanation from the public eye.

Brandon heard some kids say that Arthur killed her.

"Chopped her up, ate her, and buried the leftovers in a spare casket," Frankie McLeod had said over a cafeteria lunch, taking obvious pleasure at the way it had made the eavesdropping Brandon squirm.

Creepy stuff, sure. And maybe that was why the kids were drawn to the Field, the danger of it. But false danger, of course. Brandon didn't believe any of the talk, but he would never admit to stepping a little more quickly down the sidewalk if ever he saw Night's shiny Cadillac Miller-Meteor hearse trundling down the road.

But it was not fear of Mr. Night's old homeplace that caused Brandon to avoid the popular spot this long. That stuff about the old guy was make-believe, after all. On the other hand, the teasings (and maybe beatings) he might get from Frankie McLeod and his crew were very real possibilities. Brandon didn't understand why Frankie and a bunch of the other kids took it in their minds to be spiteful. He thought it might just be because he was new, an outsider. He did not understand why, but Brandon sensed that new people were not welcome in Brighton. It was like an exclusive club filled with old stupid families like Dennis', old places, and secrets.

Again, he stopped and considered turning back.

Dennis' voice drifted in his mind: *You gotta leave that boy be, Bekah. Make him take up for himself. You want to have yourself a little Bitch-boy?*

Bitch-boy.

Heat rose in Brandon's cheeks, and he walked more resolutely down the graveled path as the sounds of play drifted to him faintly. He would show that old-fart that he wasn't a bitch-boy. He was a man.

He was Momma's man.

❧ ❧ ❧

Brandon felt uncomfortably like he was being examined under a microscope as he walked onto The Field. There were kids there from two and three neighborhoods over as well as Brandon's own, and they all stared at him as he came.

New kid.

A few of the faces he recognized. There were the Dalton brothers, towheaded and lanky, kicking a checkered soccer ball back and forth. Danny Trenton, a big guy wearing that bored look he always seemed to carry. Porky Bill Withers from a block over. He even saw Christie Miller, the pretty red headed girl from across the street. Seeing her, Brandon unconsciously straighten from his slouch.

But any assurance this familiarity may have inspired (despite the fact that Brandon wasn't sure he could call any of them friends), washed away as Brandon's eyes fixed on a freckled face sneering from the center of the group; Frankie McLeod.

McLeod didn't live in Brandon's neighborhood; a fact of which Brandon was glad. Brandon knew Frankie was a bad boy. Brandon had once found him smoking a pack of cigarettes beneath the bridge that crossed Simmons Creek, and the boy had bragged about how he had stolen them from his old man while the geezer was laid out drunk before threatening to pound Brandon's face in if he didn't move along and keep quiet. Despite not being much older, Frankie's physique was considerably developed, and his size alone gave him an edge of intimidation. What's more, Frankie knew it.

He glared as Brandon crossed the grass. "What you want newbie? Who invited you?"

"No one," Brandon said, trying his best to sound as if he didn't care one way or the other. "I just came to play ball."

"Play ball, huh?" Frankie considered Brandon's slight frame with a sneer. "Who said we'd let little kids play."

Part of Brandon desperately wanted to turn away from the encounter, a part of him that wished right now he had chosen to look for a new Spider-Man comic instead of coming to this stupid place with these stupid people. Another part—*bitch-boy,* it whispered— rose up red within him.

"Frankie you ain't but two years older'n me. I ain't no little kid. In fact, I bet I could out kick you in a game. Bet you're just too afraid to let it happen."

All eyes suddenly turned from Brandon to Frankie. In the ritual that followed, the delicate playing out of a schoolyard challenge, Brandon would have to step delicately to avoid an outright beat down. For a younger kid to respond in such kind to someone like Frankie was unheard of. Brandon knew it, too, and braced for whatever came next.

For a moment, Brandon felt sure that a beating waited just around the corner and his legs poised to flee back up the gravel road. But the flash of anger in Frankie's eyes proved only momentary, quickly replaced by a patronizing grin.

The older boy hocked a wad of spit into the grass. "That's pretty big talk, newbie. How about we see if that's all it is. You play. Hell, you be a captain."

A warmth flashed through Brandon. Could it really be so easy?

"But," continued Frankie, "let's make it interesting." He turned and pointed to the large, black shuttered Victorian-style house replete with a spire that made it look not so unlike a haunted castle at the edge of The Field. "Loser has to go and take somethin' from the Grave-Yard Man's house."

Brandon's stomach dropped. "Steal somethin'?"

"Yeah. What's the problem?"

"Ain't you afraid of being caught?"

"He ain't there. We seen him leave an hour ago. And look, he

leaves some of his windows open on these hot days. It's easy pickings. What's a'matter, newbie?"

Brandon felt what little resolve he had managed to build up slip-
ping. He couldn't do that. That was a *really* bad-boy thing to do. And
from the Grave-Yard Man's house...

"I ain't gonna steal," he said at last.

"No problem, newbie," Frankie said with a smile. "If you really
kick like you say, you won't have to worry about it. But if the pressure's too much for the witty-bitty boy, he doesn't have to play. He
can go cryin' home to Mama like usual."

Like usual.

Those words echoed back and forth in Brandon's head.

You want to have yourself a little Bitch-boy?

The red-hot feeling returned. Suddenly none of the rest of it
mattered. He would show Frankie McLeod once and for all, here in
front of all these people. He didn't even care if Frankie decided to
beat him up afterwards. Fact is, Brandon knew two things: that he
could play well, good enough to beat out Frankie, and that if it fell
on Frankie to steal from Arthur Night's creepy house, the boy would
chicken out. What's more, Christie Miller was in attendance to see
it all go down.

All the rest was details.

"I ain't runnin', Frankie," Brandon said. "You're on."

They picked teams. In this, Frankie had the definite advantage.
Not really knowing any of the kids present, Brandon picked blindly
and hoped for the best. A small fear that maybe he had acted rashly
resurfaced, but he hushed it. This was his moment.

🏈 🏈 🏈

Game on.

While Brandon didn't know much about the other kids, they too
knew little of him. For instance, none of them knew that, until the
recent move, he had played in small soccer leagues. The satisfaction

of seeing Frankie and his goons' looks of bewilderment was doubly rewarding In a short amount of time, Brandon had already scored his team a goal.

Brandon's confidence returned. Honestly, none of the other kids were actually that good. Frankie, in particular, blundered around knocking other kids over. But Brandon proved too quick, and left Frankie more often than not doubled over gasping and swearing under his breath.

Another goal came, traded off for one made by Frankie's team. Brandon followed this minor interruption with two more scores. He noticing that the other kids cheered, really cheered, as he outmaneuvered Frankie and the goalie to score. When all of this was said and done, Brandon mused, he might have made himself into something of a neighborhood legend.

Frankie grew visibly angrier and angrier with every goal scored. Brandon loved it. He glanced over at Christie Miller on the sidelines and wound up midway down the field to take a longshot at the distant goal. At this rate, Frankie's team would never be able to catch up before it got dark, any more scores would just be more nails in the coffin.

His foot pistoned forward, sending the ball flying high.

Too high.

Brandon had been cavalier taking the shot, but even he paused over how wild it flew. For a moment, the ball became silhouetted against the amber sunset, and then it began its descent straight toward Mr. Night's house. It struck just inside the tall metal fence, bounced, and disappeared into one of the open first story windows.

All jaws dropped. Silence fell over the group.

A puffing Frankie came to Brandon and shoved him. "Nice going, you little shit. Looks like you lost our new ball."

"I—I—"

"Can it!" A smug look of satisfaction fell on Frankie's face. "Looks like you'll be taking a trip to Grave-Yard Man Land anyways."

"Wait! That wasn't what you said," Brandon protested. "That was only if I lost. I can't help that it—"

"Oh, shut up! You kicked it didn't you? That was brand new. You kicked it, you go get it. That's just fair is all. Ain't that right?" Frankie turned to the Dalton brothers, both of whom came running up angrily. "That was your new ball, wasn't it?"

"You bet it was!" said Dan Dalton, older of the two. He regarded Brandon with his narrow green eyes. "My brother and I saved up our allowances for that, you newbie *shit*. You gonna pay us back or what?"

"I was just saying that he needs to get it back for you," Frankie replied magnanimously.

Brandon blathered on, trying to think of what to say. "Why don't we wait until he comes home? We could just explain what happened and then he'll maybe give it back."

"You kidding me, newbie? That old creep ain't gonna give it back. It's lost and it's your fault. Now go get it, or I will personally give you an ass-whoopin' you'll feel for weeks."

Brandon looked around. The microscope feeling returned with full force, this time doubled by the indignation in the looks around him. It had all been so perfect, and he had screwed it up.

"C'mon newbie, don't be a chicken. Don't be a little *bitch*."

Bitch-boy.

Brandon looked toward the house which now cast a long and reaching shadow in the waning light. It stuck up like a shard of pure darkness from the field, a chunk of malignancy. Brandon shivered.

But Mr. Night was gone, he reminded himself. The Miller-Meteor hearse was nowhere to be seen and the gate to the driveway hung open. It wouldn't be a big deal to slip in and slip out, would it? He wasn't *stealing* anything, just fixing a mistake. Then another thought: if he went into the house, that would be even better than if he had won the soccer game. To be the new kid who braved the Night House? Now that would be something.

"I'll do it," he said, receiving audible gasps from some. Even Frankie looked momentarily taken off guard. "I'll go right on in. While you stand out here like a little bitch, Frankie."

Before a response could be made, Brandon cut off across The Field toward the brooding shape of the Night house.

❦ ❦ ❦

The closer he got to his destination, the harder Brandon found it to move his legs. A tremble sank into them making his footfalls unsure. With each shaky step, the house grew larger and more looming until, by the time he stood outside the tall metal gate which surrounded it, the building seemed to almost lean over him like a cat over a mouse.

The creepy stuff, it's all made up, he reminded himself. *Just a grumpy old man, is all.*

He cast a look over his shoulder. The others had followed, but only part of the way, stopping short of the house's inky shadow.

Brandon walked the fence's edge to the front of the house where looming the gate stood open at the entrance of the driveway. He noted how high the fence stretched and the cruel looking spikes that lined its top. He would need to be quick. From the look of it, this gate provided the only way in or out.

He slipped inside the fence and crept around to the window into which the ball had bounced. Like the fence, it now seemed higher from the ground. Too high to climb into, in fact. To make matters worse, a bed of thorny rose bushes occupied the space below.

Brandon walked back to the front and stood for a moment. He thought he would have to call it off. No way could he get to that window by himself. He glanced up to the front door. Probably locked, but suddenly that seemed great. He would just walk up to the front door of the Grave-Yard Man's house and try it while the others watched. Who cares if he couldn't actually get in? None of the other kids had the guts to do it, and he knew they wouldn't forget that he had been ballsy enough to do it anytime soon.

With another look back to the expectant crowd, he strode up the steps to the imposing black door. Brandon reached out and seized the old brass knob intending to give it a good wrenching just for show. To his surprise, however, it turned easily, producing an audible click as the door swung open upon an interior dark as night.

Bad boy.

For a moment Brandon simply stood there, gaping at this unexpected turn of events. He felt like a dog which, after having chased a car down the road, finally managed to catch the vehicle only to find that it didn't know what to do next.

"Go on, newbie," goaded Frankie from the safety beyond the spiked fence. Apparently, he had worked up enough gall to be a bully again. "Don't be chicken. Hurry up before the Grave-Yard Man comes back and *gets* you."

Brandon looked into the gloom ahead uncertainly, listening for any signs of something coming to snatch him from the porch. But only silence reigned. In fact, compared to the naturally noisy summer evening with its chirping crickets and croaking Cicadidae, the house seemed to emit a wave of deadening stillness.

Time ticked by, and Brandon knew a decision had to be made. He couldn't afford to stand here and risk Mr. Night coming back to find him fleeing from the open front door. He had to proceed or turn back.

"Watch. He's gonna chicken out," Brandon heard Frankie pronounce from afar.

Brandon clenched his small hands into fists. Judging from where the window looked into the house, the room he sought would not be far. It would only take a second. In, out, and done. It wasn't stealing, just getting something back. And Frankie would look more foolish than ever once he pulled it off.

With a trembling footfall, he stepped forward, leaving the pleasant summer evening behind and entering the darkness that belong to the Grave-Yard Man.

Bad boy.

The door fell shut behind him.

❧ ❧ ❧

Within those first moments, Brandon thought he would be physically unable to proceed. This was a forbidden place beyond any that he had ever thought of entering. His very presence here set his mind into a guilty frenzy.

You're being a bad, bad, boy.

As his eyes adjusted to the gloom, he found himself in a hallway that seemed to run the length of the house. Doors opened off this main hallway both to the left and right, each one looking like the foreboding entrance to some gloomy cavern. Stairs clung to the wall on Brandon's right, running with an ornate bannister to an upper level shrouded in utter blackness.

All at once another thought hit him which nearly sent him screaming for the door: What about Old Woman Night? What about the stories? Could she still be here in this house, locked up and insane, or twisted with some unknown ailment? He pictured a raving old woman, knife in hand, suddenly at his side and sticking him with a knife like one of those horror movies Dennis talked about late on a drunk Saturday night because he knew it frightened Brandon. But no screeching old woman came rattling down the stairs nor did she peak from any of the mysterious doorways. Brandon quickened his step while he still had the nerve to do so.

It would be one of the doorways to his left, of that much he was certain. He crept along quietly to the first and peered in just long enough to know it was not the one he sought. Before he came to the second doorway on the left hand side, however, one opened to his right.

Brandon glanced sideways on instinct and fell back against the opposite wall with a scream caught in his throat. From the gloom a ghastly face snarled at him. Flesh sunken upon bone looking stretched to a critical limit. Teeth twisted into fangs dripping with stringy saliva. Eyes that gleamed with a knowing malevolence.

He waited for the thing to pounce and have him by his tender throat, but it moved not a bit. In the span of seconds, Brandon turned from horror to relieved shock. Stepping closer to the doorway, he realized that the monster resided in a large canvas, nothing more than oil and paint. It appeared Mr. Night was something of an artist, though why he would paint monsters made little sense to Brandon.

A dread fascination held sway over him as he looked at the painting, and he found himself drawn into the room. He discovered other paintings, equally macabre sitting about on easels. Some showed creatures similar to the one which had nearly made Brandon wet himself, others depicted *things* (*beings*, some primordial, grown-up part of his mind whispered). They had no shape that Brandon could recognize, simply flowing feelers, tentacles, and staring, wet eyes all jumbled together in a confusing way that made Brandon feel sick. He turned quickly from their icky strangeness and hoped the images would not be remembered and give him nightmares.

As Brandon backed from room he glanced to a desk upon which an old, leather-bound volume sat opened. Something about the book seemed *wrong*, as if it oozed with sickness. Brandon dared not look too closely at the open pages. Scattered upon it, however, were small pictures which drew his eye. Not paintings like those hanging about, but polaroids. They were naughty, very, very bad boy things. With a glance at the naked, dead flesh and body parts exposed in those black and white photographs, Brandon felt sick, more a bad boy than ever before.

He hurried out of the room with renewed purpose, heading directly for the doorway through which he knew he would find the ball. Though the whole ordeal had happened over the span over moments, Brandon felt as if he had spent an eternity in the awful place, and he itched to be out again in the waning summer evening. He crossed into the room and found the ball lying on the floor a few feet from the open window. He took it up triumphantly and leaned out the window, holding it aloft for all to see. The dazed expressions of wonder on the faces beyond the fence renewed the confidence Brandon felt bloom within during the soccer game.

"Got your ball!" he called. He hurled it out the window and over the fence. "Guess that makes one of us who isn't a chicken!"

Frankie, the Dalton brothers, and everyone else looked at the ball in shocking disbelief. Brandon knew that he had shown Frankie, shown them all, that he was more than the little new kid. He thought again of little red-headed Christie and the fact that she had seen it all go down and stood a little taller again.

But his revelry came crashing down around him with the sound of an engine growling up the gravel drive.

❧ ❧ ❧

Brandon watched in horror as the other kids scrambled away from the fence. The sound of the approaching motor grew ever nearer. Heart racing, he ran back to the front door and looked out a window just in time to witness the Miller-Meteor come to a halt just within the confines of the fence. As the car door swung open, Brandon unconsciously retreated step by step back the way he had come. A large leg clad in dark pants emerged below the open door, and the rest of Mr. Arthur Night followed behind.

He wore a dark suit which Brandon thought must have been tailored for a giant. For Night towered above the roof of the Cadillac from which he had emerged. In fact, under other circumstances, seeing such a long and lanky man emerge from a car might have been a funny sight, like watching clowns pour out of a small car at the circus, but one look at Night's face dispelled all mirth. Gaunt and stretched, Night's features seemed wrong, warped. He wore a deep scowl which he directed out at The Field, presumably at the retreating kids. He then turned and strode toward the house.

You're in for it now, you bad boy.

Brandon entered full panic mode, all silly ideas of showing off for pretty girls and standing up to bullies replaced by a frantic need to escape. He thought of the paintings, the bad pictures, the old spooky book, and suddenly knew that he could not let the man find him. Already Night had made it to the up the stairs to the front door. As it swung wide Brandon jumped aside into the room with the open window. His eyes caught upon the window and the world beyond. In desperation, he ran and flung himself forward.

Only after he left the ground did Brandon recall how high the window sat above the earth below, and it was not until he felt the ripping thorns stick into his backside that he remembered the waiting rose bushes. He crashed down in a heap, struggling for a moment with the twisting plant, all the while feeling his skin and clothes tear. A distant part of himself noted absently that Momma would be none too happy with his now bloodied and tattered wardrobe.

He freed himself at last and hobbled painfully toward the front of the house, fighting back the overwhelming urge to cry. He just wanted to go home.

I'm sorry for being a bad boy! I promise never-ever to do it again!

As he peered around the corner of the house, the specter called Night came sweeping down the front steps. Brandon recoiled and hugged the side of the house desperately. The way Night walked, he seemed almost to glide upon his long strides. Brandon prepared himself to run the first chance he could move unseen and make for the open gate.

Brandon expected that Night was returning to gather something from his car before heading back inside. When the man returned once more into the house, then he would make his escape.

But Night strode past the hearse straight to the gate. Brandon watched in gut wrenching horror as he swung the tall metal closed and locked it soundly with a chain and padlock. Night then returned to the car and fumbled for a moment with keys which in his elongated hands looked like small toys. At last he found the one he wanted and inserted it into the back of the Miller-Meteor. He swung the trunk door wide and cast a wary glance around The Field.

Suddenly, Brandon realized something awful: the other kids had gone. Running off to their homes, leaving him behind. Alone.

Brandon watched as Night turned back to the car, all the while wondering how he might get over the tall fence without being seen or impaled on the wicked points at the top. His planning was interrupted, however, as he watched Mr. Night single handedly withdraw a long, pine casket from the hearse. For a moment, Brandon sat awestruck, wondering how a single man could heft one of those boxes so easily.

He thought back to Daddy's funeral, how six men had been required to maneuver the casket. But Night handled this one as if it weighed nothing. Lifting it up on his shoulder, Night turned and began to make his long strides not back up the stairs, but around the house— directly toward Brandon.

❧ ❧ ❧

Brandon hardly noticed that his bladder had given way, so consumed was his mind with a terror he could not properly articulate that he paid the warm trickle down his leg no mind.

He *couldn't* let Mr. Night catch him here. This was *really* bad boy stuff. Thoughts of the strange paintings and gross pictures kept flashing through his mind. If the strange man did find him...

Brandon fled toward the back yard. His mind raced with nightmarish possibilities of what would happen if Night found him, possibilities made more vivid by a frightened and fevered imagination. He rounded the corner of the house into the backyard in a frenzy. Eyes bulging, he surveyed the scene. Here the fence stood as tall and impenetrable as ever, and it ran until it connected with the side of the house, offering no avenue of escape around the other side. The yard lay wide open, a slaughtering ground with nowhere to hide.

Brandon bolted up the back steps of the house and tried the back door only to find that, unlike the front, it was locked tightly. He breathed some of the dirty words he learned from Dennis under his breath as tears welled up in his eyes.

Don't wanna get caught! Don't wanna be a bad boy! Don't want Grave-Yard Man to get me!

Turning back to the yard, his eyes chanced on something he had failed to notice before. There, along the back of the fence, sat a square brick structure topped by a door that sat at an angle to the ground. Unconsciously, this registered in Brandon's mind as a kind of old-timey storm cellar door. Like the one Dorothy tried to get to in *The Wizard of Oz*. He could see a gleaming padlock keeping the door closed, but half a foot of space yawned between the bottom of the door and the brick work beneath.

Just enough space for a little boy.

From around the side of the house came the heavy footfalls of Mr. Night. Brandon bolted down the steps and across the yard. Crawling on his belly, he squeezed through the small space and into the concealing darkness. Brandon found himself lying on a set of concrete stairs that descended downward to a wooden door below ground.

He crouched at the stairs and looked out to the yard in time to see Mr. Night rounding the corner of the house still carrying the coffin aloft over his shoulder. His heart beat wildly as he waited for the man's next move. Night set the coffin down on the ground and reached a long fingered hand into his pocket, again producing the set of keys. Mumbling to himself, the Grave-Yard Man turned and made his way to the back door and unlocked it.

For a moment, Brandon's legs itched with the urge to push himself out of the small space beneath the cellar door and make a break for the front of the house. His mind had already raced through several possible escape plans when Night re-emerged from the depths of the house in a flash carrying a white bowl in hand. He then picked up the coffin and turned towards the cellar in which Brandon lay hidden.

Trapped! Trapped like a rat!

Brandon squirmed away from the opening and down the steps all the while wondering how he could be so stupid. With the thought that he was gonna get caught hiding out in Mr. Night's private property came a new rush of shame and fear. He backed downwards further, and as Mr. Night fiddled with the lock above, Brandon bumped into the door at his back. On instinct, he reached backwards and tried the handle. It swung open and he fell back into a room of darkness. Scrambling to his feet, Brandon shut the door just before Mr. Night unclasped the lock above.

❦ ❦ ❦

Brandon found himself in near complete darkness. He could make out only vague shapes of things: some barrels, stacks of boxes, shelving. Feeling his way along, trying to shut out the skittering sound of rats, he climbed to the nearest corner and wedged himself behind a stack of boxes and waited.

Night entered as soon as Brandon hid himself, throwing his long shadow like an ink stain across the floor. He strode into the room and flipped on a light which sputtered to life, casting an unnatural orange glow over the room. For a moment, the man simply stood there, and Brandon felt sure that Mr. Night knew he lay close at hand, that the man had spotted some small but significant detail of intrusion. Yet, Night made no sudden move to apprehend him.

As Night stood there illuminated by the orange glow, Brandon realized just how ghoulish the undertaker looked. His skin seemed drawn too tightly, as if it were not enough to cover his frame or that his frame beneath did not befit the skin which clung to it. His eyes sat sunken in his long face and his cheeks caved inwards. Brandon thought the man looked like an exhibition in the freak show at the County fair: Come see the incredible stretched man. The thought filled him with brief pang of pity for the strange man, another of Brighton's pariahs. But the feeling quickly resolved itself; he couldn't shake the thought of those things in the house.

All at once, Night turned and retrieved the coffin, bringing it down into the room. He laid it upon a table set off to the side and threw the lid wide. Brandon felt a wave of guilt sweep through him upon seeing the contents. Night withdrew a nude girl from the wooden box, her body pale and beautiful. Her face, however, was a pulpy mess, destroyed as if by some immense blow.

"A shame," Night said, running his hand along a pale thigh. It seemed to Brandon that the man was addressing someone, though, as far as Brandon could tell, they were alone. "It was a car accident, you know. Closed casket funeral. We could take more than usual I imagine. Who would know?"

Seemingly in answer, Brandon heard a rustling in the walls. More rats.

Night grabbed the bowl he had taken from the house and put it beside the body. Brandon looked on in horror as he reached to a nearby shelf with his other spindly hand and withdrew a small container from which he pulled a selection of scalpels. Night shrugged off his coat and button down until only a white t-shirt remained to cover a body that seemed bent and twisted. He reached to the opposite wall, retrieved a dirty apron suspended from a nail, donned it.

The Grave-Yard Man went to work.

Night made a long incision and pulled the skin of the dead girl's stomach wide. With a long fingered hand, he reached into her and withdrew some piece of anatomy which Brandon could not place. Holding it aloft in admiration, Night suddenly threw it back into his mouth as if into the jaws of a waiting croc and chewed it slowly like a piece of rare steak.

"Young... choice," Night whispered. He sucked blood from his fingers.

Brandon's stomach churned. He felt seconds away from retching loudly, leaving himself to be discovered in a pool of vomit. The walls now seemed alive with the sounds of small skittering feet, and several large rats crawled over Brandon's sneakers.

"Did you hear me?" Night seemed to ask no one. "Good. Very young and nourishing. She will keep us satisfied for sometime."

The rustling grew louder still, now accompanied by an insane squeaking chorus. More rats emerged to crawl on the table around the body.

"Back!" Night swatted them away. "Wait your turns, vermin. The Lady has patiently awaited her meal."

With this pronouncement, something moved in the darker shadows of the subterranean chamber. Brandon felt a scream rise in his throat but somehow managed to stop from tearing forth. He realized that he had wandered into a living nightmare beyond any of the silly horror movies Dennis watched. Suddenly, everything else fell away: Dennis' words, the move to the new town, the kids' jeering and name calling, even that dirty name (*bitch-boy*)— all seemed alien and insignificant next to the sight before him.

The thing crawled towards the table from the deep shrouds of the shadows. Under the light's orange glow, Brandon glimpsed a maligned and disfigured body, a parody of the human form. It stalked on spindly limbs, stretched beyond natural length, joints paying no heed to the constraints of normal anatomy. Two fleshy lumps of flaccid breast swung from its front as it came. Some of its skin seemed to have fallen away, revealing a black, chitinous substance growing beneath, and thin wisps of hair hung from a head bearing sunken, large eyes. It lifted its horrible face to Night and croaked out a series of harsh sounds.

Brandon hid his face, not wanting to look at the walking nightmare, the dead looking thing which crawled from the dark. In its wasted form he saw pestilence and ruin, in its gait a defiance of nature, and in its sunken features he saw... *Daddy*. Daddy lying there, shriveled and wasted away before he had left forever.

Mr. Night cooed softly at the creature. "Come, now. I am sorry to have kept you waiting. It has been a long time since the last proper feeding, I know. But dinner's here now just as promised."

Night returned to the corpse, cutting and pulling away meat from the open abdomen and placing it in the bowl he had retrieved from the house. He placed the bowl at the end of the table, and the horrid thing began ferociously consuming the meal. Night walked calmly to the creature's side and placed a loving hand on its shoulder, rubbing gently.

"I could never forget about my mother," he whispered.

At this, Brandon's blood froze. The Old Night woman. Still alive, but . . . *changed* somehow. Brandon thought back to the spindly creatures in the paintings, not scary fantasies but family portraits. He thought of Mr. Night's strange appearance, the monstrous blood that must flow also through his own veins and wondered wild and horrible things.

Brandon fell into a ball, clasping his knees hard against himself so as not to cry out as the tears ran. He didn't care if it was a bitch-boy thing to do. He wanted to cry, he wanted Momma, he wanted Daddy!

He heard sniffing, like a large dog, then Night's voice. "What's this?" The sound of approaching steps froze Brandon's blood. He knew if he looked up now he would face a twisted silhouette looming above him in the orange light. "Mother, I smell a guest."

This wasn't right! This was meant for bad boys like Frankie McLeod! He wasn't a bad boy, honest!

He never wanted to be a bad boy.

But that no longer mattered. As he felt the ink-black shadow fall over him, Brandon realized that this was a different world from that one which promised good things to good little boys; this was a hungry world, populated by things that did not distinguish between boys who were good and bad.

Because, in the end, they all taste the same.

ONLY THE YOUNG DIE GOOD

EMILY LAVIN LEVERETT

"GRACIE!" I CALLED AND WAVED MY MUG IN THE AIR. "CAN I GET ANOTHER cup of that marvelous coffee?"

She scowled at me from the far end of the counter where she set down plates of eggs and bacon for a couple of morning regulars. She sauntered down to me, picking up the carafe along the way.

"Thanks, darlin'." I gave her my biggest grin.

Her thick, shiny hair was still mostly black with streaks of white—the kind that make a woman look wise, not old, and certainly not sixty. Her light brown skin had aged well, only a few crow's feet tugging at the edges of her eyes and laugh lines around her mouth. Thick black liner, green eyeshadow, and a dark pink lipstick had been her go-to since we were teenagers. If she ever changed, something had gone wrong with the world.

She set the carafe aside and leaned on the counter, close to me.

That's when I saw the small flickers around the edges of her face. Definitely pro work. Expensive work. My stomach dropped, and I pushed aside my half-eaten ham and Swiss omelet.

"You really okay with getting wrapped up in this?" Her voice was low, tight.

"Course I am."

She topped off my coffee and picked up my plate. "It's on the house."

"Gracie, c'mon. Don't be like that. I'm Juliet's godmother for Chrissake." I switched topics fast. "How's your wife?" It wasn't the question I wanted to ask—*how does your wife feel about you using magic?*—but it would do.

"Jenny's good," she said over her shoulder as she set down the carafe and dumped the uneaten food in the trash. "She wants you over for dinner—like we used to do." She eased the plate into the bus bin.

"Maybe when I get back," I said.

Gracie grunted her acknowledgment and moved off to refill other cups. JJ's Diner, with its black and white checkerboard floor, weathered black vinyl booths, and chipped countertop had been a go-to joint for the late-night and early morning crowds in Raleigh for a dozen decades. No joke.

Days like today, I felt like I'd been around for all of it.

Gracie, Jenny, and I had been girls together—fast friends and thick as thieves—since we were in diapers. That they fell in love and got married surprised no one, and certainly not me, but there are definitely moments where three's a crowd, so while they set up a household, taking over Jenny's folk's diner, I went my own way.

I retrieved my wallet from my back pocket and dropped two twenties on the counter. Way more than breakfast and a tip, but today was special. Ugly special. I changed one of the twenties for a five. Forty bucks felt too much like guilt money.

The bell over the door jangled, and I turned around.

The girl walking toward me, my goddaughter, was as beautiful as any I'd ever seen. She had a thousand-watt smile that damn near broke my heart. Tight, soft curls, both dark and light brown, spiraled in a cloud around her face. Sharp angles, full lips, and rich dark skin all reminded me of Jenny—she was nearly a copy. Her eyes, though, so pale blue the irises were almost white, were wholly her own.

She wore black jeans, a black tee, and black shitkickers, like me, and I took a moment to be flattered. She also wore an oversized letterman's jacket from high school.

"Hey, J-baby," I said softly. I always called her that. "Ready for your first job?"

She was ten times too happy for this world, flinging her arms around my neck. "So ready, Aunt Tanya!" Magic crackled around her, too—but it wasn't the kind you wore, the kind most folks could see. J-baby had an aura around her so bright that anyone could see it, though non-users would attribute it to her brilliant personality. She'd learn to rein in that aura, hide that magic, soon enough.

After I extricated myself from her, I took my black bomber jacket from the coat rack and slipped it on. I scooped up my black Stetson, and fixed it on my head, careful not to pull too much on my long, red ponytail secured at the base of my skull.

I jerked my head in the direction of the counter. "Do you want anything before we go?"

"Nah," she shook her head. "Mama Jenny fed me."

I moved toward the door, back to the counter. "Want to say goodbye to Gracie?" I hung my head, watching my toe kick a scuff mark on the tile.

"Bye, Mommy!" She called over my shoulder.

"Y'all be careful," Gracie called back, as if I needed reminding.

I nodded. "C'mon," I muttered. The bell jingled like always, and I didn't look back.

"Is it parked out back?" Jay trotted along beside me, and I noticed how fast I was walking. I slowed down. Jay was in good shape—like a lot of eighteen-year-olds—but she was a good five inches shorter than me.

"Yep." We followed the alley between the restaurant and the next building around to the back where Bess was parked. She was dusty black, with respectful, mysterious tinted windows, like a hearse should be. The ornate etchings—wreathes of rose buds—were only visible in the occasional glint of sunlight. I dug my key out of my pocket and hit the button. The *thunk* of heavy locks shifting back rang out across the quiet lot. And those were only the side doors. The back had reinforced steel and a complicated lock that even a couple weeks with a blowtorch couldn't bust. I supposed someone could TNT the doors off, but anything strong enough to do that would damage the merchandise, and no poacher wanted that.

Jay raced around the far side and opened the door. She took a deep breath and looked around.

"What?" I said, tensing. It wasn't one-hundred percent unheard of for a poacher to try to steal the hearse *before* it picked up the body.

"Nothing." She kept looking.

I waited. She'd get to it eventually. Neither of her moms were good at keeping to themselves.

Finally she nodded, satisfied, and dropped into the seat, slamming the door. I winced. I'd warned her about slamming—but, I reasoned with myself, it didn't do any harm now, it wouldn't do to start out criticizing every little thing, and there were sure to be more important things later.

I got in the car.

"I wanted to take a mental picture of my first day on the job."

"And?" I slipped the key into the ignition.

"It's pretty--bright and sunny." She shook her head. "There are birds singing. It's a normal winter day." She sounded disappointed.

"Yep," I agreed. "That's the thing about this job, J-baby. It's always an ordinary day."

I turned on the car and the AC popped on, too. Sure, it was in the forties now, but it would warm up some by the afternoon, and it never hurt for the box in back to be cold.

I reached for a switch on the dash and J-baby caught my hand. "Can I do it?" She asked, eyes sparkling, all eager.

"Sure." I pulled my hand back. "Have at it."

She did a little dance in her seat that reminded me of when she was a little girl—she'd get so excited about something, anything, and she couldn't be still to save her life. She flipped the switch and a silver wave spread out from the dash over the whole car.

"Did it work?"

"Hop out and check." I glanced at the clock on the dash. Arriving early for a body pick-up is gauche, so we had the time.

She heaved open the door and let it slam, again, behind her. Her eyes widened and her mouth formed a startled "o" as the magic over the car rippled and shook, but held. Hopefully that would teach her to be careful. She walked around the car, running her hands down the sides and poking it. Finally she got back in, with a gentle closing of the door.

"So," I asked, "did it work?"

"We're in a caterer's truck!" She giggled. "You have to teach me how to do that. It would be dead useful!"

It was indeed useful, I knew. Why a kid like her would have use for it was a question for another time. "I will, but we've got more important stuff to do today." I shifted the car into gear and eased down the narrow alley and hung a right to pass the diner. I couldn't help it. I didn't look to see if Gracie watched us. Jay didn't either.

The house was far from downtown in an old-money suburb. A mansion-filled community built in classic Victorian style. The heavy stone wall surrounding the neighborhood, with the towers peeking over, invoked the sense of castles behind a moat. The thick, portcullis styled gate, with its ten-digit entrance code, emphasized that.

"How was your mom when you left this morning?" I asked, trying to sound nonchalant.

"Fine." She was gazing out the side window, watching the houses go by.

I wanted to ask J-baby if she'd had problems, if Jenny had tried to stop her. Both moms had cried when I explained that Juliet's power—soul synthesis—wouldn't go away. Jenny screamed at me, calling me a liar, telling me that using magic was a choice—a moral one. We'd had the argument before, including right before I left that first time. Nothing had been the same between us since. Even when Juliet's birth healed some of the rift.

How I used the magic, that was a choice, my moral choice. But having it? That was luck-of-the-draw genetics. No one could make it come, and no one could make it go.

J-baby was willful, though, just like her mothers, and would have found her own trouble. So when they called, I agreed to teach the girl a few things.

I knew that Gracie's very nice dinner invitation was either not real—an attempt to smooth things over—or proof that Jenny had gone and lost her mind.

When we got to the house, the nicest in the neighborhood, I backed into the driveway far enough that I was out of view of the street, right up against the garage, like a delivery truck would.

Going for fairy-tale Victorian, with gables and slanted roofs, towers and a somewhat out of place turret, the house was magenta with dark green trim. Beautiful wisteria and hydrangea, lilacs, and a few purple pansies filled the front beds. A pristine green lawn welcomed visitors.

In every window, a black wreath hung. A black sash festooned the green wood slats around the porch. A heavy black curtain hid the front door and a black cloth enveloped the mailbox. She had a lot of faith in her security system to broadcast the death of her boy like this. More than a few synthers had come sniffing around, I'm sure.

I turned off the car and hit a button to keep the climate set in the back. The magic camouflage would last for a few days, assuming nothing disrupted it.

"You want to wait here?" I said when Jay hesitated.

"No." She pulled the handle and shoved open the door. She swung her leg out, but the weight of the door caused it to fall closed and almost pinned her. She cursed under her breath and fought the door, finally struggling out and letting it slam behind her.

She'd get better at it.

I followed more gracefully, grabbing a small, black, draw-string bag and slinging it over my shoulder. I led the way past the front of the house and up the steps to the front door. "You don't need to talk," I said. "But if you do, platitudes. They'll feel stupid and insufficient coming out of your mouth, because they are. But they're the best we've got. Platitudes and the assurance that we'll safely get their son where he needs to go."

"Right." Jay nodded and set her jaw.

I rang the doorbell

The door opened quick, like someone was already waiting on the other side to pull aside the curtain. The mother, a widow. She was clad in a black Victorian style dress, with a high ruffled collar and matching ruffled cuffs at the end of buttoned sleeves. The dress fell to the floor, and its bell shape suggested she wore at least one petticoat—the height of wealthy fashion. She matched the house.

I tilted my hat back on my head. "Mrs. Holland," I nodded. "I'm Tan Connors. This is Jay."

She sniffed hard and nodded. Her blond hair had been swept up into a fashionable chignon and diamond studs glittered from her ears. Her make-up was perfect. Only because I knew what to look for did I see the slight glitters of the synthesis. So she'd use it—the souls of others—but would spend thousands to make sure no one used her son's.

Jay shoved her hands into the back pockets of her black jeans and rocked back and forth on the heels of her cowboy boots.

"Would you like us to come in? Or do you want to open the garage for us and we'll handle it from there?" I kept my voice cold, even. I'd been in the business for thirty-five years.

She stared at me for a moment, considering. Even though all of this was explained in the guide I gave the families, about half hadn't decided before I arrived.

"Come in," she finally said. "He's been laid out in the parlor."

I smiled and gave a duck of the head. It was our job to box him up, too. It's a thing that chaperones have to do from time to time, but usually people with money like this had their loved ones all packed up before I arrived. It wasn't the best thing to have to do on your first time out, either. I glanced at Jay, but she was stoic. I resisted smiling—she had on her serious face. One she had made since she was a little, little girl.

I stepped in and motioned at Jay to follow. Black bunting hung from every possible surface. A table in the entry way had been made a shrine with multiple pictures of the dead young man, a candle burning in front of them.

Mrs. Henderson closed the door behind us and led us through to the parlor.

Her son indeed had been laid out. He was in his Sunday best, I assumed. He looked to be in his early twenties. Blond hair, pale skin. A black suit, white shirt, black tie. When I looked closer I saw that the jacket had an emblem on the front pocket. Greek letters, but I didn't know what they meant. Maybe a fraternity—he had been away at college when he died.

Another young man sat on the couch, facing the bier: the younger brother. He was equally pale, though with sallow and sickly colored skin. He had long black hair that hung unkempt around his face. His eyes were a dark brown. He seemed to be staring at nothing.

"Zeke," Jay said. "I'm so sorry."

The boy's eyes jerked to look at her, and I turned to her. "You know this family?" I asked.

"Yeah," she said, not taking her eyes off Zeke. "We graduated from high school together."

"Oh." I said. "I'm sorry, Mrs. Henderson, I didn't realize my apprentice had a relationship with your family."

She shook her head. "It's fine." She smiled at me, soft and sad. "It makes me feel better knowing that there's some personal connection."

"Thank you." I sighed, relieved. Personal connections meant more potential problems, like knowing how to find us later, so J-baby should have told me before we got here. No wonder she'd been eager for this job. I cast a sideways glance at her, but she stared at the floor.

"Mrs. Henderson," I said stepping between her and the body, "Why don't you and your son go upstairs while prepare for transport."

"No." Mrs. Henderson snapped. "I'm sorry," she said, voice softer. "But I want to see him off."

"Mom," Zeke rose, "it's best if we go. Just until they get Elijah in the car. Then we can say goodbye."

She looked at her son, tears welling and then spilling out of her eyes. Finally, she nodded. "Okay." She laid a hand on her dead son's cheek and stared at him for a long moment before turning to make her way up the stairs.

I looked a Zeke. "It won't take long. Maybe twenty minutes." I pointed to a doorway that seemed to lead to the back of the house. "The garage that way?"

He nodded. "Yeah, back through the kitchen." He glanced at Jay one more time and followed his mom.

"Whew," Jay said when we heard the footsteps fade up the stairs. "That was rough. Is it always like that?"

"No." I shook my head. "This is a kid—even if he is a bit older than you—that's always hard. And often the body will be ready. I didn't want you to have to do this on your first run."

"I need to learn." She waved away my comment. "What do you need me to do?"

I handed her the keys to the car. "Go open the back and pull out the gurney. Bring it in here. Okay?"

"Got it." She saluted before heading off through the kitchen, and it made me smile.

I approached the body slowly, taking in as much as I could with every step. "Hello, Elijah Leander Hanson. I'm Tan, your chaperone. I'm going to take you to the burial center, safely, swiftly, and securely." It was the motto of my business.

Most chaperones and synthers talked to the corpses, no matter what our personal views on death and the afterlife were. The only ones who survived any length of time in this job lived with the contradictions. Most religions taught that there was a *you*, a coherent self, and when *you* died, *you* left your body. What was left was a husk. The atheists believed that you were a husk start to finish. Either way, once you hit "finished," *you* were no longer there.

There isn't a synther I know that believes it's that simple.

I sure as hell don't.

That magic that Gracie and Mrs. Henderson and a million other folks use? That youth has to come from somewhere—and that somewhere is people. Vampire legends are as old as humanity—the idea that you can suck the life out of a person. Truth is, you can. But it isn't blood. And it isn't flesh. It isn't the brain or any other organ.

The cosmetics companies call it the soul synthesis—a seriously shady business. Magically taking bits of people's spirit and using them. Some synthers, like me, could take bits from the living, too. There's quite a lot of money in buying bits from people, most of whom will never be able to buy them back.

That wasn't even the worst of it. Turns out, the only thing the magic was good for was making a person look younger—the ultimate in cosmetics.

There's no nobility in leaving your soul behind, like leaving organs or blood, or even your whole body to science. Soul magic never healed anybody—maybe it made them *look* healed, but that's not the same thing.

I lifted Elijah's tie out of the way, resting it over his shoulder, and unbuttoned the three center buttons on his shirt. I slipped my hand inside the shirt and laid it on his heart. The body was cold, but that didn't mean the soul was gone.

Embalming was mostly a thing of the past—preservation was done with the same magic that un-aged living faces. The magic was almost invisible, except at the places where decomp came first. The pooling of the blood was hidden, too. And there was almost no smell.

I closed my eyes and concentrated—used the magic in me and reached out for the boy's essence. The flash of magic almost knocked me back. Pure, white energy. The mother hadn't been lying when she had called him untouched, which meant he was worth a fortune.

And that's why she reached out to me. Quietly, I had become the best chaperone in the business. I'd get her son to the crematorium, guaranteed.

I grabbed my bag and opened it.

I drew out a pouch of dried rose petals, a bottle of salt, a stick of wax, one of those long lighters used for fireplaces and grills, and a heavy brass ring.

Laying my tools out on the table in front of me, I drew in a deep breath.

"The gurney is ready, Tan," Jay said behind me, making me jump a little. "Sorry."

I glanced over my shoulder. "Be louder next time." I smiled. "I can get a bit absorbed in the process."

She stepped up next to me. "Getting ready to do the binding rites?"

"Yep." I rebuttoned his shirt and laid his tie back across his body. "It'll seal the essence in his body. Only a serious magic user would be able to break it free—and might destroy it trying." I turned to her.

"All that essence, locked away." She looked at me, annoyed. "Why? He's dead."

I shrugged. "Doesn't matter, Jay. It belongs to him. There's bad mojo around taking from the dead without permission. It's why you don't see a lot of random murders for soul essence." I laid my hands on her shoulders and pulled her to face me. "Soul synthesizing is not simple. Even when you've got the talent."

She rolled her eyes. "How much have my moms told you?"

"Enough. They don't want you to go through what I did. I ran away when I found mine. They want you to have a shot at normal." I glanced at the body. "And synthing? It's not normal."

"You seem happy enough."

I snorted. "*Seem* isn't *is*. Messing with this at all is dangerous, even when the subjects are willing. You ever seen it?"

"No," she shook her head.

I wanted to call her a liar right then, but I didn't. Time for that lecture later. "It hurts. Causing that hurt so someone else can have a pretty face? That's a karmic nightmare waiting to happen. Remember that."

"That's why you chaperone? You're afraid of karma?" She snorted. "You could be a millionaire!"

I shook my head. I wasn't going to argue with her. The kid had stars in her eyes, and only experience would clear her vision. "We've got to get going." I drummed my fingers on the edge of the bier. "We'll skip the binding," I said. "Ol' Bess will keep him safe enough. Help me get him on the gurney."

I grabbed the edge of the gurney and pulled it even with the corpse. We took his feet and shoulders and lifted him onto the cot. Together, we wrapped him in the shroud and I sealed it with a dab of wax and in impression from my brass ring. Less than a full binding, but a recognizable warning to anyone who might try to mess with the body.

This boy was one of mine.

We maneuvered the body outside and slid it against the open end of the hearse.

"It's done?" Mrs. Henderson called to me from behind. I turned to see her and her son coming out of the garage.

"We're finished up now." Behind me, the back doors of the hearse slammed.

She laid her hand on the back of the car. "You've put everything away?" she said, voice loud.

"All of the food is safe and secure for the wake," I said, confirming the story. The performance felt silly, but the subterfuge was not. If everyone believed that the wake, with the body, was tomorrow, and that we were caterers with a delivery, we'd have a safe ride today. I hoped she had kept her word and not let anyone else—even the clergy—in on the secret. Not until Elijah was safe and burned.

She gave me a hug. "Thank you," she whispered in my ear before moving to gaze into the back of the hearse.

Jay gave Zeke another hug and said something I couldn't hear. He took hold of his mother's hand and led her back into the house.

I turned to Jay. "Ready for the drive?"

"Yeah," she said, and handed me the keys.

I popped the locked and opened the door. I flicked the seat forward, dropped my bag in the back, and grabbed a bundle—my gun belt. I fixed it around my waist and settled it on my hips. Two revolvers, loaded, and extra bullets.

J-baby's eyes widened. "You didn't tell me you were armed."

I grinned and winked at her. "There isn't a chaperone on the planet that's not. It's not the wild-wild west, but it might as well be." I dropped into the car and closed the door. She did the same.

"My godmother's so cool," she mused at me.

I laughed. "Thanks." It wasn't the first time she'd said it, and though it made me smile, but it hadn't always been so great. She'd thrown that phrase at her mothers too many times, when I visited and took her out shopping, for food, whatever. That I made Jenny nervous only upped my appeal. It hurt that Jenny, and Gracie too, though I could ever harm J-baby, but I understood.

As I started the car, she went back to staring out the window.

I tried to think back to my first body chaperone. I worked for a cosmetics company—one of the first to use soul bits, though they claim the energy they use isn't a soul. It was a live carry—a person was coming to the clinic to sell some of themselves off for synthesis. He *seemed* the same after as before...

I'd visit home off and on, especially after J-baby was born, but then Jenny's dad got sick. He'd sold a lot of himself, to keep the diner, and wasn't the same guy anymore. Hollow eyed, slow, and he spent a lot of time staring off at nothing. Jenny couldn't look at me, be around me, she said, knowing I did that to people.

Accepting Gracie's dinner invite wasn't in the cards.

We'd gotten a ways down the road, following Interstate 40 to 85. It wasn't yet midday, and traffic was pretty light, when Jay tensed.

Something slammed into us from behind.

I glanced up to my rearview mirror to see the grill of a huge truck, and not much else. I fought my instinct to hit the break and instead slammed on the gas, trying to put some distance between us and the rig.

I felt the jolt as grappling hooks hit the side doors.

"Hold on, Jay-baby," I said. I hauled the wheel to the left, dragging the car into the next lane. The truck behind me slammed on its brakes. Our engine screamed along with our tires as the truck hauled us backwards against our will.

"Aunty Tanya, maybe you should—"

"I got this," I cut her off. I slammed on the brakes. We weren't getting away. Time to fight.

When the truck dragged us to the side of the road and stopped, I reached over and grabbed her hand. "Get out, but stay behind the door. If things go bad, run when I tell you. They won't chase you."

There were tears in her eyes. She looked about to say something, but stopped.

I flipped open the console between the seats and Jay gasped. I grabbed a sawed-off shotgun and a box of shells.

"You've got an arsenal!" She frowned, eyes worried.

"I used to keep grenades, too," I said. "Back when I did longer runs by myself." I shook my head. "Maybe I shouldn't have given them up. There was a time when my reputation kept people away."

I kicked open my door and hauled myself out.

The first guy was already out of the truck and lumbered toward me. I lowered the shotgun, sliding it between the door and the body of the car, and pulled the trigger. The kick knocked me back a couple steps, but I was ready for it.

He, on the other hand, was not. The blast caught him full in the chest and sent him flying back. He managed to sit up, blank eyes, blinking in confusion. Not much soul left in him, I imagined. Playing off his debt as a zombie thug for a body snatcher. Probably not what he had in mind.

I around the door and unhooked one of the grapples.

"Get the other one," I said to Jay, who, still wide-eyed, nodded and did what she was told.

The car was technically loose, but if we tried to run, they'd follow, whoever the were, because Mr. Blinky there certainly wasn't in charge.

"Can I have a gun?" Jay asked, voice shaking.

"You know how to shoot it?"

"Yeah," she said. "Mama Grace took me out a couple times."

I wasn't surprised—she owned a couple and wouldn't let Jay go without knowing how to use them. Jenny probably had a fit. "There's another shotgun in the back, wrapped in cloth, behind your seat. Don't break cover, though, okay? Just shoot from there."

"Maybe we should just give them what they want," she said as she retrieved the shotgun.

"Jay!" I was genuinely disappointed that she'd suggest such a thing. "You know this kid. You really want his soul ironing out some old bat's wrinkles?"

She shook her head but looked miserable. I didn't say it, but I had hoped Jenny and Gracie's kid would have a bit more empathy, and moxie.

The cab of the truck opened, and someone hopped out.

"Hold your fire, please." The polite voice said. A southern accent, but not a strong one, and it was familiar.

"What for?" I called back.

"I just want the body. That's it." He sounded hollowed out, empty.

"I know what you want," I said.

"Please," he asked again. "I don't want to hurt you."

I rolled my eyes. Whoever this guy was, he wasn't a professional. I rested the shotgun against the car and pulled out my revolver. I took out the mirror on the door and the window, too.

"Shit!"

"Get back in your truck and go the fuck home!" I called out. "I'll let you walk away, if you go right now."

"Can't do that," the voice said—there was a tight fear in it.

"I'm sorry for whatever ails you," I said. The desperation said he wasn't a professional body snatcher, so that could only mean he needed the soul synthesis itself. "Who do you owe?" I hollered.

There was a long pause. "Rathbone," his voice quavered a bit.

I sighed. I had really, really hoped that wasn't the case. "Not someone you want to cross."

"If you don't give the body to me, I'll tell him you've got it! He'll come after you!"

"Not likely," I said. "Especially since the body will be safely away before you report back to Rathbone. But one successful heist off me, and I lose my whole reputation."

"I'll never tell my mom about it, I promise! She'll think Lijah was buried."

A-ha.

"Fuck." A small voice on the other side of the car whispered.

I looked over to Jay.

She chewed on her lip, eyes focused on the truck before finally turning to me. "Aunt Tanya, please," she said. "Please just go away. Walk off into the woods." She turned the shotgun on me, though I couldn't quite see it, since it was below the roof of the car. Pretty hard to miss at that range.

"Put your guns on the roof," she said. "Slide them here."

I could have said no. I could have shot her right then and there. Shot her and *not* killed her. But I'd taken an oath in a church, holding her in my arms while the priest traced a little cross in holy water on her forehead. I'd promised to protect her. No matter how I sliced it, shooting wasn't protecting. I put the guns on the roof and slid them to her.

"Now open the back."

"Juliet, I can't let you have that boy. Why are you doing this? Is it money?"

"No!" She was offended.

"Then what?"

"I love him," she said. The wind caught her whisper, and that was the only reason I heard it. "Zeke."

"Don't say any more, Juliet!" Zeke came up and was standing on the other side of my open door, unarmed. He shook his head a bit, like he was clearing it. "It's none of her business." He held out his hand, gave another head shake. "Give us the keys. We'll take your hearse and go."

"Damn fool!" How much of himself that kid had lost? I shot a glare at Juliet. "You owe too?"

"No." She didn't meet my gaze. "I said I'd work for him, if Zeke didn't get the body." She looked up at me. "That's why I wanted you to teach me, so I could fix Zeke myself." She shoved her hands in the pockets of her jacket and I cursed myself for being so oblivious. There it was, right on the lapel. *Ezekiel Henderson.*

"That kind of magic takes years—decades—to learn. Taking it is easy. Giving it to someone else? That's why the companies spend millions of dollars on R & D." I looked at Zeke. "The agreement is that Rathbone would give some of your brother to you?"

"He said so," Zeke said. "Gave his word."

"He did, did he? And you spoke to him? Face to face?"

"Well, no." He kicked at the dirt. "But his guy—"

"Who?"

"It's not like you'd know them, Aunt Tanya," Jay scolded.

I snorted. "I've been in the business a long time, J-baby. I know everybody."

"You chaperone bodies." She frowned, like the thought that her godmother could be associated with anything illegal had never occurred to her. "Moms insisted that you didn't do anything illegal."

All these years, I thought they'd told her a million horrible stories about me—they knew enough of them. Turns out they hadn't. Not even one. Certainly not the truth. My heart broke.

"Aunt Tanya?" Jays eyes were brimming, tears glinting in the winter light.

"I told you it was a rough business, kid. No one's hands are clean."

I heard the sound of a shotgun cocking. Jay jutted her chin out the way she always did when she was being defiant. "Do you work for him?"

"No." I said. "*With* Rathbone, perhaps, but I only work *for* myself. When and where are you to meet?" I asked.

"Down the road at the Flying J." Zeke pointed down the highway. "In about an hour."

"Come here," I said and walked around the open door to the back of the hearse. Jay kept the revolver on me.

I opened the back and pulled out the gurney, its back feet popping out as it cleared the bumper. I waved at Zeke. "Come here." I broke the wax seal I'd made—there was no magic in it, only a show for Juliet—and opened the shroud.

Zeke hadn't moved.

"Come here," I snapped. "Roadside isn't the best place to do this, and the highway patrol cruise this area pretty frequently, so let's not give them a reason to stop and see if everything's okay."

Jay came up to me. "What are you doing?"

"Fixing your boyfriend, if he'll let me."

Zeke looked to Jay, and she chewed her lip a bit.

"J-baby," I said. "I wouldn't hurt you or your friend. He can be fixed, but much longer, and he'll be his zombie muscle over there." I glanced at the guy I'd shot. He was still sitting on the side of the road, bleeding and blinking stupidly.

"What do I need to do?" Zeke asked.

"Take my hand." I reached out.

Jay raised the gun again. "Anything funny, Tanya, and—"

"Yeah, yeah," I said. "Save the tough act for someone who might believe it."

I took Zeke's outstretched hand and closed my eyes. The kid was running low. So low that, even at his young age, he wouldn't fully regenerate over time. Taking soul off his brother was easy—he was so young and so healthy when he died—that it practically leapt from him to me, and I pushed it on, into Zeke. When I let go and opened my eyes, Zeke looked like a different kid. His eyes were bright, skin clear, brown hair shiny. A normal teen.

The dead kid looked pretty much the same. Amateur synthers would leave behind marks, maybe even aging, but I know what to take and how. Not that anyone would bother looking, but only an expert could tell he'd been synthed at all.

Jay dropped the gun and flung her arms around Zeke. They were adorable together, I had to admit. And love had smacked me around a bit too.

"Thank you, Aunt Tanya," Jay said when they came up for air.

"That's what godmothers are for, right? Magic?" I fixed the shroud in place and slipped the kid back in my ice box. The grappling hooks had torn at the magic, too, and the camouflage was a mess, so I stripped it off, returning Bess to a hearse. "So how the hell did you get into this mess?"

"Zeke's mom, and mine too, want us to go to college, but I've got my powers. We were planning on running away together."

"I see," I said, managing not to roll my eyes.

Her words came tumbling out. "I thought I could sell some soul bits for some quick cash and totally get it all back myself. But I gave too much, and I couldn't get my powers to work, so Zeke sold some, too, to get me some of mine back, but then I still couldn't make it work, and we were lost in debt. So when his brother died, it was an answer to our prayers. His mom wouldn't hear of synthing him, so I told her about you, and told my moms that my powers were acting on their own…"

"So you were going to ruin my business, rather than asking me for help." I picked up my revolver and slipped it into the gun belt next to the the shotgun that J-baby had left on the passenger seat.

"I didn't know you worked for—"

"WITH!" I snapped. "I work *for* myself."

"With," she said, voice low, "Rathbone. I'd have asked, but I was afraid you'd say no. Mama Jenny said you were a moral rock."

"Wishful thinking," I muttered. I ducked into the car, popped open the glove compartment, and pulled out a paper bag. "Here," I tossed it to Zeke.

He opened the bag. "Jesus!" He rolled the top closed again, like it might get out.

"It's a lucrative business," I said.

"So you're going to let us go?" Jay asked.

"Of course, J-baby. You need to find your own way, like I did. Your moms will understand—they won't like, but," I shrugged. "Here." I grabbed gun belt from the car and fixed it around her waist. "I hope you don't ever need them." I glanced at Zeke. "And teach him to use them, too."

She nodded. "Aunt Tanya—" she sniffed, hard.

I snatched her and pulled her into a tight hug. "You need me, you call," I whispered in her ear. "No matter what."

A sleek black hearse pulled up. It was new—shiny, with genuine chrome and a grim reaper hood ornament. The door swung open and a tall, lean man stepped out. You'd think that us sythers have a uniform. He was in dark jeans, a black button down, and a sleek black suit jacket. Five-hundred-dollar loafers, too. I was the diner version, in my discount jeans and shitkickers. He was the three-star Michelin restaurant. His dark skin and darker eyes were shrouded under the brim of a fedora, and his black and gray dreadlocks fell halfway down his back.

He eyed the kids, and they took a step toward me. J-baby put her hand on a gun.

"That the guy you were supposed to meet?" I asked, knowing the answer.

"Yeah," Zeke said.

I reached out and laid my hand over Jay's. "Take it easy. I'll handle this. You two go on, get out of here."

"That Henderson?" The man asked.

"Yeah," I said. "All set and ready to go."

He looked at the kids. "Go on now, do what the nice lady told you. We're good."

"I'm not going to leave you here with him," Jay said. "He's the middle man. He's dangerous."

Middleman laughed out loud, and I did what I could to keep from joining in.

"Go on," I said. "He and I go way back. Trust me, J-baby."

She frowned and darted in for a last, quick hug before snatching Zeke's hand and practically hauling him to his truck. They cut loose the hooks and climbed in. The truck roared to life, and I had to shield myself from the wave of gravel and stones kicked up as the truck peeled off into traffic. They left poor zombie man behind.

I walked around and inspected the my car. Relatively minor damage. Nothing that would keep her from running. The scars on the doors hadn't hit the etchings, so I was lucky there. I wouldn't have to re-magic the car.

"She reminds me of you when we were young." His deep voice had a touch of an island accent that made me smile. It always raised pleasant goosebumps on my skin. "So were you right about them?"

"It went exactly like I expected. Dumb, but not malicious."

"She know the truth?"

"That I *work with* Rathbone? That's truth enough. Maybe someday she'll learn more. But for now, she'll find her way. I did." I opened the hearse and hauled out the body. The gurney's legs sprang out, catching the ground and keeping it from falling. "You'll finish the delivery, *Middleman*?"

He barked out a laugh at the name. "Absolutely, *boss*. And I'll handle the zombie, too." He slipped an arm around my waist and pulled me up against him. He waited just long enough to see the *yes* in my eyes before kissing me. We stood there for a moment, on the side of the highway, the wind from the traffic kicking dust all over the dead body.

We broke the kiss.

"I've got to go tell Jenny and Gracie that J-baby's safe. And break the news that she's gone her own way. I doubt I'll stay for dinner." I tried to make a joke of it, but he knew better. He laughed a bit anyway. For me.

Later tonight, we'd kiss again, and his gray would vanish, and mine too, and our wrinkles with them. But for now, I needed to look like Gracie and Jenny's old friend, so I could tell them that J-baby was free.

"Meet me back at my place?" I asked.

"Sure thing, Rathbone." His voice was soft, teasing. He wheeled the body to the back of his beautiful hearse and stowed him away. I watched him get back into his car, start it up and drive away, like the kids before him.

The etches on his hearse, like mine, hold the powerful magic I'd woven into them. The body would arrive safe and secure as promised, and it would burn. The essence stored safely in the car. Everybody wins.

I got back in my car. Bess was a beater, like me, but that was all right. Looks didn't matter, not really. She purred like a kitten when I started her up.

I thought about the beautiful kids headed one way, at the beginning of their lives, and the dead boy, headed the other direction for his end.

Up and down the coast, they were afraid of Rathbone, of me, the elusive figure who controlled the soul trade from Maine to the Florida Keys. Now Juliet and Zeke would spread that fear of me like plague rats, though they didn't know I'd picked my name because I'd loved the old black and white Sherlock movies as a kid, not because it sounded scary. They'd spread my story, the faceless boogeyman and the magic godmother, not knowing they were the same person.

I'd be back at Gracie's in no time, telling the moms that everything went just fine, but that their little girl had run off with a boy for a time, but someday she'd come home to stay, unlike her godmother. J-baby would get a taste of the world, find out it was bitter, and come home. Or maybe not. Maybe the world would stay sweet, and so would the boy, and they'd come back anyway, to show us we were wrong.

To show me that not only the young die good.

THE ALBATROSS MAN

ROBERT W. WALKER

THE TWO-YEAR OLD ARTICLE READ: A PAIR OF UNSUSPECTING HIKERS FIRST *discovered the massacred birds. The married couple, after gasping in disbe-lief, took iPhone photos and posted them onto the internet. An alert internet detective in Maui's State Police center caught sight of the horror scene on his laptop, and he recognized the area, the Ka'ena Point Natural Area Reserve where the Albatross was fighting to make a comeback from extinction.*

Obviously, things were set in motion, and an investigation became the answer, a regular task-force put together on the Island, with the Island au-thorities enraged by the bird murderers, whoever they may be. But when they got to the bottom of it, the horrid decapitations, the torn apart bodies, the bashed and bruised torso, missing wings and feet, it shocked the Island Nation across all of Hawaii, as the identity of the murderers came out. It wasn't rogue psychopaths escaped from some asylum, nor outsiders who'd passed through, hoping on a slow boat back to mainland America. No, it was a gaggle of boys, young students from elite, well-to-do families who'd sneaked out at night from their expensive, elite school. Boys. Killers. Mad creatures out of some Lord of the Flies moment, gone into temporary insanity from entitlement and 'afluenza' in the end, when the courts let them slide.

When this reporter, call me Q, read of the story in the newspapers, the actual event—the affluenza killers destroying the near-extinct birds, two years had passed. Two years since the murders and the trials, which, by all accounts was a series of jokes, and not true trials. Reading of the events in that old archive collection at the newsroom, Q became curious as to where the various bird killers were today, and if they had any regrets, any remorse at all, any sense of 'an Albatross around the neck' as they say. Q wanted to know if the boys had gone on to live whole and healthy lives; if they'd gone on to become key players in the legal system, the courts, politics, entertainment, real estate, sports, teachers of young people, social workers hoping to pay back, pet store owners perhaps? In short, just what had they done with their lives after that graduation year when they murdered the birds as a sort of sick Senior Trick.

❦ ❦ ❦

Q: Question for my readers is 'Where are you and your friends at in life now? The boys who murdered the Albatrosses, Albert? And the question for you, Albert, aka Albatross Man, as some have dubbed you, you being the so-called 'ring leader' how is life going? How does it feel?"

A: I was on my way to becoming somebody when we did that sad, stupid thing with the birds.

Q: When you and the others murdered those birds, yes. Ever do anything like that before or after?"

(Note to self: A slight Hawaiian breeze lifts what's left of Albert's unusual, feathery white hair, where he leans against a headstone in the cemetery atop the lonely Oahu hilltop, where he insisted we meet. No idea why he chose this place.)

A: I could've been somebody. Now, to answer your question, all the fuck I have is regret and remorse. I *coulda-woulda* been somebody. At one time, Q, I was on my way to the top of the business and financial world.

Q: Can I quote you on that? Can I tape this interview?

A: Sure, sure. I tell you, I was assured of a future of greatness, right alongside the other fellas, my buddies."

Q: All six of you were aiming at being senators, leaders of business, shakers and takers, eh?"

A: Yes, that was me, a taker, and it suited me to be just that. Hell, we were groomed for it. Precisely what old Dad, Mom and every other influence wanted me to be.

🐦 🐦 🐦

Buried in a nesting area with broken eggs strewn about, lay the body of a bird the size of a small child. It was at the westernmost tip of the Hawaiian Island of Oahu. The state reserve, a supposedly safe haven for these creatures who were indigenous only to the Hawaiian Islands. These were the last of their breed, Birds of a rare feather. Harmless, sadly near extinct, they were being bred to save their kind in this world.

🐦 🐦 🐦

Q: What about now? Are you unhappy working in the carnival at the freak show?

A: I was once a handsome man, Hollywood material, Q. Ask anyone. Now look at me. A sad, crippled, deformed freak and getting more deformed every day. Look at these excuses for feet. I know, I know. It's like I have the feet of an ostrich. Look at what's left of my hair. I'm a young man, but I am wrinkled and shriveled and aged.

Q: You appear to have aged horribly, true.

A: This nose! Look at this nose. I'm aging in bird years, for *Christ's sake.*

Q: I should think it attracts the girls, your nose? No?

A: Big laugh! Ho-ho! Is that what you're after, a ridicule piece?

Q: Oh, please, no, not at all.

A: It's no longer a nose. (Note: Albert is indeed the Albatross Man) It's a damn beak, not a nose. I'm turning into one of them!"

Q: One of...one of them? One of whom?".

A: One of the birds you asked me about.

Q: Ohhhh...now that's a bit silly, isn't it?

A: Damn it, man, have you eyes? One of the birds that, me! The ones we massacred up there on the mountain. A place we visited days before, got the lectures on how important saving those birds was from the ranger lady.

Q: Then it's true, you didn't just stumble upon the birds. You knew they were going to be on their nests."

A: Yes, on their eggs, trying to raise their little families.

Q: There in the nature preserve? The school field trip introduced you fellas to the birds earlier the same day is what I read.

A: All too true.

Q: Then it was all planned out, a kind of kid's nasty an ambush?

A: Premeditated, yes. Meticulously so.

❦ ❦ ❦

State conservation officers determined that two dozen birds were bloodied, dismembered, and mutilated with a ball bat,and machetes and a pellet gun, all wielded by young men, who were arrested and placed on trial and given community service—after a year of nothing happening while authorities argued over sanctions to some of the state's most prestigious fathers, whose sons were involved.

❦ ❦ ❦

Q: Why? Why, Albert? Can you say?

A: Guess your readers would love to know that one, eh?

Q: Absolutely, yes, they would.

A: Why'd we do it? Why'd I do it, eh?

Q: Curious minds want to know, yes.

A: Everyone really-still wants to know that, eh?

Q: By all means, yes.

A: No one knows what we boys had to endure every damn day of our lives.

Q: Oh, you little rich boys had it rough, huh? (Note: do not snicker)

A: You got no idea. No one does. Not then and not now.

Q: Can you be more *ahhh* specific?

A: No, I doubt it; doubt you or anyone would understand.

Q: Oh, hey, watch your step, Albert."

A: Oh, it's no biggy.

Q: Not sure you should be tracking across a grave, sir.

A: He don't mind, he's dead.

Q: I detect a note of toxicity toward the dead.

A: Only this one, my last stupid buddy. It's his grave, and he could give a shit if I squatted on it and took a shit on it. Believe me.

Q: I don't know how to react to that, Albert.

A: Okay, you want a why, so here goes: it was like this—the press said we were privileged, and that our lawyers—actually our dads' lawyers—would go with the Affluenza Defense. Affluent kids had no use of morality or rules or matters that concerned others. We were raised 'above' it all. That's why.

Q: You're referring to the illness of the filthy rich? The sickness of the affluent. Some call it *Paltrowitis*, others Trumpitis.

A: What else could possibly save our asses, or explain our behavior—outright murder of innocent birds on the endangered species list. Murder too of their chicks in their shells! How shocking. It couldn't possibly be chalked up to rage, anger, desperation of soul. None of those things would fit our image."

Q: Your image? Really?

A: Yes, it was everything!

Q: You had an image at that age, a reputation?

A: Yes—boys with family crests emblazoned on our school jackets. All six of us. And besides...

Q: *Besides? Besides what?* (Note: dig deeper)

A: Be-besides it was more than just our images. *God. I mean god* forbid—our father's or our mother's images should be tarnished at the country club.

❧ ❧ ❧

Twenty-four Laysan Albatrosses, federally protected, killed and mutilated. Birds that had been the focus of a 26-year study and conservation effort. The mutilated birds had their feet cut off so the killers could take their tags as souvenirs of their 'special night'. Nearly a dozen Albatross eggs were crushed, and six additional eggs failed to hatch. Editors Note: impossible to hatch an egg if you are a dead bird.

❧ ❧ ❧

Q: Question for my readers is 'Where are they now'? You were the only one I could find for my interview, Mr. Albatross Man.

A: Each one has left us, dead. Each one afflicted with something far, far deadlier than Afluenza. Dead from a strange form of 'bird flu.'

Q: There's been no bird flu epidemic on the islands, sir.

A: All right then, a bird *curse*, whatever one might call it.

Q: Really? You believe that, do you? Can I quote you?"

A: Damn it, man, look at me! Watch this. (Note to self: Birdman just demonstrated birdlike habit of pecking at berries in the cemetery.)

Q: That's all part of your act in the circus, right?

A: First to fall was Freddie, the youngest. Frederick Remington Gains the third. He'd broken out in feathers all over his body."

Q: Feathers? Really?

A: All right, call it downy stuff. (Note: Albatross Man displayed downy, feathery stuff growing on his arms). Disgusting how it picks up so much lice and bread crumbs.

Q: I can only imagine.

A: Freddie, he scratched and tore at himself like a madman before he got his hands on his old man's most expensive item in his arsenal of six-shooters, a gun once owned by Wyatt Earp, or so the platinum plaque says still. His old man still has that thing.

Q: Really? Wyatt Earp, man. That's cool. The gun, I mean, not that your friend *ahhh* used it on himself. Sorry for your loss.

A: Frederick's father, Frederick the second, old bastard had a breakdown after that, and his mother wound up in a home for mental patients, all this after Freddie blew his brains out. He had such a promising future until...well, we did what we did.

Q: I thought you said his father still had the Earp gun, intimating that he hadn't changed a whit after his boy shot himself with that gun. Having a hard time getting my head around that. Awkward, kinda.

A: The old man insisted on the gun going into his coffin with him.

Q: Freddie's coffin? Six feet under with his son?

A: No, no, the old man had a deadly stroke, heart attack, I think, and in his will, he insisted on being buried with Earp's gun.

Q: Ahhh, I see. You know, I read about that incident, Freddie's having shot himself in the brain.

A: It was in all the papers.

Q:. What about the other boys? The other four?

A: Each in turn, gone, like I said. After Freddie, then it came for Norman Ellis Brierson, who broke out in a rash of decayed flesh—out of the blue. It just overtook him like some kind of Ebola virus, but I know now it was the bird virus.

Q: Oh my god! You mean like bird flu, right?

A: At first, the doctors chalked it up to a flesh-eating bacteria that Norman had picked up from a swimming hole.

Q: Did the diagnosis stand up under scrutiny?

A: Well, no, on closer examination, and a few more top-dollar experts, it *changed*.

Q: Changed?

A: Morphed, you might say. Meta-morphed. The diagnoses became more *ahhh* specific.

Q: Specific in precisely what way?

A: Supposedly it was a flesh-eating bacteria indigenous to certain birds of the South Pacific, such as the Laysan Albatross.

Q: Isn't that the type of birds that Norman, Freddie, you, and the others, you know, cut up?

A: You know damn well it is. Are you here to simply mock me? Embarrass me? Are you?

"Q: No, no, never. I want to understand you all. I promise to be fair when I write the article on you all, Albert.

A: Hmmm...it does appear you've done your homework, Q.

Q: Did you all go on that unchaperoned hiking trip that night with the intention of killing those animals?

A: We started out with those machetes and the ball bat in hand, knowing we'd use them, yes, of course. I told you, planned, premeditated. I don't ask for no forgiveness.

🦇 🦇 🦇

The night of destruction set conservation efforts back easily by a decade, and the incident caused more than 200,000 dollars in damages, according to state and federal authorities. It also fueled outrage from wildlife advocates, conservationists, and nature lovers across Hawaii and the globe. Those responsible were largely caught, when they foolishly posted photos taken with their iPhones and posted on social media. To date, no appropriate punishment to fit the callous crime has been meted out, and many fear there never will be.

🦇 🦇 🦇

Q: I still am fuzzy on why, Albert. Exactly why? It couldn't just be as simple as preserving the family image either that you all got off Scott free, as they say.

A: Free, ha! We were never again free from that day forward. Do you have eyes to see, ears to hear, Q? I stand before you a man defeated, cursed to follow the others into Death's night, along with all those with me that night—all now dead, a mere two years after the event. Why's that? You want to ask about a why, ask that bloody why!

Q: Then go on, tell me *that* why then.

A: No, you want to know why we did it? It's no mystery to me anymore, and not to the others either. Norman drowned himself, just like we all drowned some of those birds in the sanctuary. Tied ropes around them and threw them into the ocean and dragged them under till they were dead. Norman did more of that than the rest of us. Sick poetic justice you might say, the way Norman went out.

Q: Drowned himself, he did. Yes, I read of it as well.

A: Then there was Donald Marsten Grayson, our ringleader. See, I was not the bigshot leader.

Q: That's an interesting detail. You've always been singled out as the ringleader, Albert.

A: I always let it go, and after a while, it became part of the act— my act at the freak show.

Q: Makes sense.

A: Grayson, the tallest, strongest among us, the one who first got us kicking over the idea of murdering those nesting birds. Every one of us got excited about it, egging one another on, no pun intended.

🐦 🐦 🐦

The accused, facing animal cruelty charges and theft charges, were looking at a $2,000 fine and a year in jail. Their fines were paid by their parents and no time was levied. Only a lecture from the judge. There was much talk of keeping their records clean, so that these young men could continue to pursue their plans and goals in life, without the burden of having the bird deaths during a single night's foolish escapade, an unfortunate *mistake hanging over their heads like an albatross—or in this case an albatross' corpse.*

❦ ❦ ❦

Q: How did Grayson go out? I mean pass away?

A: Had his head cut off in an auto accident. Went right through the windshield. Something about a defective seat belt.

Q: And the others? What happened to the other boys, your buddies?

A: Listen, Q, when you can outlive a curse like the one we all fell under as long as I have, two years now, you're going to look like a *monster*, like the damn elephant man, or in my case like the Albatross Man.

Q: You're dodging the question, Albert.

A: The pressure was great, enormous, overwhelming, just to be in that prep school, a private school turned charter, just so they could milk the government cow. Hell, I would know. My father was the Head Master.

Q: I forgot about that.

A: Wish I could.

Q: I cannot imagine the pressure you must've been under to *ahhh* perform.

A: Yes, but, as to the pressure, the tense, gnawing, everyday pressure? Hell, Q, that's what everyone molded me into to begin with, a total tense dick-wad, and in truth, that's exactly why we got it into our heads that killing protected birds—protected by *adults*, protected by *society*, by all who we hated—well, the damn birds needed murdering.

Q: I think now maybe I get it."

A: No, you don't get it. No one got it then, and no one gets it now. It was and remains their only damn concern—the birds. How we could hurt *them*. Like we weren't hurt ourselves, but we were hurt.

Q: But you fellas had it made; you were given everything.

A: Hurt we were, deep down.

Q: So it was out of a deep-seated *hurt* and *anger* over that hurt that you killed the birds?

A: Shit. How else were we ever going to fight back? It was about how we could beat *them*.

Q: The birds?

A: No, the bloody parents, the school, the administrators, the faculty, the damn shrinks and all that *they* sent at us. Not a one of them figured that out. As for the cops and the lawyers, they were blind to our reasoning. Everyone chalked it up to the simple evilness that comes with being a in teen, you know, brains not yet fully formed combined with—

Q: Affluenza and evil teenagers. The undeveloped teenage brain.

A: Ridiculous shit. Like it was something we concocted alone in our heads, all by ourselves, this act that got me deformed and looking like the ugliest, oversized angry bird ever seen in a freak show. The reason you're here now, in this graveyard, the reason you paid for gas to get to the last funeral I'll ever attend, save my own, is to see this thing I've become. Here, have a good look. I'll open up my coat and shirt for you, you lousy perverted reporter punk.

🐦 🐦 🐦

With a magnificent seven-foot wingspan, the Laysan Albatross is found mainly in the uninhabited northernmost regions of the Hawaiian Islands. Creating a safe habitat for the animals has taken years of concerted effort. Since 1991 the colony at Ka'ena Point is, where some 300 to 350 Albatrosses nest, and it has been a shining example of success. The saddest part of this whole horrible event involving the young men, who had premeditated their Albatross murders, was their being students from the prestigious Punahou School from which such men as former President of the USA, Barrack Obama hailed. A part of the curriculum was a visit to the conservatory and reserve, so the students knew the history and importance of the Ka'ena Point safe haven for the birds. They took their weapons straight there, for the intent to massacre as many birds as they could in cover of darkness. "Distressing," is what the school board director and the Head Master called it.

❦ ❦ ❦

Q: You didn't tell me what happened to the other two boys, Mr. Albatross?

Q: Oh, yeah, Benjamin Willis Wellman and Charles 'Chuckie' Balmoral, whom we are here to bury today. No way to forget those two boys. The richest of our lot. One with an oil exec father, the other with an ambassador father. Bennie as we called Wellman, he fell prey to a nasty problem with his eyes.

Q: And exactly what sort of problem was it?

A: They began to grow larger and larger until they were bulging from their sockets just like how it happened that night when we strangled some of those birds to death, Bennie's preferred method of torture. He'd laugh like a mating coyote when he saw those bulging eyes popping out of their bird heads.

Q: Gross!

A: Gross in a way. Eventually, Bennie went mad, but not before both his eyes were dangling around his cheeks the size of baseballs. Something he did to himself, they said.

Q: What do they know?

A: As for Balmoral, he went out badly, too. Not sure I can talk about it, standing here within sight of his freshly dug grave, but it had to do with fire where there was no fire.

Q: How's that?

A: How's that you wonder? His skin began to bake, *spontaneously*, but not all at once. Piece by piece, extremities first, limbs next, torso, followed by face and head. Died of first degree burns on his bed at home. Dying in bed, some might say is the way to go, but not the way Chuckie did it.

Q: How's that?

A: The kid's mattress burned clear through in an outline of his body as it dropped through to the floor. Chalked up to 'spontaneous human combustion' but there was nothing spontaneous about it. His body had been lighting fires fueled by his own fat for months. This was just the big one.

Q: Weren't some of the birds set on fire?"

A: Saw Balmoral do it once to an opossum right there at the school auto shop. One of the others had trapped the animal and brought it in for laughs, but Balmoral doused it with gasoline and lit a match. The thing ran right across the badminton court until it fell over like burnt toast. Still recall how the smoke curled up off it.

Q: So Balmoral lit up a few birds, eh?"

A: Just to watch them run around like a ball of fire, yes. If it'd been the dry season, he'd have caused a forest fire. Yeah, Chuckie's doing. Chuckie was the fire bug among us.

Q: And so that brings it around to you, Albert, the last of the six teens who turned into bird killers that night, Albatross killers.

A: Yes, and how shall I buy the grave? It's coming on in my aging this way. It's rapid aging. Look at my skin, my hair, my teeth.

Q: We're all on a path to die, Albert. (Note: can't help but feel sorry for the guy)

A: We sure showed those fuckin' birds who was boss. Ha!

Q: Sure did, you did. (Note: I take back my sympathy for the guy)

A: Showed our fathers who was boss that night, too. Showed them *all*. The Head Master, the deans, the faculty, all of 'em. And now that you see what I've become, that's the real mystery, because I don't have one damn clue as to how those birds got their revenge on us all, but they sure as hell did. Look at my talon feet and fingers, look at my feathery, leathery body, my beaked nose and hawk's eyes, my crown and giblet. Look at this freak, and you tell me, how did I morph into this beast? And how did the others suffer as they did?

Q: Why do *you* think it happened like it did? How did it happen, this bad super-*karma*?

A: At first, I thought it was all in their heads, the damnable guilt my buddies carried around in their hearts and souls, you know, pure guilt getting to the others, and I scoffed at them for it, and down deep...down deep...

Q: You didn't believe it down deep, did you?

A: Even made light of it, joked about it. What did we have to be feeling guilty about when *they* molded us in the image of themselves and their gods?

Q: But your attitude changed, didn't it?

A: Yeah, how'd you know? When it happened to me. When I started changing into this horrible birdman thing, I realized it wasn't all in their minds, 'cause hell, it wasn't all in *my* mind. And, and I know now it's not imaginary shit.

Q: But if it's not in your head, not imagined, what then is it, Albert?

A: That it's *real*, that it's *physical*, and that it's *irrevocable*. Like any goddamn curse is unstoppable. Watch this!

Q: (Note: Albatross Man, in a single flat-footed leap, perched himself on the thin top of a tablet-styled headstone. The interviewer, Q, begged for a photo, and Q's wish with it granted, the photo was already coursing across the internet).

A: Photo done? Enough shots for your readers?

Q: How long can you perch like that?

A: With these talons, I could do the same with a lamp pole. I can crush cinder blocks with these babies. Hell, I do it every day in my public show, you know, the one that I do twice a day and once on Sundays, for the public.

Q: Yeah, yeah, I caught the show. Paid the guy to let me come back to talk to you, but you wouldn't come out of your dressing room to see me.

A: Sorry, but at the time, I couldn't face you.

Q: But you can now?

A: Time's passed and so has my last buddy.

Q: You shouted through the door for me to *beat it*. Quite rude, really, and I couldn't get my money back, so it was all a waste, so I was excited to get your invitation to be here today, to talk to you here at Chuckie's funeral.

A: I don't know what to say to my earlier rudeness, but showing up as you did without warning, that, too was rude.

Q: My apologies. You're right, of course.

A: A cub reporter wanting to do a story on me, and you staked me out and stalked me to my dressing room door.

Q: Well now, staked and stalked is a bit of exaggeration, sir.

A: Calling me sir, only because I look old enough to be your grandfather, when in fact, I'm only a couple-few years older than you. Staked me out or whatever you want to call it.

Q: You see, when it happened, all I could do was read the accounts in the papers. I worked for the reserve up there on the mountain where you guys did what you did. A scut-work job to be sure. Cleaned up at the dispensary, saw to feeding sick birds, washing out the cages and such. The free, healthy birds were easy prey for you boys. No bars or, locks out there in the wild."

A: Hold on. You were a worker out there on the mountain?

Q: I didn't understand you boys then or the why of it. *Why*, is still a mystery all these years on, so that's why I've stalked you, as you describe it, at from the freak show, but trust me, my coming here to see you here, at the cemetery, is only to hear it—the story—direct from the bird's mouth, so to speak.

A: Why me? Why just talk to me?"

Q: I asked the others before each passed, Albert; same as I am asking you now.

A: Really?

Q: One-by-one, but honestly, they all pretty much said the same thing over and over. 'I don't fuckin' know why we did it'. That was all they had, but you...you spin a good story, Albert Delmont Huston the Fifth, aka Albatross Man."

A: You? Are you telling me that *you* did this to us?

Q: How can you come to such a conclusion?

A: I know nothing about you. None of the others ever spoke of you.

Q: None wished it to get out; that they'd spoken with me.

A: Who are you, Q? Really, who are you and what do you really want from me?

Q: I am born Malori, from the islands beyond Hawaii, where we still practice many of the old ways. One of which is the power to place—

A: P—P—place a curse?

Q: Perceptive of you, Mr. Albert Albatross Man. But I also came to apologize.

A: Apologize? Five young men are dead! And hell, I'm to be next, and you want to apologize? This is what you and your article is all about? Was there ever an article? What kind of fraud are you, Q?

Q: Forgiveness is the theme of my article, and yes there is to be an article, and I am a journalist now with an editor and a paper.

A: Forgiveness...your intention comes late for my five school-mates.

Q: Yes, forgiveness, as I hope it is not too late for *you*, Albert, to forgive *me* for my youthful action against all six of you.

A: Sure, I will forgive you, maybe after I rip you apart with my talons.

Q: The birds were my friends, Albert. Just as X, Y, and Z were your friends. But the boss lady at the reserve, she made us wait nine days before allowing us to go out and search for all the body parts, because the only sure way to find every piece you bastards chopped up was by the smell of rot. A hellish hunt for evidence. A webbed foot here, a beaked head there, a torso elsewhere. You know how thick that guinea grass is atop that mountain.

A: I remember the smell of it like it was yesterday—the grass, that is.

Q: Like I remember the smell of rotting bird flesh. Yeah, sure, you could do that, you truly could. But without me, who will tell your story? Provide the why that you confided in me? Besides, I did not act alone in cursing you. I had help."

A: What help? Who's help?"

Q: Yes, the curse needed one ingredient from you, sir."

A: That being?

Q: Just an *nth* degree of guilt."

A: Guilt?

Q: Yes, to make it work. Now, I must hurry to get this to press on time. My editor is waiting. Have a good death, Mr. Albatross Man. Oh, and by the way, you may be interested to know that the Albatross is making a miraculous comeback.

ALWAYS ROOM FOR ONE MORE

TALLY JOHNSON

I WAS OUT FOR MY MORNING CONSTITUTIONAL... BULL, WHO TALKS LIKE THAT anymore? I was for a wandering walk just before dark, trying to figure out what was coming next. I mean, after finding out my wife of ten years was stepping out with my boss and that I was about to lose my job for confronting said boss with proof of the rather pitiful affair. But when a thirty year old attractive lady hooks up with a seventy year old man, passion isn't a real priority. Not that I was a sexual dynamo myself but still. Despite having no real interest in being outside or having no tendencies towards being a modern Dan'l Boone, I decided to just walk around and try to decide how to manage this mess. I wound up walking on the riverbank behind the old city cemetery, Saint Francis of Sales. How a cemetery in a town with like twenty Catholics decided to name a graveyard after a Saint is anybody's guess. As I came up to the old ramshackle trestle on the old rail line, I was struck by how quiet it had gotten. No mosquitoes, no tree frogs, no traffic, not even the whisper of the river. As soon as I hit the gravel marking the old railroad tracks, a good sized crow with a curious swath of white feathers on its head landed on the old mile post marking the seventy-one miles to Columbia. Being a bit phobic of our feathered friends, I decided to stay well on the far side of the gravel of it. Until it spoke to me. Literally. Out loud. In English with a hint of a German accent. Or maybe Yiddish.

"Hey, bub. HEY! You!" The crow said in a demanding tone of voice, much like my soon to be ex-boss's war cry after a screw-up in the office. Despite knowing that I was alone in the middle of the woods, I spun around and looked around for anyone else he... it... could be talking to. But, nope, it was just me and him. So, to be polite, I spoke back.

"What? You get lost flying south and need directions or something?" Not my best banter, but what would you say when accosted by a talking crow in the back of beyond? Besides, I had a worried mind.

"Wow...a regular Shecky Greene out here in the woods, you going into Vaudeville or off to the Catskills to bomb?"

I stood agog. Not only could the crow talk, but his pop culture references were older than my parents. But after a second or two, I recovered and introduced myself, Since we were chatting anyway, referring to each other as bub or hey you seemed to be rude.

"Hey, I'm Henry Jacobs. Who the Hell are you? Sorry to be so direct, but I know this isn't a Disney movie and birds ain't supposed to talk in real life."

"Easy, man, easy. They used to call me Herman Schumaker back when I was alive, but that was a while back. The guys call me Nacht-krapp behind his back. But you need to get ready to head out at any rate. He'll be along in a bit and he won't lollygag for long. So get your shit straight and be ready. We've got to make Schenectady by midnight and he's been held up over in Cornwall for a minute already.

"What the absolute HELL are you babbling about? I've got to head back home and finish packing up my crap and get some sleep. I'm going to have a real shit sandwich of a day tomorrow and I have no damn clue what you're talking about."

"Okay, shut up and sit down. I doubt the four oh ten runs on this line anymore, so you'll be okay. Sounds like your spell hasn't worn off yet, so this will all be a load to take in at one bite. Now, ask me no questions and you'll get no lies. Your day tomorrow will suck less than you think, but it will certainly be different. And if you go in blind, you'll be over your head and I'll be too busy to babysit. So sit already."

Well, I sat down. When a talking crow wants to palaver, you do what he wants. I cursed to myself for leaving my phone at home though. This crap would have made me richer than Bill Gates and more famous than a Kennedy online. So, I decided to humor it.

"Do you remember anything from before? At all? If you do, this will lessen the shock and make it easier to digest, because it's a big load to carry at one time." I shook my head no. " Hoo boy. Okay. Here it is. About six-hundred years ago, you were the Abbot of a small abbey, Buckland or Buckwood or some such, in the West of England, over in Dartmoor. Ring any chimes?"

I grinned like a mule eating thistles by the handful and shook my head again. The crow, raven, bird-thing sighed as much as a bird could. It came out like a strangled croak. Me—a confirmed and lapsed Baptist—a monk reincarnated. I had as much belief in both God and reincarnation as I did in the Easter Bunny, so this was looking and smelling like refined bullshit. I was racking my brain trying to recollect the last time I had done any drugs harder than aspirin in order for this to make sense. All that came to mind was college and that was a good two decades ago.

"HEY! DUMBASS! Eyes front! I'm trying to get you ready for a load of bad weirdness in a real short time so snap back already. You were the Abbot, the bossman of a small abbey in Dartmoor, which is where a bunch of the king-Hell strangeness in the United Kingdom comes from. One dreary Sunday after Mass you and some of your cloister mates decided to go hunting for deer. No vow of starvation for you, mister big shot. Hell, if you had been the first son, you'd be a minor noble and overawing the peasantry and trying to steal land from the abbey you were currently living in. But you weren't so you decided to indulge just once. You'd confess and beg forgiveness and do the Hail Marys and whatever other penance that the Bishop came up with. But a flank of venison would lessen the blow, you thought. But the Man in Charge had other ideas for you, didn't he? You were about to become the worse thing ever. An example."

Sounds like my damned luck sure enough. Even when I let my hair down, shit went sideways. Even as a kid, the class could be whooping and hollering to be the band, but as soon I opened my mouth, BAM, the accusatory finger and licks from a belt on a bare ass. I sagged in my spot on the tracks, but the raven took no notice, warming to his tale of the long ago.

"Yup, you were a King-Hell badass in your own mind. Even dragooned a cottage of peasants to harry the game since it would be unseemly for a good monk to have a pack of hunting hounds. Never mind that the wife was seven-months pregnant and the four children were all under ten. Hell, the youngest was barely weaned and just able to hold herself upright. Yup, you were a right well born bastard. But regardless of the ban by both God and country of hunting on Sunday, you wanted venison instead of gruel for supper. So off you and your unwilling companions went. Now if you'd been over on the chalk downs you and yours would have likely been turned into a stone circle or some such foolishness and your faux hounds would be given some sort of surcease, by being allowed to roll to a nearby brook to drink once a year or some holy day or maybe even being human for a day. But your scrawny bald ass would have been stuck there for an eternity, probably aware of the wider world but stuck fast like a roach on flypaper. Unless or until some local farmer used you to build a wall to hold his sheep or to replace a shed wall. Do you remember if your holiness happened to catch anything that long-gone afternoon?"

I was lost in my own head. The picture the raven had painted with his tongue had completely entranced me. I swear I was there, riding a brown horse, bolting through the moors and fens in my robe, cutting the backs of my unwilling hounds with a lash, uttering—based on how proficient in profanity I was at present—oaths to rend heaven and call down the wrath of all the gods. Yeah, I could see it. Didn't make it so, but damn, that bird could sure talk. My reverie was interrupted by a wing across the bridge of my nose.

"SUMBITCH! That hurt!"

"Well, well. You WERE awake. Good. Maybe this is finally sinking in. Took damn long enough. The Man in Charge has finally cleared jolly ole Ireland. So chop chop. No, you didn't catch anything. Even though you rode past dozens of likely victims. Because the Big Boss had plans for you. See, you're a two time loser going on borrowed time and too damn dumb to notice. Do you recall running into the other fella? The one on foot who met you at the Dewerstone?"

"Of course not, birdbrain. You tell a Hell of a story but so far that's all this is. A really good story killing time before either I wake up or snap out of it and head home."

"Uh huh. Sure. Stupid ass. But they always are. Anyway. He bore quite a resemblance to you. Because he was you from some five centuries before. He had been a damn sight more disrespectful than you were as the erstwhile leader of a religious house. The other you had mocked the Son. Right to his face. A ballsy move, but damn was it dumb. See, he was hauling a load of lumber up to Golgotha and you mocked him as a piss poor carpenter. Real witty, for a moron. So He fixed you with those sad brown eyes and said, "Tarry here until I come this way again." And you have. You're quite the world traveler. Set foot on every continent at least twice and in every country to boot.

But He's in no hurry to pass you on the great interstate of existence. See you made Him and the Big Boss madder than Hell and they're in no rush to let you off the hook. Since you were going to be around for quite a while, the Man in Charge decided to ask for a small favor. A sop, if you will. But he decided not to just make the call unilaterally. He got his crew together. All the big shots. Those running with him then and those to come, too. Herlechin, Dando, Arthur, Gwynn ap Nudd, Herla, Drake, Holle, Jarnik, Hackelberg, Arnau, Tregeagle, Dewer, Guthlac, Beatrk. EVERYBODY. Filled the hall and tapped out at least a dozen casks. It seems that all of them had gotten tired of chasing after small game. Unbaptized babies and children. Hunting packs gone rogue. Souls too damn dumb to know they're dead and need to go to rest. Moss maidens. They wanted something with some sense and cunning. Something to finally lather up the horses and boars and to make the tongues of the hounds loll."

"Wait, who are those people? Never heard of any of them, except maybe Arthur and Drake. And what the Hell is a moss maiden?"

I swear the raven grinned. Well, he would have if he had teeth. As it was it bobbed its head like one of those drinking bird toys you'd put on the side of a glass. It acted like I had finally caught up to him. I hadn't. I was genuinely bumfuzzled. All those names it has just spat out could have been Greek or some language from a bad science fiction novel."

"Oh, NOW, you're all curious and shit. Well, I'll humor you but the sand is starting to get real damn thin. First the short one. Moss maidens used to be called dryads. Okay, I see you didn't get a classical education, or much of any to speak of. Shit, read a book once and again. Anyway, dryads were basically tree spirits. Protectors of the trees they lived in."

"Like the Lorax?"

The raven's head sank to its breast then it shook it like it had water in its ears.

"Sure kid, if that help hurry this along, like the Lorax. Of course, the Greeks called them dryads. The barbarian hordes up in the dark forests of Europe called them moss maidens. Since, they wound up ruling the joint, their term stuck everywhere but Greece. Except over here, but that's a lesson I ain't got time for. The names. Those were the one who got second billing in the great movie called the universe. They ran their own hunts and hounds all over the place. Most of them small. Couple of horsemen, a few hounds. The Man in Charge can summon them as he will if he needs a hand or to just be a dickhead. You know from bosses, right?"

I ruefully nodded my head. Bosses, in my general experience, were bastards. Glory boys quick to put you under a bus to save their sorry asses. I felt a pang of sorrow for those weird names. Yeah, I knew from bosses.

"Now, back to where I was. The Man in Charge wasn't real thrilled at having to convince the Big Boss that what he had in mind was actually a good idea for all concerned. For one thing, it would mean that the other hunts would have to be together for a very long time and at least a few of the folks mentioned before might get ideas about being in charge. The Man in Charge could handle that normally, especially before the Son, but now it would just be a hassle and one more damned thing. Because if a man got a taste of power, he just wanted one more little bite. And a good chunk of those folks had been Kings and Counts and Archbishops and the like. Eventually, as below, so above. So he laid his plan out very clearly and carefully."

"Okay, Damn it. I'm out. This is some kind of dumbass role-playing game crap. Or I'm on Candid Camera. Y'all come on out. This crap was fun but it's clouding up and I want to get home before the bottom drops out. Hunts with packs of hounds? Look, you hunt three ways. Either up in a deer stand nailed to some scraggly pine tree covered in deer piss with a rifle waiting for Bambi to wander by looking for some tail. Or you squat under some tree branches getting your ass soaked in some swamp or pond making quacking noises at ducks flying overhead. If you're fancy, you stomp through some cut down cornfield following a lost dog with a rifle, hoping a bird might fly towards a nearby tree branch. I'm a born and bred country boy and I've only heard of stuck up inbred Brits riding after some mangy mutts chasing a fox. The immoral chasing the inedible, someone once said. So let's wrap this crap up. Come have your laugh at my expense. Shit, everybody else has here lately. And whoever threw their voice for the tame bird, damn, you should be on late night TV. Well damn done."

The raven puffed up like someone had stuck an air hose up its ass. With a croak, it flew off the mile marker towards me. It scratched at my face with claws that still had chunks of rotten flesh visible under them. I threw my hands up in the nick of time and got my forearms tore up like I had fallen through a plate glass window headfirst. For some reason, I thought of Tippi Hedren in the phone booth in the old movie The Birds. It made me giggle, despite the burning of my arms.

"Listen you damned half-wit. This isn't a prank. A cosmic joke maybe, but it sure as shit ain't funny. And the giggles will quit once the Man in Charge shows up. Because I still got shit to say and I'm in no hurry to take a permanent vacation. So shut the happy Hell up because when that 'little storm' gets here, all HELL will break loose and follow with it. Now, where was I? Damned interrupting punk. Since YOU had screwed up as bad as you did, the Man in Charge decided that everyone could just use a change of pace to fill all the vacant hours between hunts. Some of them didn't go forth but for a night and some ran all the time. He offered the deal to the junior league as they might owe him a favor. When the main hunt passed through their range, Herla, Jarnik, Tregeagle, Holle could take off after their old prey for a few nights but they had to leave security to be mutually determined to ensure a reunification afterwards. In return, he offered them prey most cunning for what may well be eternity and a respite from harrying souls to the Reaper and a chance to get off old fairy traces and grave roads linked to ley lines or old wives' tales. After some raucous discussion and more than a few cases of having to re-assert his authority, the Man in Charge convinced them to join him in his plea. So the Man in Charge went alone on the long journey up the mountain to the Gate. No sop for this watchman. Only a humble supplicating request for a brief audience. If Judas could get a day out of Hell once a year, surely the Big Boss could spare a moment for a fairly faithful servant. The watchman nodded but pointed his flaming sword at the Man in Charge's chest. Berserker rage built at the insult but quickly faded on His approach."

I confess. I sat silent, rapt even. The world was focused on this talking raven with the dirty mouth and the fantasy it could weave. The raven continued, now warming to his topic as the denouncement rushed into view.

"On bended knee, the Man in Charge made his request for new game. The Big Boss pondered and the Earth stopped spinning. The sun and moon shared space in the sky. Everything stopped. Yes, EVERYTHING. That's what happens when omnificence is thinking something over. After a moment, the Big Boss nodded his assent. But the Big Boss had a condition. He was, after all, merciful...even to those too dumb to deserve it. The Man in Charge had to give the quarry a rest. Weary prey makes mistakes and He wanted a good long run. So, every other century, you caught a break. You'd get to live your three score ten in various and sundry guises, with no memory of your role or past. BUT if the hunts got restless or circumstances changed, your break got cut short. Again, bosses, huh?"

My mind was vapor-locked like a dry engine. Almost nothing the crow had just said made any damned sense. I'd always been me. Not all that much maybe, but all me. Office drone. Mildly rebellious child. Dutiful son. Went through all the right motions in turn. This... fantasy was a bit much to grasp, even given the circumstance it was delivered in. The crow gave me no time to process though.

"Damn. It's raining already. More time, more time! There's far more to tell him before. Bah! That's why he's in charge. Damn it.

Okay, a bit about me. For every quarry, there's a courser. Someone to set the pace for the hunt and steer it to the prey. My predecessor was another writer who could not abide humanity's idiocy and made sure they knew about it. He was a greyhound. Long and sleek and could run for days on end in staccato bursts. He was a natural. I took a bit more... training. Couldn't abide being in a pack even if I was out front. But the Man in Charge whipped me into shape. Hell, I've still got plenty of time to learn and even teach whoever's next. My penance is fairly short considering. Now, like I was saying before memory lane called, you're supposed to get that seventy year break every other century. Well, things have changed and not in your favor. People don't believe like they used to even fifty years ago. Too much light, too many screens, too much distraction. So the Big Boss decided to call you back to active duty as it were. But it will be a king-Hell world tour. You've heard of climate change, right? Well, one benefit is that the Man in Charge has put the whole symphony together again. All the prey has assembled just over the horizon. You'll hear them in a bit. All that heat and crazy weather will serve to bring some Saturn level thunder boomers to pass over. So the weather is here, wish you were beautiful. And since parents don't push kids into being baptized or vaccinated for that matter anymore, the unbaptized and unshriven have hit bumper crops levels. All those dead kids and unbelievers will keep all the packs fat and happy for a few centuries. BUT me and you, kid, we're the main event. The crème de la crème as it were."

I had to ask. "Okay, assuming I buy what you're peddling, how does this work? Do I just take off at a jog and whatever this hunting pack is comes over the hill and away we go? Or is it more complicated than that? Somehow I'm sure it is the latter."

"Yeah, the light bulb finally came on. Well, sadly, you'll have to shed this guise. And before you ask, yes it will hurt. A lot. And you'll run through all your other lives and looks too. Won't take but a few seconds but it will feel like days. The Big Boss thinks it will focus your mind on the job ahead. And, you have a ways to go before you get permanently retired. But on the good foot, I expect folks will remember you after this next hunt. Folks will remember to respect nature and the old beliefs. All of them. Damn. I'm actually excited for you. Oh, here it comes. Right on schedule."

The crow half-hopped and half-flew to a branch just off the right of way. On hearing a strange huffing noise, I looked up and saw a steam engine coming around the bend. On the front was a shiny brass plate reading "Nine-Twenty-Eight." For some reason, I knew that number meant death. So I jumped up and ran for the trestle. Why I didn't just step to the side next to the crow I'll never understand. But damn, did I run. Like I'd never seen a cigarette and I was ten-years old and it was the last day of school. Like I had just won the lottery. Of course it ended poorly. The engine and the line of black cars it pulled was going a good forty-miles an hour. I wasn't doing close to that. It caught me right at the start of the trestle just as I was about to jump for the stream below. As the engine roared past, never slowing for it has many souls to collect, I heard the engineer say, "Always room for one more. But you ain't the one."

I came to with the crow pecking at my forehead. If it had had fingers, I'd swear it would be poking me in the forehead.

"Hey! Welcome back, sleepyhead! It's almost time but now for the review."

A shimmering, full-length mirror appeared before me, astride the tracks like a barricade in some B-movie car chase. I saw myself as I knew me for a second. Then it changed. From a balding, middle-aged shmuck in cheap clothes to a distinguished looking chap with his hair parted in the middle and a beard to mid-chest wearing a full suit with a detachable collar, black string tie and a vest complete with a gold pocket watch. Must have been a banker. ("Actually, in insurance," the crow mentioned.) Another shimmer, another image. Hair past my shoulders. Van Dyke mustache and beard. Sad, sad eyes. Ruffles on my shirt and what appeared to be balloons in

my pant legs. ("Courtier to Charles the First. You told him to negoti-
ate with the New Model Army. He had you hung, drawn, quartered
and tossed into the Thames. You get that a lot. Power despises being
told the truth.") Then, me but with a tonsure and in a brown robe
that looked like burlap, but I reckoned it was wool. Damn, but I had
the most Go-to Hell look in my eye. My job description said man of
God, but everything else said something different. Next, I wore an
iron helmet and chain mail and carried a long bow as tall as I was.
("Just another archer in the army of Henry the Fifth. I think you died
at Crecy. Of typhus. No glory for you, bub.") Then, a darker hue to
my skin, but still me. A long white robe and a turban. Beardless. ("A
defender of Aleppo during the Crusader siege. You died defending
Jews in the street. A Lombard knight ran you down on his charger.
You didn't even have time to draw your blade.") Then, an even darker
hue. What looked to be leopard skin around my forehead. Looked
to be nude except for a loincloth. Carrying a spear. ("Ah, Africa.
That didn't last long. You were a simple hunter in what's now Ni-
geria. Then the Moslems started towards Mecca from Medina and
you got recalled. Like a Corvair.") Another shimmer, though quicker
this time. I'm in a white toga. Grey-haired and clean shaven. Sitting
in a chair. ("Yeah, you were a Roman Senator. Of course, you were
in the last Senate before the capital of the Western Empire moved
to Milan. And you were stabbed to death in bed with your mistress.
Who was twelve. By her parents. Classy.") One last shake of the ka-
leidoscope. I looked like pluperfect Hell and refried crap. Stringy
black shoulder length hair. Huge black eyes, bloodshot. Corrugated
forehead. Hawk-like Roman nose. Mouth agape almost to my breast
bone. ("Yup. That's still you. The REAL you. Joseph Ahasver. The
Fool of Fools. The man idiotic enough to mock the Christ on his way
to Calvary. And who got what he deserved good and hard. Right in
the teeth. Stare hard because you'll be seeing it every pond, pool,
and lake for the next century or more. Assuming you ever get any
rest. NOW! GO! Fly like the fool you were, are, and forever will be!)

I heard a clap of thunder that sounded like the moon had just crashed into the Atlantic and looked over my shoulder. My GOD, what a sight I saw. A black coach and four driven by a headless man who didn't spare the whip. Hundreds of riders in black armor fully armed with halberds, swords, axes, and Heaven knows what else. Riding on coal black horses, boars, goats. Anything with a back wide enough to hold a man and four legs to run on. A man on horseback in black with his head turned all the way around, carrying a bucket in one hand. Archbishops, monks, judges; all in their finest robes. Another steam engine larger than the one that had reset my existence, this one driver-less, pulling one passenger car covered in billowing black crepe and a dozen more flat-beds, all covered with skeletal figures in blue. And the women. All topless and armed to the teeth. Riding side-saddle waving broadswords like batons. One rider's horse came up lame, missing a shoe I guess. He swayed in the saddle for a second. The dog he had held under one arm fell to the ground and crumbled into dust. The rider wailed in sorrow but the general din drowned out the noise. The noise...good God. Howling, cursing, barking, baying. The clanging of shields on armor. The pounding of hooves. The creak of leather on flesh. All of it within a mile of me and looking to run me down. Another rider tossed a bundle down towards a jogger just visible through the trees. With a choked cry, she recognized it as the baby she had miscarried the year before.

The crow, no, raven looked askance at me. "Why are you still here? The chase is eternal but the prey must be off before the hunt, not after. We'll not meet again, I expect. I hope I will have served my time and done my penance before your next rest." With that he flew up to the waiting gauntlet of his master. Odin or Woden, one or the other. My grasp of Nordic myth is shaky. Through the swirl of passing beautiful misty maidens, all of whom I would have given all my worldly goods for a night of pleasure, I saw the raven earnestly pleading my case, at least he pointed one stubby wing down to me.

Oh yes, down at me. The cavalcade was passing a good thousand feet off the ground. The old, one-eyed man with his slouch hat on his eight legged horse glared down and motioned for the hunt to halt. In an instant, I knew this was a boon not to be given again. With a shriek, I bolted to the East. Running with supernatural speed for the sunrise. Knowing that it would bring me a moment of peace but no more. You see, the Wild Hunt always has room for one more, but the prey is always alone.

🦇 🦇 🦇

"And now for some local news. A F-5 tornado touched down in downtown Hemphill last night just before dusk. Six people were killed when a tree fell on their trailer and one jogger was found in De La Rosa Park, on the path near the old trestle. She had no injuries but preliminary reports say she may have died of a heart attack. One odd note. Clothing belonging to Henry Jacobs was found on the old trestle. No body has yet been found."

THE SOLITARY PROCESSION

MACKENZIE KINCAID

WILLIAM BAKER WAS CERTAIN, DOWN TO THE MARROW OF HIS BONES, THAT IT was fate which revealed the carriage to him that night.

There could be no other explanation: that he happened to be on just the right stretch of road, on just the right evening, at just the right time, to watch the hearse appear before him, mirage-like, shimmering into the world from some other place.

It was already a God-forsaken night, bitter cold and the rain a torrent that lashed at William beneath his hat, snaked its way down the collar of his long, oiled coat, and left every inch of him miserable and shivering. His horse, borrowed from the Greens, was in just as terrible a state, but it was also a nervous creature by nature, quivering with fear every time the sky flashed with lightning or rumbled with thunder. William had to keep half his attention on the road, to try to prevent both of them from winding up broken-legged in a ditch, and half his attention on the horse, to ensure it wouldn't simply throw him off and leave him behind.

He didn't see the funeral carriage until he was nearly on top of it, partly for that reason and partly because, by the time he looked up and caught sight of it, it hadn't yet managed to fully resolve itself into the world.

It started out as a strange outline, a box where the rain splashed against some object that was not there. And then it was a sound, a jangling of harness and splash of hoofbeats in mud, a rhythmic counterpoint to the steady hiss of the rain. There was the flaring of a set of lamps suddenly lit, a gleam of light against brass, the turning of solid wooden wheels. Then it was a carriage, full and complete, the matched team of black horses at the front of it working steadily, apparently not struggling with the mud at all.

The Greens' gelding rocked back onto its hind legs, front feet leaving the ground, trying to spin and go back the way they came. When William wrenched the horse's head back again, its eyes were white-rimmed and panicked, rolling and wild. He thought for a moment that it would unseat him entirely and flee into the woods, but with his hands tight on the reins, and heels dug firm, the horse collected itself somewhat beneath him. It shook its head, wheezed out a breath as if it had run a mile, and its feet danced a frantic jig, but it submitted itself again to his direction.

He might have thought that the carriage before him was only a regular passenger cart, one that the darkness had obscured until he was nearly upon it, but the carriage itself was not fit for more than a single prone passenger. The top of it was too low to accommodate seats, and the length of it was glass encased, to allow mourners a view of the coffin.

It was a fine thing, too fine by far for the muddy road it traveled and the small, humble town that was its destination. Why it came, and where it went, no one had ever known.

For William, just then, it didn't necessarily matter. He knew exactly what the appearance of it meant for him, and there was only one thing he could do now: pass the thing by on the rain-lashed road, and run like the devil.

His horse was less certain of the plan; when he urged it on to overtake the carriage, it balked again, twisting one way and then the other, groaning and crying out like it was being asked to throw itself from a cliff. He finally pointed its head in the right direction, dug in his heels, and laid in with the crop as well, placing a series of sharp blows against the animal's hindquarters that finally drove it forward, skirting between the carriage and the trees that loomed close around it.

They paced up past the glass case, the wheels that still shone despite the mud, and drew up alongside the driver's seat, the light of the lamps casting the coachman in shades of sickly yellow. The rain poured from him, but seemed almost to roll off without leaving him truly wet.

The preternaturally pale figure, solemn in his finery and top hat, was the same one that had haunted William's childhood nightmares: long, thin face immobile, eyes white and shining like pearls. The coachman said nothing—he'd never spoken, not to anyone—but he turned his head and stared with his perfectly barren eyes, as if he could see right into William's soul.

William's borrowed horse was trembling beneath him, its head thrown up, feet scrambling though it hardly managed to move anywhere, with the bit holding it back and heels driving it forward. It groaned again, nothing like a whinny, the sort of sound that only a dying animal makes.

William gave the coachman a nod of understanding, and then gave the gelding its head and another slap of the crop. It stretched its neck out and shot into a gallop, mud flying beneath its hooves, breath heaving with terror as it passed by the carriage's perfectly matched, utterly placid pair of black horses. The gelding ran as if its life depended upon escape.

The funeral carriage kept advancing behind them: slow, steady, inevitable. They left it far behind.

❧ ❧ ❧

They entered the town at a more reasonable trot, as if William hadn't allowed the horse to bring them home at a much faster gait than was at all advisable, for the conditions. The rain had already washed the lather of sweat away, at least, and William had reined the horse in early enough that its breath had slowed somewhat. It had carried him home with all haste, as if the hounds of hell had been nipping at its feet the whole way, but it had been surefooted enough even in the wet, and it would be hours yet before the funeral carriage made its appearance.

"The doctor isn't with you," Mrs. Green said, meeting him in the street outside her house, grasping the horse by the bridle's cheek-piece to hold the beast in place while William dismounted.

"He's not coming," William reported. "Not for awhile yet. He's away."

Mrs. Green cursed, and then cursed again at the horse, shaking her hand against its bridle, uncaring when the gelding danced uneasily to one side and threw its head up, its eyes rimmed white. The poor dumb creature seemed terrified and bewildered by every part of its life, even without the appearance of ghost carriages.

"Damn this animal," she said, but there was hardly any heat left in it, as if all her emotion had drained out of her.

"Can I leave it to your care?" William asked, carefully, passing her the crop as well. "I must see to my wife."

Mrs. Green sniffled, and wiped a finger beneath her eyes, as if her tears could be wiped away separately from the rain that still poured down on their heads. "Of course," she said. She looked at him and seemed for perhaps the first time to truly see him: soaked to the bone, shivering, undoubtedly almost as wild-eyed as the horse. "You've ridden a long way, and I'm grateful to you. Please give your wife my best wishes, for her recovery."

"And the same to your husband," William said, with a nod that was nearly a bow.

When the woman turned away, leading the horse toward the little barn alongside the house, William watched her go, until she vanished into the little barn that stood next to her house. Then he turned, not for home, but into the shadowed space between those buildings, heading for the back door of her home. He moved steadily, not allowing himself to rush; Mrs. Green would be occupied for at least a little time, removing the tack, seeing the horse fed, perhaps blanketing it to wick the water from its coat. Much as she might take care with her husband's property, however, she clearly had no love for the animal, and wouldn't linger too long over bedding it in.

He would move with economy and deliberation, and the sure knowledge that fate had its hand in his actions. He could not fail.

On the little stoop, he pulled off his muddy boots, folded his sodden coat up on top of them, and placed his hat gently at the pinnacle of it all, so as not to track the rain and muck into the good woman's house. Then he strode inside, making no attempt to be quiet, letting his footfalls ring out as if he still wore his boots. He could hear Thomas' wheezing from the hall.

The man was lying in his bed, clearly fussed over by his wife, and covered in quilts that he'd thrown back from his chest, perhaps unable to bear their weight. The flesh over his breastbone was a mottled, ugly purple-black, two crescent shapes plainly visible in the mess of it, and the bone was caved in somewhat on one side. There was a bluish tint to his lips, as if he wasn't getting enough air.

"William, you've returned," Thomas gasped, each word a labor in itself. The breath in his lungs had the wheeze of a punctured bellows. Surely he'd be dead by morning, no matter what anyone did. Even the doctor would have been wasting his effort.

"I am sorry. The doctor was already gone, to reports of a sickness in Lindsburg."

"Did you bid his wife to send him?"

"I did, but I fear it will be too late." William moved closer, silent in his stocking-feet, until he leaned over the bed. He said, in a whisper, "Thomas, I have seen the hearse tonight. It's on the road, coming here."

"Oh, my God," Thomas uttered, and his face, already pale, somehow found a lighter shade of white. "Is it my time then, already?"

"I believe it is, and I am sorry for it," William confided.

Thomas stared at the ceiling for a long moment, struggling for breath, his gaze fixing on some point very far away, as if he could already see into the next world. But then he clenched his jaw, and rolled his head to the side, awareness returning entirely to the present, as if he'd had a glimpse of death and decided it wasn't for him.

It was the same look he'd had when he'd whipped his horse only that morning, and see where that had found him: pummeled by a single powerful blow from both hind feet. That he was still alive at all was some sort of miracle.

"There are others," Thomas croaked, pausing to wheeze with every few words. "The Collins boy." This pause was longer, heavier. "Your wife."

"Well, yes," William agreed, in the gentlest tone of voice he could muster. "But the hearse has the space for only one coffin, doesn't it?"

Then he snatched the pillow from beneath Thomas' head, and plunged it down mercilessly over the man's face. Thomas struggled, of course, but William's weight across his damaged chest was as effective a smothering as the pillow was, and in only moments Thomas' body went slack, his hands fell away, and his chest stopped rising at all.

William stayed in place a moment longer, pillow held tight, until he could be sure. When he withdrew at last, there was no life left in Thomas' body.

He carefully lifted the corpse's head, curling it up against his own chest in a half-embrace, so he could place the pillow back where it belonged. Where the fabric was wet with tears and spittle, he faced it down against the bed linens. Then he carefully set the man's hair to rights: smoothing back the strands that were left askew in the struggle, running his careful fingers over the beard, to lay the hairs flat again. He straightened the corpse's legs beneath the blankets, and then carefully arranged the sheets, leaving everything just as it had been when he'd arrived. He gently placed the splayed arms back onto the bed at the body's sides.

Thomas' eyes were already shut, his face slack, almost as if he'd simply passed in his sleep: a mercy, really, for the man's suffering to end so quickly.

William walked quietly to the back door, stepped outside again, and was pulling on his boots when he heard the front door open and shut. He slipped out across the yard to give the grieving widow her privacy, when he heard her begin to wail.

❧ ❧ ❧

In the morning, the hearse stood before the chapel, having arrived in the night; its glass case waited with the rear door opened, ready for an occupant to be settled within. The driver sat in his place, still as a stone, and the horses, too, were unmoving and patient, their proud heads raised. There were lights in the church windows, and townspeople already arriving, dressed in mourning black for Thomas Green.

William had seen it all from the window, early as sunrise, watched the somber-faced reverend coming and going from the chapel, a few people trickling out of their homes one by one, only to go back again to change their clothes and tell their neighbors. Soon, the square was filled with mourners, their black clothes marked at the hems with the previous night's moisture and grit.

He would have gone down immediately, to help the men with the preparations, to offer his sincere condolences to the widow, except that he had a more important task now. For the first time in three days, his wife was awake and sensible of her surroundings.

"What's happening?" she asked, her back slightly propped up by pillows, as her husband carefully spooned warm bone-marrow broth into her mouth. She could only stand a few sips at a time, but it was encouraging progress. The coachman would not take her yet. Providence had determined as much, but William wasn't averse to giving events another push, if he needed to. There was the Collins boy, and Mrs. Henry's grandmother was considerably aged. There were plenty of people in town who the carriage could come for, instead.

"The hearse has come for Thomas Green," he told her. "His horse kicked him yesterday morning, while you were sleeping, and he passed from this world last night."

"Oh, what a tragedy," Agnes said, her pretty mouth turned down at the corners. She wheezed in much the same way that Thomas Green had, but she was regaining her strength already; surely it wouldn't be long before the sound of her lungs improved. "You must go out to pay our respects. Oh, his poor widow!"

"I will, darling, but you must finish your broth first."

He kept his promise to her, though she finished only a quarter of the bowl; when the experience had exhausted her and sent her back into sleep, he dressed in his mourning clothes and stepped out onto the street.

He arrived just as the men bore Thomas Green's coffin out of the church, propped up on their shoulders. They went down the chapel steps with it, paused to lower the humble pine box between them, and then slid it carefully into the back of the hearse.

The moment the back door was shut, the coachman lifted his reins again; his team needed no command and no urging with the whip, they only set off at their usual pace, heading back to the road, to take the body who-knows-where.

It was said there was a widow once who walked after the hearse all the way from town, but no one had ever seen her again.

"I thought it had come for my Jacob," said a voice to William's left, and he turned to see Mrs. Collins there, her hand held to her mouth as she watched Mrs. Green with a gaze that was both sympathetic and relieved. "I woke him from a profound sleep, trying to make sure he was still alive, but he was, thank God. Thank God."

"I had the same fear for my Agnes," William agreed, though it was entirely a lie: he'd had faith, instead, that his actions would have the desired outcome. And he'd been right. It was not his wife the hearse carried away, today. "But she is much improved this morning. I hope your son is well."

Mrs. Collins dipped her head. "Thank you. He seems to recover, little by little."

The Collins boy seemed always to be ill, with one malady or another; the cold brought it on, and so did the summer heat, and the rains made sickness bloom in his lungs. William thought, but did not say, that the boy would probably not live to see the next summer. He expected the funeral carriage would be back for the child, before long.

The hearse receded into the distance, reaching the bend that would take it back to the road and away, and then further again to wherever it was that the wretched thing came from. They all watched it go, but as it passed from sight, the sound of it failed to fade, and then became louder, and nearer, until a second hearse appeared, making its stately way toward the chapel.

It was in the same vein as the first, though it wasn't an identical vehicle: the horses had little chiming brass bells beneath their throats, embroidered drapes across their hindquarters, black ostrich feather plumes rising from their crowns. The carriage too was different, with scallops along its top edge, the window along the side only a round inset of glass, instead of a whole panel. The coachman was a round-jowled man, just as sheet-white as the other, with the same blank white eyes.

William stared at it, utterly uncomprehending, until a man's voice very nearby said, "Mrs. Collins, perhaps you should check on your son?"

And then someone else said, "Mr. Baker, how is your wife?" with a kind of horrible tenderness.

"Very well," William replied, in a voice that felt faint and distant from himself. "She is very well this morning."

A hand rested on his elbow. When he turned, finally, he saw the butcher's face, as if in a dream. "Perhaps you should check on her?"

"Yes, of course, I will," William said, turning away from the crowd, staggering back toward the rooms above his storefront. "She's well," he said again, for the benefit of the four men who were following him, solemn-faced.

He wasn't sure why they were there. There were others down on the street, scattering, going from door to door and checking on all unaccounted-for inhabitants, even as the hearse turned before the chapel, and pulled to a stop in the same place the other had sat. It waited for them to carry out their dead, but Thomas Green's body was already gone, and so the hearse could only have come for Jacob Collins.

Agnes was in her bed, just as he'd left her, sleeping peacefully.

"You see?" William said, in a whisper, so as not to wake his wife. "She's much improved today. On the mend, I would dare to say."

Except that Thaddeus Tully leaned over her, put his hand against her wrist, and said, "She's dead."

She wasn't dead. William knew that well enough; he'd just spoken to her not an hour ago. "You've no idea what you're talking about," William snarled, and shoved Thaddeus away from the bed, snatching up the fire poker from its stand to sweep it at the whole lot of them, as they tried to advance. It was warm, still; he'd been keeping the fire lit, for his wife, and the room was hot enough to raise a sweat beneath his jacket.

"She's *dead*, William," Thaddeus repeated softly, holding out his hands in a gesture of peace. "The hearse will carry her for you, in all its splendor. Put that poker down, and we'll bear her out."

"No." He said it mostly to himself, and partly to his wife; he lowered the poker with one hand, while the other reached out to catch up the same outstretched wrist that Thaddeus had touched. There was warmth in her, though when he lifted her hand she did not move. She'd been in the same state for three days, though, before that morning. She'd laid still as a corpse, but she'd breathed.

He watched the blankets over her side, and could swear he saw them move.

"No," he said again, louder. "The hearse will not have her. It's here for the Collins boy. Go and check. Agnes will be fine."

"It's not here for Jacob," Thaddeus said. "It's come to take Agnes to the next place. She'll be waiting for you there."

William shook his head. "She's not dead. You'll not load her alive into that ghost carriage. The hearse may go away empty."

Erasmus Carstairs sighed, taking off his hat and holding it to his chest. "They don't go away, William, you know that. They sit, and they wait, and if a body is not loaded then someone else will die, and if that body is not given either, then there will be another one, until a body is given up. You've grown up here. You know as well as we all do that the hearse must be given its passenger."

William swung the iron again, the sweep of it passing over his wife's body; she did not move. "Then by God let it take someone else!"

Erasmus rushed him when the poker was gone too far in the other direction, and William couldn't bring it back in time; Erasmus's body hit him low, knocking the wind from him and the weapon from his hand. They tumbled together into the wall, then onto the floor; Erasmus's body was a crushing, solid weight, and his huge hands pinned William down easily, though Thaddeus came and helped.

William howled like a wounded dog when they pulled the blankets away from his poor wife's body. He thought of how cold she must be, sick as she was, even as they were wrapping her in her own bed linens, like a winding sheet. She made no protest, meek and gentle as she always was, even as they wrapped the shroud around her head.

When they bore her out, he shrieked and twisted like a creature possessed; he cursed their names and all their descendants, cried out an alternation of threats and entreaties. Something in his shoulder wrenched viciously and his thrashing against Erasmus's immovable bulk bloodied his nose.

"You look too hard for death," he told them. "She has been at the brink for days, but this morning she ate and spoke; she has only fallen into her exhaustion again. I tell you she is living. Thaddeus, your own wife watched over her while I was gone; let her come again and tell you the truth of it. Take Agnes's little hand mirror, and see her breath in it."

"The reverend will have the final word of her, before she's sent into the afterlife," Thaddeus promised. "She will not go to the hearse alive. I am profoundly sorry for the loss you've suffered, but she is *already gone.*"

They didn't let him loose until the sound of hooves and wheels broke the silence of the street, and even then Erasmus only reluctantly moved away.

"Go on down," he said, his face tipped toward the floor, William's blood on his sleeve. "Go down and see the carriage away."

William needed no further prompting. He scrambled to his feet, then clattered down the stairs, running through the door the impromptu pallbearers had left open behind them.

The funeral carriage was already passing his home; inside, Agnes's pale hand lay limp against the glass, having come free of its wrappings, as if she had been reaching for him.

He stumbled after the vehicle, his desperation like a living thing trying to claw its way out of his stomach. The funeral carriage came from another place, and whether from the ether or the pits of Hell, no one knew. The coachman was otherworldly, his horses like flawless puppets to his direction, but it was as solid as anything real: it could be touched. If its latch could be closed, then it could be opened, too.

"Stop!" William yelled at the coachman, running for the carriage as if he could hold it back by determination alone. "You cannot take her! She's alive! She reaches out her hand for me! Please!"

The coachman didn't so much as turn and look, even when William's fist thudded against the glass window, even when he rounded the back of the carriage and tried to slide open the simple latch. It wouldn't budge, as if it had been locked, though there was no such mechanism holding it in place.

Someone's hands tried to pull him away, but he jerked free, throwing a blind elbow behind him that seemed to reach its mark; the hands fell away again.

"Damn you!" He struck out again, this time lashing his fist against the low top of the carriage, as if to break through the solid wood. "I already gave you a body, you cursed thing, you can't have hers as well!"

He ran to the front of the vehicle instead: if the animals could not go forward, then neither could the vehicle. He grasped each horse by their inside reins, just behind the bit, pressing his fists back toward the carriage with all his might, to force the animals to a stop.

The horses, however, paid him no mind at all; the only cue they obeyed was their master's, and he had not bid them to stop. William stumbled backwards, desperately holding his grip; the horses were unnaturally strong and solid against the full force of his own body, their heads still held high where any other creature would be wrenched down by William's weight.

"Stop them," he snarled to the coachman, who was staring at him just as the other one had, when he had passed it a lifetime ago on the road. "Stop them, and give me back my wife!"

The coachman raised his head again, to survey the path ahead. He did not urge his horses to move on any more quickly, nor stop to rid his team of the unwanted nuisance. The horses drove forward at their regular pace. William pulled at them desperately, sawing the bits against their mouths, but it was like trying to push back a train.

He had the thought to try another tack: to leap onto the footboard, and try to throw the driver off, or to climb onto the carriage

itself, and let the coachman bear him away, too, whatever the destination.

He had the thought, just distracting enough to matter, and then
he stumbled over his own feet, lost his grip on the team's reins, and
fell.

The horses did not pause for this, either. His own fall and their
forward motion sent him first into the solid end of the carriage's central shaft, where it ran up between the two horses; the shaft struck
him beneath his breastbone, making something crack in his chest,
and sent him rolling to one side and right beneath the horses' feet.

The one above him did not try to trample him. It behaved still
as if entirely unaware of his presence; it drove its feet toward the
earth in exactly the same rhythm, with the same force, with very real
weight behind each footfall. William Baker only happened to be beneath it, for those few steps, and felt every inch of the impact: the
crackling of the bones in his hand as a forefoot came down upon it;
the glancing iron-shod blow to the side of his head feeling like the
strike of a hammer, the sudden fire of agony as a hind foot stepped
into the softest parts of his gut.

He watched in a daze as the singletree passed over him, the
chains at the ends of the tugs jangling, then the doubletree, and then
the bottom of the carriage as it rolled over his head without pausing,
the wheel passing close to his ruined hand but, mercifully, not rolling over him altogether.

He lay there for an endless moment, in a silence that felt almost
blessed, with pain licking at what felt like every part of his body, as if
he were on fire, as if hell had come for him early.

"What did you mean, you already gave them a body?"

The voice belonged to Mrs. Green, and suddenly she was there,
standing over him in her black skirts. She made no attempt to kneel
and aid him.

William had no answer that would give her satisfaction; he
craned his neck back, as well as he was able, and watched the car-

riage continue to draw away, well out of his reach. The sound of it seemed enormous, though it was far away.

"What did you mean by it?" Mrs. Green's voice said, strident but distant.

William had a vague awareness of others gathering around them, other voices, but all he could see was the carriage, the latched back of it, the horses' feet still on their inexorable march.

Someone prodded at William's cracked ribcage, and when he moaned, they drew back and delivered a kick. The sound of the crowd around him rose, and more blows fell, one after another. He was hardly sensible to them, already consumed by pain, as injured by a mere jostle as he was by a hit.

The sound of the carriage did not diminish. It was there still: the jingling of harness, the relentless turning of wheels, hooves against earth, the patterned breathing of the horses.

At the bend of the road, another carriage appeared.

The two coachmen turned to one another as they passed, and politely tipped their tall black hats.

MAHO TO SATSUJIN

JASON J. McCUISTON

A COLD MIST LAY HEAVY IN THE GREEN HILLS, LIKE THE GRIEF THAT CLUNG TO Shiori's heart. Her eldest brother was dead, and she had to find the wise man so that Akio's spirit could pass on to the ancestors. She had spent the previous day climbing the hills behind her village to reach the road which ran through the heart of Kyushu. She was thankful for the solitude, the opportunity to master her emotions.

Just after dawn, having slept a few hours beneath a fallen sugi tree, she finally reached the muddy, rutted path. A narrower road leading toward Hakata branched off to the west. At the intersection, beside a small shrine to the god of the road, sat an old man, his head bowed beneath a wide-brimmed straw hat, his walking staff standing upright in the mud.

Shiori gasped when she saw the black bag on his back, the long row of prayer beads and badger teeth passing through his gnarled hands. Running across the muddy lane, she fell to her knees and bowed before him. "Are you the wise man from Hakata?"

Head down, she heard him pause in his prayers. He finished with a grunt. "I am from Hakata," he said. "There are a few there who can claim to be wise... But I suppose you are looking for me. My name is Haruto... Please, get up."

She stood and watched as the old man rose to his feet with surprising grace. He was tall and lean, with a straight back and weathered face; eyes as black as his stained kimono and leggings. His straw sandals hung from his sash beside a polished fox skull; his bare feet caked with mud. He plucked his staff from the ground and stepped toward the forest behind her. "Come along, girl."

"My name is Shiori," she said, hurrying to keep up. "You... were expecting me?"

"I was expecting someone," the old man said. "The *kami* told me to come to this crossroad and wait; I was needed. Now, if you will give me one of the two rice balls in your pouch, I will listen to your story on the way to your village."

Shiori gawped. "How did you know I have two rice balls? Did the spirits tell you that?"

Haruto chuckled. "No, dear girl. Your clothes, of good quality for a peasant, are not too terribly stained. You couldn't have traveled more than a day before reaching me, and Hakata is another two days' travel from the crossroads. I assumed you had been given enough rations to make the first leg of the trip."

Shiori surrendered a rice ball, slightly disappointed. "So sorry, but I actually have three rice balls in my pouch. I did not eat yesterday."

Haruto grunted in appreciation, took the first bite. "Then you must have loved the dead person very much."

"How did you know ...?"

"Why else travel so far for a wise man? The island is thick with wandering monks and priests who could bless your crops and catches; your livestock and children; preside over your weddings and funerals. But only a wise man, a practitioner of the old ways, can open the mouth of the dead, ensuring that the spirit will find its way to the ancestors."

Shiori bowed and wiped a tear from her eye. "My brother, Akio. He was the headman of our village, Nishihama. He fell ill shortly after the terrible storm, and he never got over it. He died yesterday morning."

Haruto finished the rice ball with a nod. "Nishihama ... I have heard of that place, but not for some time... The storm, did you say? The *kami* also mentioned something about Korean pirates ...?"

"Yes. The storm drove a ship close to our beach, and some of the sailors came ashore that night. My two brothers, Akio and Jirou, were watching, fearing the Mongols had returned. When they reported it to our master, he gathered his household warriors and drove them off. I think six of the Koreans were killed. Before being executed, a prisoner told the samurai that their ship was part of a larger fleet harassing the straits. The master and his men have been away, patrolling the coast ever since.

"When Akio fell ill," she continued, "we thought it was the spirits of the dead pirates cursing him for his role in their deaths. We had a priest create a ward against the ghosts and say prayers. But they did not work."

Haruto grunted. "It may not have been the pirates. I remember now... Nishihama was once the home of a powerful witch. In the days long before the Hojo came to power. Perhaps he has returned from the dead to plague the living?"

Shiori blinked, felt a cold chill run down her spine and settle in her belly. The thought of witchcraft made her skin crawl. She was glad when the old man chose to walk in relative silence the rest of the day, quietly chanting to himself. As the return trip to Nishihama was mostly downhill, they made excellent time.

The sun was setting as they reached the outskirts of the village. Shiori clasped her hands in prayer as they passed through the old cemetery in the foothills. She tried not to look at the fresh grave that awaited her beloved brother. The priest would come at first light to purify the ground, and soon Akio would be placed in that hole forever.

"Hey!" a coarse voice shouted. "Who are you? What do you want?"

Shiori looked up as Haruto came to a halt. A shabby figure emerged from behind a row of ancient stone markers, a raised lantern in one hand, a wooden spade clotted with black dirt in the other. "Oh, it's you, Shiori," the ugly old man growled, smelling of saké and sweat. Looking Haruto up and down, he gave an unimpressed sneer. "So this is the holy man, eh? The wizard? The conman who'll make more than me, though I dug the grave *and* built the coffin, just for saying some superstitious nonsense over the corpse?"

"Haruto will suffice. And you are?"

"This is Katashi," Shiori said, forcing her revulsion of the man behind a wall of good manners. "He is the undertaker."

"Obviously," Haruto grunted, making Shiori feel foolish. "Could you show me the grave of the famous witch, Katashi?"

The undertaker flinched and looked away. "No witch buried in this cemetery," he grumbled. "Least none I know of."

"Really?" Haruto pointed his staff directly at a cracked and faded marker and said, "I thought it might have been that old one there. The one that says, 'Ren.'" Shiori blushed and looked away, embarrassed that the wise man was illiterate. The plank read "Naomi."

Katashi scowled at the marker indicated by the wise man and shook his head. "No. Ren was no witch. A bastard for sure, but no witch. Died when I was a boy."

"Thank you. If you'll excuse us, we have business in the village. I'd like to say it was nice meeting you." With that, Haruto strode through the cemetery, Shiori at his heels.

"You don't like him," Haruto said as they entered the village proper. Nishihama was nestled at the foot of the green hills, where two large streams divided a white-sand beach; rice paddies edged the northwestern stream to their left, and the master's fortified house stood higher up in the southeastern hills to the right. The fading sun glistened on the waves of Kanmon Straits, directly ahead.

Shiori frowned. "Katashi is lazy and uncouth. The only reason he's working this late is because he's digging the one grave he has looked forward to for a long time. He hated my brother. Akio never let him get away with his drunkenness and greed."

Haruto grunted. They moved quickly through the small scattering of tiny houses and huts, ignoring the curious stares and solemn bows from the villagers, until they reached the headman's house. White-shaded lanterns glowed on the porch and on the gate. The old man paused in the garden to look at a pair of sand-encrusted shovels before entering the house. This embarrassed Shiori; everyone in the family had been too distraught over Akio's sudden illness and passing to bother with cleaning the tools. She hurriedly apologized and put them in the garden shed.

In short order, they were seated on the tatami of the house's front room. The small household shrine was covered by a white cloth to prevent the spirit of the dead from entering it. Welcoming Haruto to the house, Shiori introduced the wise man to her family.

Grim-faced Jirou now sat in the place of his dead brother as head of the household; his small, plain wife, Mitsu, sat behind him, almost in the corner. Iwa, the thin, ashen-faced matriarch wept softly for her dead son; comforted by the lovely Sayo, Akio's young widow.

After pleasantries and refreshment, and the particulars of his fee were arranged, Haruto asked, "Have the proper preparations been observed?"

Jirou nodded. "While Mitsu closed and covered our shrine, Sayo gave Akio his last taste of water. And then the two of us washed his body."

Sayo somberly averted her sparkling eyes. "We then announced his death to the *kami*."

Jirou added, "I went to commission the coffin from Katashi while Sayo went to Daichi the blacksmith for Akio's burial knife. She spent all afternoon making sure that it was perfect. Meanwhile, Mother and Mitsu prepared his room, and arranged his head on the pillow, facing north until the coffin was made. Katashi was surprisingly efficient in this."

"We have made daily offerings of Akio's favorite food to his spirit," Sayo said, slight color at her throat. "And Jirou personally informed the local monk at the village shrine that Akio's spirit would soon be returning.

"Good," Haruto said, "Then it is time I performed the task for which I was summoned. Shiori, you will assist me."

Shiori felt the blood drain from her face. She had loved Akio like a father. To this point, she had avoided seeing his lifeless body. As soon as he had died, she had volunteered to retrieve the wise man in hopes of staving off this inevitable pain.

Still, she knew her duty. Bowing, she said, "Yes."

"Since you have arrived ahead of schedule, Haruto-san," Jirou said, "I must go and inform the priest and the rest of the village that Akio's wake and funeral will be held tomorrow."

As her brother left the house, Shiori followed Haruto into the back room. It was dark and filled with the thick scent of incense and pine. The stench of death and decay was also present, but she tried to ignore it. Beside the small coffin, a low table was set with a simple azalea arrangement, a stick of burning incense, and a single flickering candle. On the tatami in front of this was a bowl of rice, grilled fish, and steamed vegetables, Akio's favorite meal.

Shiori squeezed her eyes tight to cut off the tears.

Haruto placed and then lit white candles all around Akio's body. Shiori swallowed down a fresh sob, a bitter pain biting into her heart at the sight of her brother's waxy, sagging skin. She saw him as he had been in life, stern and strong, but with a twinkle in his eye; a smile that always seemed to hover just at the edge of his lips.

Haruto knelt beside the corpse's head. Chanting a spell, his fingers moved through the rosary of beads and teeth, then made the arcane signs of the *mudra*. He motioned for her to kneel at Akio's feet. Resisting the urge to vomit and shaking terribly, Shiori complied.

Haruto leaned over the dead man's face and said in a low whisper, "Go to the ancestors, Akio-san. Become a *kami* of great joy and happiness to watch over your family for generations to come... But first, tell me how you died." He then gently opened the corpse's mouth.

Shiori nearly screamed when her lifeless brother gasped, "*Murdered ... Witchcraft...*" The candles went out.

Haruto grunted, said, "I thought as much."

Shiori fainted...

𝕮 𝕮 𝕮

She woke the next morning to a bloodcurdling scream.

Hurrying from her room, she saw Haruto rushing into her mother's opened chamber. She followed. Inside, Sayo, her long black hair loose and her kimono askew, lay prostrate and weeping across a bloated corpse. It was her horrified scream which had awakened the household.

Shiori's knees buckled, tears blurring her vision. She toppled to the tatami in a heap. Bile filled her throat at the sight of her dead mother; Iwa's white, unseeing eyes staring at the ceiling. Shiori gasped, "What is happening to us...?"

Jirou and Mitsu appeared at the door and crumpled, wailing in each other's arms.

Haruto knelt over the old woman's grey, twisted face. "She was poisoned... The witch who killed Akio is growing stronger, braver, or both. Unless we do something, this entire family will most likely die; perhaps even the whole village."

Jirou, tears flowing down his face, his fists clenched on the floor, looked at the old man. "What can we do?"

Shiori blinked in surprise at the answer. "Bury your loved ones. Your sister and I will find the witch."

Arrangements for Akio's wake had already been made, so the morning was spent trying to prepare Iwa for her own burial before the mourners arrived. Haruto was a great help in this, as the family members were already taxed to their emotional limits. While Sayo and Jirou dealt with the wake's final arrangements, Shiori and Mitsu assisted the wise man in cleaning and presenting the old woman's corpse. Mitsu hurried to Katashi's hut to request another coffin and another grave.

At some point, Shiori became numb to the pain and confusion. She barely remembered sitting at her mother's feet as Haruto performed the opening of the mouth ceremony; acknowledged rather than heard Iwa's unnatural, choked answer to the question concerning her death: "*Ku* viper."

She seemed to drift through Akio's wake and funeral ceremony, which occupied the entirety of the afternoon. The ceremonial transfer of his spirit to the wooden funerary tablet; the serving of refreshments to the mourning villagers; the priest's eulogy and prayers; the farewell ceremony where she said goodbye for the last time; and the procession where she and the rest of the surviving family followed Akio's coffin up the hill to the cemetery all slid past Shiori in a blur, as if they were things happening to someone else.

Memories she would process some other time.

The brief graveside ceremony was the last stage. Since her mother was now dead, they could not begin the purification of the house until she was laid to rest as well. Shiori dug her fingernails into the palms of her hands as she watched Akio's friends toss small, symbolic offerings into the grave; polished stones, seashells, bits of silk, and other little treasures. When volunteers began to fill in the grave with the purified black dirt, the tears finally came. In the midst of all the grief, an anger welled up within her. *Where is Katashi? Why is he not here doing his job? Did he get too drunk celebrating Akio's death?*

Just before dusk, after the lengthy funeral proceedings, Shiori knelt beside Haruto at the village shrine, praying that the ancestors and the local *kami* would welcome the souls of her brother and mother, and that they would bestow a blessing upon her family. When she was finished, she asked, "Why do you need my help to find this witch? Why did you want me to assist with the ceremonies for my brother and mother?"

"Because family must be present, and you are the only one I can trust."

She blinked, understanding. "You think a member of my family is doing this?"

Haruto grunted, rubbed his chin. "I know it isn't the ghost of the old witch. The *kami* have told me that his spirit now resides in Yomi. Which means that our murderer is a living practitioner of *ku* magic; the evil arts."

"You think Jirou could have killed his own brother and mother? Or Sayo or Mitsu? Jirou looked up to Akio like a father, just as I did. And he worshipped Mother. He could never do such a terrible thing!"

"Sayo adored Akio and loved Mother as if she were her own; why else would she spend so much time and money to keep herself beautiful for her husband? Why would she spend so much time making sure Daichi the blacksmith took care of the household tools and utensils?

"And Mitsu couldn't hurt a mouse, even if she wanted to. She's scared of her own shadow, can barely stand to be around people. She spends most of her free time walking alone in the hills. The only time I've even heard her speak was when Mother would have her read scripture to her."

Haruto grunted and shook his head. "Sadly, there are many motives for family members to kill one another. Jealousy for one; thanks to his brother's death, Jirou now holds the position of headman, which also elevates his wife's position above that of her attractive sister-in-law.

"Adultery is another. Husbands are not the only men for whom wives make themselves beautiful; especially if there is a strong young blacksmith in the village.

"Then there is pure anger and hatred. Perhaps little Mitsu simply grew tired of fearing her own shadow. Tired of living in everyone else's."

"If it was another member of my family," Shiori objected, "then why kill Mother? She was harmless; old and helpless! Her death benefited no one!"

"The witch may have had a reason. Or maybe just testing his or her powers."

"I think it is Katashi," she said. "He hated my brother. He must have found the witch's grave and somehow learned *ku* magic... I've seen him creeping around our house lately. Mother must have confronted him; accused him of stealing or something. She could have a wicked tongue at times, perhaps she insulted him about his drinking and uncleanliness."

Rising and taking up his staff, Haruto said, "I doubt it is that simple. But come. We will look into it. First, I think we should stop by the blacksmith's. Just for the sake of argument."

The sun was hanging low above the western horizon when they came to Daichi's house. As he had participated in the wake and funeral along with the rest of the village, no smoke issued from his forge. They found the big man in his workshop, using the remainder of the day to tidy up in preparation for tomorrow's responsibilities. He bowed profusely as they entered. "Welcome, Haruto-san," he said. "Welcome, Shiori-san. Again, I am sorry for your loss."

"Thank you," Shiori said. Haruto grunted and let his gaze wander around the shop, taking in the details before he returned Daichi's bow with a curt nod.

"What can I do to thank you for the honor of your presence?"

Daichi asked. "Do you need me to fix something for you? Craft something for you? A new knife, perhaps?"

"Have you ever made a crown?" Haruto asked. "Of iron?"

Daichi blinked, slack-jawed. "Crown? Of iron? No, Haruto-san. But I can try if you like."

"No," the old man said with a shrug. "That won't be necessary." He turned to go, then paused, said, "But I trust you will wait the proper amount of time before you propose marriage to the widow Sayo, eh?"

Daichi's eyes widened and his mouth dropped. He fell to his knees and pressed his face to the sooty floor. "Please forgive me, Shiori-san. I am sorry, so very sorry."

Shiori blinked, amazed and revolted. She wanted to pick up something heavy and smash Daichi's skull and then go do the same to Sayo. Before she could move, Haruto took her by the hand and led her from the smithy. "Come along, my dear. There's been far too much bloodshed in this village as it is."

As they approached the beach, Shiori fell to her knees and covered her face. "How could they?" she said through clenched teeth.

Haruto knelt beside her, put an arm around her shoulder. "I am sorry, Shiori-chan. This is a hard betrayal, but at least we know it was not Daichi who killed your mother and brother."

She sniffed and wiped the tears from her eyes. "What? Are you sure?"

Haruto helped her to her feet and waited for her to dust the sand from her kimono. "Daichi may be an adulterer, but he is no liar. In fact, I'm amazed they were able to keep the affair quiet in a village this small. He was more than perplexed when I asked him about the iron crown, which means he's never seen one before. If he was the witch, he would have known what I was talking about."

"What does an iron crown have to do with anything? And does that mean that it is Sayo, after all?"

Haruto grunted and tapped the sand with his staff. "A *kanawa* is an iron circlet set with prongs for mounting candles. It looks like a crown and is worn to cast dark magic.

"As for Akio's widow, I suppose it could be Sayo. She seems to have a way of beguiling people; make it easy to keep both of her secrets... We will see."

Shiori frowned, chewed her lower lip. How long had she known her sister-in-law; trusted her; loved her? Could she really be a witch and a murderer? She was most definitely an adulteress.

"Come along then, we've others to speak to." With the clatter of his rosary against the fox skull on his belt, the old man moved toward the run-down hovel at the far end of the beach. "Unless I miss my guess, that is the home of Katashi."

"You are not wrong." The sunlight was all but gone by the time they reached the shanty. It was surrounded by clusters of tools, piles of chopped wood, stacks of pine boards, and several unfinished caskets. Black-tailed gulls screeched at them and scattered as they approached.

"Stay here," Haruto said, brandishing his staff and climbing onto the low porch. "I sense danger inside." In one motion, he flung open the sliding door and disappeared into the darkened front room.

Shiori, her curiosity greater than her fear, and still angry at the day's revelations, ignored Haruto's warning and hurried after him.

She screamed at what she saw in the shadows.

Katashi's twisted corpse lay sprawled on the mildew-stained tatami. His glassy, unseeing eyes stared at her from a face as black as coal. The foul stench of corruption filled the tiny room, and she heard a loud hiss from the corner; saw movement of scaly coils.

"Don't move," Haruto said in a low voice. "It is not a normal mamushi viper. It is a thing of *ku* magic. Very evil; very powerful."

The huge snake slithered along the juncture of the wall and the floor, its massive head aimed like an arrow at Shiori's breast. But it was more than long enough to strike either of them without warning.

Haruto's hands moved faster than Shiori could see, becoming a blur of dull light. He whispered words of power.

The viper hissed, coiled, struck.

Haruto's staff moved like a thunderbolt, crushing the snake's skull in midair. It fell across Katashi's chest in a writhing, twisting curve, dead as the man on the floor.

Shiori clutched the door for support and caught her breath. Haruto glanced at her, said, "If you are able, please light a lamp and help me search the house."

In the back room of the small hut, among the dead undertaker's squalor, they found an old red-lacquered box filled with yellowing pages and scrolls. And an iron circlet fitted with three prongs. Haruto studied the symbols on the parchment with a frown. "These are very ancient and evil spells."

"You can read?" Shiori asked.

"Of course I can read," Haruto grunted. "What kind of wise man can't read?"

He held the small iron circlet in his hands, eyeing it closely and glancing at Katashi's blackened face. "And this is the *kanawa* I mentioned, worn on the head with three lit candles to work *ku* magic during the dark Hour of the Ox."

"That explains it," Shiori said with relief. "Katashi discovered the witch's grave in the cemetery, plundered it for these spells, and used the magic to kill my brother and mother. But the *ku* snake grew too powerful for him to control."

Haruto smiled at her. "That is precisely what the real witch wants us to believe." He stared at something through the opened door, in the small garden. Stuffing the evil magic into his black bag, he moved in that direction. "Bring the lantern."

Outside, he knelt down by a pair of small indentations; barely noticeable. Pulling a pouch from the black bag, Haruto produced some dried mugwort and carefully placed it into the depressions. "Let me see the fire," he said before using the lantern's wick to ignite the herb.

He stood as it blazed and burned away. Looking back along the beach toward the rest of the village, he said, "Go back to your house and gather your family. I'll be there shortly and we will expose the witch."

"How?" Shiori asked, but the old man ignored her as he picked up one of the shovels from beside the house and strode quickly away. Shrugging, she gave one last glance at Katashi's hovel, then set off to do as Haruto had instructed.

An hour later, Shiori sat with her brother and sisters-in-law in the front room of the headman's house, knowing one of them was a murderous witch. White candles and incense burned in the corners. The shrine remained covered. Her mother's body lay in the back room, awaiting the coffin that Katashi would never make.

Jirou sat stoically in the place of honor, facing the opened door, expecting the wise man's return. Mitsu, however, could not hide her grief at the terrible and sudden losses to the family; trembling with whimpering sobs as tears ran down her face. Sayo, in contrast, looked as lovely as ever; more so in fact, her quiet, if affected, sadness adding a depth to her beauty.

Shiori balled her hands into fists, wanted to pull Sayo's lustrous black hair out by the roots. She could still be the witch and murderer, after all; her betrayal still a crime worthy of punishment. But, in honor of her family's mourning, she refrained from such a dishonorable display. Barely.

In truth, Shiori was surprised at the disparate reactions of the two women. Her mother had all but ignored little Mitsu save when she wanted some odd chore done, meanwhile doting on Akio's pretty wife, reveling in brushing her long hair while listening to Sayo's beautiful singing. She did not ponder on the surprising disparity long, however, as Haruto soon stomped onto the porch.

Jirou's eyes widened as the wise man entered the house.

"Here is what all the fuss has been about," Haruto grunted, setting a heavy, sand-encrusted iron chest on the floor. Flicking the lid open, he filled the candle-lit room with the glimmer of gold. "The Korean pirates who came ashore did so to hide this treasure in case their ship was sunk by the storm.

"And two brothers saw them do it," he said, sitting cross-legged across from Jirou. "But they did not report it to their master. They knew he would take the gold for himself. They kept it a secret. Greed is another powerful motive for murder, as it turns out."

Jirou bowed his face to the floor. "It was Akio's idea," he said. "As headman, he wanted to make sure that the village would be taken care of in times of want..."

"How... did you know?" Shiori blurted, gaping at the unimaginable wealth before her.

"The shovels outside this house yesterday," Haruto said. "They were covered with sand, yet the soil around the village is thick and dark, as displayed on all of Katashi's dirty tools. They had obviously been used to dig for something on the beach quite recently.

"It was too much of a coincidence for the troubles to have begun so soon after the pirates' arrival. Even you saw their deaths as the cause of Akio's illness. Once I considered the only reason such a small group of men would come ashore during a storm, it was easy to reconstruct what had happened. A helpful *kami* led me to where Akio and Jirou had reburied the treasure."

"You killed your own brother?" Sayo gasped at Jirou, who remained prostrated on the floor. "Your own mother? Over this gold?"

"No," Haruto said. "But he shared this secret with his wife." The old man turned his gaze upon Mitsu, who stared at the floor through tears. "His wife who had recently discovered something rather interesting near the old cemetery on one of her solitary walks in the hills."

Haruto tossed the *kanawa* to the floor in front of Mitsu. It was the perfect size for her little head.

Mitsu did not look up. "I...do not know what you're talking about," she whispered.

Haruto moved with the quickness he had displayed against the serpent. Pushing Mitsu onto her back, he exposed the soles of her tiny feet. They were burnt as if by hot coals.

"I thought so," the wise man said, releasing the cowering girl. "I burned *moxa* in your footprints at Katashi's hut. The spell punishes intruders and compels them toward justice.

"You, Mitsu, are the witch. You killed Akio so that your husband could become headman and claim this treasure. With that, you acquired a taste for murder.

"You killed your mother-in-law simply because you hated her. You killed Katashi because he knew that it was you who had plundered the witch's grave. He was snooping around here to try and blackmail you. Isn't that right, Mitsu?"

Mitsu rubbed her blistered feet. "Yes," she squeaked. "That horrible man threatened to tell everyone unless I agreed to sleep with him."

"So you sent the *ku* viper after him. And while we prepared for the wake and funeral, you planted the spells and the *kanawa* in his hut when you went to commission the coffin for Iwa, hoping I would think the mystery solved and simply go away."

"Why didn't it work?" Mitsu cried. "It should have worked!"

"Because Katashi was illiterate," Haruto said. "I ascertained that when I first met the man. Very hard to understand magic spells if you can't read them. But *you* can read, isn't that right? Your mother-in-law forced you to read to her, didn't she?"

"I tried to teach her," Mitsu sniffed. "But she wouldn't have it. *'Why should I read when I have you to read for me?'* she always said. She hated me no matter how good I was to her. She treated me like a slave!"

Jirou sat back on his haunches and stared at his wife as if he had never seen her before. Sayo's dark eyes danced from Mitsu to the sparkling treasure, her lovely face devoid of emotion.

Shiori stared at her murderous sister-in-law. She could not believe it, her mind racing along the path of clues Haruto had exposed since his arrival. She could find no flaw in his reasoning, and Mitsu no longer denied it. Clearing her throat, she said, "You are a witch and a murderer. You deserve to die."

"That she does," Haruto said, rising to his feet. "But that is up to the samurai to decide. Keep her bound and gagged until your master returns, and you should have no further reason to fear her... I will pray for this home, for this family, and for this village."

Shiori watched the old man leave as Jirou and Sayo grabbed Mitsu and held her down. "What about the gold?" she called after Haruto.

The wise man paused at the gate and lowered his head. "That, my dear, is no concern of mine." Smiling, he turned and walked away.

HEARSE

JENNIFER R. POVEY

DON'T DISRESPECT THE DEAD? HA. I'LL DISRESPECT THE DEAD ALL I LIKE. Well, okay. I exist to respect them, but that doesn't mean I don't have opinions.

Always got opinions about those I carry. Sometimes they're about the dead. A lot of the time they're about the living, too, because you can't separate the two. People have this weird idea that they're individuals.

They're not. They're an entire bundle of connections, that's why the dead don't really leave, not altogether.

That's why people fight, of course. They fight because they care and wish they didn't, because they don't have the guts to walk away. Not even from the dead.

Especially not from the dead. That's what they mean. You don't disrespect the dead because once somebody's dead you can't ever break those connections, or fix them. You end up being the young woman who's dry-eyed at her grandmother's funeral because she stopped talking to her when she was a teenager over something that seemed so important at the time. Even more so now it can't be fixed.

So they pretend, they sit on them. They always pretend.

I'm dead too, of course. Just my luck to get stuck as a ghost.

Even more my luck to get stuck haunting a hearse. It happens sometimes. It's always, when it happens, the first person to be carried by it. Just like the first person buried in a graveyard.

White Willows is the best in that regard. Somebody remembered that happens, and they buried a dog first. The dog guards the dead.

Good doggie.

I like Willow, she's a good doggie. I don't know what she was called in life. Me? I wasn't a good person as a person and I ain't one as a hearse either. Fortunately, nobody expects a hearse to be a good person.

As long as I start in the cold. Which I do most of the time. There was that one time when I had a very strong opinion about the corpse...and even if the person's fully passed on, which they haven't always, they leave a residue.

A very strong opinion. I deliberately broke down. Somebody else could deal with the murdering son of a bitch. I'd feel it for days, weeks, maybe months.

That's not the worst. The worst is when the coffin doesn't need all the space, if you know what I mean. Sometimes they're still here enough to ask me why that's all they got.

I can't answer that. I mean, we all die, we all need something like me sooner or later, except for the truly unlucky ones who are never found.

All of us.

I'm lucky, I suppose. I ain't in hell. I ain't in a bad place. But there was that one time...yes, that's the story you're waiting around for, isn't it.

There was that one time when I got to get my own, as it were. Not revenge, that would imply it was something which happened to me. It didn't. I've been in this scrap heap for fifteen years, ya know.

Hearses last a long time. I suppose I'll pass on when it wears out, I'm not sure, and maybe I'll be judged by this.

I don't care. I want to be judged.

So, again, it's not always about the dead. Sometimes it's about the living. Now, I'm lucky. Generally, I only get to carry the body.

Sometimes their spouse will be in the front seat. Sometimes. They're usually in the limo. So, I only get to see some of the fights.

Weddings are worse. Mine certainly was. Before you ask if I miss her? I miss the sex, that's all.

Yeah. Sometimes you just...realize you shouldn't have gotten married. That's the way of things. Don't marry for looks. Oh, wait. Not an issue for you, is it.

Okay. So, that particular day, we had a twofer. One morning, one afternoon. The morning one was one of the good ones. The deceased was ninety, died in his sleep, loved and mourned by children, grandchildren, a couple of greats. Those are the good ones. People are sad but appreciative, they understand it's part of the cycle.

Those are the good ones most of the time. Sometimes I'll hear them bickering about the inheritance at the graveside. It's a good thing our limos aren't haunted. If they were, I'd feel real sorry for the ghosts, 'cause I'm sure they have to listen to that the entire way.

The drivers have a window they can close, at least, to give people "privacy." Ha, it's mostly so the drivers don't have to listen.

But this wasn't one of those. Everyone seemed to be, if not getting on, at least drawn together by shared grief. Which might not be the best thing to be drawn together by, but being drawn together is a silver lining.

It was the second one that was the problem.

So, you probably want to know what I can do, as a ghost haunting a hearse. I already mentioned I can break down. I mean, it's just a matter of seizing something up and then un-seizing it later. I can feel how the engine works, it's like my heart now, except I have more control over it.

I can mess up the climate control, if I really want to express my opinion of something. I can change channels on the radio.

All of which would be more fun if I had live passengers to play with. Charles, my driver, is a decent person. Occasionally I've done something to cheer him up. I think he suspects, but he's never said anything to anyone.

Maybe he's worried they'd show up with an exorcist. I don't particularly want to be exorcised, so...I mean, I don't mind being a hearse, not really. And I can't be sure where I'd end up.

I didn't mean to do it, but I can't be sure...I don't know where people go. I know whether they go, whether they pass on or whether they get stuck somewhere, like me.

I think some people get reincarnated, too. Maybe it's the ones who believe in it or who really want it. I think I'd have preferred that. Another chance to get it all wrong, ya know. Yeah, I don't have much faith in myself.

But anyway. The second one was one of the bad ones. A teenager committed suicide. Leading cause of death for kids. They can't take it, sometimes, and I don't know whether it's in them or in the rest of us.

Probably the rest of us. Like I said, we're all connections, really. We don't and can't exist without others.

Probably the real reason I change Charlie's radio sometimes. So, I can feel that connection, because otherwise the only people I'd talk to would be on their way through and out.

And...well, it's not up or down. I don't think it's a simplistic as heaven or hell.

The kid wasn't passing on. He wasn't in any hurry whatsoever to pass on. He was raging. At his parents, who couldn't hear him. Blaming them. Maybe it was their fault. It often is. Not everyone was meant to be a parent.

Not everyone was meant to be a parent to a kid that ain't quite the same as others. I was a crappy father, too. I mean, I wasn't abusive or anything like that. Just not very good at it. Sam managed to turn out okay in spite of me. I'm real glad she managed to turn out okay. I wasn't good to her and her mother wasn't.

But she had something in her. This kid didn't. This kid hadn't turned out at all, and when they loaded in his body he was still tied to it, still raging.

I can talk to them. "Hey, kid."

"Hey..."

"Bobby, right?"

I always seem to know their names.

"You...called me by the right name."

Shock. Surprise. Even a little bit of fear.

"I always do." It's part of being what I am. I suppose, like the dog, I'm kind of a guardian. "Willow probably does too, but she's a dog."

A laugh. I had the feeling this was the first time the kid had laughed. Perhaps in a while. Perhaps ever

That he had never been happy. "What do they call you, then?"

"I don't want to tell you.

I accepted that. "They hurt you." It was true, it was deep. Perhaps I could talk him into passing on.

Perhaps I could do something else.

I could feel his anger, his rage. His pain. Nothing had ever been right for this one. Nothing had ever worked.

He blamed them.

I wished I could hear the conversation in the limo. I was glad I couldn't. I had a feeling I knew what it would be. Recriminations. Mother blaming father. Father regaling mother. Each of them trying to work out how they had failed at parenting and putting it on the other.

Threats of divorce lawyers.

That was when we had finally split, when Sam walked out.

She had walked out. This kid had done something far worse, far more final. He had left for good.

They had caused it. I could feel that.

And this was the time I snapped. Because you can't do this forever. You can't just know why everyone dies, and why everyone leaves, and why everyone fights. You can't sense all the poisoned connections and not, eventually, want to do something.

Even if it's something that might get me...dealt with.

I knew even at the time what might happen. I just stopped caring. That's what happens, somebody just stops caring. They become evil. Maybe only for a moment. Maybe for a lifetime. Maybe that moment...remember the murderous bastard...becomes the last moment.

Maybe they deserve it. We still make choices. I still made a choice. I just didn't care about the consequences to myself any more. I'm a ghost, after all. I've already died once.

You asked how much power I have. I can't really use the hearse as a body most of the time. But if I get angry enough, if I get sad enough, I can move it some. Maybe if I was angry all the time, like Bruce Banner, I'd be real dangerous and I'd have...somebody would have done something fifteen years ago, wouldn't they.

That's not what a poltergeist really is, but you know that. I bet you've gotten tired of explaining that to people. About poltergeists and teenagers and such.

About how powerful anger can be. As it slowly dawned on me what had really happened to Bobby, I got that angry.

They'd killed him. When they got out of the limo they weren't even looking at each other. I could see the guilt, the recrimination, but it was the father's words that did it.

"Well, now she won't be sinning any more."

It was those words. I knew he was blind to the truth, but the living often are. When you're dead, you see people as they really are. That includes the living. I could see how dark and hell-bound he was.

I could see how broken his wife was, but that she was no better. She'd not just let him do it, she'd genuinely come to believe he was right.

She wasn't a victim. Neither of them were.

I didn't want to involve Charlie in this. I like him, ya know. I'll miss him. He's a good man, he kind of deserves better than driving a hearse, except he enjoys it. He likes it. He says it's not makework and he doesn't have to deal with drunk assholes like he did when he drove a taxi.

So, I waited for him to go to the bathroom in the chapel. At least Willows has one. The dog gamboled after him. I sometimes thought he could see her, or at least sense her somehow. It was a good presence, a protective one.

They had the right idea with the dogs, although like most good superstitions, it had rather gone out of style lately. I personally thought that was distinctly unfortunate.

But then, I'm a ghost, I kind of exist because people are superstitious. Maybe. It's hard to tell. I know I'm real, I know there's a next place to go to. Beyond that, the whys of it, I'll leave to theologians.

Anyway. It was a gorgeous day, and there they were, arguing right in front of me.

Oops.

My handbrake failed.

She saw what was going on and no, she didn't help her husband get out of the way. I couldn't blame her, I wouldn't have risked myself for him either. She dived to one side.

He didn't.

Now, before you think anything, I'm not going that fast. Heavy, but not going that fast. I wasn't intending to kill him.

Okay, maybe I was, but I didn't. I wasn't applying quite enough force for that. He went flying, mind, and landed with a crunch, not getting back up.

He started to scream at Charles. Too late, I realized he would be the one blamed for it. Of course he would. Obviously, he hadn't parked me correctly. This might cost him his job, and I felt a guilt shiver through me.

How did I resolve this? How did I fix it? The guy deserved what I'd done. The kid was cheering.

But Charles didn't. And Charles was, while not my friend...I was too dead for friends...somebody I had a care for, a concern for.

I had to tell them what had happened. I had to make it so people would be mad with me, not him. Somehow.

I honked my horn. That couldn't happen by accident.

The priest who was there to bury the kid turned towards me. He...raised an eyebrow, then frowned.

Most people can't see ghosts. That's because they don't believe in us. Kids can. Dogs can, cats can...but I don't know what they really see. Or smell, perhaps, in the case of dogs. Smell is much more important to a dog than sight.

But he could, at least now I'd got his attention.

Maybe that would be enough. Maybe he could convince them I was to blame, not poor Charles. I couldn't be sure, though.

Charles came out of the restroom to see what happened. He looked shocked, and then guilty.

Of course, he'd think he did it too. I'd try to tell him as we went back. They were unloading the coffin now. Somebody had called an ambulance for the father, but he was insisting he had to see this through.

Even if he did seem to have a broken leg.

He deserved it. I told myself that as somebody got him into a chair.

He deserved it. The kid didn't. The kid wasn't fading quite yet, either. Maybe he wanted to see daddy carted off to the hospital.

He winked at me, but he didn't understand. I'd hurt a friend. I'd...well. I deserved to get sent to the other place.

Not for breaking a bigot's leg. For betraying a friend.

Charlie got in, and checked the brake. He checked everything.

I turned on the radio. It was playing "If I Could Turn Back Time."

"You did it," he said to me.

I couldn't answer yes.

"Why?"

I couldn't answer that, either. Will you tell him for me? Tell him what happened to Bobby, tell him why he couldn't ever be called Roberta?

The priest was doing the service. I could hear it dimly. They were grieving for Roberta, but there had never been a Roberta.

Only a Bobby.

That was what the kid wanted, I realized. Somebody, anybody, to call him by his real name. Somebody, anybody, to acknowledge him.

I couldn't do it. He knew, somehow, that I only saw what he wanted me to see.

It was the people who had driven him to his death that he needed to hear from. It was the people he had loved and who had in their twisted way loved him.

They had just loved the wrong person, the wrong image of that person. People do that. Heck, I'd done it.

I'd loved who I thought my wife was, not who she really was.

"I guess you don't have a song for that, right?"

I didn't. I could only play what was actually on the radio. I'd gotten lucky with the Aguilera. Or maybe I did have one. But it took a couple of minutes to search the satellite radio...I'd never have done it...to find "Salt" by Bad Suns. Which was all about being in the wrong body.

Charles frowned. "Oh...oh. It's one of those. You can't do anything like this again. You have to promise me."

I couldn't promise.

There was no way I could promise that I would never get that angry again, that I wouldn't act on it without thinking.

Or maybe I just couldn't find the song that explained how I felt.

So, yeah. It wasn't just that, of course. They fired Charles. He was replaced by a really stiff collared guy named Stephen.

Nobody believed Charles. Or the priest. And Stephen was boring. Any time the radio glitched, he turned it back to classical.

I didn't like him. And it was all my fault. Ghosts can get depressed, ya know. We can get upset and grieve and have all of those human emotions. They're just a little muted, thanks to not having a body any more.

The right one or otherwise. But I was still depressed. I missed Charles, and for the first time I wanted out of this situation. Even if out of this situation meant going to the bad place.

Yeah. That's how far down I was. Hell seemed like it would be better.

Somebody who knew I was there would make all the difference. Which ended up being...Stephen's girlfriend.

I don't know what she saw in him. Good in bed, I suppose. The first time I saw Maria, I wanted to tell her my story, so she would know that on its own can't make a marriage. Oh, sure, it's part of it. It's always part of it. But it ain't enough, not on it's own.

And there was something very sad about her. Something almost as sad as Bobby. Who was still hanging around.

But that wasn't the important thing. She could see me. You know that, though, as she's the one who called you.

Because I told her how depressed I was, I told her I wanted out, and she believed me. She understood. She just had no idea what to do about it.

So she'd sneak into the garage when she was here to talk to Stephen. She'd sit on my hood, in her short skirts and fishnets, and we'd talk.

She was very fond of fishnets. Was. Is. It is...tell me she's still alive? Tell me she didn't succeed in killing herself.

I told her about Bobby, because if she could see me, she could see him, could talk to him. Could give him more than breaking his tormentor's leg.

She got mad. She got real mad. Stephen wouldn't have, he wouldn't have cared. I had already told her my story.

She said she had reasons for staying with him. They weren't good reasons, though, I could tell that. They were sad reasons. She didn't tell me what they were.

But I saw the bruises, one day. And now I wanted to do something about Stephen.

Which I knew I couldn't, because she didn't want me to. It's a horrible situation, when you want to help somebody and know they can't or won't accept it.

Unless I killed him and made it look like an accident. I didn't mention that to her. I thought about it.

I thought about it a lot, and when you spend your nights in a garage and don't need to sleep, you have a lot of time to think about and plan things.

The plan I came up with would solve both of our problems. It would get me out of here, it would get her out of here.

But it took time. And I didn't want to hurt anyone other than Stephen.

I slipped up, of course. Maria had been talking to Bobby. She was convincing him to move on. She was good at that. She had me convinced too, except I couldn't. I tried.

I thought the only way out was to destroy the hearse. I was stupid enough to tell her that.

She told me not to dare. She'd find another way. Which is you, I suppose.

At least she helped Charlie. Somehow, she helped him find another job. I don't know how.

But she told me not to do it. And then she kept the closest watch on me she could. I meant to work out a way to have my fuel tank spring a leak.

I'd blow up. Stephen would be dead, I wouldn't be tied to this any more.

"You don't...it's not what you think," she told me.

"Then tell me what it is?" I was glad I could talk to her without finding songs. Glad I can talk to you, as you can probably tell from how much I've been rambling.

"He saved me."

I thought of the bruises. I doubted that. I doubted that very much. "He beats you."

"You really don't get it. But of course not. Your marriage was one of those disasters everyone but the couple could see coming, but you don't...you see what you want to see."

Sadly, she didn't leave.

I wanted her to leave. I wanted to save her from herself, at this point. I wanted her to finish helping Bobby.

No, I didn't get it. I didn't know what was really going on. Of course not. I only got to see bits and pieces of it. Stephen didn't talk to me, even the way somebody talks to an inanimate object. He didn't see me as anything other than a machine. Which was probably healthy, but...but I never did get his side of the story.

You tell me he didn't do it to her. I believe you. But at the time, what was I supposed to think?

He couldn't see me.

He couldn't talk to me. Maybe she asked him to explain and he refused. More likely, she knew he wouldn't believe her and didn't ask.

At least she told me what had happened to Charles. That he was okay. That mattered to me.

So, I was making plans to destroy myself and him. The garage was going to be a casualty. I felt bad about that, but they had insurance. It was far enough away from the chapel that there wouldn't be any premature or inadvertent cremations. I don't always respect the dead, or the living, but I wasn't going to wind up doing that to somebody and their family.

Maria asked me not to. She suspected I was up to something. Then she said she'd make sure I couldn't and walked out.

I suppose that's when she called you. I knew I'd lost her friendship.

I hesitated.

She loved him, but I genuinely believed he was an asshole and an abuser. How could I not when the evidence was on her skin?

When she said she couldn't leave him?

Any guy would think that, even one who's been dead for fifteen years. Some guys wouldn't care. Some guys would figure she deserved it somehow. I mean, that's how guys get into abuse in the first place. They get raised to think that women need to be kept on a tight leash and they never break out of that pattern.

I did. I'm not saying my father abused my mother, but he definitely expected to be the one in charge by virtue of having a cock and balls, you know.

I ended up trying to break out of that and not having a damn clue how to handle relationships with women. I don't blame him for that.

So, yes, I assumed. So, now I was planning...some lesser thing. She'd asked me not to kill him.

She hadn't asked me not to hurt him or humiliate him. That morning I refused to start. Sure, it was petty, but it made a point.

I only made him wait a few minutes. We had crying people outside. This was the short run, just from the parlor to the crematorium. We only did it for show. It would have been just as easy for them to walk and some of them did.

But some of them liked the pomp and circumstance. That's what we were selling them, after all. Pomp, circumstance, remembrance. And this group, only the kids were crying. Their father scolded them, even the girls.

"She's in a better place. Stop crying. She'll hear it and get upset."

Stupid.

You need to cry. Anyway, they got the body loaded. It seemed to be grandma. She was very light.

Cancer, maybe. But she had already passed on, so I couldn't ask her even if you asked that question.

Sometimes you just know, like with Bobby.

But we weren't going to Willows and he was hanging out there with the dog. Maybe that was the real reason he wasn't in a hurry to move on.

The dog.

We did the short run, around the block as it were. People didn't stop to watch any more. Ten years ago, they'd have tipped their hats, the guys, even if they didn't know who was in there.

Nowadays, people are in too much of a hurry for that. Well, for anything really. Anything that isn't making money.

That's why I liked Maria. She didn't...doesn't...seem to care about making money. I did a couple of other petty things to Stephen.

That night, she didn't come. That night, she didn't visit. I wondered if she and Stephen had had a falling out, or if she was still mad with me.

If she didn't trust me any more. If she didn't trust me not to act on that anger.

When I was alive, I don't think I would have. I'd like to say I would have punched him, but really I was very live and let live. Wouldn't do it myself, wouldn't go out of my way to stop it.

Fifteen years of moving bodies and talking to the newly deceased had made me much more inclined to intervene.

She didn't come the next night either. Maybe they'd broken up, but Stephen didn't seem upset. It had to be me she was mad at.

"Don't kill anyone," she'd said to me. "No matter how mad you get. You'll end up in Hell."

I'm not expecting to end up in Heaven either.

I rather like the Catholic concept of Purgatory except, now I think about it, what am I going through right now?

Yeah. I figure that's where I am. Purgatory. You still want to send me on my way, thinking about that? I mean, maybe I'm meant to be here.

No.

You know I can't be trusted not to break any more legs. Or really lose it and blow myself up. It's fine. I'd do the same thing.

What? You want to know how I died? I already told you that was a personal question. It was stupid, okay?

Oh, all right. I died because I got too plastered to think straight after my wife left me and walked out in front of a bus. Because of course I did. It wasn't suicide. I didn't want to die. I just wanted to forget for a while how I was feeling.

Most people don't want to die. Even suicides don't want to die. They just don't see another alternative. Or they're dying anyway and want to spare themselves or those they care about the trouble of dealing with whatever it is they're dealing with.

I still don't want to die. I'm already dead, but I'm afraid of what happens next. Anyway, yeah, that was my brand of stupid.

Maybe you could check on Sam for me? Don't tell her. She doesn't need to know. I'm sure she's long since gotten over grieving her idiot old man.

She was angry at my funeral, I remember that. She was angry with me for being so stupid. I don't blame her. I was angry at me.

So. I guess this is it.

I don't deserve Heaven, so I guess I'm going to Hell.

What do you mean that isn't how it works?

Wait.

Maria didn't send you at all, did she? Is she dead? Tell me if she's dead?

Oh, good. She did come on that third night. And she told me what it was she did for a living. Stephen didn't mind, because it was good money.

Yeah, it was her customers who left the bruises, and it wasn't... anything like what I thought it was. I can't bring myself to judge her.

Don't we all sell ourselves, one way or another?

But she's alive. Maybe she can get out of that trade, if she wants to. But if Maria didn't send you...

Bobby sent you? That doesn't make any sense. He's dead and didn't know any priests when he was alive.

You're not a priest, are you? I don't have the equipment to laugh. I want to, though. The wanting to makes my headlights flash on and off.

Maybe that works.

So, what was the point of all of this? Deciding whether I deserve to go to hell for breaking a transphobic asshole's leg, 'cause I don't feel sorry about that at all and if that's how you people think?

I would have deserved it if I'd actually killed Stephen, but we all think about killing people at least once in our lives, right? I mean, unless you're so sheltered or lucky you never end up hating anyone. Everyone has somebody to hate.

But for that? If I'd been alive I would have punched him and done a bit less damage. I'd have been tempted to punch mommy dearest too.

Because Bobby didn't and couldn't.

So, what are we going to do here?

I'm not allowed to know but you think I'll like it.

Okay.

Let's do it, I guess. You'll tell Maria I'm okay? Tell Charles I'm okay...because I guess I am, and it's not like I can argue.

Goodbye.

Okay, this is real strange. I'm not going to heaven or hell, am I. You've got something else in mind.

Well.

You know.

There's nothing wrong with second chances. Or third, or whatever. I'll see you around, right?

Right.

Goodbye for real this time...

Why is it so dark?

Why is it so bright?

BUFFOONVILLE

CLARK ROBERTS

WHENEVER MARIE HAD ENCOUNTERED THE WORDS GHOST TOWN, SHE inevitably experienced a chill at her spine, but the phrase *clown town* was doubly worse. *Clown town*—it just sounded so bizarre, so bastardized, and even unsound.

Marie quickly read the historical landmark sign a second time to make sure she hadn't misinterpreted the information, as the sign gave a recount of an extraordinary historical event of which she'd never heard.

It claimed *clowns* had built a settlement along the Lake Michigan coastline around 1850. Economically Buffoonville had struggled right up until the Great Fire of 1871 ravaged Chicago. In a shortsighted decision the politicians and business owners—*did they all wear **wigs and*** *clown makeup*—of Buffoonville agreed to timber off the dense forests surrounding the settlement to help rebuild Chicago in exchange for a great financial windfall. The money had begun rolling in, but without the protection of the massive oaks and tall pines Buffoonville's days had been numbered. The constant winds of the Great Lake, *always* carrying sand, had begun burying the buildings. Most of the clown residents had fled, leaving Buffoonville a relative ghost town. The black and white photos taken by a surveyor in the early 1900's, accompanying the written record, showed huge mounds of sand revealing only the peaks of a few gabled homes and businesses.

"Greg, I'm not so sure about this," Marie said.

"This is part of our country's history," her husband stated "It'll be fine. The trail marker says it's only three-quarters of a mile hike to the beach. The kids can handle it."

"I'm not talking about the hike." Marie nodded her head at the sign. "I mean a ghost town buried beneath the *sand*, it was a town supposedly inhabited by clowns of all things. The state campground is only four miles back."

The family stood at the trailhead. Despite it being a Friday evening not one other vehicle was parked in the dirt lot. Now that Marie thought about it, they hadn't seen another vehicle since they'd zipped past the state campground into what Greg reverently referred to as *no-man's land*.

"Suck it up, buttercup." Greg hitched his shoulders to resettle his backpack. "They don't even let you set up on the actual beach in the state campgrounds."

"Yeah, Mom, suck it up," Barry said from his dad's side.

"But, Greg," Marie's tone was nearly pleading, "the sign says *clowns*."

Greg shrugged a shoulder. "Yeah, I can read."

Rachel tugged at her arm, and Marie looked down at her daughter.

"It's going to be okay, Mom," Rachel said, pointing back to the sign. "The sign says the town was buried by drifting sands."

"You see," Greg grinned from ear to ear. "Even your ten-year-old daughter isn't afraid. Come on, we made great time driving. If we hustle, we'll have the tents up and everything situated before dark."

In a single file line they started up the footpath into the woods, Greg leading.

After a couple rolling hills the forest cleared completely; the trail began cutting a path through tall grass. Soft sand replaced the hard ground, and Marie began to feel the effort of each step in her straining leg muscles. They were passing some large rocks when in one graceful motion Greg turned and swung his backpack off his shoulders.

"Whew," he woofed out. He plopped down on the flattest of the rocks. "Let's take a quick break before we heft up the dunes. How's everyone holding up?"

"I'm doing great, Dad!" Barry hollered. In search of some type of treasure, he ran into the wispy grass which was nearly as tall as his waist.

"How about you?" Greg asked Rachel. "You holding up, princess?"

"I'm fine," Rachel said. She sat next to her father.

"How much farther do you think it is to the beach?" Marie asked. They'd stopped at the base of a sand covered rise. Looking up at it, the very top of the rise seemed preternaturally even. Marie could not see its end in either direction.

"*How much farther?*" Greg mimicked in his most contrived, whining voice. He squirted a shot of water into his mouth, swallowed some, and spit out a stream. He offered the bottle up to Rachel. "Jesus, Marie, give it a rest already."

"But really, Dad," Rachel broke in. She took a long drink from the bottle. "Do you think we're close?"

"*Shhhhh!*" Greg put a finger to his lips and stared down wide-eyed at his daughter. He contorted his face into a wild expression. In his goofiest voice, he bellowed, "I think I can hear the waves just over this here hill! Ayah, ayah, I think I can."

Rachel giggled. When Greg reached to tussle her hair she leaned away but continued to beam up at him.

Amazing, Marie thought, *he can behave like such a dick to me a times, but in the next instant play the role of doting father.* She forced the thought from her mind, instead concentrating on the sounds just to the other side of the hill. All she heard was the breeze blowing through the light grass.

"Mom, catch!" Barry's hollering voice broke her daze. She turned in time to awkwardly fumble but then grasp the object Barry had tossed at her. "I found it half buried in the sand!"

Marie turned the red ball over in her hand. It was about two inches in diameter. She squeezed it, squishing the foam, before turning it over in her palm. On the backside she found a slit. Realizing it for what it was, she yelped while simultaneously jumping and kicking the object as if it were poisonous.

"Settle down, Marie." Greg leaned down to pick up the clown nose. He turned it over much like Marie had, but instead of panicking he probed his thumb into the slit. "You've got a good eye, son. This is something special."

"It's a cheap costume accessory!" Marie spat. "It's disgusting."

"No," Greg answered. He wonderingly held the nose up to his eyes. "Kids, don't let your mother buffalo you. This is valuable. This is an historical artifact. Barry, exceptional find. We'll treasure this forever in our family."

Greg wedged the red ball onto Barry's nose.

"How does it look?" Barry asked.

"Looks perfect," Greg reached up and gave two squeezes. "Beep, beep!"

"Barry, take it off," Marie ordered.

"I say he doesn't have to." Greg casted a flat stare at Marie. He was drawing a figurative line in the sand, challenging her to cross it, to challenge his God given parental rights as a father.

"Mom, just let him wear it," Rachel said, sounding like the voice of reason. "It's just part of a costume. Besides, he likes it."

Inside, Marie ached for her daughter. Too many times she'd played mediator to the tiffs between her parents. Marie broke from the stare down with Greg. Her daughter was right; in the end this battle wouldn't be worth it. Still, she was shaken at the sight of her youngest child wearing that abomination. It wasn't just *part of a costume*. It was a *clown* nose, possibly over a hundred years old. She couldn't shake the feeling that some degenerate who'd not been able to add anything to society and had settled on buffoonery as a career had worn that exact nose, or even worse than a degenerate—some creep-o.

"So I can keep it?" Barry asked.

Marie shrugged.

"Glad that's settled." Greg stood, hiked his pack up to his shoulders. "Onward we march."

The top of the dune revealed the shoreline was not immediately on the other side. In the not too far distance, Lake Michigan could be seen, but in between where the family stood on the crest and the Great Lake were several oddly shaped dunes. From this vista, Marie could form the town in her mind. The larger dunes running off to either side created a sand valley between them which had obviously been main street. Beyond those main dunes were smaller sand hills that must have been homes or cabins.

She imagined the bustle of Buffoonville from all those years ago—a clown mother in chase as her rapscallion clown kids dodged horses and buggies through the street; a clown or two brushing dust from their silken suits as they left the sawmill after a hard day's work; probably there'd even been a clown blacksmith banging away and molding heated metal as his clown makeup sweated from his face all the day long. It was crazy to think they'd stayed in costume every minute of their lives, but she'd always thought of clowns the way children think their teachers live only for multiplication tables and grammar lessons.

Greg led them down into the valley. Marie shivered, feeling watched. Maybe not all the clowns had left. Her gut told her that there'd been some stubborn clowns that had refused to leave, there *always* were some stubbornly crazed occupants refusing to break when it came to dying towns. They'd been buried in their businesses, their homes. Their souls roamed these dunes. She imagined their icy stares tracking her family.

Stop this—stop scaring yourself with these silly ideas!

It wasn't difficult to believe that clowns had built the town. Marie could see the mounds literally ran right up to the shoreline. Any city planner with a straight mind would have known to leave at least the minimalist buffer zone between the lake's edge and the settlement—any city planner except for maybe a clown. Over time, the town would have been doomed even without all the lumbering that had occurred.

They passed by one more obvious valley to the periphery. Marie concluded it must have been a side road, a short route out to the residential sections to either sides of the town. Just beyond that long gone side road, the glistening lake opened up to them as vast as an ocean.

There was still a breeze building low waves. The waves crested, broke, before peacefully lapping at the shoreline. Marie didn't voice it aloud, but inside she admitted this was true beauty.

As if to remind her of the great tragedy that had occurred over a hundred years ago the breeze amped up to a gust spitting a sand that bit like teeth against her face.

Greg turned south, another hundred yards and he plopped his pack off while first assessing the layout of the beach. He faced his family and said, "This is camp."

❧ ❧ ❧

The sun had colored to pastel orange marking the turn from long evening into actual dusk. It settled down, just past the sight of where the waterline indiscernibly flowed into a postcard worthy sky.

After pitching camp and wolfing down sandwiches, they'd explored a bit, heading north to see what was beyond the point that reached out into Lake Michigan. They'd discovered more sandy beach but with significantly shorter dunes as the backdrop.

They'd put Barry's floaty wings on him, let the kids splash and swim. Swimming had been the only time Barry had removed the clown nose from his face. Greg had waded in with the kids while Marie rested from the shoreline, arms wrapped around her knees.

A promised beach fire before bedtime was what coaxed the kids out of the water. They strolled back with the water washing at their bare feet. Barry raced ahead. Rachel dragged behind.

"This has actually been enjoyable," Marie said. She reached to curl her fingers into Greg's. "Maybe I was wrong about this place."

Greg grunted something noncommittal, and that's when Barry began yelling at the top of his lungs.

"Dad! Hurry, I think this man needs help!"

Greg dropped Marie's hand to sprint forward. Marie turned back to Rachel, told her to keep up, and then she too was slapping the soles of her feet on the damp sand. Darkness was quickly falling so it was tough to see much ahead, but Marie thought she could make out the figure. What mostly stood out were the exaggerated feet. For a moment she mistook them as scuba flippers. Getting closer, she realized her error as they did not taper past the toes but actually bulged. They were bright red. The man wore a yellow jumpsuit ruffled at the neck. Marie stopped short.

The clown was splayed out like a starfish indicating he'd drowned before washing ashore.

Greg slid to his knees, prepared to give CPR.

"BOO!" Like a soldier ordered to attention, the clown quickly sat up straight.

Everyone screamed. Greg pounced to his feet.

The clown bellowed laughter, pointing directly at the faces of his victims.

"What the hell was that?" Greg roared.

The clown's face suddenly turned sober. His voice meek, he said, "Sorry, it was just a joke."

"Just a joke!" Greg answered. "My son thought you were dead!"

Marie's face flushed with anger. If the prankster hadn't been costumed as a clown she'd have joined in with her husband and lost her cool on the man. Instead, as her daughter approached, Marie put a hand out to Rachel's chest to warn her not any closer even one step.

The clown sulked, "I said I was sorry. I thought I was being—" he paused, tilting his white painted face. He squinted his eyes in a questioning recognition. "Greg? Greg Harvick?"

Greg studied back at the man before chuckling in disbelief. His tone instantly changed, he said, "Oh man, this can't be true; I can't believe it." He offered a hand to hoist the clown to his feet. The two men clapped each other's backs. "Nick Johnson! Marie, look at this. It's Nick Johnson! We graduated high school together."

Marie forced herself to shake the man's gloved hand.

"Let's get back to the camps," the clown said. "Tip back a drink and catch up on old times."

Farther down the beach, an orange glow indicated a campfire Greg had promised his children had already been built.

As they approached, Marie saw a third tent, brightly multi-colored to match Nick's curly, dyed hair, had been pitched about half a football field short of their camp.

"Marie, I want you to meet my wife Silence," Nick said.

Bells tinkled when the pert thing sprang up from one of the sitting logs arranged around the fire.

Darkness had completely fallen, but the moon was still low. A slight depression circled the summer-dried driftwood that burned. The humble fire casted the young lady in an eerie glow. Silence, although not a girl, looked young enough to still be impressionable and wore an outfit meant to leave an impression. For a camping excursion, she rocked ridiculously heeled sandals which slid over silver leggings that merely served as a second layer of skin. The leggings sheened in the glow of the fire all the way up to her slim waist, which had been accessorized with the most minimal of frilled skirts. The top she'd chosen was bare shouldered, silver and white diamond patterned, and far too snug. Her eyes matched the outfit, outlined with sparkling diamond shapes. She'd done her blonde hair up into three braids which rose in curves before bending back downward into points—a court jester's look if there ever was one.

"Silence?" Marie asked, confounded by the strange name.

Silence gently grabbed the frills of her skirt and curtsied— again the light chiming. Marie now saw the tinkle bells; they'd been secured to the ends of those tightly wound braids which lightly bounced with each movement.

"Silence?" Marie repeated the question.

"Her birth name was Stacy," Nick explained. "When we married she jumped feet first into clowning, so I named her Silence."

"That's just stupid," Rachel said. The adults stared at Rachel. In the absurdity of the moment Marie had forgotten her children were present. Rachel continued, "Why would anyone change their entire self like that for a husband?"

"Rachel!" Greg accosted. "Don't be rude."

Silence didn't miss a beat. She pressed her thumbs together and downward, while also forming joining arches with her index fingers. She displayed the perfect heart as if all present were a paying audience. Turning it to Nick, she batted her eyelashes.

"Why doesn't she talk?" Barry asked.

"Hey!" Greg whopped his son in the back of the head.

"It's a fair question." Nick squatted to Barry's level. "Silence loves me very much. She committed to being a *miming* clown when we married. Miming clowns are not allowed to speak."

"She hasn't said anything since marrying you?" Rachel sounded disgusted.

As if locking up, Silence turned an invisible key over her lips.

She glided over to Nick, and with a lacquered fingernail, teased his mouth open. Proudly, she offered up the imaginary key. Nick snapped his jaws shut and pretended to swallow.

"Your wife is just plain weird." Rachel raised her upper lip in a sneer.

Silence glared at Rachel.

"Weird or not—" Nick said, and turned to face Greg. From the man's look, Marie gathered he was making a latent accusation when he finished his thought, "—at least she honors her commitments."

❧ ❧ ❧

"You know you signed a contract," Nick said almost privately. He'd turned serious in the time it took Marie to tuck the kids into their sleeping bags.

She hadn't wanted to return to the fire, but she also knew if she'd crawled into the tent to shut her eyes without Greg she'd have been haunted with images of the nonsensical couple's painted faces twisted in menace.

"Contract?" Marie asked, sitting down next to her husband.

"Nothing, it's nothing." Greg took the pint of whiskey Nick offered over the flames. Greg wouldn't meet Marie's eyes. Instead he stared at the bottle before putting his lips to it for a deep pull. He capped the bottle and passed it back to Nick.

"It's definitely *not* nothing, Greg." Nick spoke almost under his breath. "The A.C.A. isn't a farce. Once you commit you're in; there's only one way to no longer be in."

Silence raised a sharp fingernail and mimed sawing at her own throat. She grinned over the fire at Marie.

"What's the A.C.A?" For the moment, Marie decided to ignore Silence's obviously overdone threat.

"The American Clown Association. Why can't you stop being so nosy?" Greg said, locking eyes with Marie.

Not for the first time she saw true resentment there.

"You mean," Nick expressed, "you've never even told your wife? What the hell is wrong with you?"

As if her fingers were flint and steel to set him afire, Silence quickly swiped a finger down another which pointed directly at Greg. *Tsk, tsk, tsk!* She snuggled in close to Nick like a devoted girlfriend.

Greg sighed, a vibe of frustration coming off him in waves. He stood, turned his back to the fire, and stepped away from the sitting logs

"You know they're coming here tomorrow, right?" Nick said.

Greg's attention snapped back, his face looking over his shoulder. "Who?" Marie asked.

Silence popped from her seat with the bounce of a jack-in-the-box. Her perfect smile never seemed to leave her face. She began daintily dancing and twirling.

For a moment Nick's gaze, a dull lust in his eyes, traveled with his dancing wife.

"Who is coming here tomorrow?" Marie stressed.

"Oh, sorry. It's just Silence is one primo piece if you catch my drift." Nick cleared his throat, faced back to Marie. Matter-of-factly, he finally answered, "All the other members of The American Clown Association. Who else? Buffoonville Beach is where we host our annual clown convention. By tomorrow afternoon this beach will be crawling with my kind."

Silence continued to dance and twirl, dance and twirl, dance and twirl, until she danced and twirled so deep into the darkness she was out of sight.

❦ ❦ ❦

"This is crazy, Greg." Marie zipped close her sleeping bag. Rolling away from Greg she continued, "Earlier you said we couldn't stay at the campground because you wanted solitude. Now we've got a crazy couple camped within a hundred yards of us, and it sounds like more will be coming tomorrow."

"Hey!" Greg snapped back. Throwing open his own sleeping bag, he sprang up straight-backed. "That's not just a crazy couple out there. They're *clowns,* and Nick was a close friend of mine."

"No, Greg, they're crazy. Normal people don't make a vow of life-long silence on their wedding day. *Normal* people don't stay in clown costumes like deranged actors who can't break character."

"*Shhh!*" Greg intensely put a finger to his lips. "You want them to hear you?"

Deciding to shift tactics, Marie hushed her voice to sound pleading. "Admittedly, I'm sometimes half-delusional with my phobia, but can't you see I'm a wreck? We can do this another weekend when this...this...this convention isn't happening. Can't you please agree to pack up and leave in the morning for the mental health of your wife?"

"We can discuss it first thing in the morning." Greg said. He settled back down into the air mattress. He rolled over and draped an arm across her.

"What did your friend mean when he said you'd signed a contract?" Marie shrugged out of his arm.

"It really is nothing."

"If it's nothing, you'll tell me."

Greg sighed, "When we were seniors in high school we made a pact to both join the A.C.A. I really didn't have a clue of what to do with my life. The military wasn't for me, and back then I had no ambition for college. Nick made the life of a clown sound adventurous; I followed his lead."

"Making a pact in high school isn't the same as signing a contract."

"Well...we sent in membership applications and were both accepted by the A.C.A."

"Okay, but he was so serious. You can't be legally bound to a contract signed when you're in high school."

"You never quit, do you?" Despite his obvious annoyance, Greg continued, "Halfway through our senior year, both Nick and I turned eighteen. You're not going to like learning this just now, but for the reason you just alluded to we dropped out before graduation. Believe it or not, the weekend you and I met I'd just graduated from buffoonery basic training, but you—you were love at first sight for me. I'd never connected with anyone the way I connected to you. When you explained your coulrophobia to me that night I chose to keep my clowning a secret. Right then and there I decided to go AWOL from the A.C.A."

Concern bolted through Marie. She'd never known her husband of ten years was a high school dropout. She remembered meeting him in Lou's Tavern, remembered how suave and confident he'd seemed. She'd been smitten with him, and he'd persuaded her back to a friend's apartment—*had it actually been Nick's*—where they stayed up all night cuddling on a couch. She couldn't recall the exact timeline of their conversation, but he was right that she had confided in him her deepest fear. All he had mentioned about his employment was that he was soon being relocated. After his move to Michigan, they'd stayed connected through email and phone conversations, even visited one another with plane flights. Eventually he'd won her over, and she'd jumped to Michigan to be with him.

"Don't you think that's even all the more reason to leave in the morning?" she asked.

Drowsily, he stated, "You're probably right. In the morning we'll decide." Within two minutes he was snoring.

The burning urge to pee sprang upon her. From the hanging pocket on the side wall of the tent she dug out the flashlight.

The night air outside felt cooler by degrees. Down the beach Nick and Silence's fire still burned, but she could not see them.

Probably they were in the tent having some twisted clown sex.

"Gross," she shivered the thought away and turned the beam of light towards the row of bushes just past the tents. At this time of night and on this beach no one could see her, but camping as a child she'd been taught to use a bush if nothing else. She clawed her way behind the line of wild and tall shrubbery.

She pulled her shorts down and squatted.

What if the ghosts of clowns really did still roam the dunes?

The thought and onrush of fear it provoked seemed to seal her up.

"Come on," she strained, attempting to concentrate on anything but the imaginary eyes she felt staring at her from the surrounding darkness. Finally, the piss erupted from her.

She was hiking her shorts up when nearby bushes rustled.

Marie held her breath. She forced a ten count before calling out, "Hello."

Jesus, was that a snicker she heard?

Next, she definitely heard the chiming of tinkle bells.

A shadow, low to the ground, darted and silently slipped through the brush in the opposite direction.

Adrenaline pulsing, Marie pushed her own way through the brush in order to catch that bitch Silence spying on her most private moment. On the other side of the brush line she waved the flashlight to and fro.

The beam only faded ahead into darkness.

Marie stepped forward searching the sand for clues. This far up from the waterline, the sand was completely dry and had been molded into small continuous undulations by the wind. The undulations all appeared so natural she could not say if any of them were footprints.

Facing Nick and Silence's camp she stared and listened.

"Mom?"

Marie yelped and twirled into a second beam of light.

"Is that you?" Rachel asked.

Marie squinted into blinding light. "It's me."

"What are you doing?"

"Nothing, I'm just—" *I'm just making sure no demonic clowns are sneaking up to kidnap you and your brother.* "I thought I heard something, but it's nothing."

"Oh."

"Did I wake you?"

"Kind of," Rachel paused before sheepishly adding, "I have to pee, but I'm scared."

"Oh honey, don't be scared." Marie's parental instincts took over. "I know it might sound weird at your age, but I'll stand next to you."

"Okay," Rachel agreed.

Marie stood sentry. It made her feel right again, an adult in charge. She kissed her daughter telling her not to be embarrassed before adding she could come sleep the rest of the night with her parents. Rachel declined.

Back inside the tent, this time when Marie laid back exhaustion rushed upon her and soon she was hard asleep.

***

Marie woke up and immediately shielded her eyes with an arm. The sun burned through the thin material of the tent. Sweating terribly, she threw open her sleeping bag. Greg was already gone from the insufferable tent.

How late had she slept in?

She swept a hand at the tent's floor until she found her cell. She clicked it on, and despite not having any actual phone service available it still kept time.

12:34 pm.

You know they're coming here tomorrow—

Only now did she hear outside the various noises of activity. She tried to swallow, a ball of concern clogged her throat.

On top of Greg's sleeping bag she noticed a folded piece of paper. She picked it up. Its thick quality made it feel official.

Sweat broke and tingled her palms.

She unfolded the paper. Her eyes scanned over a typeset structured letter. It was dated twenty years prior.

Dear Mr. Greg Harvick,

Congratulations on your graduation from Buffoonery Basic Training. As President of The American Clown Association let me welcome you into our cult.

A future clown's basic training is filled with rigorous training—both mentally and physically. You have studied the Laws of Clowning as they have been passed down to us from The Great Buffoon In The Sky. As current President of The A.C.A allow me to touch upon a couple of the cornerstone commandments and how they are presently interpreted.

1. Thou shalt not stray-You have committed and vowed your life's work to The Great Buffoon In The Sky. From this day forth you will be expected to follow His, and only His, teachings. His word will be adhered to before all other political, religious, or work affiliation.

2. Thou shall commit to the endeavor of recruitment-Although we are much more lenient and liberal in our interpretation of this commandment than we have been in the past, The A.C.A still requires any spouse you bring into your life to either already be an A.C.A. member or be willing to complete the process into membership. You have pledged to raise your children according to His teachings. This expectation is absolute and—harsh as it may seem—is punishable by death if broken.

My quick recap of these two laws does not in any way endorse ignorance of other commandments. It is only meant to remind you of the seriousness of the buffoon life into which you have chosen and been accepted.

We welcome you with open arms.

> *Sincerely,*
> *James 'Greasy' Jones*

Greg had held onto this letter as a keepsake all these years.

The bolts of fear racing Marie's body caused the letter to shake in her grip as she read through it a second time.

Certain phrases popped off the page—*welcome you into our cult, Laws of Clowning, The Great Buffoon in The Sky, expectation is absolute, punishable by death if broken.*

She knew without question that Greg had awoken this morning and read this very letter, studied it, and contemplated his options. Had this entire weekend been an elaborate plan for him to ask forgiveness from The A.C.A. and re-enter into clownhood?

...pledged to raise your offspring according to His teachings.

No way was Marie going to allow that to happen. If Greg was choosing to pursue a life of mockery then so be it, but she wasn't allowing him to make that decision for her children.

She tore out of the tent into dazzling sunlight and a scene even more maddening than she'd ever imagined. She was too stunned to think of her kids. The blazing sun did nothing to deter the clowns surrounding her from working like ants. There were numerous clown families pitching tents. Farther down the beach another group was setting up a stage like a rock band's road groupies. She twirled and behind her found a dozen or so clowns worked diligently with shovels, moving sand as if they were actually trying to unearth a section of Buffoonville. This was beyond terrifying and crossed into the stupefying realm. There had to be hundreds of clowns present. She stared towards the path she'd been on with her family just yesterday. In single file, a steady stream of clowns continuously hiked down into the valley of Buffoonville. All of them were in costume—tramp clowns, rodeo clowns, alien clowns, demonic clowns, animal clowns, police and firemen clowns, Little Bo-peep clowns.

It was her son's voice that broke her paralysis. "Mommy! Look at me!"

Then Rachel's calmer more mature tone: "Hi, Mom. You're missing out."

...pledged to raise your offspring according to his teachings.

Propped up in tall beach chairs, they both smiled and waved from behind freshly painted faces. Silence stood next to them waving her hands up in down as if the children were exhibits on display.

Barry wore a white skull cap with tufts of red hair on either side giving off the illusion of an aged man. His mouth was jocularly red to match that big red nose in the middle of his face. He looked ridiculous, but it was what Silence had done to her daughter that caused Marie's blood to boil. Rachel's face was slathered in glittery makeup, and her hair was done in the exact jester fashion as Silence's.

"No!" Marie screamed. She plunged forward in the sand, but something solid stepped in front blocking her path.

Greg's face was not white but pitch black as deep night. The blood red grin ended in points.

"You!" Marie shrieked. "You're a bastard!"

Filled with stoicism, Greg spoke, "I'm sorry, Marie, but this is the life I choose."

"You knew about this all along!" Unable to hold in her madness, tears erupted and ran down her cheeks in wide tracks. She balled her hands into fists and pounded at his chest. A fury she'd managed to keep deep in her belly ever since Greg had insisted they ignore her phobia and begin hiking the trail to Buffoonville suddenly burst to life. "I hate you! I fucking hate you for this! I read that letter. I know about your stupid Buffoon In The Sky!" Peripherally, she was aware that every activity in the near vicinity ceased. Every clown's attention was now directed at her. Marie didn't give a flying fuck what they thought about her cursing out the false god. "You broke that contract! You go ahead and die! You die, but they *don't* get the kids."

"It's all right now," Greg soothed. He put an arm around her and roughly corralled her near him. She struggled but his arms were like thick cables. "I don't even have to die. The A.C.A. board were the first to arrive this morning, and I discussed the situation with them. I've repented, Marie. I've repented, and they're giving me a second chance."

This close she could scent him, a smell that was distinctively Greg. This was her husband, her Gregory—just how long had it been since she'd thought of him as Gregory? He was the children's father, and he was hugging her again, and it felt so much like home. Winded from her sudden outburst, somehow she felt he was making things right.

"You don't have to die?"

"No, Marie, I've repented. I've repented, and they've made an exception. We made a deal."

"A deal?"

"That's right. Each year The A.C.A must make a sacrifice to The Great Buffoon In The Sky, and—"

"Not a chance in hell!" She shoved out of his grasp, once again wild with anger. "Not the children, you asshole. You are not sacrificing our children to some pagan clown god."

"You're right, Marie," Greg nodded. He put a hand out to her, stroked her cheek. "Not the children."

It dawned on her. Suddenly she could feel all of the clown's gazes upon her; she could feel their collective anticipating breaths. This wasn't fair. She hadn't ever agreed to any of this. She hadn't signed any stupid contract, yet the clowns continued to form a circle.

She panicked, forgetting her husband, forgetting her children. She turned and ran, prepared to mow down any clown that stood in her way. Surprisingly, the clowns parted. She sprinted through them as they continued to push outward leaving an open path. Before she knew it, she was out of the horde of clowns and racing along Lake Michigan's shoreline.

The tears were back rolling down her cheeks, but she ignored them. She glanced over her shoulder expecting to see a group of mad clowns in pursuit. There was none. In fact, she couldn't believe how much distance she'd gained.

She was sprinting south; that much she knew. She'd eventually come to the state campground beach. There she could get help. He story would sound crazy, but somebody would see her desperation. They'd save her children.

Oh God, her children. She'd left them, but there'd been no other option. She'd left them to save them, because if she'd stayed and willingly accepted being sacrificed, her children would have been doomed for life. She had to keep running for her children's sake.

She ran, and ran, and ran. The landscape seemed unchanging— one lapping shoreline and the world's longest continuous sand dune rivaling it.

To the west and over Lake Michigan, the front of slate gray clouds had appeared from nowhere and now gathered. Lightning ripped. The clouds pushed onward.

She continued.

The temperature dropped. The afternoon deepened into evening. More lightning reached across the sky. Before she knew it, the cold clouds had completely draped the sky like a grave blanket.

Just how far away was the state campground?

The beach rounded inwards, creating a bay she estimated a mile in length. A sixth sense told her that beyond the point was the campground. A second wind lifted her spirits, refocusing her thoughts.

Her children, she could make it for her children.

Fuck Greg.

She hoped The A.C.A. decided to renege on their offer and make an example of him.

Fuck The A.C.A. too, because when she told her story the feds would swoop in and crush every clown beneath its bureaucratic heel, and The Great Buffoon In The Sky would die in a whimper.

She ran, curving down and up the bay, now in the last stretch. The point was ahead a half mile. She ran harder, harder than she'd ever run before, and a hundred yards from the end she cut up and over. Her bare feet pounded on dry sand. She climbed up the lightly grassed sand dune, up to the top and was a quarter of the way down the other side before she realized the cruel joke.

There was no doubting the authenticity of The Great Buffoon In The Sky. Stunned by this turn of event she almost collapsed. She slowed until she was taking stumbling steps down the dune.

She thought of turning back, but there was no point. Impossible as it was, *here* was Buffoonville, and she unequivocally believed if she performed an about face and headed back north *there* would also be Buffoonville. Somehow, at least along this beach, The Great Buffoon In The Sky possessed the power to manipulate even the geography.

She would not turn back. She steeled herself.

If there'd been hundreds of clowns earlier the number now reached into the thousands. Their backs were all to her. The assembled stage had been completed, and all of the clowns swarmed as some Tom-foolery was occurring up there.

Marie made her way down the valley alone. Strings of hair hung in her eyes. She headed towards the crowd, and there was her Greg.

Ironically enough, there was no joy now that her wish had come true. The clowns had double-crossed him.

They'd impaled and erected Greg on a thick spear that looked to be whittled from birch wood. The spear ran through his anus, and the sharpened end thrust out of his gaping mouth angling his permanent stare skyward.

"You poor fool, Gregory," Marie whispered.

She felt no fear as she approached the crowd, because really, any fear had proven to be pointless. There was no escape from whatever was about to occur. Deep in her guts, she knew she'd fight but also accepted this script had already been written. She and her family had been nothing but marionettes swaying to the pulls of The Great Buffoon In The Sky.

She could hear a bellowing voice through the twenty-foot-tall speakers that had been assembled.

Marie tapped the shoulder of a clown that was part of the back row. The clown turned. He stepped aside and tapped the shoulder of the clown directly in front him. This clown whirled, angrily honked a palm sized horn at the sad clown before noticing Marie. He too stepped aside. Each and every clown made way for Marie until she was nearly at the front of the stage.

A portly man dressed in a red swallow-tailed tuxedo jacket was mastering the ceremony. He held a corded microphone up to his lips and addressed the crowd. "Remember, I am only a man, but I, Greasy Jones, am thee conduit for your Lord."

Greg's letter had been signed by James "Greasy" Jones.

Greasy Jones glared heavily at the crowd beneath the bushiest eyebrows Marie had ever seen. He held the microphone so close to his lips they brushed against it. He intoned, "Though shall not stray!"

As one the crowd murmured, *"Though shalt not stray."*

"Gregory Harvick strayed from the pack, yet in the end he couldn't escape The Great Buffoon In The Sky."

In unison the crowd thrust their open hands skyward. *"All hail the G.B."*

"Thou shall commit to recruitment!" Greasy Jones roared into the microphone.

"Thou shall commit to recruitment."

"Our newest members!" Greasy Jones pointed to the side where two tall chairs were being carried onstage. Marie's children perched in them.

Marie called out to Barry and Rachel, but their stupor of expression seemed not to hear her.

Greasy Jones looked straight at her. Into the microphone, he stated, "Our second sacrifice."

From behind, someone forcefully grasped Marie's shoulder.

It was Silence. Wide-eyed, Silence twice jammed a nail into Marie's breastbone. *You! You!* Next, she put her hand over her heart and mockingly stumbled in a circle. She crossed her eyes. She stuck out her tongue. She feigned collapsing to the ground in a spasm, then became still. The circling clowns whooped for her performance.

Silence stood and curtsied. Grinning, she turned back to Marie. A final time she jammed at Marie's chest. *You! You will die.*

Inside, Marie shattered, quickly reassembled into something primitive that realized this was to be the fight of not only her life, but also a fight for her children.

"Fuck you, you made up whore!" Marie snarled. She wound back with a closed fist, no intentions of an open handed slap, but rather a slug that would send this dumb Silence bitch right back to the days when Buffoonville had been its most thriving.

Another hand grasped her fist and halted the punch. Of course it was a clown, this one a hobo with oversized pants held up with green suspenders. The bloom of flower pinned to his plaid shirt let out a stream of water dousing Marie's face. The hobo clown's straw blonde hair bounced as he belted laughter—*hee-YUH, hee-YUH, hee-YUH.*

Marie lunged forward. Growling, she snapped her jaws at the fucker's nose, but suddenly other hands were on her. Marie hollered maniacally. She writhed in revolt to the assault, but it was to no avail. The hands, so many pairs of gloved hands—some pawing, some ripping, some pulling, some pushing. Marie was restrained to the ground.

From seemingly nowhere a long wooden plank was brought forth. She was placed upon it. She saw lengths of rope being passed about and then felt those very same ropes biting into her ankles, binding her wrists, wrapping her waist. She fought like hell, but the clowns knew how to tie secure knots.

Silence's jester face popped into Marie's vision. Silence honked a loogie and spat it into Marie's eyes before producing a tie-dyed handkerchief. Other clowns pried open Marie's jaws, and Silence jammed the cloth into Marie's mouth. Silence pointed dramatically through the crowd, and the clowns parted leaving a path open for Marie to look.

How could this be?

Surely the clowns had worked in shifts.

They'd actually shoveled and moved an entire sand dune to expose Buffoonville's church from the 1800s. Rather than crush the building, the sands of time had worked as a natural preservation. The front of the church was painted up as a sinister clown's face with gabled windows portraying the eyes flanking the sides of the roof's peak. A leering red mouth outlined the open double-doors.

Gesticulating her hands as if she'd just performed the world's greatest magic trick, Silence danced down the path to the church.

Marie was hoisted and suddenly she was staring at the gray sky. One of the clouds billowed hugely, reshaped into the maddening but perfect form of a clown's head with horns. Marie's eyes bulged from her sweating face. She let out the most maddening scream of her life. Her mind broke before the scream was even finished.

The plank was passed overhead, crowd surfing Marie right to the church's doors.

She felt nothing when she was dropped to the ground. She was unblinking but really saw nothing as Rachel, with her newly painted on face, kissed Marie's cheek. When it was Barry's turn, Silence held him up. Barry used the foam nose to rub an Eskimo kiss to his mother.

Still tied to the plank, Marie was carried into the church and propped against one of the lower level windows.

Her vacant eyes only saw a continuous tie-dyed swirling of colors.

The clowns stepped back outside and shut the doors.

Rachel and Barry were each handed a shovel. They tossed the first shovelfuls, and then all of the clowns jumped to help. Those that didn't have shovels grasped handfuls of sand and threw them overhand.

From above, a final bolt of lightning flashed. The clowns gazed up to the cloud above them, their God given form. They all murmured prayers that their God would be satisfied. No more lightning; the clowns went back to work.

They sweated all through the night. By the time the sun rose the next morning, another secret had been buried beneath the sand dunes of Buffoonville.

WHAT THE HEART WANTS

RICK DUFFY

THE MARBLE STEPS OF THE VASCULARIUM ROSE BEFORE ARTHUR LIKE A stairway to heaven. They seemed to get higher every year. He straightened his black tie and allowed a hand to rest over his heart, caressing the slender object in his breast pocket. But he was stalling. Arthur needed to face facts. And the facts were that no matter how hard he tried, no matter how long he prayed, no matter how much he cared, no one's heart goes on forever. Each visit here brought him closer to the day when his time with Marian would be their last.

He took a deep breath and hurried up the steps as quickly as his seventy-nine years allowed. At the top he pushed through the heavy oak doors. A cavernous chamber of pink-veined marble and stained glass stretched before him, luminous with spectral glory from the afternoon sunlight. The musty-sweet smell of old books and roses greeted him from some hidden incense spray—perhaps a bit cloying, but somehow adding to the solemnity. The Vasculariums reminded Arthur of great, hollowed-out cathedrals. Or of grand libraries, their works gone to stone.

He strode down the central finger of burgundy carpet to a side corridor. A statue of an angel, bent in grief and holding a dove in its petrified hands, stood sentinel near the entrance. As Arthur took the corner he nearly collided with an elderly woman, also in black, swaying back and forth.

"Oh! Excuse—" he began, but she couldn't hear him. Oversized headphones wrapped her head. Her eyes were closed, and her face was the image of bliss. Along this corridor, embedded in the marble walls at eye level, ran a row of cubicle-sized stone doors. Each had a label: 12-A, 14-C, 22-F, and along the line. The woman stood in front of one that was open. A pane of glass covered the niche beyond. Numbers glowed across the pane: 11000216. As Arthur watched, they dropped to 11000215. Then 11000214.

Eleven million. Damn it. With a frown and a clenched jaw, Arthur continued past.

At the next corner he lifted a headset from a bin and stripped off the plastic wrap. He came to compartment 49-F and stopped. After a deep, calming breath, he placed his hand against the chilly marble door, and for the first time that day, he smiled.

"Hello, Marian. It's Arthur."

He swung open the little stone door. The niche illuminated. Within the compartment, behind the glass and suspended in a tank of clear liquid and a web of delicate golden threads, hung the most precious thing in Arthur's world—the heart of his departed wife. He donned the headphones and plugged them into a port below the glass. Reaching into his jacket's breast pocket, he removed a thin leather case. Inside, on a bed of black velvet, rested a slender silver rod, shaped like a metal pen, or the probe of a meat thermometer. As

Arthur lifted it out, a number lit on its side. 232.

Arthur hesitated. 232. How had it come to this?

He lined up the probe and eased it into a second port. A mechanism clicked and pulled it flush. Across the upper part of the glass the same number appeared. 232.

His finger hovered over a button next to that port. He put his lips up to the glass and whispered, "Just a few today, all right, Marian?"

He pressed the button. The point of the silver object glided into the tank and through the liquid, stopping a mere sliver from the veined surface of the red organ. A gold spark flashed from the tip to the heart. The liquid effervesced and came alive with energetic bubbles. The heart shuddered and contracted once. Then again. As it picked up its beat, a sound echoed in Arthur's headphones, deep and strong, a soul-thrilling *Thump*.

Arthur shut his eyes and the rest of the world disappeared. Feelings of fullness, of completeness, reverberated through his body, from his head to his shoes, through his flesh and bones, and through his memories of Marian. He listened enrapt as each beat filled his darkness, then echoed away, leaving an almost unbearable emptiness before the next arrived.

Thump.

But even in the bliss of the moment, another thought intruded. 232.

When Marian died, her balance had been upwards of eight hundred million. That was over twenty more years of living, loving heartbeats—barring an illness, or an accident. An accident on a rainy night. He didn't remember the crash. Not at fault, they said. But he'd never forgiven himself.

Thump.

When he had lost her, vascular recovery could only save one percent of a person's leftover heartbeats. It saved less than ten million of Marian's. He'd come here ever since, to feel her life pulse through him. Over time, he'd lost touch with their friends and the little family he had—Marian and he had no children. He should have rationed better, sooner. But here he was, seven years later, with 232—

Thump.

Arthur opened his eyes—222 heartbeats left. When those ran out—well, there were recordings and simulations. But they weren't real.

They weren't Marian.

He jabbed the button. The tip of the probe retreated from the heart and the sparkling water dulled to quiescence. The heart slowed. 220. 219. 218. And was still.

The slender silver device slid out and the lights flickered off. Arthur grasped the precious object and laid it back into its small velvet casket.

"See you tomorrow, Marian." He closed the marble cover of the small, dark cavity.

❦ ❦ ❦

Arthur sat at the top of the Vascularium steps. Before him, across a narrow private lane, an orange sun melted into the reds and yellows of the autumn trees, casting shadows that spread like dark rivulets through the surrounding cemetery. That's where they'd interred Marian's body. The cold Marian. The silent Marian. Arthur hadn't gone there in years. The warm, loving Marian was in the Vascularium. The Marian he could still feel.

He thumbed through a handful of old print pictures—of Marian in their garden; on a Caribbean cruise; at her last birthday. A voice came over his shoulder. "She's lovely."

Arthur turned. A pale, thin man, younger than Arthur, stood over him.

Arthur smiled. "Thank you."

"Wife?" asked the man.

Arthur looked back to his pictures and nodded.

"May I?" The man sat next to him. "What's her name?"

"Marian."

"How long were you married?"

"Thirty-seven years." He automatically included the seven since she'd died.

"Twenty-two for Sally and I." The man held out a palm-display showing a woman with long blonde hair in an emerald green dress, grinning wide from a sofa, three children at her side.

Arthur smiled at the picture, "She's a looker."

"Died too young," said the man, and pushed the display back into his pocket. "But don't they all? The old tech saved nineteen million. You old tech, too?"

Arthur looked back at Marian.

"Oh, sorry," the man said. "My name's Tom."

"Arthur."

"I saw you inside, Arthur. About done, isn't she?"

Arthur sighed and moved to stand. "I have to—"

The man took the sleeve of Arthur's jacket. "But after five years, Sally is over twenty million now."

Arthur paused. Hadn't he said nineteen?

"That's right," Tom said and grinned. "Even with the relatives always visiting. Twenty million."

"I don't understand."

"I'll explain." The man's expression became more serious. Arthur settled back on the step. He had no place else to be.

"Today we can recover four times more heartbeats: more beats for the buck, you might say. That's not fair to people who only had the old tech. And once the procedure is done, it's done. Those unused heartbeats are gone forever." Tom made a fluttering motion with his hand, like a bird flying away.

Arthur nodded. It was expensive, too. He and Marian had been comfortable in their retirement, short-lasting though it was. But vascular interment took half his savings, plus the house. He wasn't sure Marian would want this. But she'd understand. She was his world, and death would not cheat him of their remaining years. More than that, after the accident, he owed her.

Tom continued. "It's a growing field. A good investment. They've even been working on ways to pull heartbeats from healthy people to treat sick ones. But nothing else has been workable, not yet, beyond vascular envigoration of the recently departed's own heart." The man moved closer and lowered his voice. "Except, until now: we've found a way that allows donations from a living person."

Arthur knotted his eyebrows. "I've never heard—"

"Sure," Tom said, and leaned back again. "We've done it quietly. I mean, who'd give up their own heartbeats to the dead? What law would allow it? What god? To be honest, at first I thought it sounded unnatural. Even—what's a good word?" Tom smiled. "Taboo."

"Like a bad horror movie," Arthur forced his own smile. *But this wasn't possible—was it?*

The man nodded. "Someday that attitude will change. Even so, it's not without its complications."

"What complications?"

"For starters, the transfer is inefficient, even more than older tech. But, the donor has to be compatible."

"You mean a blood relative?"

"Not necessarily." Tom stood up, looking toward the trees. Arthur stood with him.

"Hearts are picky," the man continued, seeming to speak to the sunset. "Willful. It's like they say: the heart wants what the heart wants."

Arthur gazed across the lane to the cemetery. He'd spoken to few of his visits to Marian. Now here was Tom, a stranger out of nowhere, rummaging around in his heart and soul. Maybe he should just walk away, visit Marian's grave. How long had it been? If possible, he'd gladly have parceled out his own heartbeats to keep her alive and well, timed so one night they'd fall asleep in each other's arms, and that would be that.

But then he'd dragged her to dinner that night.

He considered the man before him. Could he make up for it now?

"You're serious about this?" Arthur asked.

"I can't tell you the company's name, but you'd know it. We developed the procedure a year ago, and as you'd expect, it's stuck in red tape. Some of us don't think that's right, so we're using it ourselves, and offering it to a few others, who can keep it quiet."

"And, I assume, who can pay for it."

The man shrugged. "You understand I have risks."

Risks and profit margins, Arthur figured. "What about that compatibility thing?"

The man turned to Arthur and winked. "After thirty-seven years of marriage? I'm confident you'd be a match."

Arthur looked down the long steps. He didn't like Tom, and wasn't sure what to make of all this. He chuckled hollowly. "Got a bridge to sell me, too?"

Tom made a little laugh. "I can appreciate you thinking that. So, how about a free sample?"

❧ ❧ ❧

Rather than entering the Vascularium, Tom descended the steps toward the lane. Arthur chewed the inside of his cheek and followed. He had to know more.

The man led Arthur across the lane into the trees near the cemetery. The sweet smell of autumn surrounded him, and dead leaves crunched beneath his shoes. Marian's grave wasn't far from the path they'd taken when Tom stopped in a small grove of tall oaks, hidden from the road. Tom removed something from his coat. It was a black disc, like the chest piece of a stethoscope. Bigger, though, and with no attachments.

"This won't take long. Let's see your probe."

"What are you going to do?"

"Not me Arthur. You. *You* will give a few of your own heartbeats to Marian."

Arthur grasped for the case in his jacket. Everything left of Marian's life was inside that little silver object. "Um, I don't—"

"Sally and me, Arthur. Always together. Think of Marian." The man held out his hand.

Has it come to this? Am I so desperate that a guy with a story can drag me out here alone, like some sucker? The guy might be a mugger, but Arthur carried nothing of value. He squeezed the small case in his hand. Except this.

Arthur sighed. 218. That's just a couple weeks. Months, at the outside. And then what? Marian would be gone forever. Arthur held out the case. "If anything happens to this—"

"It will be fine. I promise." The man exchanged his black disc for Arthur's case. "Now sit here, and put that against your skin, over your heart."

Arthur leaned against a knotty tree and slid to the ground, onto a thin blanket of leaves still soft and fragrant and freshly fallen. This was a lovely place, peaceful, except maybe for the memories buried here. He opened his shirt, and placed the circular object onto his chest, where he'd placed his hand when he told Marian he wanted her for his wife.

Tom knelt next to him. "Your heart's a bit lower, more toward the center."

Arthur moved the device. Tom bent close. Suddenly it rippled, patterns looping and spiraling across the surface. After a moment it stilled and fastened onto his skin.

"Interesting," Tom said. "Your heart should be healthier for a guy your age. Maybe with exercise and—"

"Just get on with it."

"Of course." Tom removed Arthur's probe from its case and brought the point above the device. "There might be a little discomfort, but try to breathe normally. This won't take long."

As the tip came near, the center of the black disc puckered open. The skin underneath went cold. The man eased the probe into the small opening, and when he let go the slender device continued to sink. Arthur was sure the point must have penetrated into his body, but he felt nothing.

A number flashed on its side. 218.

"Okay," Tom said. "Here we go."

There came a pinch, followed by a stab of pain. Arthur gasped.

"Hang in there," Tom said calmly.

The pain grew worse, shot through his chest and along his arms. "Almost finished..."

It clawed down his legs. It became red hot. He tried to scream, but couldn't breathe. His head reeled, like he was passing out. Like—

"Done!" Tom removed the probe. It slid out as smoothly as it had gone in. Tom's device peeled off painlessly. "Take things easy a minute."

"God," Arthur wheezed, holding his chest, trying to catch his breath.

"Yeah, sorry. That happens with these quick grabs. With the full setup, it's much faster and considerably more comfortable, I promise."

The pain subsided. Arthur's head cleared, and his breathing came more easily. His chest was unharmed, other than a small red blemish.

Tom held the probe up for Arthur to see. Arthur blinked a few times and tried to read the numbers.

"218? But—"

The man handed over the slender object. "Look closer."

Arthur held it up. The number wasn't 218.

It was 1218.

Tom smiled. "What do you think?"

Arthur stared at the number. "This is legit? This is real?"

"The tech is bleeding edge, so the pull is still inefficient. That took a day off your life. But what's a day, give or take? Anyway, I said this was a free sample. Go give it a try."

Arthur placed the probe back in its case, and pushed himself to his feet, swaying as a wave of dizziness swept over him. After a moment to steady himself, they left the grove.

They returned to the Vascularium. "I'll give you your privacy," Tom said, "and time to think it over. If you're still interested, I'll meet you back here tomorrow morning, first thing. Then I'm off to another town."

The man handed Arthur a card and walked away.

Arthur watched him a moment, placed the card in his pocket and hurried up the steps. His heart pounded, partly from the impact of the procedure, and partly from his desperate hope.

With familiar routine he snatched a pair of headphones and came to Marian's niche. He opened the marble door and inserted the probe. The glass lit up: 1218. He pressed the button. Marian's envigorated heart began to beat. To be certain, he'd have no choice but to count off the 218 beats that had already been in the device's reservoir. If Tom had faked those 1000 new heartbeats, then after the 218 were gone Marian's heart would never beat again.

And Arthur would find Tom and make him pay.

He was too anxious to enjoy the heartbeats as they thumped their life away. He kept his eyes locked on the glass, on the number, as it counted off all 218, down to 1000. Then 999. 998. At 990 he ejected the probe.

"This is it, Marian," he whispered. "Now we can stay together."

He took out Tom's card. It wasn't contact information. It was a rate sheet.

And his own heart turned stone cold.

❦ ❦ ❦

The next day was chilly with a misting rain. The Vascularium opened early, but few people visited until later. Arthur waited at the top of the steps for Tom to arrive.

And Arthur was tired. He'd sat up into the night working the numbers. He knew his own remaining heartbeats: the health station at the drugstore had verified those, along with his blood pressure, which was sneaking up. And he knew the minimum, the absolute floor, of heartbeats bearable from Marian each week. From this he calculated how many of his own he needed to give, so that both his heart, and Marian's, would hit empty about the same time. It worked out to two years off his remaining eight. That was more than fair.

The problem was the cost. Tom really was some kind of racketeer. Arthur spent the rest of the night adding up assets and estimating income. But no matter how hard he tried, it didn't look good.

Tom appeared on the wet lane, dressed in a black hat and an overcoat pulled tight against the damp. As Arthur waited, resentment swelled in his chest. Tom was making obscene profits off of people's grief and desperation. Arthur was willing to risk this procedure and pay everything he had—but it wasn't right. *The guy's a parasite. If I had that thing, I'd pass it around for free.* Marian would have wanted that.

He pushed these thoughts from his mind. He'd be with his wife for the rest of his life. And Tom's morals weren't his business.

The man topped the steps. "Good morning, Arthur."

"Morning."

"You've decided?"

Arthur nodded.

Tom smiled and shook the water off his hat. "How many?"

"I want to give eight million, seven hundred and sixty thousand heartbeats."

"And you remember this procedure is much less efficient than the normal tech? We'll only be able to get eighty-seven thousand or so for your wife from that."

"I know."

"Good. Just so we're clear."

"But how did you get so many? I mean for your own wife?"

"She has plenty of close relatives, and they've each done their part."

"Well, good for you." Arthur frowned. In his case, it was only him and Marian.

Tom took out his palm display and spoke Arthur's count. He watched it a moment, then turned it to Arthur. "And there's the damage."

Arthur nodded, that's what he had figured. "I can pay half of it now, and then later—"

"The rate sheet was specific, Arthur. Up front. I can't exactly turn late accounts over to a collection agency. And at your age, you can't guarantee—"

"Yeah, okay. But I don't have it all. Not right now. Let me buy half today, for their full price, and when those run out—"

"There's a minimum, Arthur. No deal."

"Or trade? I have my own plot, and—"

"No trade. No barter."

Arthur's mind raced, searching for an asset he had missed, but coming up empty. "Wait... what can we do? What can I get? Even with half, you're still making an unholy profit. Be reasonable, Tom. That's all I'm—"

"Look Arthur, I'm sympathetic, I am. But I have my own expenses, and the price isn't negotiable." The man pocketed the display and sighed. "I've found vascular interment families to be pretty well off, people who can afford this kind of thing. I'm sorry if I've wasted your time."

Arthur panicked. He didn't know what to do. But Tom wasn't leaving, just like that, and taking away his last hope. "Please, Tom." Arthur stepped forward, and reached out like a lost child. "Please. Ask for anything. I'll get it. I'll do it. But please—" Arthur's voice choked off.

Tom frowned and shook his head. "God Arthur, you're a wreck—"

A wreck. Arthur didn't hear the rest. He saw his Marian before him, obscenely twisted in an overturned car. Cold and still and forever silent.

Tom was turning away. Arthur's face flushed hot, but his heart went cold. "You son of a bitch." He grabbed the man's coat.

"Let me go, Arthur." Tom pulled away. "We're done. I've got an-other—"

"Who the hell do you think you are, deciding who can be with their wives again? Or their friends? Or their children? No one is taking Marian away! Not again!"

Before Tom could respond, Arthur was on him. He clutched at the man's pocket, felt the flat, round device. The men struggled. Tom was younger and in better shape. "You're crazy!" Tom yelled and pushed Arthur back.

But Arthur was beyond desperate. He saw his chance, and he took it. With all his strength, he slammed forward into Tom. Tom shouted once as he stumbled back over the edge of the wet stone, and fell violently down the long, steep steps. When he hit the bottom, he lay still.

Arthur squeezed Tom's device in his sweaty hand, panting hard, looking down at the body. He glanced around. They were still alone. He stuffed the device into his jacket and descended the steps to Tom's body. There was no pulse.

The guy slipped, Arthur told himself. *It was an accident, and he slipped*. Arthur looked around once more. *But serves the bastard right*. He grabbed Tom under the arms and dragged him across the rain-slick lane deep into the trees. And he left him there.

Arthur returned to the Vascularium, hurrying now through the empty atrium and below the stained glass windows, now muted and dull in the gray clouded morning.

He arrived panting at Marian's niche and opened it. "Soon now, Marian."

He sat on the hard floor and opened his shirt. "I can give a little each day. Maybe a thousand. That should give you about a dozen. Yes, I'll start there. I can handle that."

He placed Tom's device over his heart. It suctioned into place. He took out his case, removed the probe. It read 990. He brought its tip over the device which puckered in anticipation.

"For you, Marian." Arthur took a deep breath and slid the point into his chest. He felt the pinch. And as the pain started to rage through his body, he yanked it out.

After a moment to recover, he checked the numbers on its side.

1005.

Arthur sighed with relief. Everything was going to be okay. He could do this.

He stood up, the black disc still attached to his chest, and slid the probe into Marian's port. The mechanism locked and pulled it flush into the glass.

Arthur waited. It was taking longer than usual.

At last a line flashed across the glass of Marian's receptacle. *Incompatible.* And the probe slid back out.

Arthur stared. Incompatible? He pushed it in again.

Incompatible.

His shook his head, an ache growing in the pit of his stomach. It must be the damp. He removed Tom's device from his skin, dried and cleaned it on his jacket lining. He prepared it for another pull.

The point again sunk into his chest. A pinch became a roar of pain. He bore it as long as he could, gritting his teeth, digging his fingernails into his palms, enduring it longer than he had with Tom. Finally he yanked it out.

He waited until he could catch his breath. Then examined the probe.

2325.

Okay. He raised himself up to the glass and slid it back in.

Incompatible.

He slammed his fist into the wall. "No, god damn it!" his voice a vulgar echo through the marble hall.

"Again!"

He tried a longer pull, more excruciating than the last.

4832. *Incompatible.*

"Again!"

Agony carved through his chest. His muscles, his organs, felt as if they were being ripped apart.

20412. Incompatible.

"Again!"

Electric fire seared though his veins. His world shattered in a cataclysm of thunder and soul-rending light. Then he was falling into darkness, into an abyss, going deeper, going—

Stop! Stop!

Arthur yanked the probe before he passed out, his hand pale and shaking. He could barely read the numbers.

156192. Incompatible.

His breath came in heaving gasps, each movement of his chest, each erratic beat of his heart, igniting new tortures behind his ribs. Slumped now against the wall, hardly able to move, Arthur stared at the probe in his bloodless hand.

And as his life had been draining away, his rage and anger had gone with it. That night, Marian, the crash—it had not been his fault. But Tom, pushed to his death, lying beneath the sodden trees. That was Arthur's doing.

And he thought of Marian. And Arthur understood.

The heart wants what the heart wants.

And Marian would not want this. Would not want what Arthur had become.

Incompatible.

He looked up at Marian's perfect, lovely heart, and strained his ashen hand to touch the cool glass.

"I'm sorry, Marian."

He slumped back down, and with a gentle exhalation, let the air out of his lungs, and slid the probe one more time into the device covering his heart.

❦ ❦ ❦

Two men in blue overalls, with the names Michael and Carl stitched over their hearts, were putting the finishing touches on two open cubicles.

"I don't know Mike, there's nothing I can do with it." Carl removed a small silver probe from a suitcase test unit and placed it on display inside Marian's niche. "The thing is pretty messed up."

"Save any?" Michael asked.

"Just flashes 'Incompatible.' But it's unclaimed now, so I guess it doesn't really matter. How about your guy?"

Michael placed another probe into the adjoining cubicle. "This one? Exactly one left."

"Exactly one? Wow, I hope I go like that."

"Yeah, but..."

"But?"

Michael shook his head. "This place is for people to visit, friends and relatives and all that. So what good is vascular interment with only one heartbeat left?"

"Huh. I see your point."

Michael shrugged. "But the niche is prepaid in his will, no refunds. Anyway, let's close up. We need to check the grounds: people are complaining about a smell."

They replaced the glass panes over the receptacles, closed the marble doors, and left the remains of Marian and Arthur, two hearts of flesh, alone in their stone tombs. Two hearts, with a single heartbeat left between them: Arthur's last heartbeat, perfect and pure, somehow held back. Not waiting for any visitor; not waiting for any friend or relative.

Waiting now for eternity.

Waiting, for his Marian.

CONTRIBUTORS

J.D. BLACKROSE

J. D. Blackrose loves all things storytelling and celebrates great writing by posting about it on her website, www.slipperywords.com. She has published The Soul Wars series and the Monster Hunter Mom series, both through Falstaff Books, as well as numerous short stories. Follow her on Facebook and Twitter. When not writing, Blackrose lives with three children, her husband and a full-time job in Corporate Communications. She's fearful that so-called normal people will discover exactly how often she thinks about wicked fairies, nasty wizards, and homicidal elevators, even when she is supposed to be having coffee with a friend or paying something called "bills." As a survival tactic, she has mastered the art of looking interested. She credits her parents for teaching her to ask questions, and in lieu of facts, how to make up answers.

GUSTAVO BONDONI

Gustavo Bondoni is an Argentine writer with over two hundred stories published in fourteen countries, in seven languages. His latest books are Ice Station: Death (2019) and The Malakiad (2018). He has also published three science fiction novels: Incursion (2017), Outside (2017) and Siege (2016) and an ebook novella entitled Branch. His short fiction is collected in Tenth Orbit and Other Faraway Places (2010) and Virtuoso and Other Stories (2011).

In 2019, Gustavo was awarded second place in the Jim Baen Memorial Contest and in 2018 he received a Judges Commendation (and second place) in The James White Award.

His website is at www.gustavobondoni.com

RICK DUFFY

Rick Duffy has been writing since he was sixteen—software, not fiction. When he discovered how similar writing stories felt to software engineering, he'd found a second love in life. His short stories have been published in the Providence Rhode Island Journal, the Zoetic Press Literary Journal, and other venues. He is a member of the Horror Writers Association and the Rocky Mountain Fiction Writers. Rick lives in Littleton, Colorado. Connect with him at: facebook.com/rickduffyauthor

AARON HILTON

Aaron Hilton is a new voice in the world of supernatural fiction. Hailing from Winston-Salem, he grew up on a steady diet of horror and fantasy films all the while fostering a love for the fiction of King, McCarthy, and Lovecraft. He studied creative writing at Gardner-Webb University, where he wrote a thesis on Post-Apocalyptic Literature, and began penning stories of his own while living in the countryside of Shelby, NC. Influenced by these surroundings, he cultivates a style that blends the southern rural with the Gothic supernatural. https://twitter.com/AGHilton3

LARRY HODGES

Larry Hodges is an active member of SFWA with 102 short story sales and four novels, including "When Parallel Lines Meet," which he co-wrote with Mike Resnick and Lezli Robyn, and "Campaign 2100: Game of Scorpions," which covers the election for President of Earth in the year 2100. He's a member of Codexwriters, and a graduate of the six-week 2006 Odyssey Writers Workshop, the 2007 Orson Scott Card Literary Boot Camp, the two-week 2008 Taos Toolbox Writers Workshop, and also has a bachelor's in math and a master's in journalism. In the world of non-fiction, he has 13 books and over 1800 published articles in over 160 different publications. He's also a professional table tennis coach, and claims to be the best science fiction writer in USA Table Tennis, and the best table tennis player in Science Fiction Writers of America! Visit him at larryhodges.com

TALLY JOHNSON

Mr. Johnson is a graduate of Spartanburg Methodist College and Wofford College with degrees in history. He is the author of Ghosts of the South Carolina Upcountry, Ghosts of the South Carolina Midlands, Ghosts of the Pee Dee (all for The History Press) and he also has a story in An Improbable Truth: The Paranormal adventures of Sherlock Holmes (from Mocha Memoirs Press). His newest full-length release is an anthology of Southern Gothic ghost fiction titled Creek Walking from Falstaff Books. He also has stories in two anthologies from Prospective Press. His tale "Bloody Bonnet at Blue Hole" was recently included on the Valentine Wolfe album Winternight Whisperings. Mr. Johnson was also the recipient of the first

Caldwell Sims Award for Excellence in Southern Folklore from the USC-Union Upcountry Literary Festival. He is also the Storyteller- In-Residence for Palmetto State Hangers, a hammock camping group. Find him at http://tallyjohnson.wix.com/sc-ghost-talker and facebook.com/tallyjohnson3

MACKENZIE KINCAID

Mackenzie Kincaid is a writer and artist living in the American west with one black cat and a modest collection of bones. She is the author of "The Writer's Guide to Horses," and her short fiction has appeared or is forthcoming in Beneath Ceaseless Skies, Zooscape, and the anthology Gunsmoke & Dragonfire. She can be found on Twitter, Tumblr, and Instagram as @mackincaid, and blogs at mackenziekincaid.com

EMILY LAVIN LEVERETT

Emily Lavin Leverett is a writer, editor, and medievalist English professor. She is the co-editor of several short story anthologies including Lawless Lands: Tales from the Weird Frontier and the forthcoming Predators in Petticoats. Her contemporary fantasy series, the Eisteddfod Chronicles, continues with book three, Traitor's Spring. Her historical fantasy, Marie and the Werewolf, based on the life and romantic poetry of 12th century abbess Marie de France, will be out in 2020. Her academic work focuses on Terry Pratchett's use of medieval romance tropes in his Discworld novels. Along with recent article publications, a co-edited collection of essays, Faith and Ethics in the Worlds of Terry Pratchett, will be out in 2020 from McFarland Press. She lives in North Carolina with her spouse and three cats, where they are all avid fans of Carolina Hurricanes hockey.

ROB MacGREGOR

Rob MacGregor is the author of 21 novels, including 7 Indiana Jones novels, published by Bantam and Ballantine Books. He's a New York Times bestseller for Indiana Jones and the Last Crusade. He's also winner of the Edgar Allan Poe Award for his young adult mystery, Prophecy Rock. His most recent novels are Tulpas and Time Catcher. He's also written 16 non-fiction books exploring mysteries, such as the Bermuda Triangle and alien encounters, as well self-help books on yoga, meditation, dreams, and synchronicity.

GAIL Z. MARTIN

Gail Z. Martin writes epic fantasy, urban fantasy and steampunk for Solaris Books, Orbit Books, and Falstaff Books. Series include Dark-hurst, the Chronicles Of The Necromancer, the Fallen Kings Cycle, the Ascendant Kingdoms Saga, the Assassins of Landria, the Night Vigil, and Deadly Curiosities. Newest titles include Vengeance, Tangled Web, The Dark Road, Sons of Darkness, and Assassin's Honor.

The Jack Desmet Adventures (Steampunk) series, as well as the Mark Wojcik Spells Salt and Steel series, Joe Mack Cauldron series and the Wasteland Marshals series are co-authored with Larry N. Martin.

As Morgan Brice, Gail also writes urban fantasy MM paranormal romance. New and upcoming books/novellas include Witchbane, Burn, Dark Rivers, Badlands, and Lucky Town.

Find her on Twitter @MorganBriceBook, on Facebook at The Worlds of Morgan Brice and at www.MorganBrice.com. Also @ GailZMartin on Twitter, The Winter Kingdoms on Facebook, and at www.GailZMartin.com

JASON J. McCUISTON

Jason J. McCuiston was born in the wilds of southeast Tennessee, where he was raised on a carnivorous diet of old monster movies, westerns, comic books, horror magazines, sci-fi and fantasy novels, and, of course, Dungeons & Dragons. He attended the finest state school that would have him with the intention of becoming a comic-book artist. Following his matriculation and a whirlwind tour of spectacularly underpaid and uninspired career paths, he finally realized that he was meant to be a professional storyteller.
Jason has been a semi-finalist in L. Ron Hubbard's Writers of the Future contest, with stories published in several anthologies and magazines. Other tales are forthcoming.
He lives in South Carolina, USA with his college-professor wife (making him a Doctor's Companion) and their two four-legged children. He can be found on the internet at: https://www.facebook.com/ShadowCrusade. And he occasionally tweets about his dogs, his stories, his likes, and his gripes @JasonJMcCuiston.

JENNIFER R. POVEY

Born in Nottingham, England, Jennifer R. Povey now lives in Northern Virginia, where she writes everything from heroic fantasy to stories for Analog. Her most recent book is the compelling urban fantasy Daughter of Fire. Additionally, she is a writer, editor, and designer of tabletop RPG supplements for a number of companies. Her interests include horseback riding, Doctor Who and attempting to out-weird her various friends and professional colleagues. Website link: http://www.jenniferrpovey.com

CLARK ROBERTS

Clark Roberts writes mostly short stories in the horror and fantasy genres. His fiction has appeared in over twenty publications including and most recently Mindscapes Unimagined, Terrors Unimagined, Deadman's Tome, Horror Bites, and Sanitarium. He is not a New York Times bestselling author, and for now, he's okay with that. He spent much of his teenage years reading the novels of Stephen King, Clive Barker, and Peter Straub. Mr. Roberts lives in Michigan with his wife and two children. Besides reading and writing he enjoys spending time in the outdoors hunting and fishing. He particularly enjoys fishing in the hours of dusk when trout streams whisper, and eyes open in the surrounding woods. Friend him on facebook using the following link: https://www.facebook.com/clark.roberts.39589 If you friend him, he'll confirm; he won't reject you. You'll be a lot cooler for doing this.

ANGELA ROQUET

USA Today bestselling fantasy author Angela Roquet is a great big weirdo. She collects Danger Girl comic books, owls, skulls, random craft supplies, and all things Joss Whedon. Angela lives in Missouri with her husband and son. She's a member of SFWA (Science Fiction & Fantasy Writers of America) and HWA (Horror Writers Association), as well as the Four Horsemen of the Bookocalypse, her epic book critique group, where she's known as Death. When she's not swearing at the keyboard, she enjoys boating with her family at Lake of the Ozarks and reading books that raise eyebrows. Find Angela online at www.angelaroquet.com

TIM WAGGONER

Tim Waggoner has published over forty novels and five collections of short stories. He writes original dark fantasy and horror, as well as media tie-ins, and his articles on writing have appeared in numerous publications. He's won the Bram Stoker Award, the HWA's Mentor of the Year Award, been a finalist for the Shirley Jackson Award and the Scribe Award, his fiction has received numerous Honorable Mentions in volumes of Best Horror of the Year, and he's had several stories selected for inclusion in volumes of Year's Best Hardcore Horror. He's also a full-time tenured professor who teaches creative writing and composition at Sinclair College in Dayton, Ohio. www.timwaggoner.com

ROBERT W. WALKER

Award-winning author, graduate of Northwestern University, ROBERT W. WALKER began his highly-acclaimed INSTINCT & EDGE SERIES in1982. Rob next penned his award-winning HarperCollins historical crime series: CITY FOR RANSOM (2006), SHADOWS IN THE WHITE CITY (2007), and CITY OF THE ABSENT (2008). Most recently Rob placed Ransom and a monster aboard the Titanic in an epic entitled Titanic 2012 – Curse of RMS Titanic, followed by Bismarck 2013 – Hitler's Curse, The Edge of Instinct, the The Fear Collectors, several YA titles & several short story collections followed. Rob aka Geoffrey Cain is responsible for Bloodscreams, a horror series. His CHILDREN of SALEM & other historical novels are big books! His 80th novel, done for PROSPECTIVE PRESS is Under The Dead Man's Hat. Robert resides in Hurricane, WV. Find Rob's works at www.RobertWalkerbooks.com & www.amazon.com/kindle & www.audible.com He has 3 Facebook pages and a Twitter page.

CPSIA information can be obtained
at www.ICGtesting.com
Printed in the USA
FFHW021941111019
55437704-61250FF